# Swords of Fate

## Nicole Sebastian

ISBN 979-8-9911092-0-8


Cover artist: Christina Roberts
Cartography: Leo Hartas

For my mom, who put all my extra library books on her
card so I didn't have to put any back. And for my mammaw,
who helped me read Dr. Suess books while she
watched the birds and drank her coffee.

# Swords of Fate

Nicole Sebastian

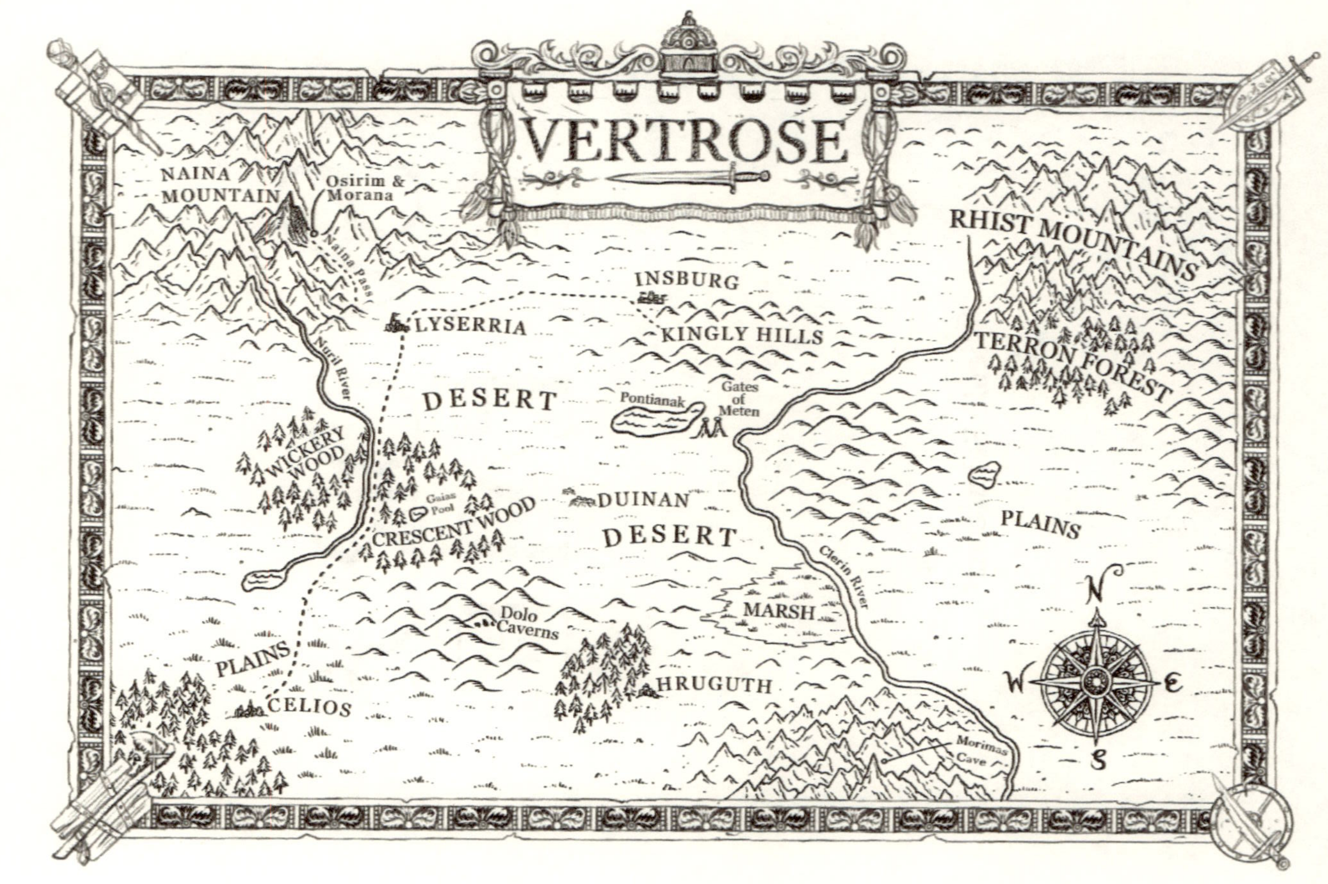

VERTROSE
NAINA MOUNTAIN
Osirim & Morana
Naina Pass
Nardil River
LYSERRIA
INSBURG
KINGLY HILLS
DESERT
WICKERY WOOD
Crescent Pond
CRESCENT WOOD
Dolo Caverns
DUINAN DESERT
Pontianak of Meten
Gates of Meten
PLAINS
CELIOS
MARSH
HRUGUTH
Mortims Cave
Clerin River
PLAINS
RHIST MOUNTAINS
TERRON FOREST
N
S
E
W

# Prologue

## Meten, twenty-three years ago

Alik stood in a great marble hall, with sword at the ready. He stood next to his best friend, Tanophis, with whom he had made so many memories just in this main hall alone. Not a bad way to go into Oblivion.

He let the steady, combined breathing of the six, all his remaining friends—his family, really—drift him into mediation. He swore he could hear the echoes of his sister, Rena and Tanophis's wife, Paxis's laughter. He drank in what he assumed would be their last moments there, in the hallowed halls that they had all once called home.

Guyt had somehow taken their powers, with a spell he had found deep in an ancient tome. Their once friend had betrayed them. Now they all stood as humans, awaiting their final fate. The clash of the battle being waged outside in the streets of Meten echoed through the now-quiet hall, as the fighting came ever closer. The building jarred and stank of burning metal and wood. Cracks had formed in the marble near the ceiling. He hated that Tanophis had ordered them to stay inside while their people died outside in the streets.

He looked at those arrayed around him, and let his angry thoughts dwell on the two missing from this last stand. It had only been a month since Ciksura and Lavinia had betrayed them, drawn like moths to the flames of Guyt's deception. He didn't really blame them; Guyt had a way of making his words sound like honey to any who were desperate enough.

Pain and hurt were etched across Faelinth and Jaylin's faces, however, the sting of the betrayal hitting them the hardest. Faelinth had lost a wife, and Jaylin a sibling.

Tanophis and Paxis stood at the head of the group now poised for battle as the great twin doors finally swung slowly open, letting in the reek and smoke from the burning streets. Ciksura entered, in flowing emerald robes and a hood covering most of their face. Alik's anger came to a head. Jaylin's sister was dead to him for this.

"I thought you might be here," Ciksura said, their voice devoid of any feeling Alik could detect.

"Ciksura," Paxis begged, "please see reason. Guyt is only using you. You are so much more than this. You are our friend. Our family."

"The time for your idle words has passed."

"You aren't meant to be what others think is normal," Paxis answered calmly, tears welling up in her eyes. "You are supposed to be special. And you are, Ciksura. You are still as precious to us as any of the other gods. Please tell us why you're doing this, and we'll try to help you."

Tears stained Ciksura's paling cheeks, and they stared with a steely resolve. "It's too late now, Paxis. I have suffered for too long, skulking these halls and watching all of you. All I wanted was to be like you. Happy. But none of you wanted to help me before. You only want to help now to keep that precious *order* you so desire. I will not be shoved back into your little box just to make you comfortable. And with your power bound to Guyt, you're useless."

Alik snarled, but stood his ground. "Bring those mud toys you make in here so I can tear them to shreds with my teeth."

"Down, dog," Ciksura spat as they arched an eyebrow.

The nuwu burst into the hall on Ciksura's command. There had to be a hundred of them or more, neutral expressions on their clay faces, all marching to Ciksura's will—mud puppets bent on destruction.

"Please!" Jaylin begged, tears streaming down her face.

Ciksura turned to their sister, but said nothing. They held only hatred in their eyes.

"I have failed you," Jaylin cried. "I am so ashamed, my dearest one. I only hope one day you can forgive us, and know how truly and completely sorry we are."

"It's funny," Ciksura smirked coldly, only letting the smallest piece of themself appear hurt. "That only once you're all facing destruction do you care."

Faelinth's tears welled up, eyes filled with hurt, as his wife, Lavinia, approached him. Her flaming red hair fell in waves down her back.

"Funny, how no one truly listens until all they have is lost," she said.

"You are not lost to me," Faelinth declared defiantly. "There is still good in you."

"NO!" Lavinia bit out. "There is not and there never was. You only groomed me to believe that I was good. I am evil and I will always be evil. I do not want to be good or kind. I want to be left alone to be whoever it is I want to be, *husband*."

"I only sought to see the good in you. And I see now, so clearly, that it was not my place. I should have let you be whoever you are. It wouldn't have changed how much I love you."

"You shoved me into a tiny, suffocating box, because it is your nature to find the good in all things. But I don't want to be 'good.' I want to be accepted and loved for myself. For the evil that runs through my veins."

Faelinth let his tears stream freely. "I cannot ever express to you how deeply I love you. It has never mattered. Your true nature has never mattered to me, nor that we were fated to be together. I have and will always love you, whether we are fated or not."

Lavinia almost looked like she wanted to drop her cold mask in that moment, but regained her steel. "But I no longer love you. Let's end this, Ciksura."

There wasn't much fighting to be done. The gods swung valiantly, and the nuwu burst into dust and ash as the swords pierced their clay exteriors. But the defenders were too few, and they were utterly devastated to not have their powers to lean on. The nuwu overwhelmed them quickly.

Alik burst into an angry war cry at their defeat. He looked around the hall, seeing his friends fall to their knees one by one. Time itself seemed to slow.

It was over before it had even started.

The gods were bound and led through the streets of their beloved Meten. Led by their friends and fellow gods. Led to Guyt.

The once-beautiful city lay in shambles in the moonlight. Fires pierced the night, and the screams of their people could be heard throughout the city. Their cries echoed through the night as the city fell.

Alik's stomach dropped as they were led out, surrounded by the utter devastation in the streets. His anger burned a hole through him. Guyt would pay for this. He would make sure of it. Maybe not now, but Alik swore to himself that, someday, he would make sure Guyt paid for every life he'd stolen.

The nuwu guard paraded them through the streets as prizes, driving them forward like animals to market. They ended the humbling trip at a tent in a once-green park that had been filled with flowers and laughing children. The park was now trampled and dead, every living thing brown and gone like Alik's soul. The nuwu dropped them at Guyt's feet.

"Your prize, my Lord," Ciksura bowed.

"Good," Guyt answered, as if speaking to a pet. He sat on a red plush seat and his strikingly blue eyes shone with psychotic delight. "Now, let us complete this curse."

"You don't need to do this, Guyt," Paxis pleaded. "We can live in peace. We trusted you for so long."

Guyt stalked over to where the powerless gods knelt at his feet. "I don't want to live in peace with you. I want to rule this world, and any other that I desire. And you and yours are in my way."

"You can't kill us, Guyt," Tanophis pointed out.

"Oh, don't I know that," he gritted out between his teeth. "Only natural causes can do the trick on you and your horrid band of do-gooders. But I've found a much better way to rid this world of you. It was not for nothing that I tracked down this tome." He pulled an age-worn book from a pedestal and held it tightly.

Paxis lowered her head, tears rolling down her cheeks. "I have failed you, my friends. I have failed our people. And I have failed Vertrose."

Guyt's gold robes billowed around him as he stepped behind the pedestal and turned the yellowed and cracked pages. He raised his arms high and closed his eyes. His long, low chant echoed through the tent, seeming to come from all around them.

The weight of uncertainty and failure nearly destroyed them.

Then Tanophis and Paxis fell to the ground and began to writhe.

"What are you doing to them?" Rena cried.

"They're getting what they deserve," Ciksura said coldly, but Alik saw fear glaze their eyes as the two afflicted gods screamed in pain at their feet.

"Ciksura," Jaylin cried. "What is he doing? Please help us. This isn't you."

Guyt's chanting grew louder and faster until all Alik could hear as Guyt continued was the great booming voice. A light appeared before them and encompassed Tanophis and Paxis, silencing their anguished screams.

"Ciksura!" Alik burst out desperately. "I will kill you and Lavinia!"

Ciksura turned their pink-stained eyes to Alik. "You can't kill me. But now you can die."

Jaylin's eyes widened. "What do you mean? What did Guyt do?"

A wicked smile slide across Ciksura's face. "He's made you all mortal. You'll age, hunger, and thirst like mortals. No longer will eating be solely a sport; it will be a necessity for your pathetic survival."

Alik turned to Guyt and struggled against his restraints. "You *bastard!*"

"Ciksura," Rena started to say, tears streaming down her face, "Please. This isn't you."

"How would you know? How would *any* of you know who I am?"

Rena clamped her eyes shut and winced. "I am so sorry...my friend."

Ciksura's face twisted in rage and hurt. "You only feel sorry that you've been bested. You were never truly my friend."

Jaylin cried out to her sibling. "Please, Ciksura. Please, hear us."

Ciksura finally exploded. "No! I will not hear you when you never heard me. You have failed me more than any of these pieces of shit. You were my sister! My *sister*!"

With that, Ciksura stormed out of the tent.

Guyt stopped the chant and watched as the light finished consuming Paxis and Tanophis. "The natural order of the world will be your killer now. And I rather like the idea of watching you all slowly and painfully succumb to old age."

The blinding light concealed Guyt's curse, and Alik couldn't see what was happening on the inside.

"What did you do, scum?" Alik demanded. "What's happening to them?"

Guyt's lip curled up as he dropped into his seat, exhausted. "I'm staking my claim on the rulership of Vertrose. I found a curse hidden deep in this ancient book that I think will fit these two quite nicely."

"Shit," Alik cursed. "If you lock me up like a dog, I will break free and ravage your bones like a beast of the wild."

Guyt laughed. "Don't be so conceited. Why would I waste my time trying to keep you locked away? You're all useless. You have no army, no powers, and your precious leaders are now gone...Or they will be, when I'm done." Guyt waved his hand, and the gods' bindings were loosened, the ropes falling away. "Go. Go and die a mortal life. You're of no further bother to me than a single flea is to a dog."

The gods stood in the tent, confused and angry. But before they could do anything, nuwu barged in and dragged them out into the night air. The mud puppets tossed the gods onto the cold grass like a child's rejected playthings, before taking up a post at the door.

Alik stood and had readied himself to burst back in when another light fractured the darkness. Two familiar figures now stood before them.

"Where are they?" Asterion asked with utter terror.

"Guyt has them," Rena answered. "He threw us out."

"Go," Dursten commanded. "Leave this place before Guyt changes his mind."

"No!" Alik and Faelinth cried out at the same time.

"My friends," Dursten said to the gods, "this is a fight you cannot win. We'll do what we can now, but you must listen to us."

"He has them in there," Alik seethed. "I will not abandon them."

"Alik," Asterion said with an unnerving, forced calm, "no curse is without a key. He must have a way to lift the curse again. We will protect them until the key is found. Now go."

The two beings disappeared into the tent. Alik felt his sister, Rena, tug on his sleeve.

A great supernatural clash knocked them off their feet. Alik burst back into the tent to see the stars' bright flash as they disappeared.

"Come, brother," Rena urged. "There's nothing for us to do now; let the stars do what they can. We're no good to them if he locks us up, too. We're no good to anyone without powers. We have to get out of here before Guyt decides that he wants to chain us. Dursten and Asterion will figure this out."

Alik forced himself to turn away from the tent. He followed the others into what he assumed would be a bleak and uncertain future.

# Chapter 1

If Mati had been honest with herself, the way she had come to be with the Masons bothered her greatly, but most days she was able to put on a brave face and just carry on. As much as her adoptive parents had made her feel welcome, she still longed to know where she truly had come from.

"Sweetheart?"

Mati was pulled from her daydreams by Carol's soft voice. Mati's adoptive mother was wearing an apron covered in flour and she swept her tousled hair behind her ear, leaving behind a streak of white flour that almost perfectly matched her graying hair.

"I'm going to miss that daydream twinkle in your eye." Carol smiled.

Mati smiled softly back at her. Carol opened her arms, and her motherly magnetism pulled Mati into a tender squeeze.

"Hey, FedEx," a snide voice echoed from the top of the stairs.

Jackson, the younger of her brothers but still ten years older than herself, was coming down with his usual arrogant swagger. She internally winced at the longstanding nickname. As much as Carol and Gary had made Mati feel welcome, their two sons had not.

"Jackson!" Carol scolded, her eyes narrowing at him. "I thought you would've outgrown teasing your sister."

A smirk slid onto the side of his mouth. "All in good fun, Mom. Mati doesn't mind. Do you?"

Mati forced a smile.

"Oh, Mati." Carol said as she turned back to the kitchen. "I almost forgot to tell you. Tyler said to tell you 'good luck.' He won't be able to make it tonight. He's got a big work meeting in the morning and doesn't want to be out late."

Mati sighed in relief. Tyler had quickly become the family's golden child after landing a supervisory position in a well-established food processing plant in town. She would not miss him. Although, if she had to choose between the two boys, Mati would gladly have had Tyler there instead of Jackson.

Mati followed Carol into the homey kitchen and settled into her usual spot at the table next to Gary.

He raised his thick gray eyebrows as she lowered herself into the seat. "Are you all packed?"

Mati nodded. "Yep."

"And you hired a mover?"

"Yes."

"Did you look up their reviews? You don't want to end up with them stealing your stuff. I can look them up here on my phone. Jackson showed me how to use the Google. What's their name?"

Mati smiled indulgently. "Yes, they are a legit moving company."

"What's the name." His finger poised over his keyboard.

"Packer's Movers."

Gary lifted one brow. "I don't like the sound of them."

"I promise," Mati assured him. "They're a real company. Lots of the kids use them."

Gary lifted one finger and hen-pecked his way through the letters one by one.

Carol leaned between them and set a steaming casserole dish onto a trivet. "Gary, leave her alone. I'm sure she has everything under control. I left some boxes upstairs for you to get the rest of your things from your old room," she added, looking at Mati.

"Thank you," Mati smiled.

She retreated inward as Gary and Carol bantered back and forth. She wanted to scream that she definitely didn't have anything under control. In fact, she was sure her life was spiraling out of control into an inescapable pit of drudgery.

She was moving tomorrow, to a new town for her new job as a teacher for a first-grade class in a larger district. She'd had high hopes of landing her dream job after graduation. She had desperately wanted to be a school counselor, helping kids like herself who had had troubled lives, and getting them some stability. But fate apparently had other things in mind. She'd been forced into taking the teaching job when she hadn't received a single call-back or second interview from any of the other schools she had applied to as a counselor, her dream crumbling before her eyes.

After having been mercilessly bullied and misunderstood all her childhood, all she had wanted was a chance to help other kids going through the same ordeal. Now, the thought of facing twenty six-year-olds in one room made her shiver to the very core.

# Chapter 2

Mati reluctantly turned away from the stars and continued packing her boxes. She looked over all her school awards, *Madison Mason* scrawled across each brass plate. She touched every one, as if she were touching the memories associated with each.

She wandered back to the window to look up at the stars one last time, and noticed something odd. One star that she couldn't place was fluttering in and out of focus. She stared at it, furrowing her brow as it became brighter—and closer.

It couldn't be. It was impossible for a star to do that, and she quickly ran through a short list of other things that it could be. An airplane, a meteor, a weather balloon, maybe? But none of those really fit the situation.

Her eyes widened as the star grew brighter. It had to be a meteor. She ducked under the window ledge with a caught breath in her chest and sat in silent terror for a moment, expecting to hear an impact that never happened. She peeked her head over the sill and saw nothing. Nothing outside was out of place or damaged.

"That's not possible," she said out loud to her empty room.

"I'm sorry," she heard a voice behind her say, causing her to spin in surprise.

The shock that hit her was one of pure terror. Standing in the middle of her small room was a tall, strangely-dressed being. Its skin glowed softly from within. It had on the richest clothes she had ever seen, and had long black hair that the light seemed to dance across. She gaped without saying a word.

"I see that I've frightened you," said the stranger. "Allow me to introduce myself. I'm Asterion, Lord of the Eastern Sky." They bowed low to Mati.

Mati stood, still silent, convinced she was hallucinating. And after a few more moments of silence, Asterion addressed her again.

"Hello, Mati. I imagine this must be coming as a shock to you."

Asterion held out their hand to her, but she just gaped, her mind running wild.

"Who...who are you?" she finally found her voice.

"I am Asterion," they answered again. "I am the Lord of the Eastern Sky and part of the Illustrus. I've come to take you to Vertrose."

She'd heard them the first time, but it hadn't quite clicked. "What is Vertrose?" Mati asked, now able to at least speak in small sentences.

"It is a land on Tera," Asterion answered, their kind face staring into her wide eyes. "It is in a different universe than Earth. And I have come to retrieve you, so that you can fulfill your destiny to set the peoples of Vertrose free from a terrible curse."

Mati thought she had composed herself, but now found herself reeling again.

"This is a joke, right? How much is Jackson paying you?"

"I know this is all very sudden," the star continued. "But you were born to help these people. The rulers of Vertrose have been cursed and the people forced under the rule of a terrible man. You were brought into this world to help save them."

"I what?" Mati gasped. This all had to be a cruel joke. Her brain seemed to buffer and freeze. "I can't help an entire planet. I can barely help myself."

"Mati," Asterion said, their look stern. "I'm not being paid by anyone, and this is certainly not a joke. We've had a terrible beginning, I fear. I brought you to this universe as a baby twenty-three years ago, and placed you in the Masons' care to keep you safe while you grew."

"Do you know my parents?" Mati wondered out loud, suddenly excited by the star's news.

"Your parents are not here and you may never find what you seek. If parents are what you need, I think you'll find that Carol and Gary are some of the best examples available." Asterion stated matter-of-factly. They let Mati stand in silence for a moment longer before continuing. "I will need to leave soon. Will you help the people of Vertrose?"

Their eyes bored into Mati like fire. Her mind did flip-flops while simultaneously going in circles.

"How do you know my name?" Mati asked, trying to find her bearings.

"I have been watching over you," they answered.

"So, you brought me here from another universe, and dropped me off in the middle of Midwest America on a strange family's porch to keep me safe from bad guys?"

"Yes," the star answered firmly. "This universe is on the outskirts of the cosmos. It's still very young in comparison to the others, and often escapes anyone's notice."

Mati closed her eyes to readjust her thoughts.

"There is nothing for you here," the star said persuasively. "Vertrose is your true home, and its people are your destiny. Its future lies in your hands. I hate to be so blunt, but we really don't have any more time to waste. I wish you had longer to process this information, but you haven't. Vertrose doesn't have the time to lose. Its people are suffering. An army is being assembled. The few lands that do remain free will not remain so for long. The gods have been defeated. The only thing waiting here for you is a job you dread and a life of struggle to fit into a world where you do not belong. A life you were never meant to fit into."

Mati pondered Asterion's words. Deep down, she knew. She had never belonged here, no matter how well the Masons had treated her. But this life was familiar, and she didn't relish the idea of leaving it for an un-known. Instinctively, though, she reached out her hand toward Asterion.

"Are you real?" she asked, feeling rather dumb.

Asterion smiled and gracefully took her hand. "Very real."

A tangible connection struck her to the core. Flashes of the star leaving a wrapped bundle on the porch of her house. A wrapping she recognized since it still lay across the foot of her bed.

A sense of relief and joy in knowing who she was washed over her. It wasn't much, but this stranger had made her feel more like herself than anyone ever had. A single tear formed in the corner of her eye. It pooled and broke free, tumbling down her cheek. She needed to know where she came from and who she was, even if she were to continue with this life.

"Can I return, after?" she asked Asterion. "As much as I want to know where I'm from, I would hate to leave my parents. It would feel wrong to leave them behind after they raised me."

"If you truly desire to return to the life you've always known," they answered, "you will be free to do so."

Asterion gave her hand a light squeeze, smiling softly as if they knew her thoughts.

With one last look at her room, she nodded to the star and grabbed their hand. "I'm ready."

⟫ ⟪

The sun beat down on Fen's neck and back particularly hard that day. The dry dirt of the barnyard swirled in the air and stuck uncomfortably to his sweat-drenched skin. He scooped up a full bucket of feed and made his way toward the animal pens. One of the sturdy beasts at the fence let out a cry.

"I'm coming," Fen answered it with annoyance. "Even you're being needy today."

"Hello, Fen," an angelic voice beckoned him from behind.

Fen tipped the feed into the trough and turned to see Aniel standing at the fence and smiling at him. Aniel was one of Fen's many admirers, and Fen thought her the prettiest by far. The village girls often smiled and batted their eyes as they passed his barnyard, and it was the only good part of his day. The attention was nice, and made his life of drudgery a bit more bearable.

He straightened up with a grin. "Hi, Aniel."

"I heard you gave Ruby a kiss yesterday," she pouted. "I visit you almost every day and you've never kissed *me*."

Fen smirked at her and strode over to stand at the fence next to her, the sun and heat now forgotten. "Ruby brought me a puff cake, since it was her coming-of-age birthday. It was just to say 'thank you.'"

Aniel deepened her fake pout and looked up at him through her lashes. "You know my mother doesn't let me cook. She says it's maid's work. Besides that, some people might say you intend to court her now."

Fen smiled wickedly. He loved making all the well-to-do girls jealous.

Aniel kept the conversation going without Fen's help. "You know my mother scolds me fiercely when she finds out I stop here. She says you aren't worth more than the dirt under your feet." Fen frowned at that, even though he was very aware of what most of the town thought of him. "I eavesdropped on her talking with Miss Lindel, and she says that Old Tauny Belger saw you headed into the saloon with one of *those* women. Is that true, Fen?"

"I think Tauny Belger is a bored, nosey old man," Fen grumbled. What business was it of anyone's where he went, or who he went with? The few times he was able to sneak off of this forsaken farm, he was going to make sure they counted. But he wasn't going to dash the innocent glow in this girl's eyes. "I was just making a delivery for Ms. Hurl."

Aniel's smile lit up her face. "I knew you would never be a scoundrel, Fen."

He widened his smirk into a flat-out grin before flexing his sun-tanned muscled arms by pulling himself back and forth on the fence. Aniel's eyes grazed over him as he'd hoped. "Well, Aniel...would you like a kiss, too? Or am I too much of a *scoundrel*?"

She instantly straightened up and turned a smooth cheek to him. "Oh, yes, Fen. But only on the cheek. Anything else would be improper."

He lightly pecked her cheek, making her giggle.

"Fennar!"

Fen flung himself around at the harsh yell of his full name from behind. The shout sent Aniel running down the road, still giggling. His guardian's gravelly voice sent chills down Fen's spine.

"Fen," she bellowed again, sounding more like a mating troggle in the pond than anything. "Come here!"

Fen took a deep breath and rolled his eyes before she got close enough to notice the gesture. "Coming."

Beside her walked a strange person, like no one that Fen had ever seen. They wore clothes that looked too expensive to be visiting a dusty, smelly farm, and the style was wholly unfamiliar. Not even the well-off people in his town wore clothing that nice.

His guardian waddled to a stop. "Fen, this is Dursten. We've made a trade. You'll be goin' with him."

Fen felt equal parts horrified and curious.

The person held out an impossibly pale hand, one that seemed to be glowing from within. "Dursten, Lord of the Western Sky."

Fen wiped as much dirt as he could off of his hand onto his pants and took Dursten's outstretched hand. "Uh, hi, I guess."

"As the kind lady says," Dursten said with a large smile, "you'll be coming with me."

"Where?"

Dursten turned to Fen's guardian with a kind and unassuming smile. "Could we have a few moments?"

"I'll be goin' back inside, anyway," the woman answered, jingling a heavy pocket of coin. "He's all yours."

Dursten outstretched their hand and gestured to the barn. Fen obliged, stepping through the open doors. "I know this is all very confusing and sudden, but you will be traveling with me to Vertrose."

"Where?" Fen asked, his mind starting to tingle with excitement.

"Vertrose. Come, sit, and I'll explain everything we have time for."

The two sat and Dursten gave him a brief description of the new world they would be going to.

Fen leapt to his feet. "Let's go! I'm ready."

Dursten smiled. "I'm glad you're taking the information so well. I wasn't sure how you would receive it."

"I'm all for fighting and killing," Fen mimed a sword fight across the hay that lay on the floor of the barn. "Are we going now?"

"Yes," the star answered. "Do you have any questions?"

Fen paused in his mock fight with a fence post. "No, I don't think so."

"Impulsive as ever, I see," Dursten said, almost under their breath. They held out their hand to Fen with a smile.

Fen took their hand with little thought. "Let's go!"

# Chapter 3

A light surrounded Mati and Asterion, and a static buzz filled her. The world went by so fast that it all blurred into darkness. Before she could even gasp out a breath, Asterion set them down in a glade of huge trees. She spun around in disbelief. The trees surrounding them were so big the only rivals they had, in her experience, were the redwood trees in California. Then it hit her...nausea. Mati turned away and unceremoniously puked in the grass, narrowly missing her feet.

"That will pass in a moment," Asterion assured her. "Traveling by light is something of an acquired taste."

They gave her a reassuring smile as she wiped her mouth. "Where are we?" she asked, trying to forget her stomach's violent protests.

"We are on the furthest edge of Vertrose," he explained. "I believe on Earth it would be the south and west. We're far outside the current patrol routes of those whom we are trying to avoid. We'll have a few days' walk to get to Celios."

"Wait? *Days?*"

"Yes, days."

"And we have no tent or water," Mati pointedly brought up.

Asterion tried to hide a smile. "Don't fret, Mati. You'll find that there are many small streams on our way, and we'll find plenty of protection from the night chill here as well. I'd be more concerned about your footwear."

Mati looked down and noticed that she was wearing a pair of sandals. "Perfect…" she grumbled under her breath. "What's Celios?"

"Celios is a great city in the plains, and the home of the madrigal. The madrigal are some of our closest allies in this rebellion."

"And they live in Celios?" Mati asked.

"Yes."

"Why couldn't we just beam there?" Mati asked, stomach still undecided about the idea.

"Traveling by light is not the stealthiest mode of transportation, as you can imagine," Asterion explained. "I don't want anyone to know you're back in Vertrose until we have no other choice."

Mati wasn't sure she liked the sound of that. "So, someone's looking to kidnap me? Great. I like how you left that out of your sales pitch."

Asterion smiled at her remark. "You could say that. I never said this wouldn't be dangerous."

"But you did conveniently forget that little detail," Mati noted sarcastically.

The star's smile grew and their eyes lit up. "Are you alright to keep going?"

Mati nodded and began to follow Asterion into the trees. Following a stranger into the woods didn't seem like a smart plan, but no matter what protest her logic put forth, she didn't have any other choice. Besides, she'd already let this stranger *Star Trek* her to…wherever this was.

"Be mindful in the forest," Asterion warned. "The pixies will likely be enthusiastic."

"Pixies? Like, little fairies?"

Asterion barked a melodious laugh. "They are most certainly not fairies. Pixies are rarely seen, but the effects of their tricks are felt most strongly. They'll throw acorns at your head, lift a tree root so you stumble, or just frolic to distract you and make you lose your way. They're very wily creatures."

Mati and Asterion walked on in silence for a while after that, but Mati's mind was loud and full of questions. How had she—an orphaned girl of no consequence—ended up in this strange fairy tale? It felt surreal, and more comical the more she thought about it, but she also felt at home here. Like this place was a distant memory from another time, and that something within her was leaping with joy at being able to return. Only a few hours ago she had been miserably getting ready to set out on her adult life on Earth, and now she was here, in a fantastical forest, following a realized star. It still seemed so unreal.

Not long into the journey, Mati started hearing skittering, and what sounded like tiny voices whispering and giggling together. She spun her head, looking in every direction. Shadows seemed to dance through the trees.

"It's the pixies," Asterion answered her unasked question. "They're very excited to have company. Be on your guard."

Almost as soon as Asterion had let out that warning, Mati tripped over a tree root that seemed to spring out of nowhere. Asterion easily threw out an arm to catch her, and smiled.

"Pixies," Mati grumbled. "This is going to be long day."

As darkness fell over the trees and their long shadows cast an eerie gloom over the forest, Asterion waved their hand over the shadows. A piece of the darkness lifted from the ground, creating a little shelter.

"Sleep," the star said to Mati.

Mati gaped at the shadow shelter, disbelieving. "How did you do that?"

"A perk of being one with the night sky."

Mati crawled into the space, too tired to ask any more questions. The ground beneath her was soft and mossy, and she fell asleep almost immediately.

The following days were spent in the same way as the previous one had been walking, avoiding the pixies' tricks, and talking with Asterion.

"Are my parents here?" She probed. "Will I get to meet them?"

"All in good time," the star answered. "All will be revealed soon."

Mati wasn't entirely satisfied with that answer, and she grumbled silently to herself as they continued on.

They walked a little further, then popped out of the trees to a great grassy plain. Dotted along the horizon, Mati saw domes of shining glass and hillocks of billowing grass.

Almost as if hearing her thoughts, Asterion said. "Those are called pastons. They are the madrigals' homes. Come, it looks as though Helian is waiting for us."

She followed Asterion through the grass, running her fingers through it lazily. This whole place felt like a familiar dream, the kind you woke from and then tried desperately to return to when falling back asleep.

A large chimera, a creature she assumed to be a madrigal, waited for them at the edge of the grass. His strong torso was human, but his body was a powerful gazelle. The madrigal was much taller and athletic-looking than she had expected. His dark ebony skin glistened in the sun, and atop his head he wore a crown made from the grass of the plains that surrounded them. He bowed with a smile as they got closer.

"I am Helian, Lord of the Plains, and this," he gestured toward the cluster of pastons behind him in the distance, "is Celios. Welcome, Asterion. It's good to see you again."

Asterion bowed. "Good to see you again, Helian. May I present Mati?"

Mati didn't know what to do, so following Asterion's lead she bowed to Helian, but Helian just laughed.

"You need not bow to me, nor to anyone," Helian spoke in a deep voice. "We are the ones who should be bowing to you."

Mati's eyes widened, but she didn't answer. What was she supposed to say to that? She was dumbfounded.

Asterion must have sensed her nervousness and caught Helian's gaze. "Are your armies ready to move?" Asterion asked, as they started to lead Helian toward the pastons.

Mati followed, not really listening to their conversation. She saw madrigals of all shapes and sizes popping out of the pastons to gawk at her, as much as she was staring at them. A few of the smaller ones peeked shyly out from behind their mothers' legs.

These people looked happy and well taken care of. Not at all what she thought the people of Vertrose would be, after listening to Asterion. But they had said that the madrigals were on the furthest borders of Vertrose. Perhaps these were the people and way of life that she was meant to protect. Her mind started to whirl again.

She could see that they were a warrior people. Many of the madrigals, men and women alike, carried bows over their shoulders and wore yellow paint on their faces and chests. The paint contrasted beautifully against their brilliantly dark skin. Even some of the children had smaller play bows and wore similar body paint to the adults. Their strong, gazelle-like bodies bent a knee as Helian passed.

She felt a hand on her shoulder and jumped.

Asterion had noticed her distant gaze. "We all have our part to play in the fate of this world. Yours may be only to bring these people comfort, or it may be to fight alongside them."

Mati's eyes began to cloud over, and she struggled to contain tears. "How am I supposed to help these people? I have nothing to offer them."

Asterion's gaze cut through her to the bone. "You can go back to Earth, but you will be damning these people to ruin. The armies haven't made it this far, but, eventually, they will. One day, these fields will burn, and the people will be killed. Your coming will help them stand and fight. It gives them courage knowing you are back."

Mati nodded, a few tears escaping and streaking her cheeks as she followed Helian and Asterion into a large glass paston. It was balmy inside, like a greenhouse. Only a few short tables and blankets lined the floor. They passed through a connective arch to a dirt paston that was just as large, but much homier inside. It was dark and cool and there were large pillows laying on top of elaborate carpets. The smell of the terrain permeated everything and calmed Mati instantly.

Across from them sat two people. One was dressed similarly to Asterion and had similar androgynous features, but with long, strikingly blond hair. The other looked to be about Mati's age, and handsome. The two were talking quietly, though the younger one was very animated. They both stood as the three entered.

"Mati," Helian announced. "These are Fennar and Dursten."

The handsome one stepped forward immediately with a cocky grin, one hand sweeping his tousled waves out of his face. "Fen. No one calls me *Fennar*."

The other bowed politely. "Dursten, Lord of the Western Sky, at your service."

Asterion came up beside Mati. "Dursten and Fen will be joining us. Fen has returned to Vertrose as well, on the same journey as yourself. The two of you will be working together."

Helian motioned for them all to sit. Asterion made a noticeable effort to seat Fen at Mati's side.

Helian remained standing. "I'd like for you all to meet my queen, Becca."

A line of madrigal trailed in, following a tall and toned female wearing a grass crown that matched Helian's. "A feast for our honored guests," she declared.

The food was in large wooden bowls and laid out on a low table in the middle of the room. Mati felt her hunger rise. She gazed at the bowls, all of them filled with grains, leaves, fruits, and vegetables she had never seen before. After Helian's wife joined them on the pillows, the feast officially began.

Fen attacked the food with the fervor of a starving animal. Mati politely smiled at Fen as he roughly stuffed a large fruit-like object in his mouth, then handed her one. She took it from him and looked it over. It looked very similar to a pear, but it was wrinkly and deep purple. She noticed utensils on the table that others had started to use to daintily slice into the various foods. She followed suit and began to cut into it before deciding whether she would eat it. The last thing she wanted to do was offend her hosts, but she wasn't fully prepared to dive in as directly as Fen had.

The table exchanged pleasantries with the stars as Mati tried to decide whether or not to eat the fruit. Finally, she couldn't avoid it anymore, as her stomach started growling impatiently. She tentatively brought it to her mouth and took a small bite.

"It won't bite you," Fen teased.

She quickly swallowed the taste and was immediately taken back to every meal of her childhood, eaten with her goading brothers. She sank slightly into her pillow.

"I didn't mean to make you mad," Fen said.

"It's fine," Mati answered softly, without looking at him. She had traded one world of mockery for another.

Mati quietly listened to the rest of the pleasant conversation, continuing to lightly munch on more food, until another madrigal approached the table. Helian had a map of Vertrose brought out and placed in an open space on the table. Fen jumped at the chance to look at the sprawling landscape. In his haste, however, he left overturned bowls and glasses in his wake. Mati immediately began attempting to straighten up the mess, along with a few of the other madrigal guests.

"Sorry," Fen apologized, and tried to pick up a glass, but picked it up upside-down. The liquid that been left in the glass spilled out, all over Mati's outstretched arms. "Sorry," he uttered again, much quieter.

The once-courtly meeting had now turned into a mess of legs, all tripping over each other trying to avoid the spilled food and drink that was now being mashed into the fine carpets. Fen turned once again, and knocked over one of the few pitchers that remained standing. Mati quickly grabbed it just before the contents had a chance to drench Becca.

Quickly but confusedly the entire room found their feet and had begun laughing.

Helian's laugh in particular boomed through the room. "We expect nothing less."

Fen's face turned ten shades of red. "I am so sorry."

"Accidents happen," Becca very calmly reassured him, as she smoothed out her pillow and sat back down.

Mati saw Fen looking at the ruined map. Smudges of various sizes and colors had blotted out many of the fine details. "I am so sorry about your map," Fen said looking at Helian.

Mati picked up a cloth and dabbed as much off as she could manage.

"Thank you," Helian said. "I think we can still salvage the important bits. If you look over by that smudge of jelly, that's the first stop you'll make. Lyserria is a harsh desert town, but your strongest ally is there."

"Who is that?" Fen asked.

"Alik," Asterion answered. "You'll have to be the ones to convince him to leave, though. We haven't had any luck getting him to budge."

"What is it exactly we have to do?" Mati asked Helian. "Asterion has been very light on the details. I'd like to know a bit more about what we're even here for."

"That is an excellent question, and one that's a bit hard to explain," Helian said with a heavy sigh. "Guyt's atrocious acts have come to a head. He's preparing an army for his final push to fully seize all of Vertrose. He's bound our leaders under a curse that we can't break without your help."

"What kind of curse?" Fen probed.

Dursten turned their eyes down. "We aren't entirely sure. We only know it was an ancient and deadly curse. It bound the gods to fully-human bodies, and we must break it before the gods perish as mortal humans."

"So, where are your leaders? Can't they help?"

"They've disappeared. Paxis and Tanophis haven't been seen since that night."

"This evil wizard guy has them?" Mati asked, still struggling to piece it all together.

"We don't know," Asterion answered. "That's where you both come in. We need your help to raise an army of allies to stop Guyt. Ciksura and Lavinia have fallen into the masterful web of lies he weaves and are now helping him raise this army."

"Who are they?" Fen butted in.

Helian smiled, grateful for the genuine interest. "Lavinia is the goddess of evil, and Ciksura is the god of pain and the supernatural."

Fen furrowed his brow in disgust. "Why would gods help Guyt if he cursed them?"

"Because Guyt is very good at bending others to his will, convincing them with sweet words and promises." Helian bowed his head in regret.

"But your return will turn the tide. You two, together, will unite the remaining free peoples to stand against Guyt."

Mati was sitting in silent contemplation, making sure she had all the information. "So, Fen and I are saviors?" she eventually asked.

"Of a sort, yes," Helian answered.

"And all we need to do is raise an army to fight the evil wizard? There has to be something else."

"There are many facets to this curse," Dursten added. "Some of which we don't know yet."

"Then where is this Guyt?" She motioned to the map.

Helian pointed to a water stain next to a giant lake. "He's overtaken the gods' city of Meten."

The remainder of the meal was quiet as Mati and Fen contemplated all the information they'd been given. The fresh foods had energized Mati and left her stomach mostly content. After, Becca showed her to her own small grass-covered paston, just across from the large one where they had eaten. As satisfied as her stomach now was, her mind had now started to feel numb and saturated as she tried to drift off to sleep.

Should she have come to this world? She had gotten so caught up in the hopes of finding her birth parents that she didn't really stop to think all that Asterion had told her. She took a deep breath to center herself and let the night noises lull her to sleep.


Mati woke up feeling so refreshed that she had completely forgotten where she was. She had anticipated seeing her old room at the farm and contented herself that everything had been a dream, until she opened her eyes. The sweet, musty, earth-scent of the paston filled her nose. She stretched and collapsed back on the giant pillow pile she had dropped into the night before. She supposed she had better get up, though she didn't know what it was she was supposed to be doing.

Mati noticed that a bowl of water had been left for her to wash. She splashed the cool water on her face and dried it with the edge of her shirt before popping out of her paston. The sun was shining brightly off the glass pastons, almost blinding her. She squinted and looked around for any familiar faces. She startled at a voice coming from next to her.

"I need some brinces," Fen moaned, shading his eyes from the gleam.

"What are brinces?" Mati asked.

"You wear them on your eyes to keep the light from blinding you."

"You mean sunglasses," Mati figured aloud. Fen's look told her he had no idea what she was talking about. "It's what they're called on Earth."

"Oh," Fen added. "So, you aren't from here."

"No." Mati replied, a bit too roughly.

Fen smiled. "Me, either. Dursten came for me on Jefy." His face turned to stone. "I wouldn't go back, though."

"Why?" Mati asked.

"I was a muck boy there. I had no life, and I wasn't going to ever have one worth talking about. At least here I can be somebody. What about you?"

Mati considered not answering. She didn't want to rub it in his face that she'd been loved and cared for. "I miss my family," she said, almost under her breath. "I had a job waiting for me...and a life. Not a great one, but it wasn't as uncertain as this."

"Must be nice," Fen added plaintively, before perking right back up. "I can't wait to kill this Guyt guy and get my name remembered..." He paused, then looked at Mati with a huge grin. "And win a fair maiden."

Mati rolled her eyes. "I feel sorry for whichever poor soul is forced to marry you."

"Oh, she won't be forced. I'll probably have to beat them back with a stick once I've killed Guyt."

Mati walked off. Fen really did like to hear himself talk. The poor girl who ended up with him had better be deaf. She was reminded of a phrase Carol had used on Jackson and Tyler; 'bull in a china shop' described Fen perfectly.

Fen was still jabbering, keeping pace with her as she walked. "Where are you going?" he asked.

"Which way are you going?" she retorted.

"I was going to ask the stars when we're going to leave. I can't wait."

"Well, I'm going whichever way you're not," Mati said, exasperated. It was too early for this kind of excitement. "I need somewhere quiet. My head feels like it's gonna explode."

She walked away from Fen and off into the field of grass through which she had followed Asterion the previous day. Once she reached a certain point, her legs gave way beneath her and her tears were unleashed. All the emotions of the last two days, both good and bad, came rushing out at once. Her doubts overcame her entirely and all she wanted was the comforting embrace of Carol.

# Chapter 4

At breakfast, Helian had announced to Fen and Mati that they would be leaving for Lyserria the next day, along with the stars and a small group of his madrigal warriors.

The rest of the day was spent in a bustle of packing and preparation. Several madrigal women had been assigned to help Mati. They were seeing to it that she was scrubbed top to bottom, and had a full travel pack of clothes and toiletries. They had swapped out her Earth clothes—which wouldn't be and hadn't been good for walking any kind of long distance—and had given her linen pants, boots, a belt, and a maroon tunic that she shimmied into. They also gave her an oversized cloak, which she stuffed into her pack. It felt strange. She looked and felt like she was going to one of those medieval faires back home.

It still hadn't fully sunk in that this was real; that it wasn't all an elaborate game of dress-up.

The next morning came far too quickly for Mati's taste. The madrigal women came in and made sure Mati was awake, packed, and fed. She stumbled out of her paston to see Fen was already raring to go. He opened his mouth to speak, but she flashed him a look that dared him to say a single word. It was too early for socializing.

Asterion came to walk beside her. "You should go walk with Fen," he suggested.

"No, thank you," she said quickly. "I like peace in the morning."

Asterion held in a smile. "Fen is quite chaotic, but you should get to know one another. He might surprise you."

"The only surprise he can offer is what hare-brained idea he'll have next."

The rest of the morning passed in relative silence as they trudged across the plains. The early afternoon light cast hardly any shadows along the grassy path they followed. Mati's look earlier had silenced Fen so far, but she knew it wouldn't last for much longer. She noticed Asterion talking with him, and she caught a quick glance he gave her. No doubt, Asterion was attempting the same push they'd tried on her.

While their walk was still quiet, Mati attempted to piece together everything she had learned in the last few days. How her very ordinary life had been flipped on its head that night. And the more she thought about it, the more her stomach started to do somersaults.

She focused instead on her surroundings, on the soft bubbling sounds of the small river the path ran beside the path, and the feel of the light on her skin. She listened carefully, and heard the gentle swish of trees as a light breeze wove through them. It was a tranquil moment that grounded her in the here and now. Until it was interrupted by a heavy splash, and a sharp yelp.

She looked over and saw Fen lying in the river. He picked himself up as the stars rushed to his side, only to slip once more. He grasped Asterion's fine garment, pulling them both back down into the water. The whole traveling party ground to a halt. The star collected the soaking garments that now hung heavily off their shoulders, and the two gingerly made their way out of the water.

Fen spluttered along behind Asterion spouting apologies. As he made it to the bank, he was helped up it by a madrigal.

"I'm sorry," Fen repeated. "I was just trying to get a closer look at a plant I saw on the bank."

However annoyed Mati had been at Fen's blunder, and how it had ripped her from her tranquil thoughts, she couldn't peel her eyes away from the wet shirt that clung to every muscle and ripple on his torso. So much so, that she clenched her jaw and forced herself to focus on Asterion, hoping no one noticed the way she had gawked.

For days they traveled on and on, along the bank of the river. Every day was the same. Each day they stopped for a quick lunch, and didn't stop for rest again until night had completely fallen. They didn't have a fire, sleeping wrapped in their cloaks on the ground instead. Each day's peace was usually punctuated by at least one commotion of Fen's making. It was mostly just small things, like having to pull stingers out of his finger after grabbing a plant he shouldn't have, or not affixing his pack correctly and having the contents fall out and roll down the bank into the river. Mati now checked his pack every morning on the sly, and had had to fix it more than once.

Mati felt like a slug after every day on the road. Slick and slimy. Her clothes both stuck to her and slid around on her. She knew she had begun to smell ripe, as well. She was attempting to adjust her breasts in her tunic when she noticed the whole party had come to a halt.

Up ahead, Mati saw what looked like a shaggy-haired dog sitting on the bank of the stream.

"What's that?" Fen asked.

Dursten hushed him. "Shush. It's a baby nenad," they whispered. "We will need to wait and not cross its path. Its mother is probably nearby."

"Let's just pass it, or shoo it into the woods. You said it's just a baby, right?" Fen started walking quickly towards the baby before the madrigal or the stars could grab him.

Fen reached out both arms to shoo the small creature away, just as a loud chuff of air sounded in the tree line, off to their right. Fen froze in place. The madrigal pulled their bows and aimed arrows at the beast when Mati yelled for them to stop.

"Wait!" she cried, hurtling forward to get herself between them and the creature. The beast that had come out of the woods was covered in long hair and raised itself up on its hind legs, waving its long, scoop-shaped claws in an attempt at intimidation.

Mati's yell had startled the mother into a frenzy. Her paws *thunked* back down onto the ground, tucking the claws underneath, and she began to charge at them.

Mati raced back to the group, grabbed Fen, and dragged him across the stream and into the forest. She didn't have any kind of plan when she bolted, except to live.

They ran through brush and around trees, accompanied by the ominous sounds of an angry mother chasing them. Mati turned for a split second to see how much of a buffer was between them. The mother was close. Her long fur trailed behind her and left her face exposed, and the sight terrified Mati enough to not look back again.

Fen's foot caught on a rock as Mati tugged him through the woods. He stumbled forward several steps and fell flat on the ground, losing Mati's hand in the process. She floundered back hastily, trying not to look at how close the nenad was behind them, and hauled Fen onto his feet again.

The mother nenad was much more agile than Mati had anticipated, and they could hear her paws thudding on the ground directly behind them. Terror and exhaustion gripped the both of them and Mati could no longer pull Fen along with her. The two skidded to a stop and let the nenad slide by. She turned on them with a quick flick and chuffed a few angry breaths into the fog that now lay thick on the ground.

They were in a silent standoff, save for the chuffing of the mother nenad. She sounded like a bull ready to charge. As they stared, Mati had an idea. A last-ditch effort.

She stared directly into the eyes of the nenad, took a deep breath, closed her eyes, and knelt on the ground. She curled over, almost bowing to the beast, trying to look as non-threatening as possible. The nenad still chuffed.

Mati cracked open her eyes and looked up at Fen, still standing like a statue next to her, clutching his arm. She was not going to die today because of this idiot. Mati reached up and yanked him down onto the ground beside her. His body crumpled like one of those thumb push puppets. He recovered quickly and knelt on bent knee, with his head bowed. After a few of the most terrifying moments of Mati's life, the nenad gave one more satisfied chuff and retreated back the way she'd come.

When she couldn't hear the soft thuds of the nenad anymore, Mati stood up and let out the breath that she had been holding.

Fen was still holding his arm as he got up onto his feet. "It's popped out of its socket, I think," he said, answering her questioning gaze.

Mati ripped off the hem of her tunic and created a makeshift sling for his arm. "That should help for now."

"Thank you," he mumbled.

Mati grinned and turned to start back toward the others. "Which hurts more—your shoulder, or having to say that?" she could hear him grumbling to himself in response, but didn't hear what he said until he spoke louder.

"What way did we come from?" he asked, looking in a few different directions.

Mati stopped and did the same. "I'm not sure."

"Let's go that way," Fen pointed to a bush. "I think we passed that while running, so we should hit the others in a moment. We didn't run that far into here."

And with that, they started walking.

They walked through the heavy fog that surrounded their feet for much longer than either one thought they should have. They had begun to get turned around and started to question their own sense of direction. They wandered for so long that the filtered sunlight started to fade. The trees seemed taller and more ominous as nighttime shadows moved in.

"Let's stop here," Fen said. "We can't keep going in the dark."

"Why haven't we found them yet?" Mati wondered out loud. "We should've found them by now."

"I know," Fen answered and slid his pack off his good shoulder. It landed with a soft *plomp* that made the fog swirl and billow around it. "We need to put on our cloaks before it gets too cold."

Mati slung off her pack, following his lead, and quickly tossed her cloak around her shoulders. Without his asking, she helped Fen slide on his as well. She'd never known him to be so quiet, and that was what worried her the most. What could scare Fen into silence?

"Let's go ahead and settle down here," Fen said and kicked a few soggy sticks aside. "It's no use trying to make a fire. Everything's too wet."

He motioned for Mati to follow him as he found a decent sized tree, then slid onto his butt and braced his back against the trunk. There was a bush nearby that he huddled into for cover. Mati sat next to him, and exhaustion soon overtook the both of them.

<br>

Fen's arm had grown incredibly stiff overnight. He hadn't slept, but had made sure Mati was tucked under his arm and safe. She fit perfectly into the crook of his arm and shoulder, as if she had been made to occupy that very spot. Mati stirred as he stretched and she blearily opened her eyes. Her face turned a violent red and she scooted away.

"Sorry," she said, averting her eyes from him and tucking imaginary hair behind her ear.

Fen grinned wide. "It's fine. I knew you couldn't resist me for long."

Her cheeks didn't lose their color but her face squinched up and her mouth went flat as she rolled her eyes. She didn't appreciate his humor, but it made Fen giggle to himself anyway.

Fen pushed himself up onto his feet and dusted off his cloak and pants with his good arm. "We'll find them today," he said, with hope lacing the words.

Mati dusted herself off as well and they started off again. It didn't take long for the light to grow fully, but through the trees and the thick fog that lay on the ground, it still looked like dawn.

Fen was hoping that they would find their company soon. His leg was starting to burn noticeably. He dared not check it with Mati there, though. After she had fallen asleep last night, he'd pulled up his pant leg to see a nasty gash. The blood had soaked into his sock and stuck to both the wound and his leg hair. Before he had another second to think about on what it might look like now, he stopped dead and threw his arm in front of Mati to stop her.

"Do you hear that?" he whispered. "Footsteps…"

Once their feet were still, the sound was clear. Delicate footsteps crunched through the fallen leaves. The utter lack of normal forest noises made the footsteps sound much louder than they really were. Fen tugged Mati behind a bush to watch and wait.

A woman emerged from the mist. The fog that laid on the ground mysteriously left an open space around her feet as she walked. She stopped as if waiting for something. "Come out, you two," she demanded in a lilting voice. "I know you're there. Your friends sent me to find you."

Silence followed, as Mati and Fen's feet stayed planted.

"Come now, Mati and Fen. I don't have all day to wait."

She didn't feel like a villain, so Fen tentatively stood, followed by Mati.

"Well, now. You two have caused your companions a bit of concern." Her voice was high pitched but soothing. Her long white dress was dirty at the hem, the color perfectly complimenting her naturally-bronzed skin and long waves of dark hair. Shiny brass pieces tied into the waves framed her kind face. "I'm Jaylin, Mistress of Crescent Wood. Come over here and let me tend to that arm and leg."

She motioned to Fen, and he complied wordlessly, not daring to defy her. As he stepped closer, the fog drew back from around all three of them. She removed the sling Mati had made and quickly popped Fen's shoulder back with a flick of her wrist.

His bones snapped into place, sending a sharp pain traveling from head to toe along the left side of this body.

"Fuck," Fen let out compulsively.

Jaylin smiled softly. "Now, let's see to that leg."

Fen didn't question how she knew. He just sat on the ground where she now knelt.

Jaylin lifted his pant leg and pulled down his sock. It stuck and pulled at the wound, making Fen wince. Mati's face was horrified. The gash now oozed and leaked yellow, and the surrounding flesh had turned a bright red. Jaylin wiped away the dried blood and pus with a small cloth she had tied to her belt. She reached into her belt bag for a salve and slathered it all over the wound, then handed the small pot to Fen.

"Make sure you use this every day until that wound is healed," she warned. "You don't want this to get infected. And don't cover it for a few days."

Fen took the salve and placed it in his pack. He tried his best to keep his face from squinching with pain. He could feel Mati's eyes boring through him as he stood again.

"Now," Jaylin said, rising as well. "Your friends are waiting around the bend in the stream. It's lucky you kept watch all night; the woodland creatures wouldn't have left anything for me to find if you had you not. Gaia had you wandering further and further into her heart."

Fen and Mati raised synchronized eyebrows.

"What do you mean?" Mati asked. "Who is Gaia?"

"Gaia is the mother of all nature. She is what draws you in with this fog and traps you...pulling you closer into her heart to feed her creatures. So, it's a good thing you kept watch. Most of the creatures of the wood fear being seen. But had you both slept, they would've dragged you to Gaia herself and drowned you in a watery grave."

Fen pursed his lips and looked anywhere but at Mati. He could feel her piercing gaze through his skin.

"Hurry off," Jaylin urged and pointed. "The tree line is straight that way. And I hope I won't see you again for a while." And with that, she turned away from them and walked off, moving like the mist, and singing a lilting melody.

Mati turned to Fen and slapped his good arm.

"What was that for?" he exclaimed.

"For not taking turns watching," she answered, her lips pressed thin. "She was talking about you, wasn't she? That you stayed awake all night."

"You were tired. And besides, I couldn't sleep because of my leg and arm."

She slapped his arm again. "And that's for not telling me about your leg! You should've told me. And you had better let me hold the salve for your leg."

"I think I can manage a salve," Fen protested.

"You're going to forget, and you probably won't apply it correctly." She held out an expectant hand.

Fen furrowed his brow. "No."

"Please, just let me have the salve."

"No. She gave it to me, and I'll do it myself."

Mati huffed. "Fine, but when you get gangrene and we have to amputate your leg, don't expect me to feel bad for you."

They turned in the direction Jaylin had pointed out to them, and in silent annoyance, started to walk. Fen limped along, stubbornly resolved to defy Mati's need to control him.

They didn't have to walk long before they found their way out of the trees. Huge sighs of relief exited them both, Fen's quieter than Mati's. They walked on to the bend in the stream and found their party waiting, discouraged. Asterion and Dursten rushed over at the sight of them.

"We thought you were dead," Asterion proclaimed. "Luckily, we ran into Jaylin this morning. Did you see her?"

Fen nodded. "Yes, she popped my arm back in and pointed us to the road again."

The stars frantically hugged them both. "We are so glad you are alive!" Dursten looked as though they were about to cry. "But you must never put yourselves into so much danger again."

Mati and Fen exchanged looks of confusion, but let it go. It had been a long morning and even longer night, and both just wanted to keep moving forward.

# Chapter 5

Lyserria was a tiny but bustling town, laying in a desert plain. The Naina mountains sprang up tall like the jagged teeth of a predator, and created a formidable snowy backdrop that directly contrasted the arid conditions where the town sat. One mountain in the center of the range stood taller than the others and appeared to be a leftover remnant from an ancient time. By the time Fen saw the town on the horizon they had already packed away their cloaks and shed all other unnecessary layers. The air was hot and dry, making the snowy mountains look inviting. It had been three days since he and Mati had gotten lost in the foggy woods, and he rubbed his still-sore shoulder.

He noticed a small creature sitting on a rock, warming itself in the sun. It only gave them a passing glance before shutting one set of eyelids and turning away. He'd never seen such a dry, hairless animal before and wandered away from the party toward it.

"I'd stay away from that," Dursten warned.

"What is it?" Fen wondered aloud, and he stretched out his hand.

Without warning, the creature turned and blew a heavy dust in Fen's face, then it made a speedy getaway. Fen coughed, spitting some of the dust out of his mouth.

Mati chuckled, and the sound made Fen's ears go hot. He hadn't heard her laugh before, and it was the most beautiful sound. It made every other giggle he'd ever elicited from anyone else sound hoarse and grating.

The party came to a halt once again as Dursten stepped over to Fen. He detached Fen's water skin from his pack and handed it to him. "Drink this," he said.

Fen rinsed out his mouth and spat the water on the ground at his feet. "What was that thing?"

"A harver," Dursten answered. "They spit dust at predators to distract them. Lucky for you, it's not harmful."

The party reconvened and started off toward the town once again. Fen could still taste the awful dust in his mouth no matter how many times he rinsed. "This stuff is awful," he complained.

"Why do you touch everything you see?" Mati asked. "If you gave more than a passing thought to anything you do, you could've avoided the problem."

Fen spat on the ground again. "I feel like there's a coating of dust inside my mouth. Do you see anything?" He stuck out his tongue and opened his mouth wide at Mati.

Mati inspected his mouth with nonchalant eyes. "There's still dust between your teeth. Swish the water around before spitting it back out, next time."

Fen slowed down and leaned in close to Mati's ear. "I thought girls liked a man with a dirty mouth."

Fen saw her cheeks go an even brighter red than the heat had made them. She shoved past him and said, with enough forced nonchalance to knock Fen down a few pegs, "We do. But *you're* not a man. Just a silly boy with dirt in your teeth."

She strode off, her pace quickening until Fen couldn't see her face. But he could almost see the steam pouring from her ears. He grinned to himself, and did as she'd told him. He was happy the dust taste was almost entirely gone from mouth after swishing.


As the party approached Lyserria, the madrigal envoy whom Helian had sent with them parted ways with their group and turned back southward. Fen, Mati, and the stars made their way into the dusty town alone.

The buildings here were low and made of mudbrick. A central courtyard held the town's only visible water supply and that was where they headed first, dipping their waterskins into the well. Fen opted to fill his first, drink the whole thing, and then fill it again before stowing it back on his pack.

"Please, don't speak to Alik," Dursten asked, almost pleading Fen. "Let Asterion and I do the talking."

"Why?" Fen asked.

"Because Alik is not one to be trifled with and you have a knack for chaos."

The stars led them through the town to a small tavern just off the central square, a place that seemed to be a favorite of the people of Lyserria. It was crawling with folks both young and old. This was Mati and Fen's first look at the variety of peoples living in Vertrose. They saw tall, lithe, pointy-eared people, a group of what looked like fauns sitting at the center table, and people of all colors and shapes eating and drinking together at small round tables. A thin layer of dust coated almost every surface and there was only one lantern that jutted from the floorboards. Despite all the patrons, the room felt lifeless and cold.

The patrons picked at plates of cheese and cured meats, but no one except the barman was even looking at them. He, on the other hand, gave Mati and Fen the most intense stare with his piercing green eyes. Fen felt like he knew this man from that gaze alone. He almost seemed startled to see them.

"I don't want anything to do with this, Asterion," the man proclaimed in a booming voice before they had even gotten to the bar. His short brown hair was mussed, and his tanned, leathery skin pulled taut over his high cheekbones. A scruffy beard covered his chin and jaw.

"Good to see you too, Alik," Asterion answered with a smile.

"I told you years ago that I don't want anything to do with this mess," Alik grumbled, while shuffling bottles around aimlessly.

Asterion laid their hands on the bar top. "Alik, you know that Dursten and I can't be the ones to help these two. You are an intricate part of this rebellion, and of Vertrose itself. You can't hide behind that bar anymore."

"Asterion," Alik replied through gritted teeth, "I don't want to deal with this fool's errand. We both know that this is a hopeless cause."

Fen's temper started to rise, and without warning, he burst out, "So, you won't even help your own people?"

Alik's gaze darted to Fen. "I don't want to be a part of a hopeless cause that will bring about the deaths of thousands. This rebellion is madness, boy."

"Madness is strictly a point of view," Fen retorted. "Mati and I have been hauled all over this place already, and you won't even stand up for it."

"I never asked you to come here." The man's face stayed stony as he looked deep into Fen's eyes.

"No. You didn't. But we're here, we're going to try to finish this, and we need help. Helian said you would help us."

Alik cocked a half-smile, the kind of knowing smile that one gave when meeting an old friend after a long separation. "Well," he finally uttered after a long silence, "How do you plan on beating Guyt? Convince me this isn't hopeless."

Fen stood in thought for a moment before answering. "We'll do whatever's necessary. I don't have a plan. We haven't been privy to any of those conversations yet. But I can tell you that I, at least—and I think Mati, too—will do whatever we need to, for however long it takes. And—"

Alik interrupted him. "No."

Fen started to puff out his chest but felt a hand sweep him gently to the side.

"Please," Mati said softly. "Fen and I are human too, but we're here to help. Asterion and Dursten seem to think that you're going to be needed if we'll succeed and I trust their judgement. Would you rather see Vertrose defeated without a fight or know that you did everything in your power to save it?"

Alik rubbed the scruff on his chin. Fen couldn't believe his eyes. Did Mati just talk this stubborn codger into going with them?

"Alright," Alik answered with a low grumble. "I'll help you as much as I'm able."

Fen didn't know whether he was more interested in thanking Alik, or giving him a punch in the face. There seemed to be something familiar about the barman, but before he could decide what it might be, Alik continued.

"We'll leave tomorrow morning at dawn." And with that declaration, he turned away to the rest of the tavern. He called back over his shoulder to Fen and the others, "I've got no rooms available for you tonight, so you'll have to sleep on the floor in my quarters. Take your things up those stairs and I'll grab us something to eat and drink."

⇒⇒⇒ ⇐⇐⇐

After stuffing themselves to the gills with the meats, cheeses, and bread that Alik provided, they sat like rocks in the small apartment above the tavern. It wasn't long until Mati's eyes began to get very heavy, and, wrapped in her cloak, she nodded off to sleep.

When she awoke, the darkness told her that it was still night, despite the hushed voices she heard from the other side of the room. She didn't open her eyes, in the hope that sleep would come back for her quickly, but before she could pass out again, she heard her own name.

"Mati has been resistant so far," one voice said. She thought it must be Dursten speaking.

"And the boy?" Alik's hoarse voice was unmistakable.

"He's shown potential, but we are not without hope," Dursten answered. "The Illustrus doesn't like us meddling, as you know. I'm not sure how long we can continue like this. We need you to help them find themselves, if this rebellion is to be a success."

"Or we will all suffer the consequences," Asterion added with a worried sigh.

"We'll go with you as far as the border," Dursten continued. "But we dare not go all the way to Insburg. There's too much risk."

The conversation ended there, and Mati slipped back into dreams.

Mati was again awakened, but this time it was by a soft hand on her shoulder. "It's time," Asterion spoke.

She stretched and stood, and grabbed her pack, then stumbled blearily down the stairs and out the front door of the tavern. The streets were still dark, even though the sun could be seen just cresting the horizon. Five horses waited for them, Fen and Alik already mounted on one each. Mati was loath to get on. She had learned to ride on the farm, but had never enjoyed it. She wasn't looking forward to the sore butt and legs she was going to have later.

"Do we need maps?" Mati asked.

Alik huffed a laugh. "I'm the map."

"Can I have a map, anyway?" Mati asked hopefully. "I'd just feel more at ease if I knew where we were going."

"We're going to Insburg to meet a longtime friend of ours," Alik answered.

Alik's choice of words was odd, since she obviously didn't know anyone here, but Mati decided to ignore it for the time being. Maybe he meant himself and the stars. Obviously, asking him again for a map would be fruitless.

The day passed slowly as they rode through the desert wilderness, listening to Fen and Alik bicker about war and weapons. Fen kept insisting that he needed to learn to fight, and that conversation led to another battle about *when* he could learn, and him not listening to Alik constantly telling him that he needed to wait. The constant back and forth between them reminded her of the way her brothers would fight.

After the first full day of riding, her backside felt sore and stiff. Fen made sure to poke fun at her unladylike gait, even though he was obviously suffering from the same problems. And every time he mocked her, or prodded at her, it made her want nothing more than to retreat into herself.

⟫⟫ ⟪⟪

Fen couldn't figure out whether Mati liked him or not. He knew that she tolerated him, for the most part, but as the days passed, he found himself almost obsessing over the question. She didn't smile much, but when she did, it was usually because she was laughing at him, or some accident he'd caused. He didn't mind that; a small price he willingly paid.

Alik woke the party up at the same time every morning—dawn. Fen wasn't feeling it that morning, and grumbled the whole time he packed up his horse. Alik walked past him with his own pack in hand, landing a swift but soft *thwack* to the back of Fen's head. Fen rubbed his head and shot a steely gaze at Alik, who didn't even turn to look at Fen's reaction.

Fen balked and stomped over to Alik, intent on confronting him. Alik turned away from his horse to face Fen, but did nothing, just waited for him to act. Fen took a swing at Alik, one he dodged with ease. Fen overshot, his arm connecting with Mati's shoulder instead, as she passed by them on the way to her own horse. Fen's eyes went wide as Mati stumbled back, stunned.

"I am so sorry!" Fen panicked. "Are you okay?" He tried to reach out to steady her, but Mati pulled away from his grasp.

"I'll live," she grunted, but she had pure malice in her eyes.

"That's it!" Alik exclaimed, pointing at Fen. "You need to learn to control that impulsive behavior of yours. Tonight, you start sword training."

Fen was too guilty to be excited about that. He had hoped that he'd learn swordplay, but not this way. Fen watched Mati get onto her horse, and realized that she was consciously keeping her eyes averted from him. That was the first time that he really felt sorry for his dumb actions. He wouldn't blame her if she never spoke to him again after that. Why couldn't he be calmer and more collected, like her?

That afternoon, Fen tried to ride up alongside Mati and apologize. He hadn't been able to think straight all morning, and needed to make sure she wasn't truly mad at him.

"I'm sorry," Fen apologized, moping. "I really didn't mean to hit you. Alik just made me so mad, and I didn't think."

Mati sat there for a long moment, still facing forward, "I'm fine. I just wish you'd go one whole day in peace and quiet."

Fen was happy that she'd acknowledged him, though it was annoying that she always seemed to feel the need to scold him. "I promise to try, if you promise to try not to treat me like a child."

"I don't know why you have to act so childish all the time," she replied instantly, but she winced as soon as she said it. "I'm sorry."

Fen straightened up in his saddle, taken aback. "You didn't think I was so childish the night I stayed awake to keep *you* safe in the Crescent Wood."

"Fen," Mati started to say, but Fen cut her off.

"You think you're so smart," Fen huffed. "You're not happy unless you're telling me what to do. I don't need a mother."

Fen squeezed his horse's sides and trotted off. In getting away from Mati, he ended up riding next to Alik.

"Troubles?" Alik asked without prompting.

"She just makes me so mad! I tried to be nice, but I can't anymore. She's impossible; always telling me what to do and trying to force me to do things her way."

Alik smiled knowingly. "Maybe she's just trying to help."

"Help?" Fen scoffed. "Help me what? Lose my mind?"

"If you let her help you, maybe you wouldn't get yourself into so many scrapes."

"You mean give in to her?"

"Compromise," Alik corrected, and reached into a large pack strapped to the side of his horse.

Fen gawked in surprise, dropping the reins, as Alik pulled out a sword and handed it to him.

"This is for you," Alik said.

Fen almost shot into the air with excitement. He took the heavy, sheathed blade from Alik's hands, and looked at it with awe. It was a beautiful sword. The hilt was finely carved with swirling shapes, had a patina, and worn as though it had already had a long life. There was a chip missing from the pommel that left Fen wondering what kind of adventures this sword had already seen. He carefully grasped the hilt and was surprised that his fingers laid almost perfectly into the worn marks left behind by its former owner. It felt so natural in his hand, as though he'd already become accustomed to its unique weight and size. It immediately felt like an extension of his arm as he pulled it from the scabbard.

"It served its former owner well," Alik added, breaking the silence. "How does it feel?"

"It feels good. I've never held a real sword before. Is it supposed to feel so right?"

Alik smiled. "If you have the right sword, it will."

"I think I have the right one, then," Fen answered, still in awe at the valuable gift. He'd never received a gift from anyone before. "Why did you give this to me?"

"I've been holding on to it for a friend. I don't think he'd mind if you used it for now."

"Was this Tanophis' sword?" Fen wondered.

Alik nodded. "It was."

"Was he a good swordsman?"

"The best I've ever faced," Alik answered, and his eyes held a light that Fen had never seen in him before. "We would train for hours and hours until Pax would force us to stop." A huge smile spread across his face. "That nick on the pommel just there has a great story. Tanophis was crazy. He leapt up over a rocky outcropping and landed behind me, but I tripped him before he got his footing. He fell, head-over-heels, down those rocks. One of those rocks nicked his sword. He was mad at me about that for weeks."

Fen ran his finger over the mark. He almost felt the pang of the landing in his bones.

"We had good times," Alik said with a sigh, before falling silent once more.

⭗⭗⭗ ⭗⭗⭗

That evening, just as Alik had promised, he and Fen had some basic sword lessons. Mati watched from the fireside where she sat with Asterion and Dursten. The stars chatted nonchalantly, while Mati tried not to look too interested in Fen. Alik was showing him several sword forms to practice, and drilling him in how to transition between them properly, before leaving Fen to practice alone.

"He's good," Alik leaned in, speaking to Dursten in almost a whisper. "But I'm not telling him that. He took to the sword quickly."

"Was there any doubt he would be?" Dursten answered smiling. "I assume he'll pick it up easily."

Alik sighed with a smile. "I suppose not. He's a natural at it. I'd almost forgot—" He stopped, noticing Mati watching him with interest. "You'll be next," he threatened, pointing at her.

Mati crinkled her nose but said nothing as Alik got a piece of cheese and began to munch on it. But as her mind wandered to the odd way Alik had stopped his original thought a moment ago, her eyes wandered back to Fen. He had taken off his shirt and was moving through the forms with ease. The sword seemed like it was part of him now, as he swirled it about. The muscles she had only previously seen in silhouette through a wet shirt, now caught her attention the most. They tensed and danced along with his movements, and she could feel her cheeks go red hot as her mind betrayed her again. Those arms had been wrapped around her in Crescent Wood...

Mati nearly had a panic attack when Fen caught her staring. He gave her a huge grin and flashed a wink as he flourished his sword a bit more widely. As he did, though, the sword tumbled from his hand and planted point-first in the ground. She couldn't tell, in the dark, whether his cheeks had gone red, but embarrassment spread across his face as he attempted to yank his sword from the dirt. Once it was reclaimed, he flashed a sheepish grin and a shoulder shrug her way.

Mati rolled her eyes and stifled a laugh. She couldn't deny that he could be kind of cute when he attempted to flirt with her. She was glad that the fire cast an orange light on her face and Fen couldn't see how warm her cheeks had gone at his grin. She couldn't let him know that. He was already a pain in the ass, and if he knew she actually liked him she'd never hear the end of it. And she was still struggling with the question of whether she would be staying here, or going back home once their job was done.

"You look deep in thought," Asterion said softly beside her.

"I am," she sighed.

"Anything I can help with?"

"I'm not sure what to do, Asterion. I do love Vertrose. It really does feel like home already."

"But..." Asterion prompted her to keep her talking.

"*But*, I'm still not sure whether I want to exchange the world I already know for one that's completely unknown. Or what role I would even play here."

Asterion smiled at her. "That is a choice you'll have to make. If I may ask though, why would you want to return to Earth?"

Mati sat deep in thought for a moment. "It's comfortable back on Earth; I know what all my options are. I miss my mom's hugs, and I miss my dad's texts to make sure I got home safe. It wasn't a perfect life, but it was the life I knew. I knew what I could and couldn't do, and what would happen next. And that feels safe. And then there's Fen. He's fitting in, and he's just able to adapt so well. I feel like I'm defective, somehow."

"You are not defective," Asterion assured her. "You're just different."

"I guess," Mati sighed. "I do have one more question for you."

"Whatever I can answer to help," the star answered.

"Are my parents here?"

"No, your parents are on Earth."

"You mean, I don't have any real parents?" Mati let her shoulders drop with a deep sigh, letting any feelings of hope escape.

Asterion placed a gentle hand on her head. "Carol and Gary are as real as parents come. They love you unconditionally, no matter where you came from or who you are. They are *real* parents."

"Why don't we have parents, Asterion?" Mati questioned. "Fen doesn't either."

"The best thing I can tell you is that you and Fen were created when the curse took effect."

"So, we just popped into existence?"

"For lack of a better explanation, yes." Asterion answered. "But beyond that, I can't say."

"I'm not even real..." Mati's heart and stomach dropped. Her whole life both made more sense and no sense at all. Everything she knew was turned on its head like puzzle pieces being dumped on a table for her to put back together.

Asterion smiled. "You're very much real. The laws of this universe aren't the laws that Earth must abide by. Dursten and I have no parents, either; does that make us any less real to you?"

"Well, you're a star. That's different."

"Why?"

"It just is. I'm just a human."

"A human, yes, but no less real than even the stars. Don't worry yourself too much over it. Keep your mind focused on your task, and you'll be just fine. Perhaps you could ask Fen to help you adjust."

"What do you mean?"

"As you said," Asterion answered, "he's adjusting well. You could ask him to help you adjust as well. It would give you two a chance to get to know one another more."

"You keep trying to shove us together," Mati said, raising one eyebrow. "Why?"

"You're meant to work together, and I just think it might be easier if you actually spoke to him."

Mati gave Asterion a kind smile. "I'll think about it."

Asterion patted her shoulder as they stood and returned to their seat next to Alik. "Please do."

Mati found some comfort in Asterion's words, but it would take a while to digest the idea that somehow she and Fen had just appeared out of thin air.

# Chapter 6

After the previous night's activity, Mati had decided to steer clear of Fen. She couldn't bear the thought of him knowing that she'd had visions of him dancing around with that sword in her head at all hours. She was sure she'd betray herself if she so much as breathed in his direction.

After three days in the desert, the wilderness had finally gone back to being green and the weather more temperate as they got closer to Guyt's territory.

Fen rode up to Dursten. "How much farther do we have to go?"

"Not far now," Dursten answered. "Asterion and I will leave you tonight, and you will continue on with Alik. We have business with the Illustrus that we can no longer put off."

"What's in Insburg?" Fen pressed further. "Who's the friend we're going to meet?"

"Faelinth, Headman of Insburg, and a valuable ally," Alik answered.

Fen sneered. "How is a headman going to help us in a rebellion?"

Alik shot him a warning look. "Faelinth is a powerful ally, *boy*. He commands the only independent army and town within Guyt's borders. He might be the only one to really be able to help us decode the curse. And you'll do well to watch your tongue when speaking about friends."

Fen rolled his eyes. "If you lot would tell us more about any of this, then I wouldn't have to watch the way I speak about them."

Alik's eyes sparked a warning, but he kept silent.

"I think what Fen is asking, ever so nicely," Mati joined the conversation, "is whether you would tell us more, without us having to ask."

"We are just trying to wait until you're ready—and until we know more—to tell you more," Asterion answered.

"We've been here for ten days. Can't you all meet us in the middle and give us a bit more information?"

"Exactly my point," Fen added, sounding irritated. "We need to know some things."

Asterion sighed a knowing sigh. "We are aware. But we are not exactly sure what we can and cannot say. Curses can be tricky, and without knowing the exact wording of this one, we can't be sure what could compromise the locks and keys."

"So, there're rules?" Mati asked. She could work with rules.

"Yes," Dursten answered. "Just as curses have keys that can break them, they also have locks that could seal them in place. If we break the lock rule—or rules—it will set the curse forever. We must tread carefully in what we reveal, in order to preserve the curse as it is and not make the situation worse. We know very little about what needs to be done."

"Can you tell me about some of the rules that other curses have?" Mati asked.

Asterion sighed in thought. "The most commonly used lock is duration—if not enough time has elapsed before a key is tried. Some locks could be about knowledge—revealing to the cursed one that a curse exists. Another lock could be triggered if there is any supernatural interference: trying to place a counter-curse to end the first curse could lock them both in place. There's just too much room for error."

As much as she hated the reasoning, she now understood why they'd been told so little. "Is there anyone that could help us? Has anyone looked for any answers in the last twenty-three years?"

"We're hoping," Alik said, "that Faelinth might have some ideas about how we should proceed. He's the only one who might have been able to figure anything out."

Mati's brain physically hurt from that news. "Faelinth is the only one who has been trying to solve the curse?"

"He's the only one who still had any hope." Alik's voice was hard. "We tried, at first, but as time wore on, we were all pulled in different directions. The task seemed impossible."

Mati felt angry that for twenty-three years they'd all just been sitting around with their teeth in their mouths and their elbows half-way up their arms—as her dad would've said—and now she and Fen were left in the dark. "No one even tried to come up with a plan?"

"We did," Alik restated. "I'm not proud that I gave up. I wish now that I had kept trying. But I didn't, and I'm trying to fix that."

Mati let out an annoyed huff—no plan.


The afternoon passed slowly, small glades of trees appearing here and there. Eventually, the party came to the first village they had seen since leaving Lyserria. It was little more than a cluster of houses and one tavern, and had no name that Alik was aware of. The party planned to only stop for a moment at the central well, to refill their waterskins.

A group of four men approached them as soon as Alik and Fen had dismounted. They were dirty, stank, and their hands rested on the beating sticks they all wore on their belts.

"That'll be two silvers…each," one stated, in a voice that made Fen's skin crawl.

Fen caught Alik's eyes, and Alik's gaze darted to each man in quick succession. "That's crazy," Fen blurt out. "Water is public property."

Alik sighed. "The boy speaks in haste. We are mere travelers and don't have any money. We only seek to refill our waterskins and to water our horses."

The same man answered, smiling with a nearly toothless grin. "Then the boy should learn to keep his mouth shut." He eyed their horses. "We'll take them as payment."

"Ha!" Fen blurted out again. "You'll have to kill us first."

The man's toothless grin widened. "With pleasure."

The other three men pulled out their sticks, and one moved toward Mati's horse.

She kicked him. "Back off!"

The man's eyes grew wide, and all four grinned with wicked delight.

"This one's a maid!" one exclaimed excitedly.

Three of the men tugged at Mati and tried to pull her off her horse. The horse started to jerk and rear up in an attempt to pull away. Mati held the reins tight and tried not to fall off as the horse continued its nervous prance for freedom.

Fen leapt off his horse, and, without thought or plan, went at the men head-first. His sword clashed against the wooden sticks, breaking one with just a few swift swings. The world blurred out of focus, and he couldn't see anything but these men. He would send those pathetic worms to their maker. How dare they try to put their hands on Mati...*his* Mati! The only girl he'd ever met that didn't seem to care too much about his looks or where he had come from or what he was. It had annoyed him at first, but somewhere in this journey they were both on, she had become to mean more to him.

His temper swelled and he saw the terrified looks on the men's faces as he got closer. They all turned to flee, and Fen tried to follow before Alik grabbed his shirt sleeve to hold him back.

"Let me *go!*" he shouted and tugged his arm away from Alik.

"No, boy," Alik answered just as angrily. "We need to get out of here before they return with friends."

He pulled Fen to his horse and shoved him toward it. "Get on."

Fen complied while Alik mounted, and the party took off out of the village at a full gallop. They passed a few villagers who had stuck their heads out of windows or doors to see what was going on. Fen was still reeling from the encounter, adrenaline pumping through his veins.

Alik led them off the main road, pushing the group as fast as they could go without killing the horses. Fen took up a position at the rear of the party and nearly choked on the dirty cloud kicked up by the horses' pounding hooves. He could barely make out Mati's horse in front of him through the dust, and he kept a close eye on her as they rode.

At dark, Alik brought them to a halt in a patch of thin trees. Mati saw that they were still near the main road, but there were bushes lining the road that would protect them from prying eyes. She dismounted and started to beat the dust off her clothes.

"You could've gotten us killed, boy!" Alik burst out as soon as he had dismounted.

"They went after Mati!" Fen retorted just as forcefully.

"There are other ways to handle things; the answer is not always having a bar brawl!" Alik answered. "You forced me into a skirmish unprepared. We could both have been injured and then where would she be?" Fen made no answer, so Alik continued. "Consider this a lesson in waiting for the opportune moment. Never go straight to a fight if there's a way out, and never go into a fight without first being sure that your partners are prepared to have your back. We'll camp here tonight. Go get some wood for a fire, boy."

Fen dismounted and stormed off further into the trees. As soon as Mati saw an opportunity when the stars and Alik were distracted, she stole away into the trees, following Fen. She only wandered for a few minutes before she found him mumbling angrily under his breath while he picked up old sticks and small branches off the forest floor. She approached him tentatively.

"What the fuck do you want?" he spat at her.

Mati recoiled. "Well, I was going to thank you for helping me. But not if you're gonna to be an ass about it."

She turned to walk away, but Fen caught her arm. "I'm sorry," he said woefully, not meeting her eyes. "I didn't mean it. I'm just angry with Alik. Are you mad at me, too?"

"No," she answered softly. "I really came to thank you, and to tell you that I think Alik was being an overgrown ass. I was close to falling off my horse when you attacked them."

Fen gave her a half-hearted smile and sat down on a fallen tree. "Thanks," he said still not looking at her.

Mati stood there, looking at him, when an overwhelming thought came to her. He had risked his life for her. Twice, now actually. She leaned down and planted a kiss on his cheek.

"I'll take that as payment this time," Fen beamed, his mood shifting immediately. "Next time, though, I'm going to require two for saving your ass."

Mati huffed a nervous laugh. What on Earth had come over her to kiss him? She started to pull away, to hide for the rest of the evening, but Fen reached out and grazed her arm with his hand. "Wait," he said quickly.

Mati stopped moving, and Fen's hand stayed, resting lightly on her upper arm. She felt like time had ceased for a moment. Fen looked into Mati's eyes, like he was searching for something there. She felt a pull towards him from deep within herself, as though her soul was trying to push its way out of her body and touch him.

He left his hand on her arm, and gently pushed her hair behind her ear with his other, then rested that hand on her hip. She immediately felt her cheeks and ears go hot, but the rest of her was frozen. His face came closer to hers and then he stopped for a moment, wordlessly asking for her approval. She stayed completely still, only the pressure from her soul beckoning him closer.

He closed his eyes and took the plunge. His kiss landed softly on her lips; to her surprise, she answered him back instead of fleeing. His hand moved from her arm to the back of her head to pull her even closer, as her lips parted for him. They kissed deeply, finding a rhythm as though they'd kissed a thousand times before. The pushing from within her seemed to thrust her forward, in a desperate need for more. Her soul became a ravenous, starving beast.

Footsteps thudded nearby. Mati was thrust back into reality and pulled away from Fen just as someone came crashing through the bushes. It was almost dark and her body flinched away, as if she had been caught consorting with the enemy.

"Where's that damn wood, Fen?" Alik thundered. "How long does it take to get a few sticks for a warming fire?" Alik was startled to a hush, obviously realizing that he'd interrupted something as soon as he saw Mati flinch away. He tried—in vain—to make a hasty retreat.

"No!" Mati exclaimed nervously before he could escape. "I was just looking for a place to pee in peace." She disappeared into the woods, just far enough away to collapse next to a tree without either man seeing her. Her hands were shaking with excitement, anxiety, and embarrassment.

She could hear Fen and Alik making their way back out of the trees, and she sat in the dark in silence. Why did she let him kiss her? Why had she kissed him back? She desperately wanted to take it back, and just as desperately needed another. When he had kissed her, it had felt so *natural*. Like they had done it so many times before that her body had anticipated his movements. And that sensation of not having been in control of her own body made her wary of her own feelings.

She finally composed herself after a period of time that she knew had been too long for a simple bathroom run. She resolved to dash for her bedroll and go to sleep immediately. She didn't feel like having to face anyone else tonight.

# Chapter 7

Fen awoke naturally before Alik had a chance to kick him awake, as he'd been doing so far this trip. He quietly packed up his bedroll and loaded it onto his horse. Then he sat in the quiet of the dewy morning, next to the remnants of last night's fire. His mind was still pitching and reeling from the kiss. He resolved to keep that memory as something to savor for the rest of his life. He knew it would ruin him, though; no other girl could possibly take up so much unwarranted space in his brain. It had also given him a bit of hope.

She had kissed him back.

Alik finally stirred just as the sun was peeking through the trees. He grunted when he saw Fen already awake. "You finally learned," he said, grumpily.

Fen smiled. "Sorry I robbed you of your amusement."

Alik smirked back at him and continued through his morning rituals.

As soon as the others were up, the stars announced that they would be departing. They made their goodbyes, then disappeared in a flash of light. Mati seemed to turn a bit green at the sight.

"Are you okay?" Fen asked.

"Just the thought of traveling like that makes me want to vomit," she answered. "You didn't get sick on your way here?"

"A little, I guess," Fen said. "Not enough to get really get sick, though."

"Lucky you," Mati said, regaining her normal color.

"Good now?" he asked.

She nodded at him and gave him a small smile that made his heart skip a beat. He returned her smile and turned to continue getting ready for the day's ride.

The day passed uneventfully and, just before nightfall, they spotted the town of Insburg ahead. It was enclosed by a high log wall, though the gate was open to all. Smooth stone streets wound aimlessly around the tall wooden houses, and the people all seemed well-clothed and well-fed. Fen couldn't imagine how that could be when Lyserria had been so poor.

"I thought life in Guyt's territory would look worse," Fen said.

Alik let out a half-amused huff. "It is. Insburg is completely self-sustained, thanks to Faelinth. He runs a tight ship and makes sure everyone in Insburg gets what they need."

They dismounted in front of an inn named The Golden Madrigal. Their horses were attended to immediately, and the group of three entered the inn. Oil lamps hung low in the space, leaving blackened stains on the wooden ceiling above. There were long rows of tables all connected together, giving the impression that all the parties seated there were friendly with each other. A fire roared on one side of the room where patrons were gathered, playing various instruments. Alik chose a spot at a table near the far end of the room, and the other customers only gave them half a glance before returning to their food and beer.

Fen had never felt so *normal* before. No one stared or sneered or whispered at his presence like they would have on Jefy. He felt immediately at ease.

"We'll wait here until Faelinth calls us," Alik said, sitting down furthest away from any other patrons. "No doubt he'll already know we're here."

Fen never sat, wandering off through the crowd instead. The food smelled so good, and his stomach had immediately begun to growl.

"Fen," Alik cried after him. "Would you get back over here?"

Fen waved him off and continued to the bar, where a grizzled old man was serving alcohol by the mug. "Excuse me," he said.

"Wait your turn, stranger!" another patron complained and pointed to a small line formed near the bar.

"Fen," Mati said from behind him. "What are you doing? Alik wants us to be ready when Faelinth comes for us."

All Fen wanted was some food. He didn't even want a drink, the way he might have if he were back home. "I just wanted to get some food. I'm starving."

The whole bar was now crying out complaints and Fen backed away. Then he spotted something out of the corner of his eye. The kitchen door had been left open and there was a massive roast animal of some kind, steaming on a table just by the door. He checked around himself, and it seemed like his retreat from the bar had once again made him invisible to the other patrons.

"Fen, no," Mati protested. "Just go wait in line like everyone else."

He ignored her completely and slid through the door, then grabbed a leg off the carcass. He had the juicy morsel to his mouth when a voice called to him.

"Aye! What you think you're doin'?"

Fen turned his head to see a large man coming through the kitchen, from the door at the other end. He had a meat cleaver in one hand and a large spoon in the other. His well-soiled apron hung to his knees, and swayed as he came after them. Fen hurriedly swallowed the large bite with a gulp.

"I will pay for this," Fen said in a panic. "I'm just so hungry. We've been riding all day."

"I don't give a dingle bartsy how long you rode for. That's for a special guest of the Headman!"

Mati tugged at his shirt. "Come on. Let's go."

Fen took another big bite of the meat. It was so good, and even the commotion he'd caused couldn't take that away.

"I'm terribly sorry for my very stupid friend," Mati yelled behind her to the angry cook, as she dragged Fen out of the kitchen by his shirt collar. "We will pay for it. I promise."

Fen allowed Mati to pull him backwards out of the kitchen as he took another large bite, still clutching the leg.

"Could you stop eating that poor man's leg right in front of him," she snarled into his ear.

Fen smiled around a mouthful of the delicious meat. It was cooked just right. He'd never in his whole life had meat that was so tender and juicy. "It's so good, though! It's a compliment to his cooking."

"Bring that leg back here!" the man demanded. He started gaining speed, swinging his cleaver and spoon wildly in the air above him.

"No one will want it now that I've eaten from it," Fen protested. "If you calm down, I'll go get the money right now."

"We don't *have* any money," Mati hissed through her teeth.

"He doesn't know that."

Fen almost fell over as Mati let go of his shirt. The angry cook had caught up with them and had the cleaver poised over his sweaty head, ready to carve Fen up like a fine dinner. Fen squeezed his eyes shut tightly, braced himself, and held the half-eaten leg over his head as a useless shield. "Take it back! I'm sorry!"

The cook paused just long enough for a regally-dressed faun to interrupt the chaos. "The Headman will see you now," they said.

Alik looked up from his table with wide eyes at the sight of Fen with his meat leg, Mati who had just let go of his shirt, and the irate cook. "What've you done now, boy?"

The cook stopped dead in his tracks at the sight of the regal faun. He dropped his arms to his sides, cleaver included. "My apologies, Litra, I had no idea these two were here for the Headman." He gave them a deep nod and shot a dirty look at Fen before turning back to the kitchen.

Fen gave the departing chef a cheeky smile, while taking another meaty bite. "Pleasure meeting you."

Mati glared at him and rolled her eyes. "Next time, I'm letting you pay for your own recklessness. You almost got us carved like a Thanksgiving turkey."

"A what?" Fen asked.

"A Thanksgiving turkey..."

Fen took another big bite of the leg. "What's that?"

"It's a holiday where I'm from. You carve a turkey up for dinner."

"What's a turkey?"

Mati let out an exasperated breath. "*That's* what you took from all this?"

Fen shrugged as Litra led them out of the tavern, still clinging to the leg as a prize.


They followed Litra through dimly lit wooden corridors and a series of locked doors, eventually coming to a small, candle-lit dining room, where a strikingly majestic man sat at the head of the table. His thick but perfectly manicured eyebrows arched over small dark eyes, and the table concealed the true length of his sandy brown hair. Not one hair or thread seemed out of place.

"Welcome," the man greeted them with a smile. "It's good to see you, Alik. It's been too long, my friend."

"And you, Faelinth," Alik answered with a smile. "You've got quite the town here."

"Yes," Faelinth agreed. "It isn't easy, but we manage to have a decent living in these terrible times." His gaze trailed over to Fen—with his leg of meat—and Mati, who both stood silent. "And you two are especially welcome."

Fen only nodded in acknowledgement while Mati uttered a barely audible "thank you."

"Sit. Sit," Faelinth motioned to the table. "Don't stand on ceremony for me. I have a hot meal being brought out now. I was beginning to get worried that you weren't coming today."

They all took their seats. Fen was still holding onto the leg he'd procured from the kitchen and was now feeling quite awkward.

Steaming food was brought out on dozens of platters and bowls by a string of servants in long aprons. At the sight Fen practically started drooling down his chin with anticipation. Then he saw a large meaty roast...with one missing leg.

"I see you've already sampled dinner," Faelinth said with a smile. "Hopefully, you found it to your liking."

Fen felt his cheeks go warm. He smiled shyly at their host. "The best."

The service was casual, and they all grabbed plates and dished their food out.

"Do you just want the serving spoon?" Faelinth teased Fen.

Fen looked up and saw Alik's scowl as Fen heaped his plate enthusiastically full. He stopped immediately, slowly returning the scoop of food currently on the serving spoon, and contented himself with the food that was already on his plate.

Not much besides pleasantries were exchanged during the meal. Their party was so hungry that once the food was officially theirs for the taking, they fell nearly silent and ate.

After dinner, Faelinth led them through several warmly-lit hallways attached to the inn and into his own adjoining residence. He opened the door to his study, then shut it behind them. The room was dark except for two lanterns that hung on hooks next to the ceiling-high bookshelves, and a low-burning fire in the fireplace across the room.

"Now, it should be safe to discuss important business," Faelinth said and sat at a large wooden desk in the center of the room. "What do you need from me?"

Alik settled himself comfortably in a large wooden armchair next to the fire. "We will need your assurance that you will send your two hundred soldiers."

"Of course," Faelinth answered. "I thought that was a given, brother. What else can I do?"

"Nothing, at the moment. We'll need to gather the others quickly...Those who are still on our side, that is."

"Yes," Faelinth answered dreamily, as if he were in a different world, before snapping back. "I'll send a few men with you now. I assume you will be traveling to the Kingly Hills for Rena?"

Alik snorted. "I'll drag her from those villages kicking and screaming, if need be."

"I'm surprised you're here, actually. I didn't think even the stars would be able to drag you out of Lyserria."

Alik huffed. "I'd never hear the end of it if I didn't. My sister, would skin my hide." His face softened ever so slightly. "And I miss my best friend. We need Tanophis and Paxis back if we're truly to win this war."

Fen was still standing awkwardly next to Mati in the middle of the room. Alik and Faelinth's disregard for their presence irritated Mati. She could only imagine what it was doing to Fen.

"Excuse me," Fen butted in, sarcasm laced heavily in his voice. "Is anyone going to loop us into this, or are we to just stay in the dark at your whim?"

Alik sighed as Faelinth's eyes snapped to Fen. "I must have forgotten myself, and who was here with us. Yes, of course you'll be *looped in.*"

"Good," Fen snapped back, and took a seat across from Faelinth, uninvited, in a matching armchair to Alik's. He motioned for Mati to join him, which she did. Then, Fen wriggled himself into the seat and continued.

"Let's start with what exactly we're," he motioned to himself and Mati, "supposed to be doing. What is our role in all this?"

"A good question," Faelinth answered. "I didn't realize you would want to be so deeply involved, but I should have guessed as much."

Alik and Faelinth exchanged a look and smile that implied they had an inside joke.

Alik took a deep, reluctant breath. "We'd like for you two to run the rebellion. And, as you know, we're here to consult with Faelinth on what he thinks we can tell you about the curse."

"And?" Fen urged, turning to Faelinth. "Can you tell us anything?"

Faelinth took a deep breath. "We can only tell you that you two are the only ones able to unite the remaining peoples of Vertrose under the banner of the rebellion. Guyt has already started to move his armies, and we will need the two of you to attend a war council called the Magnus Concilium. Your presence alone should be enough to sway the others to join us. But they may need your reassurance."

"What kind of council?" Mati asked. "And with who?"

"It will be a meeting with the leaders of the sykosee, lycans, madrigals, and banshees. We will need all of them on our side to beat Guyt's army of nuwu."

Mati's brow furrowed. "His what?"

"Nuwu," Faelinth answered. "They are mud puppets, created by Guyt's ally Ciksura to do their bidding. And since they are created from dirt, the supply of them is nearly endless. Their numbers would be enough to overwhelm any army we could hope to raise."

Mati's throat clenched. "How are we supposed to fight that kind of army?"

Faelinth turned to face her. "With some good luck, and a lot of hope that good will win out. We will also keep hope that we can figure out the nature of the locks on the curse before we need that luck."

"But we don't even know what the curse is," Fen pointed out.

Faelinth's gaze fell to the floor. "We are aware that we fight a losing battle, Fen. But we must try, nevertheless."

Mati sensed Fen's irritation brewing and stepped in to dampen the fire. "Where did Guyt find this curse? A witch's spell book, maybe?"

"You're not far off," Alik answered. "He used an ancient tome, but we have no way of knowing from where. Guyt is one of the primordial entities, and is not of this universe. He could've gotten it from anywhere."

"Why did the stars bring us back now if we're not even able to help?" Mati asked.

"Because without you, this rebellion won't happen. And we need to strike now. We have received word that Guyt is planning his final strike; some of our brethren in Vertrose don't see the imminent threat this poses to us all."

Fen huffed out an agitated breath. "We're here to break a curse that no one understands, and which could accidentally be made permanent at any moment. And you're using us as bait to bring in more allies."

Alik ran his hand down his face, resting his hand on his chin. "We would tell you the nature of the curse if we knew it, Fen, truly. And you will be more than bait. We'd like you and Mati to run the Magnus. It's your voices they need to hear."

"Can you tell us what the plan *is*?" Mati asked calmly. "I know I'd like to be more informed about where we're going, and why."

Faelinth smiled. "I think that's a very reasonable request. And I think Alik can handle that, though he's not our most communicative friend."

Alik readjusted his seat in his chair. "When we leave Insburg, we'll be headed for the Kingly Hills, to find my sister. From there we'll go to the Magnus, where you two will hopefully be able to unite the peoples of Vertrose for the final battle."

"Thank you," Mati answered, and yawned. She was trying so hard to be engaged, but her exhaustion was making the task almost impossible. She couldn't think of anything else at the moment.

"Go get some sleep," Faelinth suggested. "Your rooms are just down the hall to the right. We'll talk more when you're both rested."

Fen stood and followed Mati out into the hall. She thought, given the circumstances, she had done a decent job at acting like she knew what she was doing. But with her mind feeling blurry, she allowed herself to simply follow the servants to their rooms.

⋘ ⋙

Mati skittered into her own room and collapsed on the bed in exhaustion. She had barely stopped bouncing from her flop when a knock sounded at her door.

"Lady Mati," a female voice called.

"Come in," she answered.

The door creaked open and a tall faun came in, a bundle in her arms.

"I have clean clothes and towels for you, miss. Someone will be in shortly to take you to the bath. They're running the hot water now."

"Thank you!" Mati exclaimed, her brain coming back to life. It would be nice to finally have a real bath. She felt—and knew—she looked disgusting.

The faun hurried out of the room and shut the door behind her. And no sooner had Mati sat down again, then there was a quiet rap at the door. "Come in," she called assuming it was the faun again.

Fen popped through the door quickly and quietly shut it behind him. "Hey," he said, seemingly oddly unsure of himself.

"What are you doing in here?" Mati interrupted him anxiously. "Someone will see."

"We need to talk about this curse."

"There's nothing to discuss," Mati said. "No one knows anything about it."

"And you're okay with that?" Fen scoffed.

"We don't have a choice. It's not a mystery we can just figure out, like in *Sherlock Holmes*. We literally have nothing to go on."

"What's *Sherlock Holmes*?" Fen raised an eyebrow.

Mati waved her hand. "It's nothing."

"I think there's more to the curse than they're letting on," Fen hypothesized.

"I'm not so sure." Mati said. "Even the stars don't know what the curse is, exactly. I know they're keeping things from us. I hate it, but they've explained the stakes to us. I'm not prepared to put these people in jeopardy because I wanted to know more. We need to just keep calm and stay the course."

"You can trust them if you want, but I'm trying to help."

"I'm not trusting them. I just think that, since they're the ones who have been cursed, if they knew how to break it they would tell us. I don't want to go against their wishes. It might do more harm than good. I think we should play by the rules and it will all work out."

Fen rolled his eyes. "Are you always such a purist, doing what you're told?"

The nerve he had, to call her a goody-goody! "At least I'm not constantly surrounded by destruction and chaos."

"It's part of my charm," Fen waggled his eyebrows at her.

"It's irritating and childish, and I'm surprised it hasn't gotten you killed."

"That's what I have you here for," Fen said.

He sounded sincere instead of sarcastic, and Mati didn't know how to take that. But she hadn't really noticed until now that she and Fen seemed to be complete opposites. "Maybe that's part of the curse—a 'yin and yang' sorta deal."

"A what?" Fen asked.

"It's an Earth thing. Umm...yin and yang are opposites, but they work together, through all of nature, to bring balance. Maybe that's us. Natural duality. Maybe we really do just need to work together to bring balance back?"

Fen stood in awe. "You're very smart."

Mati jumped up and down at her discovery. She grabbed Fen instinctively and pulled him in for a hug. "Maybe that's it!"

Without warning, Fen landed his lips on Mati's. She froze.

"Sorry," he said hastily. "I thought—"

It was Mati's turn to surprise him as her instincts took over. Without even thinking about it, she planted a kiss on him just as quickly, cutting off his statement. Then she pulled back. Fen's eyes went as wide as saucers, and he grinned a cocky, crooked grin.

"You can't resist me," he joked, and pushed her hair back out of her face. "There. Now I can see your red cheeks."

Mati felt her cheeks warm from that, slapping him in jest.

Fen laughed and pulled her against his chest. They kissed, but only for a moment until a knock at the door had Mati jumping away from him again.

"Lady Mati," a voice called. "Your bath is ready. May I come in? I have some womanly items for you."

"Thank you!" Mati barked, her voice betraying her nervousness. "One moment!"

Fen choked a laugh. "Womanly items?" He was still stifling his laugh as Mati shoved him under the bed. "Really? Under the bed? You know they've already heard us, right?"

"Get under there," she loudly whispered. "And for God's sake, be quiet." She composed herself and took a deep breath, "Come in."

The servant opened the door, a shadow of a knowing smile on their face, and laid the bundle on the bed. "There's cloth, and oil for your monthlies. If you need anything else, just ask." They shuffled hurriedly out, still fighting a grin as they shut the door.

Mati buried her face in her hands as Fen scrambled out from under the bed. "They knew," Mati whispered. "How can I face these people?"

Fen laughed and teased her. "What does it matter? We were talking about important stuff...at first. At least we weren't doing anything *else*." Fen winked.

"Get out!" Mati shoved him toward the door, but she couldn't help smiling as she did it.

"Careful, or someone will hear you," Fen kept teasing, resisting her attempts to get him to the door.

"Please, just go," she pleaded. "I'd like to go take a bath before the water gets cold."

Fen purred and waggled his eyebrows at her.

"Oh, God!" Mati laughed. "Just go."

Fen opened the door and peeked out. The coast clear, he turned back to Mati and pressed a quick kiss on her cheek before disappearing into his own room.

# Chapter 8

That night, Faelinth sat in his study long after Alik had gone, the flickering candles creating a brooding scene. His mind wandered to times long past.

In his memory, Faelinth stood in the middle of a great marble hall surrounded by his friends, the gods. They were staring into the face of Ciksura—one of their own. Ciksura's sharp features and pale eyes, however, were focused on pleading with Faelinth's wife.

"Come," Ciksura beckoned to Lavinia. "Guyt is waiting. He'll give us all we dream of."

Faelinth turned, stunned and betrayed, to look at the dark eyes of his wife. Lavinia had been more melancholy than usual lately, but he had thought it was just the stress of dealing with the issue with Guyt. "What does Ciksura mean, Lavinia?"

Lavinia took one step away from her husband. One strand of her deep red hair fell across her porcelain face. "I don't fit in here."

"That's a lie!" Faelinth cried out. "You know I love you."

"I'm the goddess of evil, Faelinth. You should have seen this coming."

"How? How would I have foreseen that my wife—the woman I love—would betray me?"

"We are fated to be together, nothing more," Lavinia's now-icy stare pierced his soul. "I have never been able to love you as you have me. And Guyt doesn't ask anything from me but what I am."

Faelinth's soul broke at that statement and his voice echoed through the hall. "I have only ever asked you to be yourself. I have never once asked you to change who you are. If that's what you think, then it is an image you have conjured in your head. Name one time—just one—when I haven't accepted you!"

Lavinia's mouth thinned. "I have felt it."

Faelinth laughed in distress. "I know we've had our battles, but I have always returned to you." He looked to Ciksura. "*You* did this to her! You have turned her against me!"

"You only love me because we were created as a pair!" Lavinia burst. "Ciksura and Guyt have only shown me the truth."

"What *truth*?"

"That in any other circumstance, we would never have worked together."

"Those are Guyt's words, Lavinia, and you know it."

Ciksura stepped forward. "Come, Lavinia. Guyt is waiting."

Lavinia turned one last time to face Faelinth. "Goodbye."

Tanophis grabbed Faelinth by the shoulders and held him as he wept. Lavinia and Ciksura had turned their backs on them.

Lavinia had turned her back on him.

Guyt had poisoned her with his words and, one day, he would pay.

For now, Faelinth could only watch through tears of sorrow and anger as Ciksura and Lavinia left the hall.

Fen woke with a well-rested stretch. He'd never had such a good night's sleep. Mati liked him. And he had an actual bed, a bath, and clean clothes for the first time in weeks. A satisfied grin spread across his face. He couldn't believe that Mati actually liked him. He didn't know if it would last. He didn't even care. He would take however much she would give, and for however long she gave it. He'd never had his heart pull him so much toward someone.

A bang on the door startled him out of his daydreams. "Get up!" Alik's booming voice rang out.

"I am up!" Fen yelled back. Not even Alik's grumpy ass was going to kill the high he was feeling today.

"We're leaving by mid-day," Alik answered. "You're doing sword work with me 'til then. Let's go."

Fen rolled out of bed and slipped on his new clothes. He grabbed his sword and left his room. He turned to Mati's door as he entered the hallway, in hope that she'd be there, but sighed when he didn't see her. He knew it was stupid, but he had just wanted a glimpse of her to make sure that what had transpired last night hadn't been a dream.

Alik was particularly grouchy that morning, as they crossed swords for several hours, and thoroughly beaten Fen down before they stopped for a short break. Fen went to the well bucket for a cup of water, and looked up to see Mati at the other end of the yard. She had her hair pulled back in a long braid so he could easily see her face. She was chatting with another woman and smiling. He tried not to stare, but he desperately wanted to make eye contact.

"Fen!" Alik barked and Fen turned his head. "We're done. We need to leave in an hour."

When Fen turned back, Mati was gone. He bounded inside, partially to pack and partially to see Mati. Her door was ajar and he popped his head inside, but didn't see her.

"What are you doing?" Her voice from behind him made him jump.

He whirled around. "Looking for you."

Mati smiled. "I was just getting a few things from the laundress."

"Oh, okay," Fen stuttered, running his fingers nervously through his hair. "I just wanted to see you before we left."

Mati stepped past him into the room. "Alright, then."

He shut the door behind himself. Suddenly his tongue felt swollen. Mati continued to pack her bag with the new clothes, until Fen forced himself to just spit it out for fear of not being able to say it any other way. "Do you like me?"

Mati took a deep breath and stopped packing for a moment, clenching her eyes shut. "Yes," she answered softly.

"That doesn't sound convincing."

"I do like you, Fen." She sighed. "I really *really* like you—"

"*But?*" he prompted, perturbed.

"But..." Mati continued. "I don't know if it's a good idea. We're supposed to be working together, with this curse and everything. And we don't know what's going to happen with that. And we also don't know what's going to happen after all this is over."

"What do you mean?" Fen asked, thoroughly confused.

"I just mean that I might go back home after this."

"Then I'll come with you to Earth. There's nothing for me anywhere else."

Mati drooped onto the bed. "I don't think it's a good idea to complicate things right now. This whole issue is already complicated enough without...whatever this is."

"So, you like me, but think that after leading me on is a good time to not *complicate* things?" Fen burst out, scowling at her.

"That's not what I mean. I never meant to lead you on. I just want to make sure we're not creating an issue."

"And that's your excuse?" Fen laughed sarcastically. "I mean, that fixes everything, doesn't it? Just say you 'didn't mean it' and everything is fine." Fen threw up his hands dramatically. How could she think that would make anything better? He should have known it was too good to be true. Maybe this was how girls acted on Earth, but if you asked him, it was rotten. At least on Jefy he knew what to expect from the girls. "Why can't you do one single thing without looking at a rulebook first?"

"You know that's not what I mean," Mati retorted angrily. "You kissed me, bud! *Twice*, actually! And I'm not going to apologize for following the rules. I *wanted* to tell you that I wanted to slow down a bit, but you jumped the gun and cut me off. Why can't you just stop being so impulsive?"

"Oh no! Nuh-uh! You kissed me back yesterday. And you didn't say no. Don't even try to blame that shit on me," Fen seethed.

"You came into my room," Mati yelled. "I didn't ask you to come in here!"

"Then I'll go, *your highness*," Fen mock bowed. "Silly, impulsive me thought you liked me and wouldn't mind seeing me. Now, I know better." He stalked over to the door and slammed it shut behind him.

They mounted their horses and set out for the Kingly Hills less than an hour after the fight. Mati's eyes still stung from the tears. She was angry and sad at the same time; sad over feeling like Fen hated her and angry because no matter how much they tried, she and Fen could not agree on anything.

Alik filled the deafening silence with stories. "I thought I'd tell you about Rena before you meet her. We were very close at one time, but after Guyt's betrayal, she broke. She couldn't stand by and watch his tyranny take hold of the people, and she hated that her friends had been manipulated so badly. After we lost Paxis and Tanophis, our morale was snuffed out. The gods lost their powers, and in some cases, we lost our identities. Except for Lavinia and Ciksura. They kept theirs, thanks to their alliance with Guyt." A look of regret swept across Alik's face.

"Well, anyway, Rena and I lived in Lyserria for a while right after that, but she soon became very depressed. We argued, and she left to *help* the people of Vertrose as best as she could." Alik paused to sigh. "She's since turned to vigilante justice. She's been in the Kingly Hills, helping the poor rural families there and doling out justice as she sees fit."

Although Mati was listening, and was very grateful for Alik agreeing to tell them more, she didn't feel much like speaking. Instead, she felt hollow. Fen didn't speak, either.

Alik huffed, "Okay you two...what's the deal?"

"Nothing," Fen answered, too quickly. "I'd hate to make things complicated by speaking too much."

Alik raised an eyebrow and ran his fingers through his hair. "What happened with you two?"

"You'll have to ask Her Highness."

Any remorse Mati had been feeling nearly disappeared. "*Now* you want to keep your mouth shut and let someone else explain their side of things?"

"At least I'm trying to communicate."

Alik took a deep breath that made both Mati and Fen fall silent. "I don't know what happened, but you need to fix it. Like it, or not, you're working together through this."

The remainder of the day passed in total silence. Mati refused to be the first one to speak after Alik's scolding. She had done nothing wrong, as far as she was concerned. Fen had cut her off while she had been trying to explain her feelings to him, chewed her out, and then blamed her for being too by-the-book. She resolved to wait for him to apologize.

As the sun started to set, Alik reined in his horse, but didn't dismount. "We'll stop here tonight. There's a village over that rise. I'm going to go have a quick look, see if I can spot a friend, then I'll be back. You two start setting up camp and get a fire going."

Fen dismounted first and started unpacking his horse. He tossed his bedroll and pack down onto the ground just as Mati's feet hit the same spot. She hit the unexpected pile and rolled her foot, nearly twisting her ankle. She refused to even acknowledge the incident.

Once her pack was down, Mati went into a nearby patch of trees to see if she could find some firewood, just to avoid having to look at Fen's face any longer. It had begun to annoy her to even see it. Her blood boiled the whole time, and she muttered under her breath and mocked his voice while she picked up sticks. Damn him for being such an ass.

Mati was just outside the clearing where they were making camp when she heard Fen talking. She paused and stepped behind a tree to eavesdrop.

"How do you put up with carrying that big head and ego of hers?" Fen said to her horse. "She must crush you." He dumped the pots and pans onto the ground with a clatter, causing the horses to jump and tug at the ropes that hitched them to the tree.

"*Thank you, your highness,*" he mocked as he tried to light a bit of kindling to get the fire started, "*for letting me know I'm not good enough for your royal-ness. I'm so very grateful for the attention you paid to a mere peasant.* She's got a lot of nerve, acting like she's better than me. I mean, I know I'm not the king or a headman, and I know I get myself into scrapes, but she acts like she's better than everyone just because she follows the rules all the time."

Mati raged inside and she marched back into camp with her armful of scavenged wood. She walked over to where Fen had just coaxed a tiny wisp of flame from the kindling and dropped everything directly next to his hands, extinguishing the tiny flame. He let out a low growl of anger at the tiny thread of smoke and started to light the fire again.

"Oh," she started, in a sugar-coated tone, "I'm sorry, I didn't see you there. I think my big ego got in the way."

Fen leapt up, obviously seething. "The fuck you didn't! Make your own damn fire!"

Alik returned just as Fen jumped to his feet. "You two, knock it off. I didn't think I needed to hang around to be a nursemaid."

The night passed with their tangible distaste lingering in the air. They sat at the fire, eating silently.

"I told you earlier and I'll press you again," Alik finally said, as he got to his feet. "You'd better figure it out. We've got a long journey ahead of us and I'm not playing mediator between two grown adults. I'm going to sleep. Figure this out. I shouldn't need to remind you what's at stake if you two can't work through your differences."

Fen made a few mocking remarks under his breath while poking the fire.

Mati rolled her eyes. "You can be such a child. I'm going to sleep."

Fen huffed. "I'm not the only one."

"God, you don't get it, do you? We have to work together. I was trying to do us a favor by taking things slow, so we can really focus on breaking this curse."

Fen tossed the stick in the fire and stood up, turning his back. "I never asked you for a favor."

They both retreated to their bedrolls and fell into uneasy sleep.

# Chapter 9

Over the next few days Fen, Mati, and Alik traveled discreetly through the tiny villages of the Kingly Hills. They traveled slowly and tried to keep a low profile, while Alik sought any leads on where Rena could be. The villages they visited had some of the most deplorable living conditions Mati had ever seen. She equated it to war-torn countries back on Earth. These people had less than nothing.

"How do they live like this?" Mati wondered out loud.

"It wasn't always like this," Alik told her. "Guyt has taxed them to within an inch of their lives, and demonstrated the lengths he'll go to in order to get what he feels like he deserves. They have nothing left but hope."

"Hope of what?" Fen asked, a confused look on his face.

"You," Alik stated somberly. "The two of you are the only hope Vertrose has left. Your return will truly spark unrest in the people, and a yearning for the old lives we all led."

Mati looked at Fen, who had the same look on his face. Their eyes met, and they exchanged a shame-filled glance. These people's very lives hinged on the two of them being able to work together. And although one moment couldn't fix things between them, that one look had at least brought them back to neutral terms.

Three days out from Insburg, Alik was finally able to track down a lead on Rena, who had been spotted in a village half a day's ride away. He led them further east, until they came to another similarly-fated village. There, they found a small group of people gathered in a clearing in the middle of the ramshackle houses.

Mati dismounted and followed Alik through the crowd to the center, where a brunette woman stood, handing out small pouches to the gathered villagers. She Had sad blue eyes and was dressed in men's clothing, her hair back in a long, tangled braid. She looked straight up into Alik's face and froze for a split second, startled, before continuing her work.

Alik strode over to her. "Rena—"

"Don't start, Alik," Rena snapped. "I'll finish this, and then we can talk. I can't imagine what dragged you out of that godsforsaken desert, or made you think you could drag me back."

"Rena," Alik said more forcefully to draw her eyes. When she met his gaze again, he motioned to Fen and Mati.

Her mouth dropped open. "Oh!"

Mati felt a strange sense of familiarity around this woman, like a memory she couldn't quite recall, trapped deep down inside her mind.

Alik nodded and stepped back into the crowd to wait for his sister. Fen and Mati watched as the people walked away from Rena, shedding tears of joy, clutching the few coins she had been able to give them.

"Not used to being around poor people?" Fen asked in a low voice.

"No...I mean, we were never rich, but I've never seen this level of poverty in real life."

"It sucks. Never knowing where or if you'll have another meal, and it's rarely hot. Sometimes, I would steal a few bits of leftover food that was still recognizable from the pig slop. I would do some very nice things sometimes, to get a few coins to pay for distractions."

Mati's face drained of blood, leaving her pale. "What? You—" she stopped there, not knowing how to voice her disgust without sounding pretentious.

"Yeah," Fen answered. "You got lucky, Mati. I was little more than a slave to my *family*."

Suddenly, Fen—his essence and his being—became painfully clear. There was a grief that lay deep beneath the cocky grin and sarcasm. A sadness he strove to keep hidden, looking for distractions from his true inner pain. "I'm sorry," was all she could say, even though she knew it wasn't enough. No string of words could possibly convey that to him.

Fen grinned sadly. "It's fine. I'll add it to your bill." Mati's face must have transmitted her confusion. "Another kiss," he said, his grin now wider.

Mati let out a bark of a laugh. "Okay." She rolled her eyes and bumped him with her shoulder.

After handing out all the goods and money she had, Rena finally joined them on the grass not far from the village green.

"So, this is what dragged you out of the desert." She looked over Mati and Fen. "I feel as if I already know you two. The whole of Vertrose is thankful that you've returned to us in our time of need."

Fen gave a playful bow, ending with a flourish. Alik groaned, but Rena smiled at the gesture. Mati could see that the siblings were the exact opposites of each other, just as she and Fen were. It would be nice to have another woman around.

"So, what does this mean for me?" Rena addressed both Fen and Mati, who both looked at Alik for some kind of guidance. Rena turned a judgmental eye on her brother. "You haven't let them make any decisions or filled them in on anything, have you?"

Alik puffed up at that accusation. "I think I've been generous with the information I've given them."

Rena rolled her eyes. "You know good and well that they're more than capable of dealing with this. You've just been enjoying the chance to run the show."

"Err on the side of caution."

"Ha!" Rena turned to Fen and Mati. "It's time we had a little talk, loves."

"Rena—" Alik began to protest.

"Brother, to keep the peace between us, shut up."

Alik fumed as they followed Rena off into a nearby patch of trees, where it looked like she had set up a temporary camp for herself. They put their belongings beside Rena's for the night, and after a fire had been built and bedrolls unfurled, Rena sat them down.

"Now, loves, I'm sure my brother hasn't told you much, so I'll explain what I can, as best as I can." She settled herself onto a log with a cup of tea. "This curse that Guyt placed on us—the gods—" Fen and Mati's eyes went wide. "Alik! you didn't even tell them we were gods?!"

Alik tried to protest. "They know he placed a curse on the gods. I just didn't tell them I was a god. It was irrelevant."

Rena pressed her fingers against her temples. "Yes. We are the gods, cursed to inhabit mortal, human bodies until the curse is broken. I am the goddess of peace. Alik is the god of war. Guyt bound our powers to himself, and we have been human since that moment. No powers, no immortal bodies. We can die, but only by natural causes."

Mati's mind whirled. How could Alik not think that was important to know? "Faelinth?"

"Yes, Faelinth is a god. He is the god of good, and his wife, Lavinia, is the goddess of evil. She was manipulated by Guyt to betray us. Have you met any of the others?"

Fen and Mati shook their heads in unison.

"Okay. Then I'll continue. Guyt is a primordial spirit that was trapped in the Hell Realm, for what I can only assume were very nasty deeds. When he clawed his way out, he just so happened to drop onto Tera, and found his way to Vertrose. We didn't think he was a threat, then.

"Paxis and Tanophis gave him a place in Meten, the capital of Vertrose, but that only lasted for a while before it was no longer enough for him. He wanted the seats of power that Paxis and Tanophis held. So, he searched the universes for curses that would help him defeat us. He was able to unearth an ancient tome, a survivor from the first age of the universes, written by the First Gods many millennia ago. He dragged it out of Gaia, the great mother. The greatest injustice was what he did to Paxis and Tanophis after that. No one knows what became of them—"

"That's enough, Rena," Alik barked. "You'll lock the curse and fuck us all if you're not careful."

"I've not said anything that could lock it. They vanished from Vertrose." She paused and took a sip of tea. "But that is truly all I can tell you. I imagine it was a good deal more than my stuffy, controlling brother has told you."

"Are there more gods?" Fen asked.

Rena nodded. "Jaylin, goddess of healing and nature." Fen's head shot up in recognition. "You've met Jaylin?"

"Yes, in the Crescent Wood."

"You've been *inside* the Crescent Wood?" Rena barked, then glared sharply at Alik.

"*That* was before they came to Lyserria," Alik justified loudly. "You can blame Asterion and Dursten for that one."

"You can bet they'll hear from me." Rena continued. "I'll make sure of it. But Jaylin's sibling is Ciksura, god of the supernatural and pain. They...well, I assume they are still a they—"

"What's that supposed to mean?" Mati asked.

"Ciksura is a troubled soul, love. And they hated the way they felt, even though we all loved them. We didn't know it then, but we know now. We all made mistakes. Then there are Paxis and Tanophis—gods of order and chaos."

Mati sat in thought for a moment. "So, all the gods come in pairs, and are opposites of one another."

"Yes," Rena smiled. "To keep the natural balance."

"Do other universes have gods? Like Earth?"

"Universes get gods once they mature to an enlightened state. Earth's universe is too young for gods; it's only just starting to bud. One day it might. I believe Earth still only has humans and a few beings that are using it as a quaint escape. I think the Illustrus have been keeping tabs on things."

"Aliens..." Mati said. "Are the Illustrus aliens?"

"I'm not sure I understand," Rena said with a furrowed brow. "What are aliens?"

"We have these stories about flying crafts and beings that come to Earth. Sometimes, people see them and get taken by them. Gray or green beings with big black eyes."

"Hmm..." Alik mused. "I'm not sure."

Fen quickly changed the subject. "What can you tell us about this rebellion? Alik did tell us about a meeting that's coming up soon."

Rena turned and made a wry face at Alik. "So, you did at least tell them that a Magnus Concilium had been called? That was nice of you." She took another sip of tea. "The Magnus Concilium is a meeting between all the peoples of Vertrose. The mingled folk are represented by the gods. Then there are the madrigal, sykosee, lycan, and banshees. They will all be represented at the Magnus. I assume the stars called this meeting, yes?"

Alik only nodded, his look sour. Mati was sure he was about to spout fumes out his ears.

"Where *are* Asterion and Dursten? I thought for sure they'd be running this circus," Rena asked.

"They had business with the Illustrus," Alik answered.

"Ah, so they had to go explain to that great light in the sky why they aren't assholes for giving a shit about the little people."

Mati was very grateful for Rena's honesty; it was nice to finally get details. "Is there anything else you can tell us about the Magnus? I'd like to know what we're walking into."

Rena smiled widely. "Don't let Gruthlan or Vrutuuk intimidate you. And that statement will make more sense when you see them."

Mati sat in thought for a moment before adding. "What are the mingled folk?"

"Ah," Rena started. "It's all the peoples who live together. Fauns, elves, and humans, mostly. I imagine you saw some of all of them while in Insburg, especially."

The conversation lulled after this, leaving them each to their own thoughts.

As she stared into the fire, Mati started to wish things were different. Her mind drifted to Fen. While she was grateful that they had gone back to at least neutral terms, she found herself missing the excitement that he brought to her days.


The next morning came with a fright they didn't expect. A blinding light woke all four of them with a start. Asterion and Dursten appeared a split second later, as the light faded. Alik had leaped to his feet, sword in hand, only to drop it when he saw who stood in their midst.

"Apologies," Asterion said with a hint of a smile. "We felt we needed to join you as soon as we could."

"Good thing," Alik replied, now relaxed again. "You two never told me when the Magnus was."

"Did we not?" Dursten questioned. "We are sorry. It's set for three days from now, in Dolo Caverns. Is it safe to stay here until we leave? Asterion and I will beam the group there, I suppose, since we won't make it otherwise."

Rena leapt up and gave both stars a welcoming hug. "Yes. The people of this village are loyal to me. We'll be safe for a few more days."

"Good," Asterion said. "It's settled, then. I could use a cup of your tea, Rena, if it's not too much trouble."

Rena set to stoking the small fire and boiling some water while Mati and Fen rolled up their bedrolls. Mati had hoped to finally just have an easy morning, but Alik had other plans. He had tasked Fen with training Mati to use a sword.

It was a truly cruel task, in Mati's opinion. She barely had the strength to lift a sword, let alone to swing it around without risking decapitation of herself, or someone else.

Unable to escape the lesson, Mati followed Fen to a small clearing in the trees.

"Here," he said, and handed her one of the swords.

She took the sword and nearly dropped it to the ground. It was heavy and didn't feel right in her hand. Fen stifled a laugh. Mati shot him a dirty look.

Fen raised his sword effortlessly and stood in front of her. "Follow my lead," he said and started moving his sword in a controlled pattern.

Mati followed as best as she could, but it just didn't work for her like it did for Fen. He was so fluid and natural with his movements, and she was just...not. "It's no use!" she burst out in frustration. "This thing is too heavy, and I'm not cut out for physical confrontation. I avoid it at every opportunity."

"You're thinking too hard about copying me exactly," Fen said. "This isn't something you can just read about and do. You have to feel it."

"That's easy for you to say. You're Mr. Happy-go-lucky."

"I don't know what that means."

"It just means you're more able to go with the flow than I am."

Fen nodded and smiled. "I think I understand. You're trying to say I'm way cooler than you."

Mati smiled and relaxed a bit. "Yes, that's exactly what I'm trying to say."

"What's your instinct telling you?" Fen asked.

"My instinct tells me to put the sword down."

"Guyt won't give you the chance to 'just put the sword down.'"

Mati let out a drawn-out groan of defeat.

Fen put his sword on the ground and came around to stand behind her. "Can I help?"

Mati held out her arms in defeat. "You're welcome to try."

Fen sidled up close to her back and placed a hand on each of her wrists. "Hold it like this, and just feel the sword."

Mati tried to focus on the task, but her mind was wandering. She tensed her muscles to keep from doing anything she might—or might not—regret.

Fen tried pushing and pulling her arms in different directions. "Loosen up. Your arms are way too tense."

"Sorry." Mati took a deep sigh and loosened her muscles, so Fen was able to guide her into a better stance.

"There you go," Fen praised. "You've got it."

Mati wanted to smile and feel proud as Fen guided her and they found a rhythm, but she kept her breathing even and forced herself to stay focused on the movements. Fen let go of her and let her continue through the stance on her own.

"Look at you," Fen said smiling ear-to-ear. "I might trust you to be my partner someday."

Mati's focus cracked and she let out an excited squeal. The sword took a hard right, landing in the dirt.

"Easy," Fen said jumping back a step.

Mati met his eyes and the joy that filled her was nothing she'd ever experienced. Fen was proudly smiling at her. "I did it!"

Fen laughed. "You did."

That night by the fire, Mati eased herself down onto a log. Rena joined her, handing her a cup of tea. "How are you holding up?" Rena asked softly.

Mati sighed and took a sip. The heady flavor was exactly what she needed. "I'm okay, all things considered." Mati allowed her gaze to sweep over Fen who, unsurprisingly, was swinging his sword around on the other side of the fire.

Rena followed her gaze. "You know...I had a lover, once. We loved each other with everything we had in us. But he was mortal..." She trailed off. "Don't let a temporary problem ruin your happiness."

"What did you do?" Mati asked, staring deep into her tea now.

Rena gave a heavy sigh. "I told him to leave, because I was scared. I thought it would save us both some misery if I ended it before I inevitably lost him. I thought I was doing what was right."

"Did it work?"

"No. We both lived in misery for longer than we ever needed to. I could have had almost a century of happiness with him. Instead, I ended it, and we both lived through a century of misery. Don't let the fear of losing someone later stop you from living *now*." She laid a hand on Mati's shoulder, then moved to sit next to Asterion.

Mati sat in thought for a while, and let her eyes trail back to Fen. She knew exactly what Rena had meant by telling her that story. And at that moment, she thought that maybe it was what she wanted, whether it made sense or not.

# Chapter 10

The next few days were spent at Rena's camp. Fen spent his days training with Alik during the morning and teaching Mati in the afternoons. In the evenings, Mati would help him with his speaking and ways of engaging with people.

They hadn't been butting heads as often, which was a relief to Mati. He still irritated her more than any other person ever had, especially with how frenzied he always made a situation, but she had started to find it more endearing. After her talk with Rena, she had decided to just take things with Fen day by day. She still hadn't made up her mind whether or not to return to her old life, after all, and she wanted to be absolutely sure of what she wanted before she made any decisions that might rock the boat that they'd just steadied.

She'd been in Vertrose for almost a month, if she had counted her days correctly. It had felt more like a return to something familiar rather than a true upset in her life. It had surprised her how quickly she'd become accustomed to this place, and these people. And with every day that passed, returning to Earth seemed to occupy less and less of her thoughts.

The day of the Magnus Concilium had finally arrived. Rena had taken their horses and given them to the people of the village, and all the other packs were readied.

Asterion and Dursten grabbed everyone's hands, pulled them into a circle, and with little warning beamed them into space. They landed on a damp, fern-covered forest floor with a dull thud. Mati fell on her butt and immediately started hurling up the little breakfast that she had eaten. Fen was next to her, trying desperately to keep his own breakfast down.

Alik slapped Fen on the back and barked a laugh. "You'll get used to it eventually."

Asterion led them through the forest, following a cliff face that wound around the corner from where they had landed. Once they turned the corner, Mati gaped at the great, elaborately-carved archway that stood in front of them. It had to be at least twenty feet tall.

The stars led the way through the archway into the equally enormous tunnel system. The sounds of the forest vanished, leaving them in complete darkness for a split second before they saw a light up ahead. They followed the tall tunnel into an enormous chamber lit by a large hole in the ceiling that was dripping with vines. Water poured from the hole into a small pool in the center of the chamber. Behind the pool lay a dais of hewn stone, with ten carved seats arranged in a circle.

As they walked further into the chamber, Mati saw creatures carved along the walls, images of all the peoples that lived in Vertrose. Some of them she recognized, and some she didn't. The most impressive were the ones that looked like dinosaurs, but not like any she had seen in children's books. These ones wore armor and stood on two legs, with thick tails and massive wings spread out behind them. Certainly, they couldn't be real.

"This is the Magnus Locum." Dursten announced. "It's an ancient meeting place for the peoples of Vertrose, a neutral ground. We haven't had a Magnus in quite a while, since before Guyt took over. This will be quite the event."

Fen sat down on the dais as they waited. Mati could see his leg bouncing, and his back rose noticeably as he heaved in breaths.

"You'll be fine," Mati encouraged. "You're a natural at speaking."

"What if I mess it all up?" Fen met her eyes and she saw true terror laced in them. "I always mess everything up."

"You won't mess this up."

Fen scoffed at her. "I'm a fuck up. I don't ever think things through. Even you say so. I know I annoy you because I'm not as thoughtful as you are."

Mati smiled. "You do annoy me. But you've got a secret weapon now."

"What's that?"

"Alik and Rena and me. I'll help where I can. You're better with people than I am. Plus, you've got this talent of just figuring things out as you go, by listening to your gut and letting instinct take over. Like, how are you so good at sword fighting already? I can still barely pick it up and you're over there charging around like a knight. It's actually really aggravating."

Fen finally fully looked at her, and he smiled. Her confidence had given him the tiniest of boosts. "You just need to listen to your gut and let instinct take over."

⟫⟩ ⟨⟪

The first to arrive at the great cavern were the delegates of the reptilian warriors known as the sykosee. Mati looked at them with awe and fear. She recognized them as the dinosaur creatures that she'd seen earlier, carved into the walls. They were much more impressive in person and very real. The leader wore thick leather armor, had a massive sword at his side, and great pterodactyl-style wings that folded behind him. They looked like something straight out of a science fiction novel, yet here they were. She remembered Rena's warning from a few days before and decided this must be one of the two species Rena had said to not let herself be intimidated by. She hoped it was, anyway. She admitted to herself that she'd failed on that count. Fen, on the other hand, had gone striding over without hesitation to introduce himself.

"I'm Fen," he reached out a hand, which was not taken. He bowed at the waist, then quickly bowed only his head. He oozed nervousness. "Who are you?" he finally asked and winced.

The warrior reached out a scaled hand and linked his arm with Fen's, forearm to forearm. He didn't seem to mind Fen's blunders. "Vrutuuk, leader of the sykosee," his voice was gruff and hissy. "It's an honor to finally meet you. My people have been suffering lately at the hands of Guyt's patrols, and we believe he's ready to strike us any day now. We're looking forward to having help defending our kingdom, as well as Vertrose."

"That's why we're here." Fen answered and tugged Mati forward in an unexpected move. "And this is Mati."

Mati sheepishly reached out her hand to Vrutuuk, who took it graciously and softly. She took a page from Fen's book and mustered every ounce of gut instinct she could find. She held out her hand further and with more confidence. "An honor," she forced the words out, while dipping her head to him respectfully.

"The honor is entirely mine," Vrutuuk answered.

Once Vrutuuk moved on, Mati slapped Fen's arm on the sly. "Why'd you do that?" she whispered to him angrily.

"I panicked," Fen said in a rush. "I didn't know what else to say to him."

"At least warn me when you're going to throw me to the wolves."

They both looked up when the room erupted with a howl that reverberated off the walls. The whole cavern froze, and all those present turned to face the entrance.

Entering the cavern with a burst of energy, like football players bounding into a stadium, were a group of ten-foot-tall bipedal wolves. Covered in gray and white fur, and wearing rough-hewn armor, they looked like they would rip your head off as soon as look at you.

"What was that about wolves?" Fen whispered to her.

"What the fuck," Mati breathed out, and gave Fen a little shove forward. "Go greet them with your *gut instincts*. That must be Gruthlan since we've already met Vrutuuk."

"You're hilarious," Fen remarked, his voice dry and sarcastic. He took a breath and tugged Mati along with him as he headed for the group.

"You must be Gruthlan."

You wouldn't even know, Mati mused to herself, that Fen's head was almost completely tipped back to look at Gruthlan towering over him, or that he had been sweating bullets less than an hour ago. By his tone, one might think they stood completely equal. Eye to eye. "I'm Fen."

The wolf leader sounded like he was almost barking and growling his introduction. "I see my reputation precedes me. It is an honor to meet you, Fen." The great wolf bowed his head.

"The honor is all mine," Fen answered, lowering his voice to match Gruthlan's deep baritone and bowing his head to match. Mati almost rolled her eyes at him, but caught herself.

"And who is this?" Gruthlan asked, looking to Mati.

Mati took a deep and resolute breath and stepped forward. She was determined to not let Fen steal all the thunder or make her look like an imbecile. "I'm Mati," she said simply.

Gruthlan tipped his head to her in greeting. "It is a great honor to finally have you both back among us."

"It's an honor to be back and help our people." Mati wasn't sure where that came from. It sprang out of her with the most effortless feeling. Maybe Fen was right; maybe all she needed was to let instinct take over.

Mati and Fen had a moment of awkward peace after that, before they were greeted by Helian, Becca, and their envoy. Mati let herself show a broad smile, and this time she was the first to stride up to them. The madrigal king smiled just as warmly and embraced Mati.

"I'm very glad to see you again," he said, nodding to Fen as well. Then he winked at them. "You will do fine. You've made it past Vrutuuk and Gruthlan, after all."

"Barely," Mati answered under her breath.

"Truly," Becca said softly, "you are doing just fine."

The final group to arrive were actually the ones who scared Mati the most. Which was saying a lot, considering that two of the groups of attendees were already pure nightmare fuel as far as she was concerned. These people were all women. They glowed from within with a pale blueish white light. Their heads were covered by thin veils, and they wore long, translucent dresses to match. The lead woman seemed to float over to them.

"I am Clíodha, chosen figurehead of the banshees," she said, in a low, powerful voice that slid over them like warm butter.

Fen introduced himself a bit more formally this time. "An honor, my lady." And he bowed low.

Mati stepped forward. "Mati," and she too bowed low.

Without any other words, Clíodha floated directly to a seat on the dais. That seemed to be a silent signal for the others to join, and each delegate took a seat in one of the stone thrones that, Mati now noticed, had been specially designed for each race. Vrutuuk's throne had the back left open to accommodate his massive wings, while Helian and Becca's thrones were a flat stone table so they could easily rest their gazelle-like bodies. Rena and Alik stood off to the side of the dais, and the stars ushered Fen and Mati to two thrones alongside the others.

Fen took his seat with a natural ease that suited him, while Mati felt like a child sitting at the adult table at a Thanksgiving dinner.

Asterion stepped into the center of the ring. "We want to thank all of you for coming to this Magnus," they began. "I believe you all know one another, but there are a few new participants today, and I will be letting them run this Magnus." They gestured for both Fen and Mati to join them in the center of the dais.

Mati's stomach dropped. She was terrible at public speaking, but luckily Fen took the lead as he'd done with the introductions.

"Thank you all for coming," Fen announced. There was a tiny croak in his voice, almost imperceptible to anyone but Mati. "Welcome, Vrutuuk of the sykosee, Gruthlan of the lycan, Clíodha of the banshees, as well as Helian and Becca of the madrigal." As he said each name, the delegate bowed their head in acknowledgment. "Mati and I are happy to be in Vertrose to serve you. And we'll need all the help we can get from you all, the free peoples of Vertrose. We beg you to join us and fight against Guyt's evil. Do we have your allegiance?"

Silence sliced a bitter knife through the cavern, when all that could be heard was the dripping of water.

Finally, Vrutuuk stood up. "You will have the sykosee warriors. Our people are close to the current border of Guyt's territory, and we've experienced his armies trying to expand past that boundary and take over Duinan too many times. Our people are already under attack and will be joining this rebellion with our whole hearts."

Fen dipped his head in thanks and in reverence to the great reptilian warrior, who returned the gesture.

"You will also have the madrigal," Becca announced proudly. "Our army is currently moving toward Duinan in response to Vrutuuk's plea for help. Helian and I will be proud to stand alongside you all, should you choose to fight."

Again, Fen dropped his head in silent thanks, before picking his head up and turning to the other delegates. But no more of them stepped forward.

When it was clear that Fen was reaching an internal crisis point, Mati stepped up. "We need everyone to join together for us to have a chance of a real fight."

Gruthlan spoke first. "My people are far from the border. I think it would be unwise to align ourselves now. It could force Guyt's army to move faster in order to destroy us. I believe we should wait. It will be many years before he reaches us."

Vrutuuk leapt to his feet. "You would let innocent people—*my people*—die in return for a few more years of peace for yourselves?" he shouted accusingly. "How typical of the lycan to be so selfish. I shouldn't have expected any less, even with these two returning."

Gruthlan's black eyes bored holes through Vrutuuk. The bitterness in the air became palpable.

Then Clíodha spoke, before a fight could erupt. "I feel the same as Gruthlan. Our borders at the Terron Forest are safe. We should wait—"

"Wait until when?" Fen exclaimed. "Until anyone who would've allied with you is dead?"

Mati saw both perspectives, but she also saw a crucial flaw. She interjected before Fen really offended anyone. "Wouldn't it be better to strike Guyt's army before he was prepared for it? It just seems to me that it would be better to have the element of surprise, yeah? He doesn't know that Fen and I are here yet, right? So, wouldn't now be the perfect time to strike with all our combined forces?"

"Correct," Fen stated firmly. "You can't wait so long that either he is prepared, or all your allies have been destroyed. That doesn't serve any purpose besides being stubborn and selfish."

That statement seemed to make the circle pause in thought for a moment, before Gruthlan spoke again. "The lycans will wait for further guidance. I will consult my council once I return to Hruguth. I will not make a decision without involving the Beta."

"And I will consult with the rest of the banshees." Clíodha agreed. "We are governed by vote, and I would not deny them the right to have voices in this decision."

Fen visibly deflated. "But what about the people who have been and will be slaughtered, while you take your time deciding?"

Mati could feel Fen's anger starting to boil over and she doubted an outburst would win over powerful and proud rulers like these. She stepped forward and laid a calming hand on his shoulder. "You can only think for so long before you will be required to take action. We can give you a few days to decide."

Gruthlan and Clíodha nodded in unison, apparently happy with Mati's ultimatum.

"What about Morimas?" Becca asked.

"Hmmm..." Asterion thought aloud. "Perhaps she could be persuaded. But not easily."

"Who's Morimas?" Fen asked, looking to Asterion.

"Morimas is the great dragon. She is notoriously reclusive. She could be an exceptional ally, if she could be persuaded to join the fight."

"Not likely," huffed Gruthlan. "No one has seen or heard from her in a hundred years. She could be dead, for all we know."

"That is unlikely, but you are right. It's equally unlikely that she'll join," Dursten replied.

"The greatest question," Helian added breaking his silence, "is how, exactly, are we supposed to overthrow Guyt? He is a primordial spirit.

A mortal blade can't kill him, and I would not trust a cell to hold him for long—even if we did manage to get him into one."

"Ah," Dursten stepped into the center to stand next to Mati and Fen. "Asterion and I have been thinking on this matter. We believe that a sword created by Morana and Osirim might kill him."

"Who are they?" Mati asked.

"Morana," Dursten answered, "is the spirit of death. Along with her brother Osirim, the spirit of life, they might be able to create a weapon to kill Guyt."

"And how do we get them to create a weapon?"

"You and Fen would need to travel to the Naina Pass and up Naina Mountain, to implore them to create a weapon that can kill a primordial spirit like themselves. You're the only ones who might be able to sway them."

Fen sighed in irritation. "So, all we have to do is beg a death spirit to make a magic weapon to kill Guyt. And if we do that, will the lycan and banshee join us?" Fen turned to face both leaders square on.

Gruthlan nodded. "If you're able to convince the spirits to make a weapon which can kill Guyt, we will most gladly join the battle." Fen let out a victorious sigh at first, until Gruthlan continued. "But I doubt you'll be able to convince Morana to create a weapon that could also be used to kill her brother and herself. You won't be the first to have asked."

"Even better..." Fen added with heavy sarcasm, before turning to the stars. "Were you planning on letting us know that we were going on a fool's errand before or after we climbed a mountain?"

"It's not a fool's errand if they agree," Asterion answered curtly. "You'll have to put that mouth of yours to good use."

Before Fen had a chance to spout any more remarks that could quite possibly chase off their potential allies, Mati stepped in. "Good. So, we'll travel to Naina Mountain and ask Morana and Osirim for a weapon. Then when we have it, you'll join us, yes?" Mati stared at Gruthlan and Clíodha, who both nodded. "We'll hold you to that."

A great blinding light and clap of thunder rumbled through the Magnus Locum. By the time the attendees had blinked, Asterion and Dursten had vanished. Their sudden exit seemed to have shocked everyone present.

"What happened?" Fen asked Alik.

"Nothing good," Alik answered stiffly. "It seems the Illustrus have caught on to their endeavors. Looks like we'll be walking to Naina Mountain."

"We still expect your word to hold, with or without the stars." Fen spun, directing his words at Clíodha and Gruthlan.

# Chapter 11

The next day, Alik, Rena, Fen, and Mati started out for Naina Mountain. The Magnus had ended abruptly the day before, with the sudden exit of both stars. It had put everyone on edge and the delegates left with their envoys almost immediately after. Alik was too quiet for Fen's liking. It made him nervous.

"Without horses," Alik wearily told them, "it'll be a long trip. We should get to Lyserria to restock in nine days, if we don't have any trouble along the way. We'll cut through Crescent Wood to save time."

"Wait, what?" Fen retorted. "The forest that tries to eat you?"

"Yes," Alik answered smartly.

"Oh, good. That'll be fun," Fen sneered.

"It'll save us several days instead of walking around. And we need to make as much haste as possible."

The four companions walked on without much more fuss, but Fen felt the heavy weight of their journey as they traveled.

"What are the banshees, exactly?" Mati asked Alik, who walked alongside her.

"The banshees are spirits," Alik answered. "Women who died in terrible ways and have chosen to return for another kind of life."

"So, they're only women?"

"Yes," Alik nodded.

"Human women?" Fen asked.

"Not all," Rena replied. "Some are other races. They all had tragic ends, however, perishing before they should have."

"You mean, they were murdered and such?" Fen pieced together crassly.

Alik nodded.

"How did Clíodha become the queen?"

Rena answered that question, heaving her pack higher onto her shoulders. "She isn't the queen. She's just their chosen leader. They decide things as a group. They're very tight-knit, as you can imagine."

"What about Vrutuuk and Gruthlan?" Mati asked. "How do their societies work?"

"Vrutuuk was voted in as sykosee leader for the length of his life," Alik replied. "When he dies, there will be another vote. And Gruthlan is king of the lycan."

Fen furrowed his brow. "Then who is Faelinth in all this? And why wasn't he at the Magnus?"

"Faelinth is just a headman in Insburg," Rena answered. "You and Mati are here to represent the mingled folk."

Fen tried to puzzle it out. "So, then the mingled folk are—"

Alik cut off his train of thought. "The humans, the elves, the fauns, and all other folk who don't separate themselves into their own exclusive kingdoms."

"And Helian is king of the madrigal, and they are a separate kingdom?"

"Yes," Alik answered. "But he and Becca share power equally."

Mati sighed. "Welcome to Vertrose politics 101..." The others turned to face her, confusion on their faces. "It's an Earth thing. I have another question. Why didn't you fight back against Guyt when he first started?"

Alik and Rena dropped their gaze to the ground.

Rena answered first. "He manipulated Ciksura and Lavinia. Ciksura can create puppets from mud, and they had created an entire army against us. It all happened so quickly. He stripped us of our power without warning, and we had no army to counter his."

"How did you not have an army?" Fen asked with surprise.

Alik huffed. "We had always used Ciksura's creatures until that moment."

The party remained somber as the day wore on. Rena and Alik's dark memories had leeched out into Fen; he certainly felt the sharp sting and overwhelming heaviness of the loss as his own.

"You did well with the Magnus," Alik said to Fen without warning as they walked. "I was impressed. As was the rest of the Magnus, I presume."

Fen almost tripped with a stunned grace. "Thank you. Mati helped me a lot. And some of it just flowed out."

"Was that a compliment?" Rena teased Alik. "Be still my beating heart. Even after—what has it been, several millennia?—you're still able to surprise me."

Alik grumbled under his breath and stomped away ahead of the group.

"No, wait, Alik," Rena kept teasing as she hurried after him. "I thought I saw a tear in your eye just then. Perhaps, since you're feeling so tender, we could also hold hands and skip together."

Alik was fuming, still trying to get away from her, but she was relentless. "Come on, big brother! We haven't hugged in such a long time." Rena laughed mercilessly.

Fen grinned from ear to ear. Having that reassurance from Alik had meant more to him than he realized.

"Don't let that go to your head," Mati said, bumping him playfully with her shoulder.

Fen smiled. "You did good, too."

"Thanks," Mati smiled shyly. "I just let my instincts guide me."

Fen gaped mockingly. "You listened to an annoying, thoughtless—"

Mati cut him off with a laugh. "Yes."

"Well, listening to you helped me."

They walked in comfortable silence for a while before Fen couldn't contain himself any longer. "I know it's late, and maybe obvious, but—friends?"

"Yeah," Mati said, with a shallow sigh. "Sorry. I'm still not sure what I want. I really don't want to hurt you and I just need some more time to be really sure."

Fen shrugged. "I figured. If it's any help, I've never been to Earth. I wouldn't mind a trip."

Mati laughed. "I'll remember that."

They walked in comfortable silence as Fen wrestled to not cross Mati's boundaries. He wanted to sweep her up and give her the biggest hug. He'd missed their conversations.

The days spent trekking through the hills of Dolo Caverns were rough, but, to Fen's delight, the land finally evened out as the Crescent Woods started to glimmer on the horizon. They made a small camp just outside the line of looming trees and heavy fog.

"We'll start out at dawn," Alik announced to them while they sat munching by the fire. "I'm hoping we'll be able to get all the way through the woods by nightfall."

"Will we meet Jaylin again?" Mati asked.

"Perhaps," Rena answered. "I wouldn't mind running into her. I haven't seen her since..."

"Since when?" Fen asked naively.

Rena sighed into her tea. "Since the day we lost Vertrose and were turned mortal."

"Why has it been so long?" Mati wondered aloud.

"After turning us mortal, Guyt let us go. We were all scared that he would change his mind, or perhaps come after us for sport. So we all hid in plain sight, kept a fairly low profile for a few years, and tried to stay invisible."

"Except you," Alik cut in.

"Pish posh," Rena waved him off. "We've been over that already; no need to drag that back out from under the carpet. Like I was saying... Guyt didn't feel threatened by us and has mostly left us alone. We are, after all, just mortal now. No powers, no real pull with the people, and no longer truly immortal. We age like humans." She splayed out her hand on her lap and looked at it. "I saw my first gray hair a few years ago," she smiled sadly.

"And you really can't tell us what Guyt did to Paxis and Tanophis?" Fen asked, hoping she would have a different answer. Or at least a less cryptic one.

"No," Rena said. "We truly don't know what became of them. The stars showed up and sent us away. We haven't seen or heard from either of them since that night."

"And why me and Fen?" Mati asked. "Why were we chosen?"

"Because you are opposites, perhaps. You represent the gods. We are each the opposite of our counterparts. I am peace and Alik is war."

"Ha!" Alik barked. "You're as peaceful as a crocat stuck in a window on Fulltide."

Fen and Mati understood the gist of the joke, at least, and giggled.

Fen hadn't thought of it like that but, judging from Mati's knowing look, she'd pieced that part of it together already.

The next morning, exactly on cue, Alik woke them just before dawn. They packed their bags and set out into the misty Crescent Wood. A feeling of secrets long kept hung in the air. It clung heavy to every tree branch, leaf, and rock.

"Keep your wits about you today," Rena warned, mostly looking at Fen. "We can't afford any jokes or setbacks. This wood will have you turned around before you can blink, as I'm sure you recall."

Fen nodded and strode to the front to walk with Alik. He remembered all too well how muddled this place could make you.

They passed briskly but cautiously through the forest. The further into the heart they went, the eerier the surrounding trees felt. The sensation of being watched and stalked was everywhere. It made every nerve and hair he had stand on end.

Alik pressed them on and on. He very much wanted to be out of the forest by dark and Fen had to agree. By midday, Alik said they were close to Gaia. The air here was so thick and raw that it almost felt like you were suffocating when you breathed it in—like trying to breathe in water. Their feet trudged through the thick fog like they walked through fresh mud. Fen kept swiveling his head to keep his mind satisfied that there was nothing lurking just behind them, ready to pounce.

Rena pressed close between Mati and Fen, linking all their elbows. "Stay close, loves. We're very near Gaia's pool. I can feel her pulling us in to her depths."

"What is Gaia, exactly?" Mati asked, her voice sounding heavy.

"She's a primordial spirit, like Guyt. She is the mother of all universes; all of us sprang from her. Her pools can create worlds, or destroy them. They are vast and endlessly deep. We believe it's through one of her pools that Guyt crawled out of the Hell realm and entered our own. If you fall in to one, you disappear from this world."

"Happy thoughts," Fen replied dryly. He loosed his arm from Rena's, placing his hand on the hilt of his sword. He made sure to keep one eye on Mati as they walked on.


By afternoon, they had finally traveled far enough away from Gaia that the air was starting to get lighter and breathable again. They were well on their way to escaping the Crescent Wood by dark, at least that was what Fen hoped. He had no intention of spending another night inside the Wood. Once in a lifetime was more than enough for him.

As the sun started to disappear behind the tops of the trees, Fen started to feel uneasy. Just like before, the Crescent Wood was silent, with none of the usual noises of a normal forest. All the creatures seemed to be waiting for the right time to strike—and they were the prey. The longer the day went on with them still in the Wood, the more curdled his stomach felt. He caught up to Alik at the front of the group.

"We've been in these woods too long, Alik," Fen opened, unease lacing every word.

"Hush," Alik silenced him. "We're being hunted. They sense our unrest."

"Hunted by what?" Fen laid his hand on the hilt of his sword to comfort himself.

"A creature I would not wish to meet, should I be given the whole world." Alik paused, directing his eyes in every direction but keeping his head forward. "It's a morest. They are unnatural creatures. If you get caught in this forest too long, the Wood itself changes you—turns you into one of its creatures."

"Great," Fen whispered. "Can it be killed with a sword?"

"Yes...but only if you see it before it catches you, and only if stabbed through the heart."

"I knew there was a catch..." Fen said, and dropped back to where Mati had been walking alone in the middle of the group. Rena was bringing up the rear on high alert, her hand on her sword as well.

"Whatever you do," Fen whispered to Mati, "Just stay close, and don't do anything stupid."

"That's rich, coming from you," Mati whispered nervously. "What's going on?"

"We're being hunted by a darling little beast called a morest."

"What's that?"

"I'm not exactly sure. But it has Alik scared, so it's not a puppy."

They walked on, anxiety creeping into Fen's bones. It poisoned the air around them. Mati clung tight to Fen's belt, her touch the only comfort he had other than his sword.

Everything happened in a single shocking burst. A blur sprang from the trees above them and dropped directly on top of Alik, who managed to roll out of its way just before it crushed him.

Alik jumped back onto his feet to find a tall, bony wraith of a creature standing before him. It had thin, dirty patches of hair on its body, like it had suffered from mange; long, thin claws on each hand; and its eyes bulged from its head.

Fen drew his sword in a flash and charged toward the creature. Mati was dragged forward with him, until she released her hold on his belt and tumbled to the ground.

Alik had just landed on his feet when the creature hurtled at him, teeth bared, and long, clawed fingers reaching out toward him.

Fen reached them and swung his sword with a grunting yell. Alik was still off-balance as Fen's sword connected with the creature's arm, but the blade simply slid away. To Fen's surprise, it didn't do any damage.

Fen recovered, planting himself in front of Alik, stunned by what had happened. His swing hadn't even dented the morest's skin. How was that possible?

The morest swatted at Fen, one of its sharp claws digging deep into Fen's forearm. He let out an angry, curdled scream as the claw popped out the other side of his arm, pinning the two of them together.

"Bastard!" Fen screamed. His body roared as the pain radiated through him in a constant wave. His eyes watered and his legs buckled.

Alik was back on his feet and ready, raising his sword in the air as he attacked. Rena came in behind them, sword ready to slash. Alik and Rena's heavy blows connected, stunning the morest long enough for Fen to rip his arm free.

"RUN!" Alik ordered, but no one listened.

Fen was too angry to run. He defied his body's cries to give up and readied his sword with fervor. He was going to kill this creature if it was the last thing he did. Rena landed another hard and well-placed *thwack* to the morest's spine as it spun to face her. Alik took another swing at an arm that was reaching wide to take a chunk out of him.

"Now, Fen!" Rena cried out.

Fen's eyes narrowed and time seemed to slow. Rena and Alik had created a small opening for him where the creature's chest was undefended. Fen let out a cry so unnerving that he shocked even himself. He drew back his sword and thrust with as much force as he could manage. The power of the strike lifted him into the air. The sword hit true, and with enough force behind it to pierce the morest's hard chest. It let out a gasping breath and stopped in its tracks. It seemed shocked that the blow had hit its target.

Fen landed on the ground again, his sword still buried deep in the chest of the morest. He sucked in air, his breath heaving, and the morest looked deep into his eyes. It seemed to be *peaceful* somehow, as though Fen had released it from a dream. It let out one last breath and went completely limp, its weight borne by the sword, bulging eyes still staring into Fen's.

Fen yanked his sword free, and felt a clap on his back.

"Good job," Alik said, proudly but breathlessly. "I haven't had that much fun with a sword in a while."

Rena snorted. "Only the god of war would get excited for battle."

"Come on," Alik ushered them. "Let's get out of this damned wood. We're only about a hilston away from the end, I think. Fen, keep that wound covered. We can deal with it after we get out of this cursed forest."

Fen wasn't sure how far a hilston was, but he hoped it wasn't far. The pain in his arm was far worse than he was willing to admit.

# Chapter 12

Mati ran up to Fen's side and kept pace with him while they raced the setting sun to the edge of the Crescent Wood. He held his arm cradled against his chest and was using his other hand to try and wrap the open wounds to staunch the bleeding.

Mati took hold of her tunic and ripped a long strip off the hem. "Here. Let me see your arm."

His face had started to drain of all its color but his eyes were clenched shut. "It's fine," Fen lied through clenched teeth.

"Would you shut up? Your arm has a gaping hole in it. I'm not dragging your heavy ass through these woods when you pass out from blood loss." She wrenched his arm away from his chest and started wrapping it tightly with the makeshift bandage. He drew in a sharp breath as she tied off the bandage over the wounds. "There."

Mati watched Fen closely. She could sense something was wrong. Fen was one of the toughest people she knew; she hadn't even noticed when he'd hurt his leg during their first trip through the woods. And now he was visibly wincing with every heavy step he took.

The Crescent Wood was darkening just as they cleared the tree line. A weight lifted from Mati's shoulders and a deep exhale left her lungs.

"We'll make camp here," Alik announced, also sounding winded.

They all dropped their packs and nearly collapsed on the ground, all heaving in breaths of fresh air.

Alik prepared a fire while Rena readied a salve for Fen's arm. "Come, sit," she commanded. Fen complied wordlessly. "Mati, you too. You'll do well to learn how to dress a wound properly. Though it looks like you've done a decent job already."

Once Fen was sitting beside her, Rena started to remove the bloody bandage that Mati had rigged for his arm.

"It's nothing, really," Fen protested.

"You think that now," Rena chided him, "but when it becomes infected and Alik chops your arm off to save your life, you'll be thinking differently."

Mati stepped closer. Fen winced and clenched his teeth as Rena unwound the layers of linen. The wound had already swelled up, turning bright red and purple around his injuries.

"What the hell is that?" Fen burst out, looking down at his arm.

"Shit," Rena exclaimed, grabbing a small blade that she had laid out next to the fresh bandages. "There's a stinger stuck in there. I need to get it out."

"Stinger?" Mati gasped.

"Alik," Rena called out urgently, "I need your help holding him."

Alik dropped what he was doing and rushed over, grabbing Fen by the shoulders and bracing Fen back against his knees. "Mati, grab his hand."

Mati pushed herself forward and grasped Fen's hand tightly, as Rena started to explore the wound with her blade. Fen's whole body tensed, and he let out a gut-wrenching scream as blood started to well up and drip off his arm.

Rena withdrew the knife from inside Fen's arm, shaking her head. "Hold him. I can't get it with this. I gotta use my hand. I'm going to try to push it through."

Fen clutched Mati's hand with all his strength and screamed again as Rena's searching finger plunged into his arm, pressing tendons and muscle to the side as she dug. He heaved frantic breaths into his lungs, and Mati's heart wrenched at the sight of seeing tears in his eyes.

"Got it!" Rena declared, as a small, pointed claw-tip dropped from the bottom puncture wound in Fen's arm onto the ground below.

Fen continued to pant, and Mati became painfully aware that she was still holding onto his hand and stroking it gently.

Rena took a scoop of salve from a small wooden container and made sure to pack it down into the bloody gouge. Fen tensed up again and puffed out his cheeks, trying to control the pain.

Mati gently squeezed his upper arm with her free hand. "Relax the muscle, or it will hurt worse."

She felt his tension slowly abate, allowing Rena to finish tending to the wound.

"Here, Mati," Rena handed her the clean bandage. "You did an excellent job with the other one. I need to go wash my hands."

Mati took the bandage and sat next to Fen, taking his arm gently into her lap. She felt, rather than saw, Fen's gaze boring into her.

"Thank you," he said, as she re-wrapped his arm.

Mati looked up into his face then and saw the gratitude written on his face. She'd never seen him look at her like that before, and the intimacy made her squirm. "You're welcome."

Without another look or word, Mati finished wrapping his arm and went to join Rena by the fire.

"No training for a while," Alik said firmly to Fen. "That wound'll need to heal a bit first."

"What the hell was that?" Mati asked.

Rena wiped her hands dry and began to steep some tea. "The morest have a stinger on the end of one of those claws, one that breaks off inside their prey. I didn't think it had done that this time, since the claw went all the way through Fen's arm."

Fen dragged himself over to them, slumped, exhausted, against his bedroll, and shut his eyes.

"Sit up," Mati told him gently. "I'll unroll it for you."

"I'm fine," he said sleepily.

Mati heaved him forward. "Move, you big lummox. You'll be stiff as a board tomorrow morning if you sleep like that, and I'm already going to have to hear you whine all day about that little cut."

Fen smiled at her and complied with her demands. He watched with heavy-lidded eyes as she unrolled the bedroll and helped him in. His limbs were little more than dead weight, and Mati nearly couldn't shove him underneath the covers. She kept an eye on his bad arm, laying it gingerly on top of the blanket as he settled.

"Thanks," he told her softly, his eyes drooping shut.

She sat by him as long as she could, before crawling into her own bedroll that she had set up next to his. She knew that injury was hurting him far worse than he let on. One of these days, she mused, he was going to get himself killed. Then consciousness slipped slowly away from her.

⟫⟫ ⟪⟪

Fen woke up nearly face to face to Mati, with no sense of the hour. It was still pitch-black outside, though, and they were no longer in the forest. Ease washed over him when he saw her sleeping face. She'd stayed next to him, and even though he hadn't actually known that while he slept, he thought that somehow, he had still been aware of her, right there. A satisfied smile crept over his face, he leaned over as far as he could, and kissed her forehead. The throbbing pain the movement triggered in his wound was worth it. She was warm and unharmed. And that was all he wanted. A feeling of familiarity had laid claim on him from the moment he had first seen her in Celios, and the feelings he had for Mati now were more potent than even he wanted to admit.

"Come on, you lazy lot," Alik grumbled. "I've let you sleep a full hour past dawn. Let's go."

Fen rolled onto his wounded arm and let out an audible sharp gasp. "Fuck!" he exclaimed.

Mati jolted up from her position sleeping next to him. "I'm sorry. Are you okay?"

"I'm fine," Fen grumbled, holding his arm against his chest. "I forgot about my arm for a second." Fen pushed himself up onto his good arm and tried to heave himself up to standing.

Mati leapt up and stretched out a hand to him. "Grab on."

Fen took her hand and nearly pulled Mati over onto him as he tried to get up. He laughed a bit. "Sorry."

"I'll add it to your tab," Mati teased.

They followed the stream bank that morning, the same route that Fen and Mati had taken with the stars on their way to Lyserria not too long ago. The day was getting hot as the sun climbed too high to allow the trees to shade them, and every misstep made Fen wince in pain that he was trying to hide.

"How's your arm feeling?" Mati asked, seeing through his façade.

"It hurts like hell, to be honest," he answered her, being more frank than he usually was about these things. "It'll be fine, though. I wouldn't want you to have to listen to me whine," he teased, shooting her a smile.

She returned his smile sheepishly. "I didn't know you could fight like that."

"I didn't, either. I guess I'm better under pressure." Fen shrugged. "Although I'll have to add that to your tab, too."

Mati laughed. "You saved Alik, not me. Perhaps you should add it to *his* tab."

"What tab?" Alik asked as he walked by.

Mati smiled. "Fen wants a kiss for saving your life."

"Ha!" Alik barked a laugh and reached out a hand to grab Fen. "Come here, then..."

Fen couldn't dodge him without falling on his arm and Alik was able to get him into a gentle headlock. "Let go!" Fen fought.

Alik made kissing noises at him. "Don't you want a kiss?" Alik laughed.

"Big, smelly, and bearded isn't really my type." Fen wriggled to free himself, but not before Alik landed a purposefully slobbery kiss on his cheek.

Mati laughed so hard at the scene that she started to double over.

"Yeah, it's so funny," Fen grumbled, wiping the slobber off his face with his good arm once Alik had released him.

"Come on," Alik called to them, still laughing. "Fen, you can walk up here with me."

"I'll pass," Fen grumbled. Even though he was irritated, the camaraderie with these people felt right. They felt like family. He'd never had that before in his life. It was a surprisingly satisfying feeling to have a group of friends to laugh with.

⚜

Other than Alik's joking around earlier that morning, they'd been walking for hours in mostly silence—a silence Mati was tired of. It only made her mind wander. She still didn't quite know how to feel about the knowledge that she had no parents. It was a mystery that she had focused on so much as a child, and all the possibility that she would ever find them was now gone. She felt almost lost, in a way that she couldn't place. She longed for some sense of family and friendship.

"Rena," she finally asked, breaking the silence. "What were Paxis and Tanophis like?"

"Oh, gods," Rena smiled. "They were the glue that held our family together. They would bicker and fight, but, oh, they loved each other so much. And they loved playing pranks." Rena laughed. "Alik, do you remember the Fulltide celebration when Pax and I had you and Tan locked in the pantry?"

Alik grumbled something inaudible.

"What's Fulltide?" Mati asked.

"Fulltide is a day when the darklight and daylight are both in the sky at the same time, for the whole day. We call it Fulltide, and everyone spends that day at home."

"Like a holiday?" Mati wondered out loud.

"I'm not sure what that is," Rena said. "But in Vertrose, the Fulltide changes people's behavior, heightens their emotions, and makes personalities run wild. It's why everyone stays home—to keep their crazy families locked up and away from everyone else's crazy families."

"Oh," Mati said. "So, it's exactly like Thanksgiving."

"What's that?" Fen asked with a raised eyebrow.

Mati smiled. "It's a holiday on Earth, when extended families all get together. They eat food, act like crazy people, and if there's not at least one fight it's a miracle."

"Sounds pleasant..." Rena said, her face showing her confusion.

"If everyone hates each other," Fen said, "then why do they get together?"

"Because its *tradition!*" Mati answered.

"Sounds stupid."

"You're not wrong," Mati admitted with a laugh.


Lyserria hadn't changed at all since they had last been there, almost a month ago. Alik led them to his saloon, and they lost Rena somewhere in the streets as she met friends and paused to catch up.

Mati dumped her pack onto the floor of the apartment. Dust and grime covered everything. She picked up all her clothing and headed for the door. "I'm going to go wash all this."

"I'll come with you," Fen replied. "I need to wash my stuff, too. And find a new shirt." He thumbed the holes in the torn sleeve of the one he was wearing.

Mati nodded and together they went in search of the well. The town was as cheerful as she remembered and now, after seeing the Kingly Hills villages, she understood why they were so happy. They lived poor lives in this desert, but they lived free. She had a newfound appreciation for their journey.

The well, once they found it, was busy. People were gathered there chatting, washing clothes, and just visiting friends. This seemed to be the town center. Fen and Mati got a bucket of water and started to wash their clothes. Fen nearly knocked over his bucket trying to wash his with only one hand.

"Give them to me," Mati said.

"I can do it, really." Fen argued with her.

"You're using one hand." Mati sent him a sidelong glance. "You'll never get them clean like that."

"Thank you," Fen sighed, and handed over the clothes. "You know I don't expect you to do that, right?"

"I know," Mati flashed him a smile. "I just don't want to smell you if you don't get them clean enough. I know you won't do it right."

"You think you're so funny," Fen mocked her.

Mati just answered him with a smile.

Fen was able to help, in the end, by taking the clean clothes and holding them as Mati handed them to him, so they didn't get dirtied all over again.

Mati woke the next morning from her bedroll to find Fen looking over at her from halfway across the room. "Good morning," she stuttered.

Fen's cheeks went red. "Morning," he said, and quickly looked away.

Once the rest of the party was up they left Alik's apartment, stopping briefly in a small shop to pick up a few longer-sleeved tunics.

"Here," Mati said, adding another tunic to the pile in Fen's already laden arm.

"I don't need that," he argued, rolling his eyes.

"You'll thank me later," she insisted.

Rena was beaming after having spent the previous evening with old friends, and Alik wasn't nearly as grumpy—as usual—either, so the party chatted nonchalantly as they walked. It was a strangely cheerful day, and that made Mati nervous.

"How long until we get to Naina Pass?" Fen asked.

"About half a day's walk," Alik answered him. "Rena and I will camp at the bottom of the Naina while you and Mati hike up to Morana and Osirim."

Fen's mouth dropped open and he shot Alik an angry glance. "And you're just now telling us that we're hiking up a mountain alone?"

Mati was also shocked that Alik and Rena had kept them in the dark, but knew that Fen was about to lose it. "Calm down, Fen. I'm sure they had a good reason for not telling us." She turned to the others. "You *do* have a good reason, right?"

Alik couldn't form any words in defense, so Rena spoke up. "My brother would tell you yes in order to appease you, but I won't patronize you. We just didn't want you to worry about it for longer than necessary. It's a treacherous climb."

"This is bullshit!" Fen shouted.

Alik seemed shocked by Fen's anger. "I—"

"I don't give a fuck," Fen interrupted him. "I—*we*—don't have to be here. We could take off right now, and leave your asses to break this mystery curse yourselves."

Mati put a calming hand on Fen's arm. "That's enough," she said softly. "Go cool off before you say something you'll regret."

"No!" Fen shot back. "This is bullshit. You can't possibly agree with this shit, can you?"

"No, but yelling about it isn't going to help. Go walk ahead of us and I'll take it from here. Please, Fen."

Fen stormed off to walk a little way ahead, while Mati talked to Alik and Rena.

"I know he came off very strong, as usual, but he's right. You have to stop keeping these things to yourselves. You can't tell us we're supposed to lead a rebellion and then turn around and treat us like children."

Alik took a deep breath. "I'm sorry. We only want to protect you."

"Give us a chance to make those decisions, at least," Mati said. "I know we're not millennia-old gods, so I'm sure we seem like children to you. But if Fen and I are going to unite these people and lead a rebellion, then we need you to trust us. You obviously trust us enough to go up the mountain and talk to the spirits by ourselves, so you can't pick and choose what *adult* things we do and do not get told. Agreed?"

Alik and Rena nodded in unison. They looked like children being scolded by a parent. Mati waved for Fen to come back and join them.

"What?" Fen blurted abruptly, obviously still irritated.

"Settle down," Mati directed him softly. "Alik agreed that we'll be included in everything from now on. No more picking and choosing what we're told. Right?" Mati turned to Alik and gave him a stern look that surprised even her.

"Right," Alik answered her. "I am truly sorry, Fen. I'm not used to dealing with such young people, and I made a mistake in not trusting you. I just wanted to keep you safe."

Fen nodded, looking a little calmer now. "Thank you. Is there anything else we should know before we continue?"

"No."

"Okay," Fen nodded again. "I appreciate you trying to look out for us, but I've been practically on my own for a long time. The time is long past for me to need a father. But I'd be okay with a friend."

Alik nodded to Fen and patted him on the back. "I can do that."

# Chapter 13

After making camp for the evening, Fen grabbed Mati sneakily and half-dragged her out of ear-shot from camp. "Thank you for taking over, earlier," Fen said. "I know I flew off the handle."

"It's not a big deal," Mati answered. "You were in the right. Maybe just not so loud next time," she suggested, and smiled.

"And thank you for being on my side. I've never had anyone do that for me."

"We're a team, right? That's my job. I'm the brains and you're the brawn."

Fen laughed. "I can be okay with that. I'm glad we're friends now."

Mati looked down at the ground. She couldn't risk looking him in the eye and have him somehow see just how badly she wanted him to lean in and kiss her. "Me too," she said, still looking at her feet. "We make a decent team."

"Yeah, we do." Fen added, and then paused.

Mati didn't know what else to say either, not without being awkward, so she blurted out the first thing that came to mind. "Ready for tomorrow?"

Fen's face screwed up in a grimace. "As ready as I guess I'll ever be, not knowing what to expect. I've never climbed a mountain before."

"Me neither," Mati replied. "I mean, I went hiking with the Masons a few times as a kid, but never anything like this."

"The Masons?"

Mati felt a twinge of guilt twist her stomach. "Yeah. My family."

"Oh, I keep forgetting you had one of those," Fen said, in a jokingly sarcastic tone.

"It wasn't everything you think it was," Mati said softly. "I never fit in with them."

They sat in silence for a moment, contemplating lives that would never be the same again. For good or ill.

"Well," Fen blurted out, "I think we'd better be getting back before Alik comes searching for us."

Mati nodded in agreement and smiled. "Although he probably won't dare after the last time he found us."

Fen let out a cackle. "I forgot about that. You missed the look on his face after you disappeared. He was absolutely humiliated. And if I hadn't been just as mortified, I'd have died of laughter."

Mati started to giggle at the thought. "I imagine he was."

And then, as though they were both remembering the situation that had led to Alik finding them, that last time, they nervously let out a few more forced chuckles.

"We really should be getting back," Mati said, in an attempt to work through her jitters and force some kind of normalcy between them.

As they approached the camp, a bright light blinded them. Asterion appeared in the center of the light.

"Asterion!" Mati exclaimed. It was good to know that the stars were okay, after the abruptness of their last parting.

Asterion bowed their head with a smile. "Hello."

"I'm so glad you're okay."

Asterion's smile faded quickly as their face went grave. "I need to ask for your help, Mati."

"With what?" Mati asked.

"I'm going to see Morimas. And I'd like you to come with me."

"I'll do what I can." She glanced quickly at Fen. "But we're going to hike Naina in the morning. Would we be back in time for that?"

"Yes," the star answered. "I'll beam us there, and bring you back immediately afterward."

"Okay," Mati decided. She remembered the conversations about the dragon at the Magnus, and hoped she could bring Morimas to their side. She held out her hand to Asterion, and the too-familiar light wrenched them through space.

Mati clamped her eyes shut in hopes of not puking when they landed on the other side, but as soon as they halted, she retched up that morning's breakfast. Being queasy wasn't how she would have wanted to meet a dragon.

"Come," Asterion called. "We don't have much time. Morimas is a cunning creature."

When Mati looked up to get her bearings, she noticed that they were standing on a high outcropping of stone, in the middle of a vast mountain range. The wind whipped past her face as she looked out over the snow-capped peaks and valleys in between.

Asterion led her around a tight corner and into a huge cavern that appeared to have been dug out of the rock. The sight frightened her to the core. She had read fairy tales as a child, but never really imagined herself meeting one. She mentally prepared herself as best as she could.

The moment they stepped into the colossal tunnel, a loud voice rang out. It reverberated off the rock, the echo making the words sound even more ominous.

"I know that smell," it said.

Mati's stomach lurched. *Great; she smells lunch.*

Asterion didn't answer the dragon, so Mati stayed quiet as well. They wound further into the tunnel, and the deeper into the darkness they went, the more the smell of age-old decay hung in the air. It wasn't a foul odor, but a heady one that left Mati feeling heavy.

Mati heard a low rubbing and scraping noise ahead of them. The air moved in the tunnel, a slight fluttering breeze. Everything was dark now, and gave her a strange, displaced feeling. She couldn't tell what was up or down. A low light broke the darkness and Mati saw a small ball of light appear in Asterion's hand. She finally saw that they'd come to the end of the tunnel. They stood before a chamber so large that the small light couldn't reach the top, or the other side.

Another wave of air hit Mati in the face. This time the air was musty and cold, and she became suddenly hyper-aware that they weren't alone. Her stomach spun wildly in anticipation of what awaited her.

"Morimas," Asterion said. "We are here to beg for your allegiance."

Mati jumped as a single large brown eye appeared from the darkness beyond, into the ball of light the star held in his hand. "I don't concern myself with young mortal beings. They're fickle and temperamental."

Mati tried desperately to regain her composure, but was frozen solid.

"But you are part of this world," Asterion said. "You are part of the symbiotic life-cycle."

"It's none of my concern." She disappeared back into the darkness, followed by a rush of wind.

"Why does everyone in this world seem to be so unconcerned about anyone else?" Mati thought out loud.

The eye reappeared in a flash, and Mati twitched in surprise. "Life goes on," Morimas declared. "An endless cycle in time, forever repeating itself. It does not matter whether I care or not. Life will continue."

"What a bleak outlook."

"When you have lived as long as I have," Morimas rumbled, "you too will stop interfering."

"I'm not sure how old you are," Mati replied. "But it can't be as long as Asterion. And the stars still care about life."

A deep, low chuckle filled every inch of the chamber. "Everyone has a vice. Sticking my snout where it does not belong is not mine."

Mati was taken aback, and couldn't resist arguing. "I'd rather have the vice of helping others to create a peaceful society, than the indulgence of sitting in my cave and judging others."

A snort disturbed the air, blowing Mati's hair around her face.

"You are very precocious, but I am unmoved." And Morimas fell back into the darkness of her cave.

Mati huffed. "Fine! Go back and hide in the lonely, black."

A great wind and flapping sound broke through the black silence. "I am not hiding!"

"You could've fooled me." Mati added calmly. She'd definitely hit a nerve. "We were warned that you wouldn't come. That you'd been hiding in this cave for hundreds of years."

More flapping stirred the air and now Mati heard scraping on the stone walls. Asterion grasped her wrist and started to pull her out of the chamber.

Mati wrenched her arm free. "You'll cower in this cave as the world crumbles. You'll be known by all as a weak and useless creature. And don't think for one moment that Guyt won't come for you next."

"Mati," Asterion warned. "I think it's time to go."

Morimas let out a roar that had Mati clamping her hands over her ears. She didn't pull away from Asterion's grip this time, allowing them to pull her out of the dragon's chamber. The small light went out and the blinding light took over, as the star beamed them to the safety of camp.

Mati still had her hands over her ears when she saw Fen sitting by the fire.

Alik and Rena raced over. "How did it go?" Rena asked excitedly.

Mati took a few deep breaths to control the nausea before answering. "It went...well?"

Asterion laughed. "You certainly made quite the impression."

"Did she give you an answer?" Alik asked.

"No," Mati sighed. "We had to leave early. I may have made her a tiny bit mad."

"Lovely," Fen snorted. "So, we have no dragon."

"Only time will tell," Asterion answered. "I wish I could stay longer, but I must go."

And Asterion disappeared in the light.

***

The next morning came far too quickly for Fen; he was dreading the task ahead. The breeze off the mountain was too cold and he knew the sun wasn't going to offer much warmth.

Rena fussed over them like a mother hen, flitting from one bag to the next, checking to be sure they had everything they needed, and then everything else that she could shove into them. Alik, meanwhile, was trying to explain to them the easiest way to get up the mountain.

"We'll be fine," Fen said firmly. "You better have hot tea waiting for us when we get back," he said, mostly to Rena, who was still too busy fussing with Mati's bag to answer.

Fen gave the mountain one long scan before setting out. Naina was probably as inhospitable as it had looked from Lyserria. Cold, lonely, and miserable. It was going to be a very long day.

They had wrapped their scarves around their faces to cut the icy wind that swept through the narrow, rocky canyon, so talking was almost impossible without screaming. It made the trek even more lonely, and Fen was left to fester in his own thoughts undisturbed.

They trudged through the damp, rocky terrain in silence for an hour, until the ground started to turn white with a dusting of snow. A narrow canyon loomed up ahead, reminding Fen of Alik's words last night. Alik had definitely taken their request for information to heart, as he'd dumped a load of background on them at camp last night. The most important pieces had been the explanation that Morana and Osirim weren't particularly fond of the gods, and the spirits would be more likely to create the sword if Mati and Fen went by themselves.

They trudged up and over the slippery rocks with effort as the day continued on. Their faces were frozen from the icy wind that zipped through the canyon, and their muscles ached and threatened to seize up.

Fen's arm hurt almost as badly as it had four days ago when it had first been skewered. He tried to keep it tucked into his chest and under the scarf as much as he could, but that offered little protection from the biting wind.

When Dursten had first showed up to take him, almost thirty days ago, Fen would never have guessed that *this* would be where his path would lead.

Mati's face, feet, and hands had been numb for the last hour. With every footfall, she felt her skin tighten and scream. Her teeth chattered uncontrollably beneath the useless scarf wrapped around her face. Even the gloves she wore felt pointless against the cold. But in the moment when she was about to give up, she saw an end to the steep canyon. She'd been slipping on the rocks for hours and now, bruised and battered, she could see the flat ground just within reach.

Fen took her hand and heaved her up. She could feel his muscles tense through his hand as he lifted her partially with his injured arm. He took a deep breath after Mati stepped up onto the thin ledge overlooking the canyon. "Well, I guess this is it."

A dark, uninviting opening in the mountain face stared them down, daring them to enter. Mati twined Fen's hand in hers. "Here goes nothing," she said, as they walked into the wall of dark that yawned open before them.

As soon as they passed through the opening, a room beyond lit up, like they'd walked through a portal into a new world altogether. The warmth of their new surroundings instantly started to thaw their frozen bodies. The packs they had been carrying had vanished.

The room was a huge hall made from polished rock, lit from nowhere and everywhere at the same time. Across the hall, seated on two enormous stone thrones, were Morana and Osirim, as though they had been waiting patiently for them. Morana was clad in a mantle spun of pure gold, and Osirim wore a green robe, with bright green eyeshadow carefully painted across each eyelid. Their deep, russet-brown skin and black hair matched each other perfectly.

"We've been waiting for you," Morana said, and stared at them blandly. "We felt you as soon as you set foot on our mountain."

Fen stepped forward. "I'm Fen," he started. "And this is Mati—"

"We know who you are," Osirim interrupted. "What we don't know, is what you want."

"Right," Fen started again, a bit nervously. "We're here on behalf of the peoples of Vertrose to beg for your help in destroying Guyt. We need a weapon that will kill him."

"We're not in the business of acting as mercenaries," Morana declared with an air of distaste. "Vertrose will need to rid their land of Guyt themselves. We don't intervene in the natural order of things."

Mati stepped up, recalling a story Rena had told them. "But Guyt isn't a natural part of Vertrose. He was never supposed to be here."

"Are you an authority in the ancient arts of the Seeing Eye?" Morana asked sarcastically.

"No," Mati answered.

"Then how could you possibly know that Guyt was never meant to be here?"

"I don't, exactly," Mati said, suddenly aware of how unsure she sounded. "But I know that he came into this world from another one. And I know that if we don't kill him, he won't stop at just taking over Vertrose. He'll soon come after the both of you as well. He's too power-hungry to settle."

"What you suggest is not possible," Osirim answered haughtily. "Guyt couldn't destroy us."

"I'm sure the gods thought the same thing...until he staged a coup. Are you so confident that he won't try someday, that you'll risk not helping us now?"

Morana and Osirim looked at each other for a long moment. They seemed to be having an unspoken conversation. Mati met Fen's eyes and willed him to not speak up yet. They didn't need to irritate the spirits.

"We," Osirim announced finally, "do not believe that it is our duty to entrust you with such a powerful weapon."

"You mean that you don't want to give us a weapon that could potentially kill you as well," Fen said. Mati put a gentle hand on his arm to stop him.

"We understand your hesitation," Mati interceded. "But if you know who we are, then you must also know that our intentions are not to harm you."

"Not *your* intentions," Morana replied. "But this weapon may not rest in your hands for all eternity."

"We could bring it back once Guyt has been destroyed," Fen jumped in desperately. "We could swear it. Then you would have nothing to fear."

Morana and Osirim held another telepathic conversation. Mati and Fen stood in silence, Mati struggling against the desperation she could feel growing inside, until Osirim finally spoke.

"We will create this weapon, but *only* on the condition that it is returned to us once its purpose has been served. You must also accept any consequences that your actions could incur from this act. You both must share in this responsibility, and perform a blood oath to hold yourselves true to your word."

Mati looked at Fen, who agreed without hesitation.

"Very well," Osirim replied. "Come forward."

A tall stone table appeared out of nowhere in the center of the room. A roughly-hewn obsidian knife and crystal bowl appeared as well, as the two stepped up to the table.

"Take the knife. Each of you must shed blood into the bowl." Morana motioned to the table.

Fen took the knife and held the blade inside of his fist. He closed his eyes and ripped the knife out with his other hand. Blood trickled into the bowl as he handed the knife to Mati, then wrapped his hand in the hem of his tunic to staunch the blood.

She took the knife, unease settling in her chest. The knife was heavy and still covered in Fen's blood. She carefully wiped the tip off onto her sleeve and used the sharp blade to cut the tiniest slit in the heel of her hand. In direct contrast to Fen's larger wound, which had bled easily, she was forced to squeeze the cut a bit to get any blood to drip into the bowl.

Morana and Osirim immediately began a low rhythmic chant. The blood in the bowl began to swirl and steam. Fen and Mati watched, almost forgetting the stinging in their palms until the cuts began to burn.

Fen opened his hand to see what was happening and Mati followed suit. The cuts on their palms were black as night and hot as fire. It was almost too much to handle as the hypnotic chanting pounded through them like drums, the sound filling them up with what felt like white-hot lava.

Mati almost collapsed in pain when the thudding in her body finally ceased, slowly taking the piercing pain with it. It ebbed, then stopped, and she came back to her senses as the table, knife, and bowl disappeared.

"The covenant has begun," Morana announced. "If you do not bring back the weapon following Guyt's demise, you will die and be bound in the Hell Realm for the rest of eternity."

"But how do we get the weapon?" Fen asked looking around as though he expected to see it manifested and waiting.

Osirim sat up a bit straighter. "We require you to bring us two things in order to forge this weapon. Magic swords are not created out of nothing."

"We need," Morana continued where he left off, "a flask of water from Gaia's pool, and four gords of raw, ancient metal from the bottom of the Pontianak Sea. Bring these things here to us and we will make you a weapon to kill a spirit."

Fen nodded and grabbed Mati's hand. They turned to leave, still in a slight daze.

"Wait," Mati stopped Fen. "Where are our packs?"

"We have taken those as payment for disturbing our peace." Morana answered.

"But we need those to get back to camp."

"Then you'll die on the way and won't require a weapon." Osirim answered blandly.

Fen tugged her forward and she let him. Mati could feel their wounds pulsing against each other as they retraced their steps, back out through the magic portal and onto the mountainside.

They both let out deep sighs once out in the snow again, a sigh of both relief and determination.

# Chapter 14

The sun had begun to sink low in the sky as Fen and Mati started their trek back down the steep, snowy canyon. All they had now were the clothes they'd had on when they had entered the spirits' chamber. All their other warm clothes, whether helpful or not, were gone.

"Come on," Fen tugged Mati's hand. "I don't wanna be stuck up here when the sun goes down."

Mati followed Fen as they descended lower and lower, trying to beat the setting sun. The temperature had already started to drop; Mati could feel her fingers going numb again.

"Fen, I don't think we're going to make it."

"We have to," Fen answered resolutely.

Mati's heart sank. She knew how dangerous it would be to be stuck on the mountain overnight. The climb wasn't easy, either. After slipping twice, they had to slow themselves down to a crawl. The weather had become almost unbearable. The biting wind sliced through her clothes, only stopping once it hit her bones.

The sun set abruptly, almost like a light switching off, throwing the mountain into near complete darkness. Mati's eyes adjusted a little, but it wasn't enough to keep her from stumbling over the huge rocks and dips in the ground. Keeping control of her own body was nearly impossible.

"Fen," Mati pleaded, her teeth chattering uncontrollably. "We need to stop. I can't see. It won't help if we fall off a cliff, or trip and get hurt."

"I know," Fen answered over the howling wind. "We'll take cover there."

He led her to a small outcropping of rock that had managed to block the snow from building up on one side. They plopped down onto the ground with their backs against the rock. Fen tucked her up against his side, while Mati shook uncontrollably.

"Don't sleep," Fen warned her. "If we fall asleep, I'm not sure that we'll wake up. Keep your body moving and awake at all costs."

Mati could barely keep her eyes open, and she shook as though she was having a seizure. "I'll try," she forced out, between her chattering teeth.

"No, Mati. You *have* to stay awake."

"I don't know if I can. I'm so tired, Fen."

"Mati, if you close your eyes you will die." Fen paused before going on. "And if you die, I don't think I could live with myself."

"This isn't your fault," she said, trying to stay awake. "I was looking forward to you visiting me on Earth."

"Don't you dare talk like that, Mati. You will *not* die on the side of a fucking mountain."

Mati's eyes drifted shut for what felt like just a moment. It was warm behind her eyelids. She thought she was in her bed at home, warm and tucked up under blankets. Then, she was ripped from that place back to the biting cold by a slap on the face.

"Mati," Fen shouted and clutching her shoulders. "No, no, no. Wake up!"

"I'm still here," Mati mumbled, as if through a dream. She was enveloped in warmth again, but this time it was Fen's body clinging to her. He'd pulled her even closer to his chest, and kissed the top of her head.

"Mati," Fen said into her ear, "I love you."

Mati's senses perked up a bit at his declaration. Part of her thought that maybe she was just lingering in that warm dream. She came to her senses again with a start. Fen was still clinging to her. "You can't love me, Fen."

Fen went quiet for a minute, but kept her tucked against his side. Then he started to sing what should've been a lively tune, but was barely audible through his dry, cracked lips.

"What are you doing?" Mati asked.

"Singing," Fen answered. "It'll keep me awake." Then he continued singing the tune.

Mati's lips tried to curl into a smile. "I'd slap you for making me listen to your awful singing, if I wasn't frozen in place."

"Well, if you have to listen to me sing, you won't fall asleep." Mati just knew he was smiling by the way he said it.

After a minute of listening, Mati found herself being drawn into the song. The words repeated themselves, the tune was catchy, and she started humming along to keep herself awake. Fen pulled her even closer, making sure to sway with the tune every now and again, movement which helped her not pass out again.

The night passed slowly but steadily as they took turns humming and singing. It felt like an eternity since they'd been warm. Fen tucked Mati's hands into his tunic, against his bare chest, to keep them as warm as possible.

Mati would've blushed, in different circumstances. She could feel the rock-hard muscle at which she'd often snuck glances, and wished, like never before, that they were back in the woods, by a warm fire, with Alik and Rena.

When the first dim light started to brighten the darkness, Fen knew they'd survived. And he would've celebrated, if he weren't so exhausted and frozen. As things were, though, Fen squeezed Mati and that was the only celebration he could muster.

He rose to his feet and lifted Mati up onto her wobbly legs. They began to trudge down the rest of Naina Mountain, one foot falling in line in front of the other without thought or intent. They held onto each other's waists and shoulders to steady themselves. They moved slowly and cautiously on frozen toes, their feet barely lifting as they shuffled through the light snow and over the rocks.

Fen turned at the feeling of Mati's hand yanking away from his own. She'd fallen face first into the snow, too exhausted to go on. He dropped to her side and tried to heave her up onto her feet.

"I'm sorry," Mati breathed out. "My legs—"

"It's okay," Fen interrupted, as he lifted her up. Her lips were a sickly blue-gray color through the cracks. "Lean on me. We have to be getting close."

He pulled Mati's arm over his shoulder and held her tight around her waist. Pain ripped through his body and his injured arm felt like it had been lit on fire. He clenched his teeth, pushing his body to keep moving forward, most of Mati's weight now on him.

The snow was getting deeper. They couldn't lift their feet, and pushing through the drifts was the only option.

"Just leave me," Mati said hoarsely.

Fen heaved her up again in protest. "Like hell I will."

Somehow, through the freezing mist, Fen thought he heard his name on the wind. *Is this what it feels like to die? The cosmos calling out to you to let go?*

Again, he heard his name, clearer this time, followed by Mati's name. He tipped his head up just enough to see a figure bounding through the snow, coming for them. Alik—it was Alik.

Fen dropped to his knees at the sight, his body giving in at long last as help drew near. His world went dark and calm, lulled into a warm and peaceful dream.

⟫⟫ ⟪⟪

Alik raced to the pair, calling for Rena as he ran. They had waited up all night in terror, setting out at first light to search. Alik had feared the worst right up until the moment he saw the two slumped and slowly-moving figures through the cold mist.

"Rena," he called frantically. "I found them! Over here!" Alik dropped to their sides. "Fen? Mati? Stay with me. You're safe now."

Rena joined him. "We need to get them back to camp. I don't know how they've held on so long. Their breathing is shallow. And where are their packs?" she demanded.

Alik and Rena dragged the half-dead bodies of Fen and Mati back to camp. Rena started two fires on either side of them, while Alik covered them with every piece of clothing and blanket he could scrounge up. And then they waited.

⁘⁙⁘

It was nearly midday before Fen started to stir. He blinked a few times, adjusting to the harsh sunlight. His lips felt slick, a thick salve smothering them. Where was he? He blinked again and looked around. There was Alik, and Rena was tending the fire.

"What happened?" he rasped.

Alik whipped around to stare at him. "Thank Gaia, you're alive!"

"What happened?" Fen asked again, starting to wiggle out of the cocoon of cloth.

"You and Mati nearly died of exposure."

Fen immediately remembered the night, even though it had all felt like a dream. The overhang, the singing, the bitter cold. Mati falling beside him. He pushed himself upright. "Where is she? Is she okay?"

"She's still sleeping," Rena said, as she pushed Fen back down into the cocoon and handed him a cup of tea. "As requested," she smiled.

"But is she going to be okay?"

"She'll be fine," Alik replied. "She was a bit worse than you, but she'll be fine."

Fen passed the rest of the afternoon being force-fed hot tea by Rena, and drifting lazily in and out of sleep until, finally, he saw the ball of blankets next to him stir. He shot up to seated again.

Mati blinked and squinted at him. "Fen?"

"It's about time," he teased. He didn't dare let on how relieved he was. "We thought you would sleep the entire day."

"What happened? The last thing I remember is asking you to leave me."

"Yeah, I'll punch you for that later," Fen scowled. "Alik and Rena found us. You've been asleep all day."

Mati tried to sit up but was promptly stopped by a cup of steaming tea in her face.

"Drink that and don't even think about getting up," Rena warned. "You're both staying right there."

"We have too much to do," Mati protested. "Morana and Osirim—"

"Can wait," Alik interrupted. "You'll be of no use to anyone if you can't even walk. But we would like to ask you how it went with the spirits, if it's not too much."

Fen scooted up to sit comfortably, leaning against the makeshift pillow to answer. "They agreed to make a weapon, but only if we give it back to them once we kill Guyt. They made us swear a blood oath on that."

"Well, that's good news," Rena said. "We honestly didn't even think you would be able to convince them."

"A blood oath is of little consequence in our dire situation," Alik added. "But where is the weapon?"

"We have to get them two things before they can make it," Fen said, glancing at Mati with a protective eye.

Alik raised an eyebrow. "What do they need?"

"Water from Gaia's pool and metal from the bottom of the Pontianak Sea."

Alik and Rena's faces went blank. Alik sighed again. "We have no choice..."

"Alik," Rena interjected. "These items are nearly impossible to get. It's madness."

"No more impossible than getting the spirits to even agree to make such a weapon," Fen retorted. "I don't think we have many options, so we just need to get on with it."

"Do you have any idea," Alik said dryly, "what the Pontianak is?"

"No," Fen retorted. "But does that change our lack of other options?"

"That's not the point. The Pontianak is a sea well within Guyt's territory, and one that he has patrolled. And it is home to a lethal sea spirit of the same name."

"Regardless, we still need that metal," Fen said.

"Unfortunately, yes," Rena replied.

"So, when will we leave?"

"When you and Mati have rested enough," Alik answered. "Maybe in two days' time."

That night, after Alik and Rena had gone to sleep by the dual fires they still kept burning, Fen lay wide awake.

"Are you awake?" he asked the air. Mati was still tucked into the blankets directly next to him, so close he could hear the gentle in and out of her breath.

"Yes," Mati answered in a whisper.

Fen laid in silence for a moment before saying anything else. "Do you need me to sing you to sleep?"

Mati let out a chuff of a laugh. "No," she said, with a smile that he could hear. "I can go the rest of my life without hearing you *sing*. If that's what it can be called."

Fen laughed softly so he didn't wake Alik or Rena.

Fen could tell just how closely they were laying to each other. Damn Rena for not letting them get up. He wanted to know—and just as equally did not want to know—how many layers of fabric were currently between them. Definitely not enough.

Mati shifted further down in her blankets, and patted around the space between them until she came into contact with Fen. His breath caught in his throat as she ripped her hand away.

He willed his body not to respond, but squeezed his eyes shut when his body betrayed him in the worst possible way. He tried to turn away to escape Mati, with speed but no accuracy. He rolled so fast that the blankets yanked her along with him, slamming her into his back. She grunted in surprise, but said nothing.

"Sorry," Fen forced out in terror, trying desperately to untangle the blankets and set her free.

"It's fine," Mati responded, as much terror in her voice as he was feeling.

Fen reached over and, in the confusion and the dark, his hand grazed Mati's chest. "Shit!" he exclaimed.

They scrambled silently to untangle themselves and once they had, promptly scooted as far away from each other as the blankets would allow them.

Even in his mortified state, Fen felt his blood diverting. He thought of anything that might curtail his current state of distress, but found his mind exceedingly stubborn.

His first order of business, once it was light, was to get far *far* away from Mati.

# Chapter 15

The morning they left the mountain pass to begin their trek back into the Crescent Wood was especially cold. The dawn light had barely touched their camp and a mist hung low on the mountain top. They traversed the Naina Pass silently, the weather slowly warming as they reached the bottom of the pass. Mati was never happier to finally be able to shed some layers as the sun started to warm her.

They bypassed Lyserria this time and headed straight for the Crescent Wood. The landscape changed from desert wasteland to grassy woods and open fields over the days of walking. They passed some familiar landmarks and, once again, started following the river that ran between Crescent Wood and Wickery Wood.

Mati walked behind Fen, watching his every move. She and Fen had recovered from their blunder in the blankets, but had admittedly been a bit shyer with each other since then. It was childish, she knew that, but she couldn't shake the embarrassment. She argued with herself that it had been four days since the incident, and she resolved to be the first to bring it up.

"Hey there," she said to Fen, with forced confidence.

Fen almost jumped out of his skin. "Hi," he replied, with a raised eyebrow.

"Jumpy, huh." Mati smiled, trying to force them back to their old teasing banter.

Fen half-smiled. "Yeah, I guess. I was just thinking."

"About what?" Mati inquired.

"About you, actually."

"Oh." This was good. He was thinking about her, too. "What about me?"

Fen's face flushed a bit red, and he started scratching unconsciously at the bandages that were still covering the wounds on his arm. "Well," he started, then stopped. "I...uh...wanted to apologize for the other night. I never—"

"Oh, that!" Mati interrupted nervously. "It's nothing. I'm sorry, too."

"It's fine, really. I just—" Fen stopped and looked Mati straight in the eyes. "Fuck this. I'm not sorry at all. I'd be lying if I said I hadn't thought about something like this before. I'm sorry about how awkwardly it happened, though."

Mati was taken aback by Fen's brazen confession. "Please, don't—"

"What? Tell you I love you again? No, I won't."

"Thank you," Mati said, letting out a mental sigh. "Not to sound like a parrot, but I really do want to go slow with whatever this is."

"Do you, now?" Fen smiled cheekily at her. "I'd be willing to go slow, if that's what you actually want. But you know that grabbing my bits isn't exactly slow."

Mati's face heated with embarrassment. "Dick!"

Fen started laughing harder, drawing the wary eyes of Alik and Rena. "I'm sorry!" he said through his laughter. "I couldn't help it."

"I take it all back!" Mati raged at him, though she found herself more annoyed than anything, and not really meaning it. "I don't want anything to do with you." She tried to storm off, but Fen caught her arm.

"I'm sorry. Truly sorry," he said, that teasing smile still on his face.

"No, you're not."

Fen composed his face as best he could. "I am very sorry I teased you."

Mati wasn't really mad, just mortified, and he knew exactly how to get her riled up. But she couldn't resist his smiling eyes. She smiled in return. "No, you're not," she said again. "You're only trying to smooth it over now."

"Is it working?" He flashed her a cocky grin.

She rolled her eyes, smirking. "Yes..."

Fen composed his face for real this time. "So, you still want to take it slow?"

"Yes," Mati answered uncertainly. "I don't like being just your friend, but I don't want to get too involved, or make a big deal of everything while we're trekking all over the place. I know Rena is okay with it all. I think she is, anyway. But I'm not sure how anyone else will take it. We should try and keep things discreet for a while, and not rock the boat."

"The way you talk confuses me sometimes, but I think I know what you mean. And that seems fair," he finally answered after much thought. "I'm the king of no fuss," Fen stated, with dramatic flourish of his arm.

"Yeah," Mati rolled her eyes again. "We've both been very dramatic thus far, and you know it."

"Thus far?" Fen repeated mockingly. "Don't you sound fancy." Mati gave him a sidelong glance. "Okay, okay. No drama. I vow I won't make a public spectacle by kissing you…" He moved in closer to her and stroked one finger down her arm. Then he stepped in even closer and whispered in her ear. "Or touching you…"

She threw a quick look ahead to make sure Rena and Alik hadn't seen them. "You're off to a fantastic start."

"Consider that payback for grabbing my—"

"Yeah, yeah." Mati interrupted. "I get it. I'm serious, Fen."

"I know you are," Fen said as they walked on. "I'm just happy you're finally giving in to my devilish good looks and charm."

"Ha!" Mati huffed in amusement. "You act like you haven't been drooling over me this whole time."

"I have, and I don't feel the need to act like I wasn't. I only got mad when you acted all wishy-washy with me."

Mati duck her head. Admittedly, watching him work out shirtless, and the incident in the blankets, had pushed her to make this decision. Her cheeks started to burn at the thought. She composed herself and pushed the images out of her head.

"Low key…" she warned, shooting him a glance and pinching him on the arm. "I can just as easily change my mind."

Fen narrowed his eyes and leaned in close. "Give it time, you won't want to change your mind."

"You do think highly of yourself, don't you?" she teased, trying desperately to not think about the feeling of his warm breath on her neck. She was helped by Alik's voice suddenly pulling her out of her own head.

"Keep up, you two," Alik called from ahead. "We're getting close, and I'd like to make this as quick a trip as possible."

The Crescent Wood was just as looming and hard to breathe in as before. They could tell that Gaia was close, by the butter-thick air that clung to every branch and leaf. Instead of going around it like they had done before, however, Rena and Alik led them directly into the thick air.

Fen had thought the air was unbearable before, but soon realized that had been nothing compared to the overpowering and impenetrable air they were walking through now.

"How much further?" he asked with difficulty, sucking in a rough breath.

"We're very close," Rena answered, with just as much difficulty. "You and Mati will continue on alone."

Fen nodded and took Mati's hand.

"Just keep going straight," Alik said. "You should reach it in no more than five minutes."

Fen led Mati into the dense wall of cloud that surrounded the outer ring of Gaia. "Are you okay?" he asked Mati.

"I'm fine," she answered, sounding choked. "Let's just get this over with."

After the few minutes Alik had predicted, they finally reached what Fen could only guess was Gaia. The cloud cover completely dissipated and he and Mati stopped suddenly, before they could plummet into the pool that laid at their feet.

The pool was dark and looked more like tar than water, despite the stray leaves floating on its surface.

"Do we talk to it?" Fen wondered out loud.

Mati shrugged. "Hello? Gaia...?"

"I can hear you, mortal," an eerie low-pitched voice answered from everywhere around them, the sound rippling across the murky water of the pool. "What is it that you have come here for? It's not often that one of your kind visits me."

"We need to take some of your water," Mati answered. "To make a weapon to kill an evil spirit."

"Spirits are not evil," Gaia answered. "Some just have different motivations than others, making them seem evil."

A silent pause followed, as neither of them knew how to proceed.

"So, can we have the water or not?" Fen asked, in a snappy straightforward tone.

Mati shot Fen a look that said *settle down and don't screw this up.*

"No," Gaia replied.

"But—" Fen started to object.

"I said no, mortal. Do not test me."

"Please listen," Mati chimed in. "We've got to have that water."

"Mortal concerns are no concern of mine."

Fen rolled his eyes. "Seems to be a theme," he muttered under his breath.

"Your snide remarks aren't helping," Mati snapped in a rough whisper before continuing her plea to the spirit. "Please, just listen to me for just a moment. And excuse my partner. He's an ass."

Fen gave her a look of contempt, but he kept quiet.

"Very well," Gaia answered. "Go ahead. But I make no promises about changing my decision."

"That's fair. We need this water so that Morana and Osirim can make us a weapon. We have already gotten their word that they will do so, but, but we need just enough water for them to make it. Guyt must be defeated."

"I will say it again, your mortal problems are none of my concern."

"But what concerns Vertrose, concerns you."

"My dear, I was here long before even Tera was here. What makes you think I require such a temporal pin in this universe as a pool in a wood?"

"Nothing. We're aware that you don't," Mati lied. "But wouldn't it be easier to just help us out now? Then you can continue to sit here undisturbed for a good long time to come."

Gaia let out a long chilling laugh that echoed in the pool.

"Will you help us?" Mati asked again.

"No," Gaia stated.

Fen had enough. "You let him into this world, and now he's going to destroy it. The very least you can do is give up some of that muck you swim in to help us get rid of him."

The little ripples on the water turned to larger splashes. "I didn't *let* him into this world," Gaia refuted Fen's accusation, almost sounding offended. "He escaped my clutches."

"So, you failed Tera and let this monster out," Mati shot back. "Then you can help us get rid of him. We don't have all day to chat. We will be taking that water."

"You wouldn't *dare*!" Gaia raged.

"Watch us!" Fen replied already removing the cap from his waterskin.

"How dare you speak to me that way. I am a primordial spirit!"

"Yeah, that's great. Look, Mati tried to convince you her way, and frankly, I'm done playing nice. We have no time to squabble with you. Either give us permission, or I will take the water from you."

"You'll have to take it from me, if you dare!" Gaia spat. "I will not give you permission."

Fen reached down and filled the waterskin with no further fuss from Gaia.

Mati stood and watched, confused. "Hang on. Why were you so against us taking it, but now you're letting us have it so easily?"

"What?" Gaia asked, sounding surprised.

"Why are you so scared to give us permission?"

"I'm not," Gaia replied, a little too evenly.

"You're hiding something from us," Mati thought out loud. "Wait! Guyt is a primordial spirit too. Is that why you can't help us officially?"

Fen looked up at Mati curiously, with the same epiphany hitting him. "You *did* let him out, didn't you?"

The waters of Gaia's pool went devastatingly still. "As I've said, I didn't *let* him out."

"Then what happened?" Mati asked.

"Guyt is my brother," Gaia answered, her waters still unmoving. "I broke him free from the prison into which our parents had thrown him. All of Hell was created just for him. But I believed in him. He was my brother. And I broke him free. I brought him into my world and let him stay in the pool. I thought he would stay here and be happy. But I was wrong..."

"He escaped..." Mati whispered.

"Yes," Gaia's voice was mournful. "I have failed this universe."

"I'm sorry," Mati said softly.

"Long ago, I promised him that I would not willingly help destroy him. It is an oath I have upheld."

Fen and Mati exchanged a look.

"Thank you," Mati said and laid her hand on the ground next the pool. A trail of murky thickness came up from the bank to meet her. "I promise you, we will make it an honorable death."

Gaia fell silent once again and her waters went deathly still. It was as if she had left the pool altogether.

Fen slid his hand into Mati's and tugged her away from the waters. "We should go."

# Chapter 16

F en and Mati rejoined Alik and Rena. The mist and choking air seemed a bit lighter somehow to Mati, even though it was still heavy in the air.

"Did you get it?" Alik asked with a worried look.

Fen held up the waterskin. "Yes."

Rena's eyes widened. "How did you convince her?"

"We'll tell you as we walk," Mati said.


They made camp just outside of the edge of the Crescent Woods that night. Rena couldn't believe their story and was still mulling over the details with Mati while she made them all tea.

Fen and Alik decided to bring out their swords and get some of the day's nerves out while they waited for their tea. The wound that Fen had received from the morest had finally healed enough that he was able to start training again.

"Tea's ready, you two," Rena called. "Come over and rest."

Mati had unashamedly been watching Fen while helping Rena, and that didn't go unnoticed.

Rena handed a cup to her and sat next to her by the fire. "You and Fen seem to be on good terms again."

Mati took a sip of tea. "Yes," she answered politely.

"Very good terms..."

"We're just not arguing about anything at the moment."

Rena took a sip and looked over the cup edge at Mati, whose eyes had wandered once more to Fen on the other side of the fire. "Mmm... was it something that happened that night on the mountain?"

Mati's heart lurched to a stop. "What?" she asked, trying—and failing—to seem composed.

"The night you got lost," Rena clarified. "Did something happen?"

"Oh, that night." Mati sighed. Rena raised an eyebrow. "He told me that he loved me. But he thought we were going to die. We're just taking things slow for now, to see what happens."

Rena smiled into her tea. "Slow? More like an old married couple."

Mati narrowed her eyes. She didn't care for Rena's words, even if they were true. "Just friends....ish," Mati emphasized.

Rena took another sip of tea. "Okay," she replied coolly. "I'm just glad that you're beginning to accept that chaos is a part of the calm of life, and that by denying a little chaos, you were quite literally creating it."

"What's that supposed to mean?" Mati really didn't like the connotations Rena was throwing out.

"All I mean is that your need for calm and order was creating chaos. We all see how taken Fen was—is—with you, and that you two were at odds. Creating chaos, you see..."

Mati didn't answer, focusing on her tea instead.

Rena finally turned to face Fen and Alik, who were in the middle of a debate about combat stances and battle procedures, as usual. "Is that all you two talk about?"

"Not always," Fen answered. "But it seemed appropriate now, since we're heading straight for Guyt's southern border."

"That's a fair point."

"Alik says it'll take a while to get there." Fen grabbed a piece of dried meat from his pack and began chewing.

"He's right," Rena answered. "I wish we had horses."

"Is there anywhere in between here and the Pontianak where we could get some?"

"No," Alik replied, gulping down his tea. "We don't have enough time to waste by going into the Kingly Hills, or back to Lyserria. The sykosee would be the closest allies on our way."

"Can we stop there?" Mati asked.

Alik paused in thought. "We could maybe swing by Duinan, but the sykosee don't have horses."

"Oh, yeah," Mati recalled glumly. The wings. They'd look pretty ridiculous riding around on horses when they could just spread those massive wings and fly away.

The conversation lulled, then moved to more pleasant topics until they all decided to get some sleep.

Mati tucked herself quietly into her bedroll. Did Rena know what had happened with Fen at camp *that* night? She was asking a lot of questions, and Mati didn't really like it. Her thoughts, however, were interrupted by a voice near her ear.

"Follow me," Fen's voice whispered, his breath almost tickling her.

Mati carefully unwrapped herself and stood up as quietly as she could. The last thing she wanted was to wake up Rena or Alik. Fen clasped her hand and led her quietly away from camp.

"Where are we going?" she whispered.

Fen dragged her a few more feet and stopped. "Here," he replied, turning her toward him.

"For what?"

Before Mati had a second for another breath, Fen leaned in and landed a kiss on her lips. Not the hesitant kisses like they'd been before; the kiss he gave her now had pent up energy in it, like a released spring.

Fen steadied her with a firm hand cupping the back of her head. He wrapped his arm around Mati's waist and pulled her against him. She could feel every muscle as he moved against her, and she was suddenly very aware of something else that that now pressed against her lower abdomen. That was the moment Fen attempted to push her slightly back and hold her at arm's length.

Mati was having no part of *that*. She had asked for this quiet relationship, but she was aching to do more than peck him on the cheek. She moved closer to him once more, needing to feel him against her. Even if they didn't do anything else—which she hoped they didn't right now, since it was pitch black and she didn't feel like picking sticks and leaves out of places that sticks and leaves should definitely not be—she still wanted to feel his weight and warmth against her.

He let out a low, guttural growl as she took his bottom lip between her teeth and bit down lightly. Mati was undone by the primal sound that escaped from him, feeling the sound vibrate through his body and into hers. But she had to stop. *They* had to stop. She pulled away this time, but kept her hands planted firmly on his chest. He drew back as well, moving his hands to her waist. The night was wholly black around them, and she couldn't even see his eyes. No moonlight bounced off of them.

"We should get back," Mati forced out breathlessly. "Rena is suspicious, and I'd rather not have her wake up with more questions for me."

"Alik is getting suspicious too," Fen said, his voice low and husky. "He mentioned it while we were training, earlier. He asked if we were together. I know he wanted us to be friends but I really couldn't figure out if he was okay with us being more."

Mati sighed. "Then we'll have to be extra-careful. I kinda have the feeling that Rena is okay with it, but Alik—or anyone else we have to deal with—might not be so accepting. We're supposed to be unlocking the curse that's on them, not dating. They might see it as a distraction that could fuck their chances of reclaiming their land and powers. I think we need to test the waters before being too open. We still have to get Vrutuuk, Gruthlan, and Clíodha to join the rebellion, and if we offend them or they're not receptive, then we could risk them pulling out. And it's not worth it right now."

"As much as I hate to say it," Fen answered softly, "I think you might be right. I couldn't gauge whether Alik was supportive or not." Mati nodded and he took her by the hands. "I do love you, Mati."

Mati froze, her heart skipping several beats. She was a deer in headlights, stunned by his words.

"And I don't expect to hear it back. I just wanted you to know that I do."

"Fen," Mati sighed. "I do like you a lot, but I can't say that yet."

"No, I get it. I just wanted to tell you." He paused for a deep breath. "I just really felt like I needed to tell you."

"How are you so open and caring, after all you've been through?" Mati asked, not realizing how the question might catch him off-guard.

She felt his shoulders shrug. "I don't ever want you to feel the way I've felt most of the time. The way I grew up was horrible and I don't want you to ever wonder about your worth, or your place in my life."

Mati's heart sank to her toes. He wanted her to feel wanted and loved because he had never felt that. And she couldn't tell him that she loved him. She wasn't completely sure that she did, and she definitely didn't want to say it if she didn't. A heavy sense of guilt washed over her, and she drooped her head. "I'm sorry."

Fen took back one of his hands that still held hers, and lifted her chin. "It's okay. I didn't expect to hear it back tonight. I'm sorry I made you feel bad." He leaned in and kissed her lightly on the forehead.

She felt a little better after hearing those words. "I'm sorry," she said again.

Fen left his forehead resting against hers. "You have nothing to be sorry for. I'm sure you have reasons."

Mati sighed and felt tears welling up in her eyes. "I had a boyfriend in college. I ran into a store to grab a few things and I saw him there with flowers. I thought they were for me, so I didn't say anything. I didn't want to ruin the surprise. But later that night, he came over and he didn't bring the flowers. I didn't say anything. I didn't want to cause problems. The next day I went to my friend's dorm to walk to class together." She stopped and drew in a ragged breath. "I saw the flowers he had bought, sitting on her desk. When I asked her about them, she told me that her friend had given them to her. I tried not to let it bother me. A week or so later, I got home early and I found them on the couch... kissing."

Mati couldn't hold in the tears anymore. They started pouring down her face as she sobbed.

Fen pulled her into his arms and laid his hand against the back of her head, resting his cheek on her hair. "He didn't deserve you. I'm sorry."

He kept her wrapped in his arms, tight to his chest, until Mati was able to staunch her tears. "Let's get back," she said softly. "They'll be wondering where we are."

⟫⟫ ⟪⟪

After a week of traveling, the party had all become grumpy. The landscape was turning hot and dry again, and the sand and loose dirt kicked up every time the wind blew. Their boots, hair, and eyes were filled with grit.

The weather was particularly hot that day. There were no clouds in sight and no scraggly trees for shade. All that stretched ahead of them was barren desert, until Mati saw shimmering dark spots on the horizon.

"What's that?" she pointed ahead.

"It's nothing," Alik waved. "Just a heat image."

"No, look. It's moving."

They stopped walking for Alik to squint off in the distance. "Just a mirage. Let's keep going."

"It's not a *mirage*," Mati emphasized, getting irritated. "I'm not an idiot."

"I see it too," Rena chimed in. "There's definitely something there."

"We're still too far from Duinan," Alik stated.

"So, you believe *her*," Mati huffed, letting the irritation of the sand and heat get to her.

Alik gave Mati a sharp look. "Rena knows more about this terrain."

"But I'm an idiot?"

Fen placed his hand gently on Mati's arm, the way she did for him when he was getting testy. "We're all just feeling this heat."

Mati took a deep breath. Fen's hand did comfort and steady her, so she decided to let it go.

Rena cupped her hand over her eyes and squinted. "It's definitely getting closer, Alik."

Alik squinted toward the horizon as well, his breath catching in his dry throat. "It can't be…"

"What?" Fen asked, not liking the worried tone in Alik's voice.

"It looks like dralin."

"Fuck!" Rena exclaimed.

"Who or what is a dralin?" Fen asked, his hand still firm on Mati's upper arm.

"The dralin are a people that Guyt has brought in from another kingdom in Tera, to help him take over Vertrose. They're not a group I want to meet at the best of times, but especially in the middle of the desert, exhausted, with nowhere to hide."

"Great," Fen said sarcastically. "So, now we just wait to be killed or captured?"

"No," Rena replied, looking up into the sky. "We wait for them."

Mati looked up, following her gaze as a dozen swooping figures darted across the sky. Sykosee flew by, firing arrows and throwing javelins at the running figures with deadly accuracy. Then Mati realized that the dralin weren't running *toward* them, but away from the sykosee.

"Shit!" Alik exclaimed. "Run! They may not realize we aren't dralin until it's too late."

Fen grabbed Mati's hand and pulled her away from the approaching dralin; hopefully they could put enough distance between themselves and the dralin to set themselves apart.

"Shouldn't we be helping the sykosee?" Mati asked as they ran, tripping in the sand.

"If you would rather be skewered by an arrow or javelin, then be my guest." Fen kept tugging her along. "But I'm not going to stop and hope the sykosee notice that we're human."

An arrow whizzed past their heads and stuck in the sand ahead of them. "Point taken," Mati replied.

They continued to run as the fleeing dralin started to gain ground and mingled in with them. They had lost Alik and Rena in the panic, and the sykosee swooped over their heads. Mati looked around frantically, trying to make sense of the confused mass of bodies. No Alik or Rena to be seen. Fen dragged them sharply to the left as an arrow came screaming up behind them.

Fen tossed Mati unceremoniously off to the side once they had finally reached the edge of the mass of bodies. "Fuck this," he exclaimed, whipping out his sword with a flick of his arm as if it was already second nature.

Mati watched from the side as Fen began to take swings at the dralin. They seemed too concerned with self-preservation to notice Mati cowering next to a large rock.

The sykosee began to land, pulling out swords and joining in the ground battle that was now raging. Fen moved with such speed, accuracy, and natural ability that Mati found it hard to believe this was his first fight. He was too much of a natural and seemed to thrive in the heat and chaos of combat. Dark blue blood flew from the dralin as every strike hit its mark.

The dralin were nightmare creatures that looked like they stepped out from the darkness beneath a child's bed, monsters of the imagination. They wore leather armor and wielded massive broad swords. Their faces were distorted, marked and scarred with red tattoos that traced across their green-gray skin. They didn't lumber as their massive bodies suggested; they were agile and precise, with wide, callused feet that sat on top of the sand.

It was one thing to see Fen spar with Alik or with a tree, but to see him charging at the dralin with such skill and precision made Mati's jaw drop. She might've admired it more if she wasn't terrified for her life. There was a part of her that wished she had practiced more, wished to be helpful, but as it was, she could still barely swing the sword accurately twice in a row. And, as Fen so lovingly pointed out to her during their lessons, she would be more of a hindrance than a help in a real fight.

⤜⤛ ⤜⤛

Fen attacked the dralin, darting between their swinging swords with ease. He was only able to take one quick glance in Mati's direction to make sure she was staying put before he had to focus on the battle again. The dralin were powerful but they took too long to swing, giving Fen every opportunity to strike fast and hard.

Their blood dripped down his arms and face. The dark bloody splotches smelled like rotting flesh and permeated Fen's nose. It lay on top of the sand in thick puddles. He had butchered the animals when he was a muck boy, but they never fought back, and he had never had to slaughter more than one or two at a time.

He let his body take over his movements. The weight of the sword was so natural, his movements entirely by instinct, as he sliced and cut.

The sykosee must have realized they weren't on the side of the dralin, since Fen was slaughtering them left and right. There were a few dralin that had managed to escape, and the leader of the sykosee sent his soldiers flying after them in pursuit. Fen had forgotten how formidable the sykosee had been at the Magnus, with their armor and massive wings. Now he looked up as those wingspans flew over his head.

The leader strode up to Fen on all fours. "I thank you for your assistance, but who do I have the honor of thanking? We don't get many visitors out here."

"I'm Fen. And who did I have the honor of fighting with?"

"Trantu, leader of this band of wretches," he answered.

Alik and Rena came striding up, both covered in the same dark blue blood, their swords dripping onto the sand.

Trantu turned and raised up on his hind legs to greet them. "I was just saying to young Fen here that we're grateful for your help, Alik."

"The pleasure is all ours, Trantu," Rena replied. "We weren't sure whether you would see us or not."

"I know I'm not a hatchling anymore, but I'd like to think I can still tell the difference between friend and foe," Trantu laughed and nodded to greet Mati, who had returned hesitantly to the group. "And you must be Mati."

Mati nodded and smiled. "Yes."

"It's an honor to meet you," he bowed low, bringing his wings off the ground. "What are you doing out in the desert, so close to the gates?" he asked Alik.

Alik finished wiping blood off his face with his sleeve. "We're on the way to the Pontianak."

Trantu's beady eyes widened. "Why there?"

Fen was the one who answered. "We need some of the metal at the bottom of the lake so the spirits will make a sword for us to kill Guyt."

"That's no easy task. The lake is haunted by a deadly spirit."

"We've been told," Fen answered, giving Alik and Rena a sidelong glance. "But we need that metal and we're going to get it."

"Ah, well... What if we take you to Duinan with us, and then after we clean up and have a hot meal, we'll fly you to the Pontianak ourselves? I'm sure Vrutuuk would approve, since it's such a noble mission."

Fen sighed deeply. "We'd be forever grateful."

"Then it's settled." Trantu motioned two of his soldiers over. "You'll ride on our backs. We're not generally fond of being ridden, but we'll make an exception for friends."

# Chapter 17

The flight to Duinan was interesting. Mati and Fen rode on the back of one sykosee, with Alik and Rena on the other. Mati giggled and teased Fen the whole trip. She was used to flying in airplanes, albeit not in the open air, but she loved it nonetheless. Fen, on the other hand, buried his face in Mati's neck and refused to come out. He squeezed Mati so tight she was sure he'd cause internal damage.

They flew over the desert until Mati saw some small hillocks rising out of the sandy ground next to a low-lying plateau. The sykosee glided down and landed on all fours.

Fen leapt off so fast that Mati hardly saw him move. "LAAAAAND!" He cried in only partial jest, falling dramatically onto his knees.

"Good grief," Mati rolled her eyes. "Get up. You're going to offend the soldier."

"I'd rather take on that morest and all the dralin by myself than be up in the air again," Fen said as he got back up onto his feet.

Trantu led them to an enormous wooden door erected on the side of the plateau. He swung the door open with a lurch and the smell of earth and spices tickled their noses. Mati was shocked when Trantu's long tongue popped out and back in again.

"The women have a dinner ready," he said.

He led them under the ground through large and inviting tunnels, lit by oil lamps swinging on the walls. The air in the tunnels was warm, like a cozy blanket wrapping around them, and Mati could smell the savory food. It was a completely different feeling to Morimas's caverns, that had been dark and uninviting.

Fen's stomach growled so loudly that Mati could clearly hear it. "I'm so hungry," he complained. "It smells so good!"

They entered the dining hall following Trantu. The cavern was enormous, with hanging banners and flags covering the earthen walls. Trantu led them to an empty table at the front of the hall. The seats were an odd shape and as soon as Trantu sat in one, she realized why. The backs of the chairs were curved up on only one side so that the sykosee's mighty tail could slide underneath the other. Mati looked around. There were a few other sykosee in the hall, but the majority of the tables were empty. She noticed that some of the sykosee didn't have wings.

"Sit," Trantu invited them. "The food will be out in just a moment. We're late for the normal lunch that's served, but we'll still have a feast to satisfy a warrior's belly."

The party plopped into the chairs surrounding Trantu and his soldiers. Mati took the seat next to Fen.

"Why do only some of them have wings?" Mati leaned over to Rena and asked quietly.

"Only males have wings," came her answer.

Within minutes, Trantu's promise came true. A line of servants brought out heaping trays of cooked meats and breads, and laid them out on the table. Fen was practically drooling at the sight.

"You want a napkin to wipe your face?" Mati teased.

Fen dug in immediately, without waiting for anyone else. "I haven't had real food for so long," Fen said, his mouth already full of meat.

Mati rolled her eyes and smiled at him. "You like that meat, huh?"

"Don't you dare ruin this for me!" Fen retorted, giving her a side-long look. "There's nothing you can do that'll keep me from enjoying this food."

"Are you sure about that?" she teased him.

"Not entirely." Fen squinted at her. "But please just let me eat this and enjoy every bite."

Mati laughed and started to grab food to put on her plate. There were several different meats to choose from and Mati took a small piece of each along with a few slices of bread. She delicately placed a slice of meat between two of the bread and took a bite. Fen looked over at her and started smiling, with that goofy grin of his.

"What?" she asked.

"Oh, nothing. It's just that it seems you look like you're enjoying that meat, too."

She gave him a mild slap on the arm. "Stop!" she warned, but she couldn't help smiling.

He laughed and flinched away from her hand. "Don't dish it out if you can't take it."

They continued eating until everyone had almost finished. Then, Trantu eyed Fen. "So, you're on the way to the Pontianak?"

"Yes," Fen answered easily, now stuffed and sitting back in the chair. "Morana and Osirim require some metal from the bottom of the lake to make that weapon we talked about."

"Hmm. We should have an audience with Vrutuuk. Your mission is of some importance, and I wonder if he'll assign some of our warriors to fly you there to speed up your journey. I'll go arrange that meeting now." A timid sykosee came up to the table and stood next to Trantu. "In the meantime, Cern here will take you to your rooms."

They all rose lazily from the table, grabbed their packs from the floor, and followed Cern down several winding tunnels, all lit by those warm lanterns. She stopped in front of a wooden door.

"Alik," Cern said, "This room is for you. We remember how you like to stay close to the hall. The others are assigned to the next three doors."

"Thank you, Cern." And Alik disappeared inside his room.

Rena took the next one, which left Fen and Mati with rooms next to one another. Cern took her leave with a courteous bow. Mati turned to Fen before she went inside her own room. "Come over in a bit, if you can manage it without being seen."

Fen joined her and opened her door. "I'll come over now, since no one is in the tunnel." He tugged her into the room and shut the door behind them.

The room was warmly lit by the lanterns, just as the tunnels had been. It made Mati instantly sleepy, especially after having stuffed herself with food and drink. The bed in the corner of the room had been made up with pale green linen sheets and blankets, and a small table sat in the corner closest to the door. Then Mati spied the most precious thing in the world, set in a little alcove across from the bed... a copper tub filled with steaming water.

Fen walked over to the bed and collapsed on it. "Don't get your grubby self on my bed," Mati fired at him.

"Well, I'd take a bath, but I imagine you're calling first dibs on that."

"You know, you probably have a bath of your own waiting in your room."

Fen sat up. "Would you rather I leave?"

Mati smiled. "No... and yes. I really want to take a bath. And you need one, too. You reek."

Fen looked at the blood stains and smears on his clothes. "I guess you're right. I'll be back later, though."

Mati smiled and gave him a quick peck on the cheek as he left.

After Fen had gone, Mati took a bath and put on clean clothes from her pack. She hadn't bothered changing them in a long time; she hadn't seen a reason, considering all the walking and camping. It felt amazing to be clean again.

Before Fen could come back, Rena knocked on her door. "Trantu wants us to have that audience with Vrutuuk now," she called through the door.

"Okay," Mati answered. "Coming."

She opened the door while Rena grabbed Fen, and the three of them traced their way back through the tunnels into the main hall. Trantu and Alik were waiting for them in front of an archway on the opposite side of the hall. Trantu led them down several more winding tunnels until they reached a massive set of wooden doors, decorated with banners and gold hardware.

He pushed the doors open. Fen and Mati gaped at what was revealed. This cavern wasn't anything like the rest of the tunnels. The walls were lined with wooden panels and gold mirrors that allowed the torchlight to dance and bounce over all the other surfaces. As a result, this room was almost blindingly bright after the low lantern light elsewhere. Straight ahead of them, sitting on a glistening gold throne, was Vrutuuk. He wore no crown or any other object that would indicate his position, other than the sheer force of his presence.

"Ah," Vrutuuk greeted them pleasantly. "Come in. I was surprised when Trantu informed me of your arrival."

They walked through the room to stand before Vrutuuk. Alik stepped forward one more step. "Thank you for your hospitality, Vrutuuk."

"It is our honor to be hosting you," Vrutuuk bowed his head. "Trantu also tells me that you're headed to the Pontianak."

This time Fen stepped forward, drawing level with Alik. "Yes, we are."

"That's a very dangerous area now, considering both the spirit's presence and Guyt's patrols on the move."

"We know. But we haven't got any other choice. Trantu said you might let him and some of the others come with us on our mission, since we need all the speed we can get."

"He was correct. We would be honored to assist you. I will send four of my warriors with you."

Fen was the one who bowed his head this time. "Thank you. We appreciate your help."

"Please," Vrutuuk said, as he descended the steps from his throne to stand on the floor with them. "Tell me all about your travels so far. I'm most interested in your plans for this war."

Alik opened his mouth to speak, but Fen had a quicker tongue. "Certainly. We'd love your advice as well. You've been fighting Guyt's patrols, is that right?"

"We have." Vrutuuk motioned them to follow him to several couches set near a wall. "And it would be my pleasure to give my advice. I'm honored you'd think of us."

Alik looked flabbergasted as they all sat. "It's a very wise decision to ask for your advice," Alik offered. "Your input would be a valuable asset to our plans."

The plans they began to discuss involved the Gates of Meten and the Clerin River. Mati had no idea where those were, but Vrutuuk used some small objects on the low table to stand in for the locations, to give them a better idea of the geography. They spoke about battle strategy for a little while before Vrutuuk changed the subject, wanting to know more about their travels.

Mati sat back and listened to the conversations, happy to let Fen do one of his favorite things—talk. They spoke at length about all the events of their journey so far, Fen leaving out some of his more chaotic blunders. Vrutuuk was happy to hear Fen's stories, and Mati felt herself relaxing a bit.

After she escaped the long meeting, Mati lay on the bed in her room. She let her brain rest in the silence of the room. She was startled by a light tap on the door as it opened at the exact same time. Fen popped in silently, closing the door lightly behind him. "How's that for *low key*?"

She rolled her eyes and sat up, smiling at him. "It was quiet, at least."

Fen strode over to the bed and plopped down in a way that felt familiar, as if he had done the same things a thousand times before. Mati was surprised by his boldness. She was struggling hard with the two parts of herself—one which kept thinking that this longing for Fen was right and familiar, and the other which still wanted to keep him at arm's length.

Fen turned to face her. "What's wrong?" he asked, furrowing his brows.

"I'm just still getting used to *this*." She gestured at him and the bed.

Fen laughed. "Sorry, should I pretend to be more timid?"

"No," she replied quickly. "I'm just not used to it." She paused. "It's nice, though. It's just different."

"Yeah, I get that," Fen replied. He paused and wrinkled his nose.

"What?" Mati asked. "What's that look for?"

Fen smiled. "I was hoping you'd let me crash in here with you tonight… but it's fine that's too weird."

Mati sighed. "Not tonight. I told you I want to go slow and not draw attention to ourselves, until we're positive it won't cause any damage to the rebellion."

Fen rolled his eyes and smacked the pillow lightly in defeat. "I figured. I know it's probably for the best. At least that's what Alik thinks. I'm sorry if I'm being pushy."

"You're not," Mati said. "What was that about Alik, though?"

"A while ago… Alik told me that I should let you help me so I didn't get into so many scrapes. That it might make things easier. Or something like that."

Mati grinned. "If it's any consolation, I love how much you like me."

"Not really," Fen gave a defeated grin. "But I'll take it, because you haven't given me another choice. I hope you don't think I want… you know… that I just wanted…" He trailed off until his voice was completely inaudible.

"I didn't assume that," Mati assured him.

"Good," he said, then fell silent.

A long, awkward pause dragged out between them, until Mati said, "Anyway, what plans did you work out with Vrutuuk?"

Fen perked right up back up. "Some really good stuff. He's sending four of his warriors with us—including Trantu—to fly to Pontianak. And then he'll allow two of them to fly us back to Naina, so we can get that weapon. Then we'll meet back up with everyone here."

"Flying, huh," Mati teased. "That'll be fun."

Fen scowled. "Go ahead, tease me all you want."

Mati laughed and Fen gave her a goofy grin. "What?" she asked.

"I just like to hear you laugh."

"Did you hear Alik tell you that you were wise?" she asked, excited for him to hear the compliment.

"Yeah," Fen said dryly. "He was probably patronizing me."

"No, he wasn't. Rena even said later she was surprised. She said you've really grown into your role in the last few weeks."

"Really?" he asked, seeming half-excited again. "I mean, I'm just doing what I feel I should. They said we have to lead this rebellion, so that's what I'm trying to do."

"Well, I'd say you're doing a good job."

"We," Fen corrected.

"No," Mati argued. "You. I'm only here for moral support. I haven't done anything useful. I can't use a sword, or talk to people like you do."

"Hey," Fen gently tipped up her chin so she had to look him in the eye, "you don't need to be good with a sword or at talking to people. You have brains, and you're good at calming me down so I don't do stupid things. You don't think I know why you lay a hand on my shoulder all the time? And you make sure we've got a plan. And you went to see Morimas."

Mati flushed. "But that's not helpful. We don't even know if Morimas will join. I just made her mad."

"You are the *only* one who can calm me down so I can think straight. That's very helpful. I wouldn't be able to talk to people like I do without your help. And I'm sure Morimas will come."

Another long awkward pause stole over the room. Mati got up onto her feet. She didn't know why but she needed to do something... anything. She walked over to her pack and started to fidget with it. "Did you three decide when we're leaving for Pontianak?" she asked.

Fen flopped back onto the bed, sprawling out and tossing one arm under his head. "Yeah. Not tomorrow, but the next day. Vrutuuk's soldiers need to rest a bit."

"Good," Mati choked out, still fidgeting with her pack and the stuff in it.

"Do you want me to leave?" Fen asked, his brows raised.

Mati was having a hard time with Fen's compliments. She had never had anyone say stuff like that besides Carol. She turned to him but couldn't look him in the eye. "No. I'm sorry. I'm not good at the gooey stuff. I'm not used to it."

Fen let out a burst of laughter and Mati scowled at him. "I'm sorry," he said, covering his mouth. "I've never heard a compliment called *gooey stuff* before. But I think I know what you mean."

"It makes me all nervous and sweaty, for some reason."

Fen sat up. "Then we'll just have to practice."

"Okay," Mati said glumly.

"Come here," Fen patted the bed next to him. "Can we just enjoy this moment of finally being alone? No Alik or Rena about to burst out of nowhere to interrupt..."

Mati nodded and sulked over to the bed. "It's still weird."

She sat down on the bed and Fen pulled her up closer to him. "I'll admit that it's weird still. *But* that just means we'll have to practice a lot." He pinched her sides to tickle her and Mati curled up in an attempt to keep him away. "And I'm perfectly fine with that."

"I'm glad we're trying this out," she said, scooting down to lie with her head next to his. His being so close just felt right.

"Agreed," he said smiling. "Tell me more about Earth."

"What do you want to know?"

"Everything. Jefy was awful. I'd like to hear what a better place is like."

Mati sighed. "I'm not sure Earth is any better."

"Okay, so tell me about how you grew up. You said you had a family. The Masons, right?"

A ping of hurt shot Mati in the chest. "Yes. They adopted me after Asterion left me on their doorstep. I knew I wasn't one of their biological children, but Carol always made me feel loved. She and Gary had other kids, but I never fit in with them. They used to call me names."

"Assholes," Fen said sharply.

Mati continued, staring off into space. "They called me FedEx kid. And they called me 'weird' or 'loony' because I was always drawing pictures of who I thought... wanted... my real parents to be. I didn't fit in with anyone. I decided that I wanted to be a school counselor to help other kids like me. To give them someone to talk to and feel like they had a friend. To help them make some order in their lives.

"I loved Carol and Gary, and I loved the farm, but I hated the town and everyone else in it for hating me."

"Doesn't sound all that different from how I grew up," Fen let out a deep sigh. "Dursten left me with a family that already had four kids. They basically used me as their slave. They fed me if they had anything extra, but sometimes I had to fend for myself. I hated it. Once I got a bit older, I started to get some attention from the girls in town. Honestly, that's what kept me going. They made me feel human. It didn't take much convincing for me to go with Dursten. I thought it couldn't possibly be worse than Jefy, even if I thought they were crazy. Why'd you come here?"

Mati thought about her answer for a minute. "Because I felt the same thing. I didn't get the job I really wanted as a counselor. I did get a job as a teacher, but I knew I was going to hate it. I was scared, and... I guess I knew I wasn't ever going to really be happy there." Mati gasped suddenly.

"What?" Fen asked in surprise.

"My job! They'll have given it to someone else when I disappeared. Oh God! Carol and Gary! They'll be beside themselves. How could I not leave a note, or anything?! How could I be so stupid?! I can't go back to Earth now. I'll have no job, and I'm sure the Masons will clear my room out, thinking I've gone insane and left for good. I've got nothing left there."

Fen put his hand on her leg. "You have me..." he said, gently and quietly, in a way that made it almost sound like a question.

Mati's lips curled up at the corners, but the smile didn't reach her eyes. "Thank you. I don't know how I could be so rash, and leave without even a note. It wasn't like me. They might think I was kidnapped, or murdered."

"I'm sure, when you go back, they'll just be glad to see you're okay. And you'll get a better job too, I bet."

"Thank you..." Mati looked him in the eyes. "What do you plan on doing after this is all over?"

Fen thought carefully, his hand still on Mati's thigh. "I'd like to go to Earth with you. Even if it's just for a visit. I'd like to see it. And, you know, maybe see you, too. Honestly, though, I haven't given it much thought. I haven't had time. Every time I turn around, we're being chased or attacked or almost dying on the side of a mountain."

Mati sighed a knowing sigh. "I feel that. I like being here in Duinan. It feels safe and comfy. I wish we had more time here."

"This place is amazing," Fen agreed. "I never dreamed there could be an entire city underground."

They lay side by side in silence so long that both fell asleep in the quiet comfort of knowing the other was there.

# Chapter 18

Mati woke up the next morning and stretched. She didn't remember falling asleep, but it was the most peaceful sleep she'd had in a long time. Her arms reached up and over, then came into contact with something hard. She over, startled. Fen! She panicked.

Fen grunted. "What the—" He bolted upright, but Mati was already sitting up and staring at him with horrified surprise.

"We fell asleep," she pointed out.

"I see that," Fen answered, relaxing and giving her a wide grin. "Sorry."

Mati wanted so bad to feel the horror she had initially felt but as the moments ticked by, she found herself content and okay. No one had found them. No one would know. Their mission wouldn't be compromised. There was nothing to fear... she hoped.

She let her posture relax to match Fen's as the initial shock wore off. "No, you're not," she replied cheekily.

Fen's grin turned cocky. "You're right. I'm not. At least now I know that you don't kick or snore in your sleep."

Mati smiled. "You hope. Maybe I was just too tired last night."

She snuggled down into the bed. Fen wiggled his arm around her and pulled her in close. Being with him felt both familiar and unfamiliar. She couldn't quite put her finger on the details of the feelings, and she wished they would go away so she could just enjoy these little moments of calm.

"You better get out of here before someone comes looking for us," Mati said after several more minutes snuggled in Fen's arms.

"Nooooo..." He groaned. "Just a few more minutes."

"Two," Mati said, as Fen leaned down and pressed a kiss on her forehead.

"Five," he protested.

"No. Two."

Fen leaned down a little further and tilted her chin up with his fingers. "Five," he repeated as his lips met hers.

He pulled away from her slowly. "Still two," she said with a grin. "Don't think you can just kiss me and get what you want."

Fen crinkled his nose in playful annoyance. "She-devil..."

A knock at the door followed by Alik's booming voice grabbed their attention, and they both jumped. "Mati," Alik boomed.

Mati slid off the bed. "Hide," she loudly whispered to Fen.

Fen rolled his eyes and got under the bed begrudgingly as Mati walked to the door. She looked back to make sure Fen was hidden before opening the door. Before she had a chance to say anything, Alik exclaimed.

"Do you know where Fen is? We need to talk to Trantu, and I haven't been able to find him. His room doesn't look slept in."

Alik kept darting his head like he was trying to look behind her. Mati's face flushed hot as she feigned a calm demeanor. "No," was all she managed to squeak out without giving herself and Fen away.

"I thought he might be in here. I've noticed you hanging around together more often these days."

Mati's blood froze. Alik definitely seemed irritated. Maybe he wouldn't approve if he knew. "No," she finally answered. "He's definitely not in here."

Alik huffed. "Where did that boy get to? Just when I thought he was starting to come through. If you see him, tell him I'm looking for him."

"I will," Mati breathed a sigh of relief as she shut the door.

Fen popped up directly behind her, startling her as the door clicked shut. "The nerve of him!" Fen fumed.

"It's your own fault," Mati replied. "You had better go and find him... and come up with a good excuse as to why you weren't in your room."

"Yeah, yeah," he continued, grumbling and muttering under his breath. He started to open the door but leaned in first, stealing another quick kiss before disappearing.

Mati spent the rest of the day with Rena, making sure their packs were all stocked and ready to go for the next day. She was bursting to tell Rena about Fen but kept silent. Rena might be alright with the idea of the two of them, but she didn't want to cause any more tension between Rena and Alik than there already was. Her mind flip-flopped between the two all day, distracting her from the majority of conversations around her. At lunch, she finally resolved to keep things a secret, allowing herself the rest of the day to take in Duinan and its stunning beauty.

Fen spent his day with Trantu and Alik. After he left Mati's room, he sprinted after Alik, busy concocting the story that he'd woken up early to explore Duinan. Alik seemed to buy the excuse and stopped grumbling at him. Fen was grateful; he had very much started to look up to Alik as a father figure, and desperately wanted to impress him again today, so he remained extra vigilant when talking to Trantu about the next day's plans for Pontianak. He also worked very hard to keep his mind from straying to Mati.

Trantu seemed impressed with Fen's involvement, as well as with his ideas and plans. This sort of stuff just somehow seemed to come naturally to Fen. They planned to leave before dawn—Alik's favorite time of day—and would hopefully arrive at Pontianak just after sunrise. They planned to have two of Trantu's warriors go out into the sea and retrieve the metal from the seabed. Vrutuuk had told him that sykosee were good swimmers, despite living in a desert, because of their powerful tails. And if their luck held, they wouldn't encounter the Pontianak spirit at all.

Fen and Mati didn't cross paths again until dinner, when they gathered again with Trantu, but were joined by several other sykosee who were unashamedly trying to see and be seen with their party. Most of them looked much younger than Trantu. Fen made sure to snag himself a seat next to Mati. She scooted closer to Rena to make room for his chair, hoping no one noticed.

After a long day of talking and planning, Fen wanted to take a few minutes to just exist. He sidled his leg up next to hers so that they barely touched. She didn't pull away. In fact, she pushed closer, taking up any space Fen had left between them. He dropped a hand under the table, careful not to draw attention to the movement, and brushed a single finger across her thigh.

Mati's cheeks flushed and she pressed her lips together to keep a smile hidden. Pleased by that response, Fen put his hand back on his own lap. But Mati slyly and slowly took his hand beneath the table, and placed it back on her thigh.

"Mati," Rena prompted, staring at her expectantly. "Are you okay?"

Mati whirled her head to look at Rena. "What? Yes. I'm fine. Sorry, I was just thinking."

Rena leaned forward, elbows on the table, to look past Mati at Fen, who was grinning like the cat who had eaten the proverbial canary. "Uh huh," Rena said blandly before looking back to Mati. "I was trying to ask you whether or not you had been told about the Pontianak spirit yet? But it seems your mind is otherwise engaged."

"I was trying to remember whether I packed some things, is all," Mati lied... badly. "But no, I haven't heard anything about the spirit, other than that she's dangerous."

"Very," Rena replied. "We'll need to stay alert tomorrow. The spirit shouldn't bother us, but she'll definitely go after the others. She feeds on male organs."

"Huh?" Mati asked, her confusion obvious. "What do you mean?"

Fen leaned in to answer her, feeling like he was going to puke. "She eats *organs*... you know, the manly bits."

Mati's face crumpled up in disgust. "Holy shit," she replied. "That's... uh... unfortunate—for you." Rena giggled at that, and Fen scowled. "I'm sorry. It's just very funny. What a specific diet. I wonder if she eats them raw, or cooks them first?"

Rena burst out laughing while Fen removed his hand from Mati's thigh and laid it protectively over himself. "That's not even funny," Fen said.

"Just a little funny," Mati answered, still snickering.

"You're just mean," Fen retorted teasingly.

"Maybe this is obvious," Mati said, "but why can't me and Rena go ourselves, with a couple of female sykosee?"

Rena's smile faded and she leaned in very close to Mati. Fen leaned in as well, to hear what Rena had to say. "The sykosee are very strict about gender roles."

"That's dumb," Mati said perturbed.

"It's not for us to judge," Rena answered. "Also, they don't have wings, and it won't help us at all if we have to go by land."

The rest of dinner went much the same way, except Fen kept his hands to himself. He did still leave his leg pressed up to Mati's. And then they retired early, since they all knew it was going to be an early morning. Fen didn't even try to sneak into Mati's room this time; he didn't like the way Rena had been eyeing him at dinner, like she knew something was going on between him and Mati.

⋙ ⋘

The next morning, Mati made her way out of her room. She checked Fen's room, but he was already gone. She met Rena in the hall, and they walked together to the meeting point, where Fen and Alik were waiting with their escort.

"Let's go, since we're all here," Fen said, in a way that sounded almost commanding. "Better to get to Pontianak as quickly as possible."

Each human was paired with one sykosee this time. Mati saw how hesitant Fen was to get onto the sykosee assigned to him. She giggled, and Fen shot her a glare. She giggled again when she saw Fen huddled as close to Frunat's back as he could get when they lifted off.

Mati, on the other hand, loved every second of the flight. She looked out and saw an enormous body of cerulean blue water. It shimmered in the sunlight. Further off, she saw a pair of columns that stood between the sea and a great river. The sykosee glided down and landed on the far west of the Pontianak.

Fen leapt off the sykosee almost before they landed, followed more gracefully by the others. "You know I don't mean to insult your flying abilities, Frunat," Fen said to the warrior.

Frunat smiled. "None taken, sir."

Trantu, however, seemed on edge. "Be on the lookout. The spirit could come out of the water at any time, but if we're lucky, she's busy elsewhere." He turned to his warriors. "Frunat and Dun will go in after the metal. Hopefully, we'll find what we need close to the bank."

The two warriors stepped forward with leather bags and headed for the water.

"Be careful, my brothers," Trantu added. "The metal should look like smooth, green rocks."

"It's our honor," Frunat replied, and the two sykosee waded out carefully into the water.

They disappeared under the inky blue-black waves. The rest of the party kept their heads on a swivel so Trantu could monitor the water. After several minutes, the two still hadn't surfaced. Mati felt a knot form in her stomach.

"They should've come up for air by now," Alik said with a tinge of fear.

"I know," Trantu replied, and pulled out his sword. "Ready yourselves. I fear she knows we're here."

No sooner had Trantu finished his sentence than the water erupted, and they heard an unholy screech. The sound was high-pitched, with low under-notes, and chilled them to their bones. The creature that had burst from the water landed on the bank, screaming and rushing toward them. Its hair billowed in the air as if it were still under water, its eyes black as the swirly depths, and its body was skeletal but toned. The defenders drew their swords as the spirit glided rapidly toward them, clawed fingers at the ready.

Mati pulled a small knife out of her belt. It felt impossibly useless in such a fight. Even Rena, former goddess of peace, had a sword drawn and was standing ready with the others.

Impossibly fast and without warning, the spirit moved through the air heading for Trantu. The party stepped in to defend him, but the spirit moved too quickly. Even though she was seemingly over-matched and outnumbered, she held her own by dodging and weaving around them, vanishing and then reappearing elsewhere. She slashed at them with knife-like claws, screeching all the while.

Mati was looking on, horrified, when she saw something out of the corner of her eye. She turned and saw the mangled, intertwined bodies of the two sykosee warriors floating on the surface of the sea. Blood and torn flesh filled the water around them.

"Rena!" Mati called. "We have to go get that metal while she's distract-ed."

Rena nodded and dropped her sword, following Mati to the water. They heard the clash of metal on claws over the terrible shrieking that continued behind them as they dove into the sea.

The water was freezing, and Mati's body tried to seize up and steal her breath. She forced herself to move with the adrenaline that now coursed through her veins. She swam over to the carnage that had once been Frunat and Dun and took the two floating bags that they had carried. She gave one to Rena. They both took deep breaths and sank below the surface.

It was pitch black, but Mati swam down until she felt rocks beneath her fingertips. It was impossible to tell if what she was grabbing was the metal or just rocks, so she just grabbed handfuls of anything that she could reach and returned to the surface to examine it. She pocketed the green ones and let the others fall. Rena was doing the same. She popped up above the water just as Mati was about to dive back down. The sound of the battle on shore was a stark contrast to the numbing silence under the water. Mati had only a moment to glance over to see Fen still standing, and swinging masterfully at the spirit.

"How much do we need?" Rena asked.

"They said 'four gords,'" Mati answered. "How much is that?"

"We don't have enough," Rena said without answering her question. "Keep going and hurry!"

Mati and Rena repeated their dives over and over until Mati lost count—diving down, grabbing handfuls of rocks, returning to the surface to sounds of the panicked skirmish on the bank, keep the green ones, toss the rest. Dive again.

Rena came up one last time. "Have you filled your bag?"

"Yes," Mati answered hopeful. The task seemed to be attainable.

"We need to help them," Rena said, commanding and calm, but with a sense of urgency.

They swam as fast as they could to the bank, hauling themselves up despite the sopping clothes that weighed them down. Rena gave Mati her bag and raced for her sword, still laying on the grass where she had dropped it. Rena brandished it and sprinted into the fight with a war cry, while Mati scrambled to get a good distance away from the water. She looked up when a furious, bloodcurdling scream broke through the air.

⋙ ⋘

Out of the corner of his eye, Fen saw Mati and Rena race for the water. He needed to keep the Pontianak busy long enough for them to complete this godsforsaken task. He doubled his efforts, even though that put him squarely in the line of fire.

The spirit whisked through the air with supernatural speed, attempting to strike everyone. Her claws lashed out in his direction, and he narrowly dodged them. He slashed his sword deftly but it missed the mark, as the spirit disappeared and then reappeared in front of Alik.

"Don't you dare," Fen grunted and shoved himself toward the Pontianak spirit. "Come here!"

Fen carved his sword through the air and caught the spirit's claws before they could rake Alik. It disappeared again, letting out a haunting wail.

He fought on beside the others, but none of them landed any major blows. He gave a quick look towards the water. Mati and Rena were coming out of the sea, but had been spotted by the spirit, which turned in their direction. Fen launched himself in front of the Pontianak.

Time slowed down, as the spirit let out an angry wail and its claws struck Fen's back. His back and chest felt warm, but he thrust his sword up into the spirit's body. He had to keep it there. He had to save Mati.

It let out a final bloodcurdling wail before it retreated.

⟫⟫ ⟪⟪

The spirit had given up and vanished back into the murky water. No one was relieved. There was no time to even catch a breath. They scrambled to remount the remaining two sykosee. Mati instinctively scanned the group for Fen and her breath caught in her chest. Fen was covered in blood and his shirt was torn to shreds. His torso was covered in so much blood that she couldn't tell what had happened, or to whom. He stumbled more than ran to Trantu, where Mati joined him, still clinging to the bags.

"Get on, Mati," he pleaded, an agonized grimace on his face.

She had stopped dead when she saw Fen up close and realized that there were several deep gashes in his flesh.

"Mati," Fen called again, more urgently.

She snapped back into focus and scrambled onto Trantu.

Fen reached out a bloodied hand to her and she helped heave him up behind her. Mati felt Fen collapse against her back as Trantu took off.

"Fen?!" Mati called back to him frantically as Trantu leveled off. "Fen, answer me, dammit!"

"I'm here," he forced out, his voice weary and barely audible over the whoosh of wind.

"Don't you dare die, you asshole."

"I'm trying my best. It hurts, Mati."

Tears started to fill Mati's eyes. "I know. I know it hurts, but you have to stay with me. Do not close your eyes."

Mati felt Fen start to slide from her back. "He's falling, Trantu!" Mati called as she reached a futile hand behind her to keep Fen upright. "Trantu, I'm going to turn around. Keep us steady."

"I'll do my best," Trantu called back to her.

Mati slung both bags of rocks over her shoulders and carefully maneuvered her feet up onto Trantu's back. She steadied herself with one hand, keeping the other firmly on Fen. She took a deep breath. The rush of air around her made her wobble for a split second, but with one quick Hail-Mary spin, Mati pushed herself around and dropped her legs on either side of Trantu's back. At the same time, she threw her arms around Fen and pulled him toward her chest. She latched onto him and held on for dear life.

Adrenaline coursed through her veins. Her heart thumped in her chest. Her only thoughts were of keeping Fen from falling. She had to save Fen.

The journey back to Duinan seemed like it took four times longer than the trip there. Trantu was wounded as well, and carrying the extra weight of a second person, he had to fly much more carefully. Mati felt her shirt starting to cling to her as it soaked through with Fen's blood. She buried her head in his shoulder, her arms wrapped around his trunk. He would survive. He had to. There wasn't another option.

Trantu glided down and landed next to the massive door that led down into Duinan. Rena raced toward them as soon as her sykosee hit the ground.

"Let go, Mati," she pleaded, and tried to pry Mati's hands apart. "We have to get him help."

Mati refused to let Fen go. The tears she had been holding in started to pour down her face. Alik was immediately behind Rena, practically ripping Fen from Mati's arms. Rena helped Mati down off Trantu as Alik carried Fen's limp body into the city.

Mati wailed and fell to the ground. When Fen was taken from her, her soul felt as if it had been wrenched from her body as well.

"Come on, love," Rena said sorrowfully, and attempted to heave Mati to her feet. "Let's get you inside."

"I want to be with him." Mati cried. "Take me with him!"

Rena wrapped Mati in her arms. "Love, the healers are going to help him. We need to get you cleaned up."

Rena was able to lead Mati into the city door and down to her chamber. The sykosee had all rushed up to see the returning party as word quickly spread of what had happened.

The world slowed. Mati gasped for breath between wracking sobs. She followed Rena into the tunnels with stumbling steps.

Rena had led her every movement since they had returned to Duinan, ending up in her room. Mati was numb as she stepped into the copper tub. "Take me to him," she ordered through the anger and tears that suddenly poured out of her.

"Mati, you need to rest," Rena implored. "And so will Fen, once the healers are done."

"Take me, Rena." Mati's voice was hard and resolute in her grief. "Or so help me, I will tear this city to pieces until I find him myself."

Rena let out a sorrowful breath of defeat. "Okay. I'll take you."

Rena led Mati through the tunnels, past the gawking crowds. Mati barely noticed them. The only thing holding her together was the thought of getting to Fen.

Finally, Rena rounded a corner and they entered a large cavern filled with beds. A small crowd of sykosee surrounded the first one. Mati burst through the crowd, unconcerned for who was there. Her first glimpse of him made her chest clench and tears begin again.

It was Fen, laid out on a stone table like a dinner. His shirt had been removed and Mati could now clearly see the deep lacerations carved into his chest. A female sykosee was tending to him, while the others surrounded them for support—and some, merely out of curiosity. Alik had collapsed onto the floor and leaned against the wall, his head buried in his hands more from exhaustion than sorrow.

Mati rushed to Fen's side and grabbed his hand. The attending healer didn't even look up from her task. She was chanting and coating Fen's cleaned wounds with a thick salve. Mati knelt by that stone table for what felt like days. Time slowed and her brain formed no thoughts. All was void and empty. She simply watched as the healer continued her chanting and stitched Fen's wounds with a long-curved needle.

After an eternity, the healer finally stopped her chants and laid down her needle. "I've done all I can. Hopefully it is enough." She dropped her head in weariness. "You can take him back to his chamber. It will be better for him to be away from all the curious eyes."

The healer left, and two other attending healers gently carried Fen back to his chamber. Mati never left his side, a silent sentinel of hope grasping his hand tightly. Rena helped Mati tuck him into his bed, then took her leave. She looked haggard and tired as she closed the door.

# Chapter 19

Now alone, Mati begin to cry again, deep woeful sobs that made her body shudder. She crawled up into the bed next to Fen, being careful not to touch his chest. She didn't even want to look at his injuries, for fear that even her grazing eyes would hurt him. She clasped his hand, kissed his cheek, and fell into a tearful sleep.

When she woke, Fen was still sleeping. She stared without breathing to see if Fen's chest still rose and fell. As soon she saw his chest go and up and back down in shallow breaths, she let out a breath she hadn't realized she was holding and cuddled up next to him again. She had no idea what day or time it was. They had returned from Pontianak at midday, and she was sure that the healer couldn't have finished with Fen until late at night. She guessed that it must be morning on the next day as she lay curled up next to Fen's chest. His breathing was shallow and his body much cooler than normal, almost forcing Mati to get a blanket despite the warm lanterns.

At some point, Mati fell back asleep, and woke with a start. Someone moved, and it wasn't her. She whirled to see Fen blearily squinting at her. A laugh and cry escaped her at the same time.

"Fen!" she cried out, tears of joy filling her eyes.

Fen grunted and blinked several more times. "Mati?"

"Yeah. It's me." She latched onto his hand and laid her head on his shoulder.

"Where... where are we? What happened?"

"You let that spirit almost kill you, you ninny. We thought you were going to die."

"I wouldn't dare," he smiled feebly.

Mati let a smile emerge through the tears. "Do you need anything?"

"Yes," Fen answered. "I'm charging you twenty kisses for my services this time. And I'd like to cash them in now, please."

"I'd hit you if I hated you more."

Fen smiled again and his eyes began to shut. "I'm sorry," he said. "I'm just so tired."

Mati kissed him on the forehead. "Sleep. I'm not going anywhere."

Fen's smile only faded once he'd fallen back into a healing sleep. Mati sat up and wiped the tears from her face.

She crept out of the room and tapped on Rena's door. Rena answered, and when she saw Mati's tear-stained face and red eyes she had to hold back tears of her own. "Is he okay?" she asked in a panic.

Mati smiled. "He woke up a few minutes ago. Only for a few minutes, though, and then he went back to sleep."

"Praise the spirits!" Rena cheered, happy tears rolling down her cheeks. She pulled Mati in for a hug. "Is he in pain? Is he okay?"

"Well, he had his wit, so I guess he's good for now," Mati answered, holding on to that hope.

"Good," Rena replied.

"I should get back. I promised I would be there when he woke up again." Mati started the walk back to Fen's door.

"He's very lucky to have a *friend* like you, Mati," Rena said pointedly.

She was caught by Rena's words and turned back to face her for only a moment, giving her a half-smile. Rena just spun back around in silence and disappeared into their room. Rena definitely knew something, Mati thought. Or thought she knew something, at the very least.


Fen didn't wake up again that afternoon, so Mati contented herself with reading one of the books Rena had sent in with lunch. She curled up on the bed next to Fen and snacked lazily, keeping a wary eye on Fen's chest. The healer had come in once to redress the wound, but that had only taken twenty minutes before Mati was left alone again. Alik and Rena hadn't visited him yet, but Mati was fine with that. She wasn't really ready to share him with anyone.

Eventually, she changed into night clothes that the sykosee brought her. They were ill-fitting on her human form, but she appreciated the sentiment. She curled up again next to Fen, but just as her back pushed up against his side, he groaned sleepily.

"I'm sorry," Mati jumped up.

"You're fine," Fen answered, slowly lifting his hand and rubbing his eyes. "In fact, if you don't lay back down, I'll stage a formal protest."

Mati smiled. "Will you?"

Fen smiled up at her. "Yes. Plus, I'm an injured man."

Mati laughed out loud. "Already pulling that card, huh?"

"Yes."

"How do you feel?" she asked.

Fen sighed and tried to scoot up to a sitting position, but Mati saw him lurch in pain. Mati laid a hand on him and pushed him back. "Don't get up."

Fen groaned again. "I need to move."

"Not yet." Mati said with a sternness that dared Fen to disobey. "Tell me how you feel."

"I feel like a carved-up meat dinner."

The smile returned to Mati's lips. "You look like one, too."

"Thanks," Fen grunted. "What happened to us? The last thing I remember is climbing onto Trantu behind you."

"You passed out and almost fell off. I had to do some fancy moves to keep you on his back."

"I'm sorry," Fen breathed out.

"It's not your fault. Don't you dare apologize."

Fen laid quietly for a moment, then tried to crane his head to look at his chest. "Will I get a cool scar?"

"Several cool ones, I think," Mati explained. "She got you good."

"Can you help me sit up?"

"I can try, but I doubt I'll be able to pull you up myself. I can ask someone to help me."

"Won't that break the *low-key* rules?" Fen teased.

"Ha, ha," Mati laughed sarcastically. "I think that ship has sailed. I'm pretty sure everyone knows now and, so far, no one seems to mind. I caused quite the scene when we landed." Her face flushed with heat.

"Then, in that case, yes, please go get help. I can't lay flat on my back any longer."

Mati kissed his temple before scampering out the door. She tried Alik's door first but got no answer. The dining hall was sure to have someone strong enough to help, and she headed down one of the tunnels. She rounded a corner and ran square into Alik's chest.

"Sorry," Alik apologized before realizing who it was. A panicked look crossed his face. "Is he okay?"

"Yes, yes." Mati answered, rubbing her nose where she collided with Alik. "He's awake and wants to sit up in bed, but he can't pull himself up and neither can I. Could you help me?"

"Of course," Alik answered happily.

He followed Mati back down the tunnel to Fen's chamber. She knocked on the door and waited for Fen to reply before going in, Alik trailing behind.

"Good to see you awake," Alik boomed cheerily. "I don't mind saying that you scared the piss out of us."

Fen smiled at the joke. "It'll take more than a screaming demon to kill me."

Alik's smile went wide, and he strode over to the bed. "I hear you're feeling like sitting up."

"Gods yes, please."

Mati placed a pillow across his stomach and chest. "Hold this, and put pressure on it as you move."

Alik hooked an arm under one of Fen's and Mati got the other.

"Alright," Mati said, taking charge. "Just be careful. I don't want to have to explain to the healer how his stitches broke or have him bleeding all over the place."

Fen rolled his eyes, then grimaced in pain as the other two heaved him up.

"Are you okay?" Mati asked nervously.

"Yes," Fen answered her, though his expression was pained. "It's just a little sore."

Alik and Mati heaved one more time and got Fen sitting somewhat upright. Mati padded his back with pillows and fluffed them until Fen waved her away. "I'm fine, Mati," Fen protested. "Stop fussing over me."

Mati harrumphed and finished fixing a pillow. "Are you sure you're okay?"

"Yes, I'm fine."

Alik smiled. "Glad to hear your tongue wasn't damaged." Fen furrowed his brow. "I'm glad you're okay, *boy*."

Fen smiled at Alik's last word. He hadn't called Fen that in almost a month. Mati was sure Alik meant it as a term of endearment these days, instead of the insult it had once been.

"Thanks," Fen replied.

"I'll leave you two be," Alik said. "Can I tell the others it's okay to come by and see you tomorrow? You have quite an adoring public anxious to see you."

Fen looked to Mati, who just shrugged. "Sure, I guess," he answered Alik.

"Good, good," Alik said and strode out of the room.

Mati sat on the bed next to Fen. "I'm so glad you're okay."

Fen looked down at his chest, still covered in bandages. "How bad is it?"

"Bad," Mati answered with a sigh. "You're going to have scars, that's for sure. You lost a lot of blood and tried to give it to me."

Fen tried cocked his head. "What do you mean?"

"When you fell unconscious on Trantu's back, I had to hold you on and do acrobatics to keep you on his back. You owe me a new shirt and pants.

And you're lucky it washed off the rest of me." She smiled weakly, trying her best to keep the mood light.

"So, a *lot* of blood."

"Yeah."

Fen tried a deep breath and winced. "Guess it'll be a minute before I can fight."

"I think you've done enough fighting for a while."

"Have Trantu or Alik spoken to Vrutuuk? When are we leaving for Naina? We need to get the water and metal to Morana."

"Settle down," Mati soothed. "You won't be going anywhere today. I imagine that we'll have to wait for you to get better."

"We don't have that kind of time. We need to get that weapon."

Mati twined her fingers in his. "Then you should consider not being the hero next time, so you won't need to heal before we can do anything."

Fen grumbled. He carefully lifted his arm and draped it around her shoulders, then leaned his head against hers. "You know what would help me get better?"

"I'm sure I'm going to regret answering you," Mati snorted. "But what?"

"Kisses." Fen grinned widely. "You owe me twenty, I believe."

Mati laughed. "I guess I do."

She sat up and turned to face Fen. Just last night, she had been fearing for his life, and now she was perfectly happy beside him. She drew closer and could feel his breath on her lips. She closed her eyes, and her lips found his. She pulled back. "One."

Fen looked at her as if she were the beginning and the end of every-thing. He brushed his fingers lightly along her cheek and then down her jawline to her chin. He held her there and moved himself forward. "Two," he breathed against her lips.

"You should get some rest," Mati managed to say.

"Would you just hush, woman, and let me kiss you? I've had a very bad few days and I'd very much like to just sit here peacefully and exist with you."

"Okay," Mati whispered and leaned in for another kiss. "Three..."

They stopped counting after that, but Mati was sure the final tally was more than twenty. The strangeness had started to wear off, which pleased her.

Then Fen took Mati's face between his hands, slid one hand down to her shoulder, her stomach, and then rested it on her hip. She felt a knot twist up in her stomach.

"Not tonight," she said quietly. "There's no way. You almost died twenty-four hours ago."

"I swear, I feel fine. And there's no telling when we'll have time alone again…"

"No." It pained her to say it.

"You're no fun," Fen grumbled, idly trailing his thumb across her hip.

Mati closed her eyes as the knot in her stomach got tighter and moved lower. "No. No. No," she managed to say, more to her body's reaction than to Fen.

"But—" Fen protested.

"No."

Fen deflated. "You're serious?"

Mati laughed. "Sulk all you want, but I'm being serious, Fen. Your wounds are still oozing God-knows-what. And I'm not going to be the one who has to run the healer in here at midnight and try to explain why your stitches are ripped."

"Fine." Fen sulked.

"You'll have to content yourself with other things…" Mati shot him a devious smirk.

Fen returned her grin, seeming to pick up on her hint. "What if I suggested another option?"

"Which is what?"

"I thank you for all you've done for me over the last couple of days." He trailed his hand from her hip to her thigh, then up to the hem of her ill-fitting night-dress. He ran his fingers back down her leg, now touching skin. Mati's muscles tensed. Her mind blanked of anything except his touch, and that sent chills through her entire body.

She fought to keep her composure, setting her jaw. "What do you have in mind?"

Fen's grin turned almost manic, and his eyes seemed to darken as his pupils went wide. He wiggled his fingers between her thighs, encouraging them to part, before drifting gently up her inner thigh. He leaned in close and let out a growl that Mati had never heard a human make, tickling her neck. "I have some ideas," he purred.

Mati was no longer composed and couldn't even pretend she was. Her thighs had spread easily at Fen's touch and that feral, teasing growl of his had tightened every muscle in her body. She moaned while Fen danced his fingers tantalizingly close to her most sensitive nerves.

"I'm going to make you beg," Fen promised, his voice dark and low.

He lifted one finger and let it trail across her wet entrance and up to the nerve center. She moaned again and spread her thighs even further apart, leaving her vulnerable in the best way. She didn't realize how in need for touch she had been. Her body moved unconsciously in response to every one of Fen's movements.

Mati was completely undone. She laid open her thighs for Fen to better work her. He tugged at her night dress, already unceremoniously hiked up to her waist. She pulled it off and tossed it to the floor while Fen was already sweeping his fingers up to her breasts, his gaze fixed on them. His attention was so fixated that his hand stopped moving entirely, and he reached his other hand over to grab them both. He cupped both her breasts in his hands and squeezed lightly, before lightly pinching her hard nipples. She saw him wince, his movement obviously causing him some pain, but she couldn't form a coherent sentence to protest.

Ecstasy overtook Mati and she let out another much longer moan, her head tipping back.

"Get on your knees," Fen commanded.

Mati scrambled up onto her knees and sat back on her heels. She braced her hands behind her on the bed. Usually, she would have been more timid, being so intimate with someone this quickly, but she felt completely safe with Fen, and allowed herself to bare every inch of herself to him.

Fen let out another feral rumble at the sight that sent goosebumps on her skin. "Fuck, you're gorgeous."

He didn't leave her in anticipation any longer. He dropped one hand to cup her, the other continuing to pinch and tease her nipple. He ran his palm along her entrance and across all those sensitive nerves, and then pulled away to look at what he'd done.

She smiled wantingly at him. She needed him as much, or more, as she needed air to survive. "Please," she begged.

He held up one finger then two, and she watched hungrily as he inserted them into her. Tingles raced through her body like lightning as he placed his thumb against the cluster of nerves and gently caressed it, while he moved his fingers in and out of her.

"Fuck, I want to fuck you right now," Fen burst out in that low, husky voice.

Mati closed her eyes and smiled. "Then you better heal up fast."

He moved his fingers in and out of her a little faster now, and she fell into the rhythm he set, rising to meet him, then falling back. Her moans were nearly constant now; she both craved release and wanted the moment to keep going. His fingers moved expertly over her body, until she couldn't take it anymore. He was purposefully keeping her on the edge of bliss and she knew it.

"Please, Fen," she begged him.

A devilish grin crept over his face. "I told you I'd make you beg."

He intensified his efforts at her plea, masterfully coaxing her to sweet release. She shuddered and let out a loud cry of ecstasy, which Fen covered immediately with one hand over her mouth.

Mati rested like that for a moment, panting as she tried to catch her breath. She felt exhausted in the best way. Her legs felt like jelly, but she had never felt as satisfied as she was at that moment.

Fen scooted his pants below his hips, wincing again. Mati was still breathing hard and bared to him as he reached down and began to work himself. She watched him from her same position in a state of satisfied exhaustion. She made sure to log every movement he made in her memory.

"Want me to help?" Mati asked, her heart racing.

"No," Fen answered just as breathless. "I want you just like that. Panting, naked, and legs open, covered in your own come."

Mati made sure to stay where she was but twisted slightly to watch Fen, whose head was tipped back as he moaned. He opened his eyes long enough to get a good look at Mati, still spread wide in front of him. Inspired, she grabbed her own breast and bit her lip, looking right into his eyes.

Fen released with a loud "Fuck!"

Mati smiled, satisfied, and went to grab a cloth from the adjoining washroom. She quickly washed herself off and brought a clean, damp cloth for Fen.

"Thank you," Fen said. his chest heaving as he cleaned himself up. "And not just for the cloth. You are the most beautiful creature I've ever seen."

Mati blushed and took the laundry back to the washroom. "You're not so bad yourself," she replied when she returned.

"I hate to ruin the good thing we've got going on here, but that really did me in. I'm exhausted." Fen carefully wiggled himself back down. "Come here, you."

Mati tossed her nightdress back on, grabbed a blanket, and curled back up next to Fen. This time, she wasn't crying. She was perfectly happy, tucked up into Fen's protective embrace, and her sleep that night was the best night sleep she had ever had.

# Chapter 20

For days, Fen received well-wishers whom he suspected were more curious than concerned. They all wanted to see the wounds from the spirit's claws, and they all wanted to have an audience with Mati and himself.

"Just be nice," Mati pleaded through a fake smile, as yet another group of sykosee trailed in. "They mean well."

The healer had instructed Fen to start walking around and using his muscles as much as he could without serious strain. Mati didn't agree, trying to keep him in bed as much as she could. Fen wouldn't be contained, though, and she usually lost that battle. He was currently sitting in a plush chair that Mati had brought in for him, greeting the endless line of the curious. He was starting to feel like a sideshow act.

"We should start charging admission," Fen whispered. "We could make a fortune."

Mati slapped his shoulder light, avoiding his injuries. "Hush, and be nice. I'm going to shut it down after the next one."

"Thank you," Fen replied, exasperated.

And right on cue, after the next couple turned to leave, Mati stepped in. "I think that's it for now. I'm sorry. Fen needs to be careful about overexerting himself." Fen smiled, his mind diving headfirst into the gutter. "No, no, no... Stop it." Mati hissed at him.

The door closed behind the guests with a click, and Mati promptly smacked Fen's shoulder again as he burst into laughter. "Not funny."

"You said it, not me."

"Such a child..." Mati smiled and pointed to the bed. "Go. Now."

Fen shook his head. "No. I'm tired of being in bed."

Mati smirked. "That's not what you said last night."

"Now whose mind is dirty?" Fen shot her a devious smile.

Mati laughed. "You're entirely responsible for it. Now get to bed."

"No. I'm going to get up, walk to the dining hall, and eat with everyone else today. It's been almost a week and I've barely been out of this room. I'm going to go crazy." He stood carefully, the sore muscles in his body throbbing.

Mati sighed, defeated. "Fine, but no hanging around. You go out, you eat, you come back."

"Deal," Fen said, and started to gingerly shuffle for the door.

The dining hall was packed when they walked in. Fen was being careful, and it took him twice as long to walk there than it should have, but Mati wasn't complaining. He'd already popped several stitches since he'd started walking from trying to pull himself up too fast. The healer wasn't at all amused and had given him four kinds of evil glares every time she had to come stitch him back up.

They sat down at a table with Trantu, Alik, and Rena. Fen heard the names of Asterion and Dursten mentioned as they approached, and joined the conversation. "The stars? Where have they been?"

Alik turned to him. "That's what we're discussing. They've never been away for this long before."

"We're getting worried," Rena added.

Fen slowly lowered himself down into his seat and waved away Mati's attempt at assistance. "We can still continue as planned though, right?"

Trantu nodded. "We should. I think it would be a mistake to wait."

"I think we should give them a few more days," Rena replied, setting her mug down.

Trantu shook his head. "I think that would be a grave mistake. Our patrols have seen too much movement from Guyt's armies. They're preparing for something, and we need that weapon if we're going to stand a chance. Guyt isn't going to wait for the stars to return to make his move."

"He's right," Alik pursed his lips in thought. "Rena, we need to move now."

Rena shook her head. "If we don't move with caution, then we risk Guyt finding out that Fen and Mati are back."

"How do you know he doesn't know already?" Fen cut in again. "Weren't those his minions we ran into in the desert?"

"They were," Alik answered.

"Then wouldn't it make sense that Guyt is moving *because* he knows?"

Mati took a gulp of her drink. "He's right. There were a few dralin that escaped. I don't know much about war, but I do know that if only a few of my men returned, I'd want a play-by-play of what happened. And they certainly saw the four of us."

"She has a point," Rena agreed. "I'm sure Syradax would've wondered."

"Who's Syradax?" Fen asked.

Trantu had opened his mouth to answer when he was interrupted by screaming and commotion in the main tunnel. They all turned at that noise, Trantu and Alik both leaping up and immediately racing off.

Fen tried to rise as well, but Mati stilled him. "Let them handle it."

Fen dropped back into his seat, grumbling, as Rena stood, now panicked as well. Alik and Trantu were sprinting back to them, leaping over hastily-abandoned tables and chairs.

"Dralin!" Alik's booming voice called over the commotion.

Rena sprang into action. "Go, get Fen back to his room," she commanded Mati.

"Fuck!" Fen cursed.

"Come on," Mati urged.

Trantu and Alik skidded to a stop. "They're in the city," Trantu said, his alarm evident. "Get Fen and Mati out of here."

The commotion in the main tunnel grew louder. Cries of terror and pleas for help mixed with the clang of metal on metal.

"Where should we go?" Mati asked.

"Out of the city," Trantu answered, falling silent as he fixed his attention back on the tunnel. Then, all he said was, "Syradax."

"Fuck!" Alik exclaimed. "Trantu, get Mati and Fen out of here. You'll have to fly to Naina tonight. We're out of time."

"We don't have the metal or the water with us," Fen said.

"They're ready by the back door," Alik directed him. Then Alik moved across the room brandishing an enormous broadsword.

Syradax had entered. He was a dralin, but much larger than the ones they had fought in the desert. His skin was far deeper gray and more badly scarred, and one of his eyes was wholly black. It oozed a yellow goo that he let trail down his face and dry in flaky chunks. Years-old blackened blood was splattered across his armor, in equal proportions to the new red.

"So, it *is* true," Syradax said, his voice gravelly. "I couldn't believe my luck when my pathetic men came back from the desert with the story of four humans fighting alongside the sykosee. When they described them, I knew it had to be you, Alik. And I knew there wasn't anything short of the return of these two that would drag your sorry ass out of that hellhole you call a refuge."

Alik stepped forward, his sword readied in front of him. "Go," he commanded Trantu. "Rena and I will hold him off as long as we can."

"Oh, look, Ciksura," the new voice was unnervingly calm. "It's our old *friends*."

The two now moving through the chaos looked at the group with cold eyes. The one who had spoken wore leather and a red cloak that matched her hair. She had a look of dark superiority about her as she walked slowly into the hall.

"Yes, Lavinia," Ciksura replied coldly. Their white hair fell around their shoulders, and the acid-green robe they wore almost seemed to billow even without wind. "How funny to meet you both here, Alik and Rena." Ciksura prowled through the hall toward them, as if stalking prey.

Lavinia stopped in front of Fen and Mati. "Are these the precious two? So young, aren't they?"

Fen didn't like the way the newcomers looked at them. Their gazes were cold and calculated, and made a chill run down his spine. Fen seethed with the need to hold himself back. He had no weapon, and probably wouldn't be able to wield it even if he did.

"Go," Alik hissed through clenched teeth.

"Let's go," Trantu tugged Mati's arm.

She grabbed Fen's hand, and together they ran after Trantu and out of the dining hall.

Ciksura and Lavinia moved as though to dart after the three, but Alik moved with desperate speed to block them. He could not allow the traitors to reach Mati and Fen. Rena followed him almost as quickly, throwing up her sword to block Ciksura's path. The sounds of battle moved into the dining hall as Alik's blade clanged against Lavinia's.

Dralin poured in through the main doors, their massive frames every inch a match for the sykosee. Alik cleared his mind and focused on the opponent in front of him.

"Go, Syradax," Lavinia ordered the massive dralin. "These two are ours."

"You will *not* harm them," Alik insisted as he thrust Lavinia's sword back at her.

"Careful, Alik," Lavinia warned. "You're a mortal now."

"I'd sooner die here than let you or Guyt get your hands on them again."

Lavinia thrust her long, elegant sword with malice. "That can be arranged," she snapped.

He blocked her strike, their swords clashing against each other with the ringing sound of deadly metal as the four began to battle in earnest. The dining hall was filled with ebbing and flowing crowds of dralin and surprised sykosee, a terrible party of dancers and their partners, each trying to get the upper hand.

A cry tore out of Rena and ripped through the space. Alik could only spare a millisecond side-glance to see her and Ciksura embroiled in a tense fight.

Ciksura's sword raked down Rena's face, slashing it and leaving a shallow cut that ran from Rena's brow, down her cheek, to her jaw. Rena's wound beaded with blood, droplets collecting and starting to trail down her face.

"Fighting you brings me no joy, Ciksura," Rena called through the blood that begun to drip from her lips and chin. "I had hoped to never have to fight you again. I refuse to kill you, my friend, but I will do anything else in my power to keep you from hindering our mission."

"Fight me!" Ciksura seethed, while dealing blow after blow. "Kill me!" she roared.

"I will not kill a friend," Rena stated again, fighting through the pain. "This isn't truly you."

Ciksura leapt forward. "You don't know me! You never did. And now it's too late."

Lavinia managed to push Alik back twenty paces or so from where they had begun their fight, taking full advantage of his hesitation to end her life. He almost couldn't hate her for it. It was a good move.

Sykosee poured into the hall in greater numbers now, overwhelming the dralin forces. Their grotesque bodies were strewn across the stone floor, the tiles now stained with their blue blood. For all their might, they weren't the most intelligent strategists. Alik didn't know how many dralin had been in the raiding party, but it wasn't a smart plan to attack Duinan. Hopefully, if Fen and Mati could get away, then their enemies would abandon the fight. They only had to hang on for a few more minutes.

Lavinia pushed him further and further back. "Why not fight me, Alik, God of War? Have you grown incapable?"

Alik snarled at the challenge. "Your death is not mine to bestow. It is your husband's right to make that decision. Nor would it be in my best interest to strike you down yet. Like it or not, you're still one of us."

"I have no husband, and I do not wish to be one of you!"

Their swords clashed again and again, Lavinia's attacks becoming more and more frenzied and uncontrolled with her growing rage.

Then Alik's world toppled. He tried to retreat from Lavinia's hectic swings and tripped over a fallen dralin. The last thing he remembered was how devastatingly blue and slick the hard floor had become, before he struck his head on something and blacked out.

Fen caught one last glimpse of Alik in the battle with Lavinia before rounding the corner and running out of the hall.

His wounds burned and screamed at him, but he steeled himself to push through the agony. He couldn't let Mati see how much pain it was causing him. They had to get out of there, fast, and this was the only way. He heard Syradax's angry cries behind them as he attempted to give chase, but they ran down tunnels not designed for Syradax's powerful but lumbering frame.

Trantu led them through tunnels they hadn't seen before, winding down staircases and through unlit passageways. They finally stopped at a heavy, locked door guarded by a warrior. "Unlock the door," Trantu ordered.

Fen noticed the bags of rock and the waterskin, sitting ready for them by the door. Mati followed his gaze and saw them as well, heaving the bags over her shoulder as Fen grabbed the waterskin.

Thankfully, the fighting must have slowed Syradax down. They had been given just enough time to get out.

The guard hurried to open the door, and Trantu shoved past him to do it himself. "The city is under attack. Go fight. Help your brothers. Stop Syradax with your life, if necessary."

They followed Trantu out into the dark desert night. "Get on. We have no time to waste."

Mati shoved Fen up onto Trantu's back and then climbed up herself, dragging the bags with her. Fen felt her watchful eyes on him, but ignored them. His chest was in agony, and he was taking the shallowest breaths he could manage to try and avoid the roaring pain. Not even adrenaline could keep it at bay any longer.

Trantu lifted them up into the sky just as an arrow whizzed past them, then another. Fen looked down and saw several dralin on the ground, their bows aimed at the flying sykosee and his passengers. Trantu expertly dodged the missiles as they took off into the night, but the evasive movements jarred Fen's insides and made his stomach lurch with nausea. He managed to hold himself together with only the thought that Mati would worry even more if he couldn't. And he shuddered to think how many warriors Syradax would have to strike down to get out that door.

The cool quiet of the night sky as they flew was too much for Fen, after the chaos they had just escaped. "Talk to me?" Fen asked, his arm wrapped around Mati. "I can't stand this silence."

"I don't know what to say," she answered. "My mind is frozen."

"So, I guess Guyt does know we're back," Fen said.

"Seems like it. Which means we don't have any time left." Mati paused. "How's your chest? And don't lie to me."

"It hurts," Fen replied blandly, and refused to elaborate.

They flew all through the night, the cold wind rushing through Fen. He tried to keep Mati as warm as possible, but unfortunately his arms only offered limited warmth and she still shivered slightly. Once the sun peeked over the horizon, Fen guessed they'd been flying for eight hours or so.

Trantu flicked his wings and they started to glide down toward the trees. "We'll land here," he called back. "I need a break." He descended in slow circles and landed gently on the grass. Fen winced, regardless, as Trantu's feet hit the ground. Mati slid off his back and helped Fen down as well. He squeezed his eyes shut, trying to hide his pain, as he gingerly slipped down the reptile's back to stand on his feet.

Trantu stretched his wings and flapped them a few times, shaking off the fatigue before plopping down, exhausted, onto the grass. "We'll continue in a few minutes. We should get to Lyserria in the next hour."

"And from there," Fen added, "we can walk to Naina. You can't go into the mountains with us, right?"

Trantu nodded. "I've never tried it, but I can't imagine I'll be much help if I freeze to death."

Fen remembered their experience with the cold, and didn't relish the idea of facing it again. They'd have no one to help them if they got lost this time. He was standing there on the grassy plain, his chest still screaming at him, when Mati came over.

"Let me see," she said.

"I'm fine," he objected, and tried to wave her away.

Mati gave a quick jab to his chest that momentarily stunned Fen as he sucked in a sharp breath. "Sure, just fine..." she scowled at him.

She took hold of his shirt hem and pulled it up. He was sure that some of his wounds had reopened, the stitches popped. Mati scowled at the blood and rumpled bandages. "We'll have to fix that before we hike Naina. We can't afford to have you getting worse up there."

Fen rolled his eyes and swatted her hands away, tugging his shirt back down. "I'm fine."

"Whatever," Mati rejected his evaluation. "But I'm not dragging your unconscious ass down that mountain if you lose too much blood."

Trantu laughed at their bickering and got up onto his feet. "Let's get going. I want to get to Lyserria as quickly as possible."

Mati hopped on first, and offered a hand to Fen as he mounted. "Stubborn ass," she chided.

Fen smiled, wrapped his arms back around her, and gave her a little squeeze. "You'd be more worried if I wasn't being an ass."

Mati didn't say anything in response as Trantu flapped up into the dimly-lit morning sky.

"Do you think Alik and Rena are okay?" she asked, tentatively.

"I think that they've been around a long time and can handle themselves." Fen only half-believed his own words. He knew that trying to face Syradax, Lavinia, and Ciksura would be an uneven fight. He just hoped that Alik and Rena had been able to escape, if nothing else.

They flew in silence for a little while until Mati's silence started to worry Fen. "Are you okay? You've been quiet."

"I'm fine," she replied.

Fen laughed softly. "You know I'm the king of *I'm fine*, right?"

Mati's brow furrowed. "Really, I'm fine. I'm just tired. Or have you forgotten that we haven't slept all night?"

Fen worried for her. She wasn't telling him everything. "What's wrong?"

"Nothing. Just please, leave me alone."

"Okay," Fen replied quietly, and leaned back to give her a little space.

His thoughts raced as he tried to figure out why Mati had snapped at him like that. Was she really still peeved about the whole 'swatting her hands away' thing? He hadn't meant it to come across as a rejection; he just hated how she always pestered him, like a mother hen.

He'd never had anyone show him that much attention and care before and, if he was being honest with himself, he didn't know how to deal with it. He was very adept at hiding his emotional incapacity with humor and sarcasm, but actually receiving more than a passing glance from a silly girl was out of his expertise. He knew how to give it...or he liked to think he did, at least. Receiving was quite a different set of skills.

# Chapter 21

They finally caught sight of Lyserria on the horizon as Trantu started to make his descent. They landed on the loose dirt just outside of the town. Curious onlookers had gathered to see what and who had just arrived.

A young woman wearing a white turban and brown slacks stepped up to them. "You're Mati and Fennar, yes?" she asked.

"Yes," Mati answered her hesitantly.

"I thought so," the woman replied. "I remember seeing you come through before, with Alik and Rena. I'm Pelka. Can I be of service to you? It'd be my honor."

Mati nodded without pausing to think. "Yes, Pelka. We could use a healer for Fen, and some food and water for all three of us."

"Of course, my lady," Pelka answered her. "I'll take you to Mother Grint. If she can't fix up the lord, then no one can."

"Thank you," Mati said, and they began following Pelka through the city streets.

"I'll go find us food. We'll lodge in Alik's apartments," Trantu called after them. "I'll meet you there."

"Okay," Mati answered back.

Fen was now visibly in pain and wasn't hiding it anymore. Mati held out her hand to steady him a few times, and she was surprised that he took it.

Pelka soon stopped in front of a mud brick house close to the center of town and knocked on the door. They heard shuffling inside, and an elderly woman stood before them once the door opened.

"Mother Grint," Pelka began. "The Lord and Lady need your help."

Mother Grint shuffled back, opening the door wider in an invitation. "'Twill be my honor to assist them. Come in. Come in."

Fen and Mati stepped inside. The walls of the house were lined with bundles of dried herbs and flowers, and shelves upon shelves of jars, tokens, bits, and odds. "Come over here, my lord, and let me get a good look at you."

He stepped forward to face the plain-clothed elder with a certain amount of surprise.

"You're wondering how I knew it was you in need of healing," she said, looking up at Fen.

"Yes," he said in wonder.

"Your shirt." She smiled kindly at him. "It's covered in blood."

"Oh," Fen laughed, then winced at the pain it caused him.

"Take off that shirt so I can see what I'm dealing with."

Fen obeyed painfully and handed the shirt to Mati. Mother Grint removed the wrapped bandages, carefully soaking them and peeling them from his skin where the blood and pus had stuck them together. She looked him over thoroughly with her keen and critical eyes.

"How long ago did this happen?" She asked him.

"Almost a week," Fen answered.

"And what caused these?"

"The spirit of Pontianak."

Mother Grint kept prodding around the wounds. "Dear gods... why would you mess with that unholy creature?"

"I didn't do it for fun," Fen objected. "I was trying to save a friend."

"Hmm..." she eyed him carefully before turning and bustling around the main room, pulling different jars and oddities down from everywhere. "I think I have something here to help it heal and to take that pain away. And I'll need to redo some of the broken stitches. You had a skilled healer taking care of you, it seems."

She finally gathered all the supplies she needed and dropped them all onto a counter where she began mixing and crushing things in a small mortar and pestle. "So why were you bothering the Pontianak? She's a testy devil, so I hear."

"Well," Mati started to explain, "we were trying to get some of the metal in the sea to make something we need."

"Well, I'm glad you survived. Just barely, mind you, by the looks of him." She finished mixing her ingredients, added a bit of water, and remixed it all together into a paste. "Bend down, my lord, or I'll not be able to heal anything but your knees."

Fen tried to comply, but winced as he attempted to kneel. Mati steadied him with a hand under his arm.

"Thank you," Mother said, and began smearing the paste over his wounds. "This will sting."

Fen winced the moment she said it.

"This will help protect the wounds from infection. You're lucky you didn't do more damage than just pulling out a few of those stitches. Normally, I wouldn't add this paste until after I'd stitched you up, but the paste will help the needle slide through your skin and cause you a tad less pain than it might otherwise. Even if it does make my job a bit trickier."

Fen nodded in thanks. He was gripping Mati's hand so tightly that it was turning a bright red and purple in places.

"I suspect you're in terrible pain already, and I'll not make it any greater if I can help it." Mother Grint set the bowl of paste on the counter and wandered off into the small parlor.

"Fuck, fuck, fuck," Fen mouthed under his breath once she had turned away. "I'm sorry," he added as he looked at Mati's squished hand.

"It's fine," she assured him and laid her other hand on his shoulder.

Pelka had taken a seat at the table and was fidgeting with the ingredients for the salve. "I'm honored to be of assistance to you, my lord," she said, now eyeballing Fen's bare chest.

Mati shot her a dirty look. She was positive Pelka wasn't admiring his injuries. "Thank you, Pelka," she stared flatly. "We're most grateful for your help. Aren't we, Fen?"

Fen nodded without much enthusiasm, and Mati wondered if he was even paying attention.

Mother Grint came back to them with a freshly-threaded needle. "I'll be quick, and then I can give you that pain herb."

Mati glared daggers at Pelka as the healer began to sew up the re-opened injuries on Fen's chest. How dare that little trollop stare at Fen... *her* Fen? Pelka did have the good sense to look away, but it did nothing to quell the animosity simmering in Mati's gut.

Mother Grint was quick as she promised, then handed an herb to Fen. "Put this in your mouth and leave it under your tongue until there's no flavor left."

Fen took it and popped it into his mouth. "Thank you," Fen said to her. "It tastes like tea. Not at all like any medicine I've ever had."

Mother Grint nodded. "It was my honor, my lord. You just heal up, and that will be thanks enough."

Fen smiled. "I can't make any promises."

Fen's smile drew Pelka's eyes back to him again. She was practically drooling.

Mother Grint slapped the table in front of Pelka, the loud noise snapping her out of whatever daydream his smile had conjured. "Stop ogling, girl," she chided. "Can't you see he's taken?"

Mati's face blushed hot but her heart jumped with joy. *Ha! that'll teach Pelka to keep those wandering eyes to herself. Or, at least, on men who aren't taken.*

"Let that plaster dry before bandaging it up," Mother Grint said, handing Mati a roll of white linen.

Mati hugged Mother Grint in thanks, both for helping Fen and for scolding Pelka. "Thank you. You've helped us tremendously."

She returned Mati's hug. "You're welcome, my lady. I leave it up to you to make sure the Lord doesn't strain himself overmuch... in one way *or another.*"

Mati's face felt hot as fire. She thought she knew exactly what Mother Grint meant with her last words. "I'll try. But he can be very stubborn."

"I bet he causes lots of chaos in your lives," Mother Grint smiled up at Fen with a twinkle in her eye.

Mati rolled her eyes. "You have no idea."

Fen smiled that cocky grin of his. "We really should be going. Trantu is waiting for us, and we need rest."

"Thank you, truly," Mati said again as they left, following Pelka into the city.

Pelka led them back through the dusty streets. "You're going to Alik's barroom, yes?"

"Yes," Fen replied. "Thank you for taking us to Mother Grint's."

Pelka looked over her shoulder to smile widely at Fen. Mati was sure she saw Pelka flutter her lashes at him... or maybe it had just been a shadow.

"It was my pleasure," Pelka said coyly. "I'll find you a new shirt to wear." Her eyes trailed over Fen's broad chest and muscular arms again.

Mati made sure to step in front of Fen protectively. "That would be very helpful," she said through gritted teeth, with a fake smile. "Thank you."

Pelka's eyes widened, she turned back around, and that was how she stayed until they got to Alik's. "I'll find you that shirt and drop it off at the bar. I've got to be getting back to my chores now, or my mum will skin my hide."

"Thank you," Fen called to her with a smile that faded when he glanced back at Mati's seething face.

"*Thank you*," Mati mocked Fen.

Fen burst into laughter. "You're cute when you're jealous."

"I'm not jealous," Mati lied. "You're just making a fool out of yourself with that child."

"Child?" Fen laughed. "She's the same age as you or me."

Mati feigned nonchalance as they started up the back stairs to Alik's apartment. "Could have fooled me. She barely looks older than twelve."

"You know I only goaded her on because I liked seeing you jealous."

"I'm not jealous," Mati stated firmly again. Of course she *was*, but she didn't want to surrender to Fen and his irritating smirk.

Trantu was already there once they got to Alik's apartment, and had a feast laid out. He was helping himself while he waited. "Looks like you got all fixed up," he said, looking up from his meat at Fen.

"Good as it gets for now," Fen replied, eyeing the food.

Mati passed Fen and headed straight for her dinner. She hadn't realized just how hungry she was until she saw it laid out in front of her.

The two joined Trantu at the table and they all made quick work of the meal. After, Mati let out a yawn and fell back in her seat. They hadn't brought anything with them by way of packs or bedrolls, thanks to their rapid escape. She wasn't thrilled about sleeping on the hard wooden floor, but it was better than nothing. And at least it was safe.

"Come here," she looked at Fen. "I need to put these bandages on you now. The plaster looks dry enough."

Fen complied and Mati wrapped the linen around his torso, covering all the gashes.

Trantu was perched awkwardly on a stool, almost falling off and looking very uncomfortable. "Damn human furniture," he grumbled, half under his breath. "Your chairs don't accommodate my tail or wings, and these stools are damned uncomfortable."

Mati tried to hide a smile as he twisted and fidgeted, trying to get comfortable. She hadn't realized before just how large he looked in a human setting. "Fen, when do you think you'll be ready to hike?"

Fen reached down and patted the bandages experimentally. "Tomorrow. We don't have the luxury of waiting any longer than that. This pain herb is already working miracles."

"I'm afraid he's right," Trantu agreed. "By now, Guyt definitely knows that you've escaped his three generals. He'll be preparing for a full-scale war."

Mati wasn't thrilled that Fen would be traveling so soon, but she understood the reason in their need for speed. "Okay. We'll leave at dawn."

Fen nodded as he yawned. "I'm going to turn in."

"I think we all are," Mati said yawning again in reply.

Mati and Fen had become too familiar with pre-dawn awakenings. They sluggishly prepared themselves, Fen retrieving the shirt Pelka had left for him downstairs, and Mati rooting around the tavern for any food they could take with them. With Fen still badly wounded, she knew he'd need more food than usual to keep his body upright.

Trantu woke up to see them off. Mati wrapped the reptile warrior in a warm but awkward hug. "We'll be back soon. Thank you for everything you've done for us."

"It has been an honor," Trantu replied, returning her embrace. "Can I show you the sykosee way of saying goodbye?"

"Of course!"

Trantu bent down to her level and ran his scaly snout along her cheeks, on both sides. "I'll be waiting here for your return."

They started off on the path to Naina once again, laden with packs, Gaia's water, and the two sacks of rocks. This time though, they were alone, and it seemed to Fen that it was fitting. Everything and nothing had changed since they were last here. The nature was all the same, but he and Mati had changed. They had started on this journey as children, completely naïve to what this world had in store for them. And now they walked this path alone for the first time, the weight of their task laid heavy on his shoulders.

That was when it clicked. All of Alik's grumbling, coarseness, and training had been in service for this moment.

They were quiet all day as they walked, Naina an ever-present finish line. The mighty weight they carried would affect an entire world. And the pivotal players in this game of fate now walked from desert into snow... alone.

They camped at the bottom of the pass that night like they had before. Huddled together, neither seemed to get any sleep, but they at least got to rest their feet. Fen's chest had been tolerable until the chill of night set in. He refused to let Mati know how much it bothered him, even then. He kept her tucked against his side all night as he silently waited for dawn's first light to start the climb up the Naina.

⟫⟫⟫ ⟪⟪⟪

Mati reached over and laced her fingers into Fen's. The morning was cold, and the wind ripped through the canyon as they climbed. "How're you feeling?"

"I'm doing okay," Fen answered. He wasn't completely lying. He was mostly uncomfortable now, as opposed to being in actual pain. "Don't worry about me. I'll be fine."

The path had become steep and snowy by this point, and memories of their last trip flooded back to them. The cold air had begun to sting his nose and lungs, and Fen's chest began to ache sharply as the wind hit.

They climbed up and up until they finally reached the deep crevasse that led to the spirits' magical portal. Mati held Fen's hand in a tight grip as they climbed.

Fen's mind was consumed with taking one breath after another, one step after another, to just keep moving. Mati's hand in his was the only thing keeping him on his feet. The thin air provided little support for mind or body. His body ached to just sit down, to just take a little break, something that he knew would be fatal.

They both let out audible sighs of relief as the cliff face in front of them flattened out to that familiar flat rock surface. They trudged onward and passed through the portal. The spirits were sitting exactly where they had been before, in exactly the same clothing.

"Welcome back," Osirim greeted them, emotionless.

Fen and Mati bowed with the best effort they could muster. "Thank you," Fen said, exhausted. "We have the two items you require for the weapon."

"Good," Morana said dryly. "I must remind you of your oath, that you return the weapons to us once they are used."

"Yes," Mati answered. "We know the oath."

Morana nodded and, with a simple blink, the stone table and crystal bowl appeared before them as they had before. "Place the items on the table."

Fen removed the waterskin from his belt, and Mati laid the sacks on the table next to it. With magic, not moving from the throne, Morana poured the contents of the waterskin into the crystal bowl and then dumped the minerals in after. Fen jumped back as the bowl began to resonate with sound through the cavern, as though an invisible finger ran along its edge.

Morana and Osirim began a low chant. The green hunks of metal and the crystal bowl both began to melt. The heat was so intense that Fen could feel it from where he stood several feet away. The swirling, molten liquid floated into the air. The chant seemed to fill the room, and the liquid morphed and shaped into twin blades. They took shape right in front of Fen and Mati's eyes, as if an invisible blacksmith was hammering them out. After completing their transformation, the swords floated to Mati and Fen, one in front of each. They appeared to be identical in every way.

"I can't take this," Mati protested. "I can't use a sword."

That was when Morana stood. "It chose to forge itself for you. And you would do well to take it."

Mati reached out a shaky hand and took the blade that offered itself to her. "I don't have a belt."

Osirim waved his hand through the air. As he did, a pair of glittering belts and scabbards appeared before him. "This should do," Osirim said and bumped one through the air toward Mati.

Mati reached out her hand and caught it, with a little effort. Fen grabbed his sword directly out of the air and had begun to swing it gracefully as Mati thrust hers into the scabbard.

"Thank you," Mati said soberly, bowing low to the spirits. "We truly appreciate this. And won't ever forget your assistance."

Fen held the sword and looked it over, familiarizing himself with the weapon. The blade was a jade-green color, and wrapped around the hilt and trailing down the blade were crystal designs and runes that Fen couldn't read. He carefully sheathed the sword and bowed as low as he could, pushing through the pain and trying to hold in a wince.

"You come to us injured," Morana said, her eyes on Fen. "I felt the pull of your soul wanting to cross over in the moment when it happened."

"Yes," Fen answered, resituating his shirt against the pull of the sword, so it didn't lay so tightly across his chest.

"You've shown great resilience in climbing our mountain while so badly injured," Osirim said. "My sister was sure you would pass into the shadow."

"It'll take more than a pissed off spirit to kill me," Fen answered resolutely.

"Come," Morana beckoned Fen over to her.

Fen confusedly strode up to the thrones. Osirim rose from his throne and came down the stairs to meet Fen. "Open your shirt."

Fen complied with Osirim's command, unbuttoning each button until his chest was laid bare. Blood and pus had seeped through the new bandages as well, and had crusted over. Fen felt the tug of the bandages against his skin with every breath and movement. Osirim closed his eyes; heat and vibration coursed through Fen's body, and a bright green light burst from Fen's chest.

Mati rushed to his side as Fen was hit with a rush of pain and fell to his knees. "What are you doing?" Mati demanded, panic in her voice.

"Hold, child." Morana said. "All will be well."

The pain in Fen's chest would have had him fully doubled-over if the green light wasn't tugging him forward at the same time. He let out a howl as the pain crescendoed, but as the green light faded, the pain subsided as well. It all left Fen fighting for air, falling over on his face.

"Fen," Mati pleaded, worried and sounding almost as breathless as he felt. "Are you okay?"

Fen took a few deeper lung-filling breaths before rising on his knees once more. He looked down and pawed at his chest. The bandages had been evaporated by the green light and jagged white scars had been left behind. "I'm... fine?" Fen said in disbelief.

Only remnants of the salve, pus, and dried blood remained on his chest. Fen's gaze flashed to Osirim, who looked drained and tired.

"Thank you," Mati breathed in wonder.

Osirim nodded, accepting her thanks. "You have shown the valor only a true hero would exhibit, to protect a people they do not know. It was well-deserved."

"Thank you," Fen replied as well, as he stood and buttoned his shirt back up without the sting and pull of stitches.

"Go, now," Morana said to them. "You have little time to waste. The people of Vertrose need you. And I hope to one day meet you both again, in happier times. Your strength and courage will, I believe, turn the tide of this war."

Mati nodded. "Thank you again, to you both. We'll see you again once Guyt's reign has been ended."

The two turned, fingers laced together, and stepped back out onto the dark, snowy mountain, carrying the weight of the world on their hips.

# Chapter 22

It was the wee hours of the next morning when they finally stumbled back into Alik's sparse apartment. Trantu woke with a start at the clatter they made coming in. One small lantern left on the table created just enough light so they could walk in without tripping over themselves.

"Sorry," Mati said as she shut the door behind them. She collapsed on the floor face-first.

"Did you get it?" Trantu asked before he saw that they both carried weapons. "Two?"

"Yes," Fen answered, as he too collapsed. "They made one for each of us." Fen unsheathed the green sword and handed it to Trantu.

Trantu held it with awe, spinning it around and watching the blade and hilt sparkle in the low lantern light. "This blade is like nothing I've ever seen."

Fen sat at the empty table, hanging his head low. "Hopefully it works."

Trantu handed the blade back to Fen. "If the spirits gave it to you, then I imagine it works."

"I'm exhausted," Mati interjected. "Can we sleep now and talk about the pretty swords tomorrow?"

"Of course," Trantu said, narrowing his eyes at Fen who had already started nodding off at the table, his forehead resting on his palm.

Mati removed her belt and sword and lay down on the floor unceremoniously. Fen stood up as well, removing his own belt and sword. He stumbled across the room and lay down next to Mati. He stayed awake long enough to hear Trantu blow out the lantern, before falling into a deep, exhausted sleep.

Fen woke with a crick in his neck to find the room now fully illuminated by the sun. He squinted and propped himself up on an elbow, rubbing his neck, wondering how long he had been out for. Trantu was nowhere in sight, but Mati still slept beside him. He smiled at the sight of her, curled up into a ball with her arm under her head. He liked having her beside him when he woke.

Fen gently placed a hand on her shoulder. "Wake up," he leaned over and crooned at her. Mati grunted incoherently. "Come on, lazy."

"No," she grunted, tucking her knees further up into her chest.

Fen laughed heartily. He shook her shoulder and was swatted away by her angry hand. "You need to get up. It's full light out."

Mati let out a long groan. "Fiiiine..." She stretched, then collapsed again, yawning. "What time is it?"

"I'm not sure," Fen answered. "But I think we should try to leave today, if we can."

The pair sat, Mati still yawning, as Trantu opened the door carrying a tray of food and drink. "Good," he said, setting his tray on the small table and sitting down. "You're up. I was hoping I wouldn't have to wake you. My goal is to leave as soon as we've finished eating. I'd like to get back to Duinan as soon as possible."

"That's what I figured," Fen grunted, getting up off the floor and making his way over to the food.

"Your wounds seem to be doing well," Trantu pointed out observantly, as he took a bite of bread.

"Oh, that!" Fen said excitedly and whipped open his shirt. "Osirim healed them."

Trantu's eyes went wide. "A spirit healed you. That *is* a miracle. They're not exactly known for benevolence towards humans. They must have thought very highly of you."

Fen shrugged nonchalantly and grabbed a piece of fruit from the tray. "He said something of the sort."

Within an hour of waking, Fen and Mati were once again seated on top of Trantu. The flight would take less than eight hours this time, with Trantu fed, rested, and uninjured. The day was warm, and the sun bounced off the sand with a bright gleam. Their spirits were tentatively high as they took off into the blue sky. Mati knew there was a chance Duinan had been destroyed, or that their friends had been killed, but she pushed those thoughts away.

They soared and glided through the sky just under the clouds. Mati felt like she could reach up and touch them.

"You love flying, don't you?" Fen asked, his grip tight around her waist.

"Yes," Mati smiled. "It feels free and endless. Like anything is possible." She turned her head to glance at Fen behind her. "And you don't, I presume, considering the vise-grip you have on me."

"No," Fen said, almost smiling. "I'm not a big fan."

"This seems like it should be just your thing, though. The whole rough-and-tumble free-spirited nature of it."

"I get that," Fen replied. "But I prefer the free-spirited nature of the ground."

Mati laughed. "Fair enough!"

Eventually, they sighted Duinan in the distance through the clouds. Mati couldn't tell from that distance whether anything was wrong, though. She and Fen kept staring, almost holding their breath, as they glided lower and closer.

"They're alive!" Fen shouted joyously. "Look! There're guards posted outside the door."

The warriors spotted them gliding in and raised their bows, but quickly realized who it was and lowered them again. One stationed at the door popped into the shadow of the opening, before reappearing moments later with Alik, Rena, and Vrutuuk.

Trantu landed gently and Fen and Mati slid off. Rena was already racing toward them. Mati saw a nasty cut down her cheek, but otherwise she seemed okay.

"Thank the spirits, you're safe!" Rena called out, tears welling in her eyes. "We were so worried about you." She flung her arms around both Fen and Mati.

"We were worried for you as well," Mati said, her own tears of joy streaming down her face.

Rena pulled away and looked them over. "Are you well? Do you have the swords?" She leapt back suddenly. "Oh my, Fen, I'm sorry! I forgot about your injuries."

"It's all good," Fen said. "Osirim healed me."

Rena froze in shock. "Oh," she said, amazed. "That is a great honor."

"So I'm told."

Alik and Vrutuuk joined them then, and Alik clapped Fen on the shoulder. "I'm glad to see you're well, Fen."

Fen nodded and pulled out the sword to show it off. "We have them," he announced triumphantly, with a little too much flourish.

Alik and Vrutuuk's eyes were glued to the sword. Alik reached out to run his fingers along the crystal runes. "It's like nothing I've ever seen before."

The crystal hilt glinted blindingly in the desert sun. Vrutuuk traced his scaly finger down the smooth green blade. "It's a gorgeous weapon, to be sure."

Fen slid his sword back into its sheath, protectively laying a hand on the hilt. "How is everyone here?"

Vrutuuk slumped his head. "We lost many good warriors, but Duinan still stands. We will need to move to a war camp if we can. I'd like to keep the fighting away from here, if at all possible."

Fen nodded. "I figure we need to go hold Gruthlan and Clíodha to their word, too. Show them that we have the swords, and make sure their armies start moving as quickly as possible."

"Very wise," Alik agreed, with a hint of pride.

"How long until Guyt's armies are assembled, do you think?" Fen turned to Vrutuuk with his question.

"I fear they're already on the move," Vrutuuk answered. "We don't have more than a week. My patrols have told me that there is a lot of movement at the Meten Gate."

"Where's the Meten Gate?" Mati asked.

"Close to the Pontianak," Rena answered. "It's the main gate into our once-great city. We'll have to choose our battlefield carefully."

Fen nodded. "Yes. You both can be in charge of that, for now. I don't know enough about the terrain to make that decision."

"When will the madrigal be here?" Mati asked.

Alik turned. "Helian said they had already left for Duinan when we were at the Magnus." He paused and counted silently. "If they make good time, they could be here within the next two days."

"Good," Fen said. "Then Mati and I will leave tomorrow morning for Hruguth. And I dare Gruthlan to go back on his word once he sees these."

The assembled party all nodded in agreement.

"I'll send Trantu with you again, if that pleases him," Vrutuuk offered, with a look at Trantu.

"It will be a great honor," Trantu bowed. "And I'd consider it a slight on my honor if I wasn't chosen." A prideful smile slid across his face.

⇛ ⇚

Vrutuuk led them through the battered city door. The tunnels had been trashed, marred with gouge marks and streaks of blood. The main tunnel had been the most badly damaged from the assault; as they wound further into the city, the damage seemed to lessen slightly.

"We're still cleaning up," Vrutuuk explained. "Almost all the residential tunnels were destroyed. We've had to move the families to my wing to give them somewhere to live in the meantime. I'll leave only a few soldiers here for defense when we move to the battlefield."

Mati was hit most heavily by the stench of the once warm and inviting tunnels. The metallic tang of blood still hung heavy in the air, and some tunnels were now almost completely dark, as the warm orange lanterns that had once lined the walls had been shattered.

Vrutuuk stopped them in front of a set of double wooden doors, then opened them and led the group inside. "These are my personal quarters," he explained. "There's enough room for you all to stay in here with Alik and Rena. Your previous chambers had to be given to families."

"This is perfect," Mati said. "Thank you so much for all you've done."

Vrutuuk bowed and exited, closing the doors behind himself and Trantu. His quarters turned out to be a small suite of rooms, all decorated with the crest of the sykosee. The sitting room had a bedroom attached, containing a bed that was even larger than those in their old rooms, with a washroom off the other side.

Rena gave them both another hug. "I'm so happy you're back and safe."

"We're happy to be back and to have somewhere to return to," Fen said.

"You'll have to tell us everything," Alik said, sitting on the large couch against the wall.

"As will you," Fen replied, sitting next to him. "What happened after we ran?"

Alik sighed and Rena and Mati joined them on the couch as he began to speak. "It wasn't easy. The dralin nearly took the city, but luckily the sykosee are mighty trained warriors and already well-versed in fighting dralin. They hadn't brought a full force with them, which helped. Syradax managed to weasel his way out after you, while we were distracted fighting Ciksura and Lavinia, but he must've been too late." Alik paused.

"Alik and I," Rena picked up the story, "fought Lavinia and Ciksura until they tried to run after you two as well. After you escaped, Syradax returned, and they pulled their forces out of the city."

Alik cut back in to tell the rest of the story, "If I had to guess correctly, I'd say they had orders to capture you two at all costs. With that opportunity gone, they fled."

"But what happened with you and Trantu?" Rena asked.

Over the next half an hour, Fen and Mati rehashed the story of their journey to Lyserria, Mother Grint, the climb up Naina, and their interactions with Morana and Osirim.

Alik sat and stroked his chin in thought the entire time, drinking in every detail as they spoke. "You did well," he finally said. "I have never heard of Osirim ever bothering to use his gifts on humans before; he must have thought you a truly worthy beneficiary."

The next morning, the company prepared for their separate journeys. Alik and Rena helped prepare for the armies' move to the new camp, and Mati and Fen gathered their packs and met Trantu at the city door.

Mati climbed up on his back first, but her leg caught on her sword, and she nearly fell off. "Damn sword!"

Fen held in a snicker and helped steady her so she could get her footing. "It won't feel so foreign forever. You'll get used to it."

"I hope so," Mati grumbled as Fen easily swung his leg over Trantu's back, his sword moving like it was a natural part of him.

"Be safe," Rena called out to them.

"You too," Mati answered as Trantu flapped his massive wings and took them up into the sky.

The air was warm and dry, and the sky had no clouds. They could see for miles out over the desert and Mati's heart was lighter than it had been in a while. Alik and Rena were alive, Fen had been healed, they had the swords, and things were looking up. She'd almost completely forgotten about the curse. No one had even mentioned it since the Magnus, and that made Mati nervous.

"What're you thinking about?" Fen said in her ear, the question jarring her out of her thoughts.

"About the curse," she answered, almost sighing. Her chest felt heavy again at the reminder, ruining the few moments of lightness she'd had.

Fen sighed for her. "No use thinking about it. There's nothing we can do."

"Given how much as they wanted us to work together, I thought that might be the way we were supposed to break the curse," Mati exasperated. "But then why hasn't it broken?"

"How do you know it hasn't been?"

"Because Alik and Rena would know. Their powers are bound to it. I assume they wouldn't keep it from us if their powers had returned."

"Good point," Fen replied.

"Exactly," Mati huffed. "It's just bothering me. What use is this war if we can't break the curse and Guyt just comes back?"

Fen shrugged against her back. "I don't know. If we were doing something wrong, I'm sure Alik, at least, would let us know."

Mati smiled faintly. "I guess you're right."

Fen leaned over her shoulder and popped a kiss on her cheek. "So, stop worrying about it."

Mati turned her head and returned the gesture. She breathed deeply and tried to focus on the wind on her face. "I'll try very hard to not let it worry me."

"Good," Fen smiled. "You wanna know something?"

"What?" Mati asked, her brow furrowed.

"I don't really care about the curse," he answered. Mati shot him a shocked look. "I mean it. I'm just glad everything is working out so far. I'm afraid that if, or when, the curse is broken, that I'll be sent back to Jefy. Or just left to lead a normal, boring life."

"And I'm glad you're healed. You had me worried for a minute."

Fen feigned a shocked face. "Almost as if you... dare I say it... *care* about me?"

Mati rolled her eyes. "Of course I care about you. You think I don't?"

Fen smiled a cocky grin. "Can't resist me."

"Oh geez," Mati rolled her eyes again. "I'd push you off, if I thought it'd do any good. With my luck, though, it wouldn't even dent your hard head."

Fen pecked her on the cheek again. "I do love you, Mati. You know that, right?"

Mati's heart stopped beating for a split second. "Fen, please don't. Not now."

"You don't have to say it back, remember. I just want to make sure you know. I don't ever want you to wonder."

They went silent for the rest of the flight, but Mati was left reeling. She knew Fen had gotten more out of this relationship than she had. She had tried to forget that he'd said that to her before, and she couldn't fathom that someone truly loved her. She had always questioned whether her parents even loved her. She had just been a kid who was dropped off on their doorstep, after all. To think that Fen loved her was an unfathomable idea.

# Chapter 23

They spotted Hruguth through the rain. The sky had gotten dark what had felt like forever ago, to Fen. Trantu expressed his apologies for not being able to avoid the weather, since the city was directly in the middle of the storm. He was just glad it was only rain and not lightning.

They couldn't land fast enough. Fen had thought he hated flying in nice weather, but flying in the rain and wind was far worse. Rain poured down his face and had long ago soaked him clean through. He could feel Mati shivering with no way of warming her, but he held onto her tightly anyway.

Hruguth was a great stone fortress sitting against a backdrop of tall evergreens that, to Fen, looked dry and welcoming where it would usually have looked foreboding. Stone houses and a city surrounded the central fortress.

Trantu aimed for an open courtyard near what appeared to be the main entrance. He landed with a splash on the stone streets, and Mati and Fen slid off instantly.

"Where do we go?" Fen asked, shielding his face from the pouring rain. "This wasn't exactly how I planned on arriving."

Just then, the large iron door at the head of the courtyard opened behind them, and a lycan beckoned. "Fen? Mati?" the gruff voice questioned over the howling wind.

"Yes," Mati answered hurriedly.

The lycan opened the door wider and the three scurried in like rats. No one asked where the door led, or who the lycan was, choosing to wait with their questions after they had escaped the torrential downpour.

The room was dimly lit by a warm fire and a few wrought iron lanterns that hung on the walls. The room was sparsely decorated otherwise, and they noticed another closed wrought iron door on the other side of the room.

The lycan shut the front door behind them and shook off the rain that had splashed on him. "Stron, master of doors for King Gruthlan," he introduced himself. "Sad you came into our great city on such a miserable day." Fen and Mati nodded their thanks while Trantu bowed. "Come in by the fire and get yourselves warm. I'll inform the king that you're here."

Stron headed to the other iron door, drew out a ring of keys, unlocked the door, and disappeared through it. Then they heard the lock click on the other side, as Stron locked them in.

"Trusting folk, aren't they," Fen said acidly.

The three waited in silence, trying to warm themselves by the fire. Mati still shivered as water dripped off her, forming pools around her. Trantu was trying in vain to hide that he was also shivering as he stood in front of the fire. Fen seemed to be the only one whose teeth weren't chattering. Not that he wasn't cold, but he was able to hide it better so that the others could take the prime spots in front of the fire and not feel obligated to take turns.

He gritted his teeth against the cold and, to occupy his mind, wrung out the excess water that soaked his clothes.

They heard padding footsteps and nails clicking against stone, the sounds coming toward the door. The lock clicked again, and the door creaked open as Stron and Gruthlan appeared. Gruthlan was wearing a crown of silver atop his head, and a long silver robe flowed out behind him. He looked more like a king now than the warrior that they'd first met at the Magnus. Fen straightened up out of instinct and placed one hand on the hilt of his sword.

"Fen," Gruthlan greeted him. "It's good to see you. I was beginning to wonder if you were coming. I'd feared that the spirits had turned you down." He turned to Mati and Trantu. "Mati and... I'm afraid I don't have the honor of knowing your friend."

"I am Trantu," the great lizard answered. "It's an honor to meet you, Your Highness."

Gruthlan held out his arm to Trantu and the two embraced forearms. "An honor to meet you, Trantu," Gruthlan greeted him as Trantu nodded. Then he turned back to Fen. "I see you have a sword there. Is that *the* sword?"

"It is," Fen answered, unsheathing the sword and holding it up with authority for Gruthlan to inspect. "And we hope that you still plan to honor your word."

Gruthlan let out a guttural grunt. He reached out for the sword. Fen drew back and skillfully re-sheathed his weapon before Gruthlan could touch it. "I beg your pardon," Gruthlan said. "I meant no offense."

"None taken," Fen answered. "We have a blood oath to return them, and I'd rather keep it close than risk losing it. No offense meant to you, either."

"None taken." Gruthlan let his arm fall back to his side. "That's a wise decision. A warrior should always keep his weapon secure."

"I hate to press the issue, but we don't have much time." Fen walked over to the fire to warm his hands. "Will you keep your promise and join us?"

Gruthlan stood in thought for a moment, drawing out the little patience Fen had. "I'd be remiss if I went back on my word, when I made it in such revered company. We will be honored to join you."

Fen nodded in relief. "I was hoping you would say that."

"Well, now that our business is taken care of," Gruthlan said. "Will you be staying for the night?"

Fen looked at Trantu and Mati, who both nodded enthusiastically. "Yes, we'd be honored to stay. I think this storm has delayed our plans for our next trip."

"Good," Gruthlan said, turning and preceding them to the iron door.

Stron led the way and unlocked the door, holding it open for the three of them to follow Gruthlan. After they passed through, Stron shut and locked the door behind them once more. The air was cold and damp in the hall, now that they were away from the fire, and the hall was lit by iron lanterns hanging from the ceiling. Banners and tapestries filled with great crests and battle scenes lined the stone walls. The stench of wet dog made Fen's nose curl. It reminded him of being back at the farm.

Gruthlan led them up a circular set of stairs that wound several stories up into the fortress. A female lycan waited for them at the top. She was older than the others, as far as Fen could tell from the much lighter patches of gray fur around her neck and face. She looked surprisingly kind, even through the menacing wolf-like appearance.

Gruthlan stopped in front of her. "This is Prethon," he said, gesturing to the female. "She'll make sure you have rooms, clothes, and food for the night."

"Thank you," Fen said. "I'd like to have an audience with you after we've eaten, if you have a moment."

Gruthlan nodded. "Of course. I'll have a servant bring you to my study after you've refreshed yourselves. But for now, I must leave you in Prethon's care." He bowed and disappeared down the winding stairs.

"Ah," Prethon said, with a smooth but gruff voice. "Let's see what I can do, my lord and lady." She turned to one of the younger lycans scurrying by. "Hujan, take them to the baths and get them some clothes. I believe we have some put away for just such an occasion. They'll need to change into some warm clothes before the poor creatures catch their death. Very unlucky to not have a warm pelt to keep them warm in this weather." She paused only long enough to grab the arm of another female who was passing by. "Gert, go immediately and light fires in..." She looked to Fen and Mati. "Will you require one or two rooms?"

"One," Mati answered, before Fen could speak. His heart leapt a little at hearing that single word.

"Okay, my dears. Gert, light fires in two of the south hall rooms and make sure there's extra wood in this gentlemale's room." She gestured to Trantu. "I'm sure he'll need a little extra warmth. Go on, child! We don't have all night. Hujan, go ahead and take them away. I'll have dinner brought to your rooms in a burrowtuck."

Gert scurried off down the hall on all fours at top speed, while Hujan led them through more halls to a set of rooms that held deep, steaming pools of hot water. The room was so warm it felt like a sauna, and a small crew of lycan appeared wordlessly to set up privacy screens around each pool.

"You can each pick a pool and take some time to soak," Hujan instructed. "It'll help warm you. I'll be waiting in the hall when you're ready to be taken to your rooms."

Hujan disappeared and each of the party made their way to a pool. Mati eagerly skipped to the closest one, while Fen took the one next to it. The warmth of the room alone was soothing to his cold and aching bones. He took off his wet clothes and one of the servants took them as he stepped into the steaming water. He melted into the water with a luxurious smile and his body gave one last shiver, evicting the last of the cold from his bones.

"God," Mati sighed out from inside her partition. "This feels so good."

Trantu let out a long, satisfied hiss. "I thought my body was going to seize up with cold." He stretched his massive wings over the top of the screen before they disappeared back down into the water with a splash.

"Fuck," Fen said, fully satisfied. "This is amazing. I need one of these."

They lazed in the water for almost a quarter of an hour before they collectively decided it was time to get out. Servants brought them new, dry clothes and offered them to Fen and Mati. They didn't fit well, but they were better than the soaked ones they'd arrived in. Fen strapped his sword back around his waist, while Mati just carried hers.

Trantu replaced his leather straps and weapons, and led them out into the hall where Hujan waited.


As they followed Hujan, Fen leaned in close to Mati. "That's the first time you've acknowledged us being together—to anyone."

"I know," she answered quickly. She wasn't entirely sure why she'd answered in that way, but it had felt right.

"What happened to *low key*?"

Mati shrugged. "Honestly, I forgot. I got so used to being in one room in Duinan. I suppose I've just gotten more used to the idea. I'm pretty sure everyone knows, anyway. I was worried about what other leaders would think, but Gert asked and I just answered. I suppose we can't hide it forever."

Fen let out a low, warm laugh and brushed his knuckles against her fingers. "I'm glad."

"I still don't want any major PDA, though. Let's keep it professional in public."

Fen's face screwed up as he tried to figure out what Mati had said. "PDA?"

"Public displays of affection," Mati explained. "Keep them to a minimum. We're getting ready to go to war with a primordial spirit and we still have a job to do. I just want to keep things professional in public."

Fen gave her a crooked grin. "I'll try."

Hujan stopped them, and opened a wooden door. "This is the lord and lady's room."

"Thank you," Mati smiled and dipped into the room with Fen.

There was already a large fire roaring, and it made Mati want to curl up like a cat on the thick rug in front of it. The bed was large and covered with a thick and colorful woolen blanket. A low-hanging iron lantern cast a warm orange glow through the room. Mati crossed to the rug next to the fire and sat on it, placing her sword on the floor next to her. Fen pulled the blanket off the bed and joined her. He draped the blanket over her shoulders and tucked it around her neck before sitting next to her on the rug.

They sat in comfortable silence watching the dancing flames, listening to the storm that still raged outside. Mati's eyes started to droop closed, but a quiet knock on the door opened them.

"I'll get it," Fen said, smiling sweetly to her as he rose.

He opened the door and Gert came in with a tray laden with fruits and meat and ale. She placed it on a small table in the far corner of the room and scurried out again without a word.

"Thank you," Fen called, as he shut the door and turned back to Mati. "Talkative, isn't she?"

Mati stood, still holding the blanket around her, and sat down at the table. "Maybe she's shy. Or maybe they have rules about talking to guests. We don't know their customs."

Fen grunted in acknowledgment and joined her at the table. He grabbed a circular piece of meat from the stack and popped it in his mouth. "I'm eager to get going. We have to make a visit to Clíodha and hope she keeps her word."

"We need rest, though," Mati replied. "And it's no good arriving at the banshees' territory in the middle of the night. I don't think they'd take too kindly to that."

Fen grunted and stuffed a large piece of red fruit in his mouth.

"At least we have Gruthlan's allegiance," she continued. "Plus, there's this storm. I don't think Trantu would survive it, him being cold-blooded and all."

After they'd all eaten, Hujan led Fen, Mati, and Trantu into a large hall. Despite the lanterns and fires, the room still left them feeling cold. A constant stiff draft blew through the room as they crossed to a large iron throne where Gruthlan waited proudly. Lycan of all shapes and sizes lined the walls as well as the long rug leading to the throne.

"I apologize," Gruthlan began gruffly as they approached, "but I thought it would be better to meet you in the throne room instead of my study. My subjects were very curious to see whom it is they will be following into battle."

Fen and Mati bowed, while Trantu hung back. "We completely understand," Fen replied.

"Good. I was hoping you wouldn't mind. We can discuss our action here with my general—and brother."

A lycan with the same girth and commanding presence as Gruthlan stepped forward from the gathered masses. He wore a sword at his side and a long blue cape held on by a clasp at the shoulder. His face twisted with a hint of disgust at the sight of Fen and Mati, but dipped his head in greeting none-the-less. "Rugrul, General and Prince, at your service."

Fen and Mati both dipped their heads in return.

"Your services and those of your people are greatly appreciated," Mati said. "Fen and I are honored to be here with you." She turned to acknowledge Fen and she was met with the most tenderly surprised expression on his face.

They snapped their attention back to Rugrul and Fen mirrored her sentiment. "Yes; we will be honored to fight alongside such warriors."

"Ha," Rugrul burst out, his eyes narrowing in contempt. "*Fight*? Can you even hold a blade? You're not old enough by half to be making decisions that affect an entire world." He turned to face Gruthlan. "Brother, please listen to reason. This is a waste of our resources. Are we really going to follow these pups into battle?"

Mati could see the fire starting to rage deep in Fen's eyes.

Gruthlan narrowed his gaze at Rugrul. "We've already discussed this, brother. I gave my word to them at the Magnus. And they upheld their side of the bargain."

Fen cut quickly across the floor, unsheathing his sword with a sharp angry *swish* and leveling the tip at Rugrul's heart. The lycan snapped his head toward Fen with a snarl, moving so that the sword was no longer touching his chest.

"How dare you threaten me, *pup*," Rugrul growled. He bared his teeth, his ears laid back against his head.

Fen neither lowered the sword nor backed down, but instead moved so that the sword once again pointed at Rugrul. Fen met Rugrul's stare with an authority that was palpable. "You insulted me. And I will not be spoken to as if I'm a toadstool."

Mati stepped up to Fen's side, nudging the sword away from Rugrul. "It's not worth it, Fen."

Gruthlan stalked authoritatively down from his throne and met them on the carpet. He glared at Rugrul and stepped between the two, directly into his brother's line of sight. "I said that we are fighting, and that's the end of it. You'd be wise to remember your place, or I will remind you."

Rugrul continued to grimace, but stood down as Fen lowered his sword to his side. Mati moved to stand between the two as Gruthlan stepped away.

"Now that you two have gotten that out of your system," Gruthlan said, facing them again. "Let us retire to my study to finish this conversation."

Gruthlan led them into a considerably smaller room lined with wooden shelves, with an iron desk in the center. He took his seat at the desk and the others filled in the space around him. Fen walked around the desk and immediately took the only other chair in the room. Rugrul sneered down his snout, but was forced to stay on his feet as Fen made himself comfortable.

"Now, Fen," Gruthlan started. "When do you require the lycan army to report for battle?"

"Two days." Fen turned to Trantu. "Correct?"

Trantu nodded. "The madrigal should be arriving tomorrow to join the sykosee army that's already gathering."

Gruthlan gestured to Rugrul. "Have the armies ready to march by morning."

"We won't be able to gather the full force by then," Rugrul stated flatly.

"Have emissaries sent out to gather the rest of the able-bodied lycan, but I want at least the company based here in Hruguth to move out by the morning. You'll remain behind for two days and await the others."

Rugrul bowed stiffly, still eyeing Fen, and left the room.

"I apologize for my brother's rudeness. He's loyal and means well, but I'm afraid that he has our mother's short temper."

"No need to apologize," Mati said, before Fen could answer. "We understand that we're new and inexperienced. I'd be more surprised if we hadn't met any opposition. He's just trying to ensure his warriors' chances of survival."

"You're quite wise for ones so young," Gruthlan said with a smile before turning to Fen. "Will you be leaving tomorrow?"

"Yes. We still need to meet with the banshees, and hope we're not too late. How long will it take your army to reach the Meten Gate?"

Gruthlan pondered for a moment. "Two days at a hard run. Then Rugrul will be two or three days behind that."

"Hopefully, that'll be soon enough. We fear Guyt is already on the move, and Vrutuuk and Helian won't be able to hold off his legions alone. And in the event that Guyt doesn't wait to attack, I want to be sure we have options."

"Faelinth promised us two hundred, as well," Mati pointed out.

"True," Fen answered. "I'd forgotten about that. How many fighters can you provide?"

Gruthlan leaned back in his seat with a conceited curl of his lip. "Eight hundred."

"So many?"

"We train our males and females alike. There's no need to keep our females defenseless, since they are just as capable of fighting as the males."

Mati hunched her shoulders and folded her arms across her front, suddenly feeling very inept and useless. She'd not trained enough to even be able to swing her sword with any degree of accuracy, and there were warrior females out here in Vertrose. A guilty twinge crept through her gut and turned her stomach sour.

Fen stood, followed by Gruthlan, and he held out his arm to the king. Gruthlan accepted the gesture and they linked forearms.

"I think we'll retire to our room now. We'll leave at dawn, so I may not have a chance to see you again before battle. I'm honored to be fighting alongside you."

"It's a great honor to be going to battle with you," Gruthlan said, and he dipped his head.

# Chapter 24

Back in their room, Mati sulked on the bed, staring at the sword lying on the table.

"What's wrong?" Fen asked, pulling his shirt over his head.

"I can still barely lift that thing."

Fen laughed. "You've only practiced a few times, that's why."

"I know," she huffed. "Can you teach me now?"

His smile reached his eyes. "Come on."

Mati leapt up from the bed and drew the sword from its sheath. Fen stood behind her and helped her hold the blade. She could feel his chest pressed against her back and she struggled to concentrate. She willed her brain to focus.

"Good," Fen said, letting her go and moving around to stand beside her with his own sword in hand. "Follow my lead."

Mati copied Fen's movements, swinging and lunging into every position.

"Not bad," Fen praised. "It takes practice, but you've got the basics. Plus, it looks hot." He winked at her.

"No, no, no," she replied, still moving through the stances. "I won't be able to concentrate if you do that."

Fen smirked and wrapped his arms around her from behind, his hardened length pressed against her butt. She tried fruitlessly to continue practicing as he ran his hands up her legs and stomach, finally landing on her breasts. "The last time we were alone in a warm room, I was not in the position to give you all you deserved."

Mati kept practicing, with Fen glued to her backside and moving along with her. "If I hit you with this sword, don't blame me."

He grabbed the hilt with both hands and guided her through the stances one last time. Her breath caught in her chest. "Maybe," he breathed into her ear, "you should stop practicing. Core muscles are very important to build up first. Luckily, I know a few exercises to help."

She closed her eyes, trying to shut out the heat building between her legs. "I'm sure you do," she said.

Without warning, Fen seized her hips and spun her to face him. He grabbed her sword mid-spin, keeping it between them. Mati kept her hands on the hilt with Fen's now wrapped over them, guiding the blade to his throat.

She drew a sharp breath. "What are you doing?"

"Just go with it," he answered slowly. "And if you don't like it, we can stop. Trust me."

Mati let him lead her. She let him drag the sword carefully along his own neck and, when he let go, she saw the heat in his eyes. She curled one side of her mouth in a smile. "Are you ready?" she asked.

His brow furrowed ever so slightly. "Ready?"

Before he had a chance to ask anything more, Mati pushed her hand against his chest and walked him backward, sword at his throat, until his back hit the wall. She leaned in. "You think I don't know what you want?"

He grinned manically. "I didn't think so at first, but I'm reevaluating that assumption." He grabbed her ass and slowly squeezed her up to his chest. She deliberately steadied her hand to keep the blade precariously poised against his throat.

Mati pressed a gentle kiss to his throat as she ran the sword tip down his neck to his chest, stopping just shy of the V of muscles created by his hips. "You better hope I'm decent at controlling this blade."

Fen leaned into her, his breath tickling her eyelashes. "I trust you."

She kissed his cheek lovingly before dropping to her knees. She pushed the blade tip into his skin, drawing a tiny drop of blood that fell onto his waistband.

Fen drew in a deep breath and let out a soft moan. He deliberately wrapped his hand around the hilt, taking it from Mati's grasp, and tossed it on the bed with a dull *thud*.

He attacked Mati with a force she didn't see coming. He spun her around so that her back was now the one against the wall, and pressed his hard length against her with a long low growl. Mati caught her breath. Just as she did, Fen ripped her shirt down the front and tore it open, exposing her chest. Her nipples hardened at the chilly breeze as his mouth closed over one and he massaged the other with his fingers.

"Fuck," he let out, breathless.

Mati had no time to recover from that move before he yanked her pants down to her ankles, pressing himself against her again. Her core heated despite the chill of the stone against her back. She felt the wetness swelling between her thighs and compulsively reached out to touch Fen's chiseled chest. Her hands ran over his skin as Fen feverishly touched her whole body, kissing her neck.

Fen dropped his pants and grabbed Mati's hips, all in one fluid motion. He pulled her away from the wall and clasped her tightly to his chest. She could feel his dick sliding through her slickness as he walked her backwards across the room, stopping at the foot of the bed. Her legs hit the wood, making her fall back onto the edge of the bed, with his length directly in her line of sight.

Instinctively, she moved forward and took it in her mouth. A low growl ripped from Fen, a sound that Mati felt vibrate through her body as well as his. His fingers gripped her hair as she slid him in and out of her mouth, nipping the tip with her lips. He flinched but moaned and thrust himself back into Mati's mouth again and again.

With a growl, this one more of determination than pleasure, Fen pulled away from Mati and pulled her to her feet. He looked deep into her eyes before pulling her into a fervent kiss. She nipped his bottom lip as she pulled away, eliciting another guttural moan from him.

Mati wanted all of it, hadn't realized how much she needed it until now. All her instincts were on high alert; she knew him, as if this was the fortieth time they'd made love instead of the first. Their inability to form words emphasized the feral nature of this act so far. They were insatiable.

Fen spun her around and bent her over the edge of the bed. He paused, just long enough to let Mati catch a single breath. "Fuck," he exclaimed, which drew a giggle from Mati.

"It's your fault," she said sweetly. "But could you just fuck me now, please?"

Those words sent Fen over the edge. He thrust into Mati's core so forcefully that they both groaned. He sat inside her for a moment before pulling out almost completely, then thrusting again. Mati moaned in mingled pleasure and anticipation.

"Fuck me like you mean it," she managed to get out.

Mati felt every hard and fast thrust of his dick into her. With every hard stop into her, he sent her closer to the release she crazed. Fen slapped her ass, and the sting sent chills through her.

"Fuck," he said again. "You feel amazing. Why did we wait so long?"

"Because we're constantly surrounded by people," she answered, moving her hand between her legs. She moaned louder as she grazed her fingers over the sensitive bundle of nerves there.

Fen grabbed her hips and pulled her toward himself as he thrust. Mati could feel herself coming close to release.

"I'm going to come," she warned Fen. And with one more sweep of her fingers over the nerves, she exploded like she never had before. She let out an animalistic cry, one that sounded more like Fen had murdered her.

"Fuck," Fen exclaimed once more, as she twitched and tightened around him.

Mati felt him stiffen and let out a loud groan of his own, before he collapsed across her back with an exhausted sigh. They both lay limp on the bed for a while, breathing heavily, but happy. Fen's smile spread clear across his face, and Mati still felt that satisfying pulse below.

Fen wrapped his arms around her, drew her close to his chest, and they fell blissfully asleep.

Mist covered the ground of Hruguth as Fen and Mati walked across the courtyard to prepare for their journey to Terron Forest. Trantu was already waiting for them.

"How do people live in this cold, wet environment?" he asked, dropping onto all fours for Mati and Fen to mount.

"They *are* covered in fur," Mati answered, while Fen pushed her up onto Trantu's back.

"Give me the dry, warm desert any day," he replied back.

Fen heaved himself up behind Mati and got settled. "At least it's not raining."

"That is a good point," Trantu agreed. "I don't think I've ever been so miserable as that."

The flight to Terron ended up being far more enjoyable than the previous day's flight had been. The weather began to warm as they flew over the Clerin River, and into the marshlands below.

Trantu set them down for a quick rest, in a lush plain of blue grass beside a large lake that had formed in the lowlands just south of the Terron.

"How much further?" Fen asked, stretching his legs.

"See those mountains?" Trantu pointed and Fen nodded. "Those are the Rhist Mountains, and the Terron lies at their feet. I'd say we have another hour of flying time."

After a few more minutes of rest, Trantu urged them to get going.

"If I never fly again, I'll be happy," Fen said, wrinkling his nose as he climbed back up on top of Trantu's scaled back.

They landed next to the scattered beginnings of a forest on the plain. The thick forest ahead didn't welcome them like a forest typically did. It left them on pins and needles when they entered, a prickly tingle rolling up their spines.

"We're here," Trantu announced, with no excitement in his voice. "I'll let you go in alone. I'm in no hurry to enter the Terron."

His tone didn't ease Fen's nerves.

Fen laid a hand on the hilt of his sword. "How do we find them?"

"They'll find you," Trantu answered, with a less-than-excited look on his face.

"Great," Mati replied sarcastically.

"I'll wait for you here. I'd like to be able to head back to Duinan tonight, if possible."

Fen nodded. He took hold of Mati's hand as they walked with trepidation into the heart of the Terron.

The forest was at least alive with birds and animals, which helped ease the eerie sensation they had of being watched. The sun shone as golden rays through the branches, casting long shadows across the forest floor. Fen swore he saw something moving through those shadows and squeezed Mati's hand. She squeezed back as she placed her footsteps with more care.

An hour passed quickly, with their nervous glances darting from left to right and the oppressive feeling of unease becoming almost too much to bear. A familiar voice made them stop in their tracks.

"You are either very brave or very stupid to come into the Terron," Clìodha's voice sounded from all around them.

Fen squeezed the hilt of his blade where his hand had been resting since they had parted company with Trantu. "We came to hold you to your oath to join the rest of Vertrose in the fight against Guyt."

Clìodha floated out of the trees toward them, joined by a company of veiled women wearing almost transparent, floor-length shifts. Their clothes floated and waved around their forms as though they were under water. Shadows seemed to creep around their feet and around the trees from where they had stepped. It gave Fen an uneasy feeling in the pit of his stomach.

"Where is the weapon you promised?" Clìodha demanded.

"Here," Fen said, and drew the green and crystal blade from the sheath, holding it up for all the banshees to see.

"How do we know that's a real spirit sword?" one asked, gliding forward.

"Settle, Luciel," Clíodha said, with a calm that seemed forced. "Hold out your hand." Luciel did as she was commanded, and held out the palm of her hand to Fen. "Cut her."

Fen looked at Mati for direction. "Do it," Mati answered. "It's the only way they'll believe us."

Fen took hold of the banshee's cool, pale hand and placed the sword against her finger. He pulled back, grazing the edge across her skin. A cut formed, and a trickle of silvery liquid dripped out. Luciel's surprised eyes pierced Fen's, and she drew back her hand.

"It works," she announced, stunned. "It's not healing."

Fen sheathed the sword and looked at Clíodha with authority. He scanned the rest of the women. "So, now that you're satisfied that we aren't lying to you, will you join us as your delegate promised?"

"What is your answer, banshees?" Clíodha addressed them all.

A high-pitched shriek went through the crowd, a sound that had Mati covering her ears. A chill ran through Fen's entire body as the eerie sound erupted and then died all at once.

"They agree," Clíodha interpreted. "We will fight with you against Guyt."

"Thank you," Mati replied, with a bowed head. "We don't have any time to lose. Can you be ready to leave for the camp today?"

Clíodha's patronizing laugh stilled them and made Fen's blood boil. "We will leave now."

And without more explanation or warning, the banshees vanished back into the shadows of the trees. Fen and Mati had no idea where they'd gone, but the pervasive feeling of being watched had gone with them.

"I guess we rejoin Trantu," Mati said with an annoyed sigh.

"Guess so," Fen replied, turning to leave.

Then they stopped, blinded by a great light. Fen shielded his eyes with one hand and Mati turned her face away. Had the banshees returned?

"Apologies," another familiar voice said.

Mati smiled at the sound and whipped back toward it. "Asterion!"

Asterion and Dursten stood before them. "Yes," they answered her. "We have returned."

Mati pushed forward and hugged them. "What happened to you both?"

"Ah," Dursten answered. "The Illustrus called us back—rather forceful-ly—to discuss our role in the universe."

"And you're okay?" Fen asked.

Yes," Dursten continued. "It took us much longer than we expected to get back here, however. It has been expressly forbidden. We're here now, though only for a moment."

"But Asterion came back to see Morimas," Mati said.

Asterion gave her a wry smile. "I was not supposed to be here then, either."

Mati skewed her face in disgust. "Will they hurt you if they find out you're here with us?"

"We'll be okay," Asterion answered with a kind smile. "We didn't mean to scare you. But we thought you wouldn't mind."

"Not at all," Fen said. "A lot has happened since you've been away."

"We know," Asterion answered. "We have already met with Alik and Rena. They informed us of everything."

Dursten cut in. "We're glad you have the swords. I can't lie, I had little hope that Morana and Osirim would create them for you."

Fen patted the hilt at his side in confirmation. "You said you were only here for a moment?"

"Yes," Dursten said. "We have another errand that we must attend to, but we will return to you once it's complete."

"Wait!" Mati stopped them. "Could you beam us back to Alik and Rena? It'd be a lot faster that way, and I'm sure Trantu would welcome not having to cart our asses around Vertrose like a chauffeur."

"I don't know what a *chauffeur* is," Fen added, "but I think I get the meaning, and she's right. I'd like to get back to the camp as soon as possible."

The stars looked at one another for a moment before Dursten spoke, smiling. "I think we can do that."

The party set out to meet Trantu. The mood of the forest had lightened, no longer feeling so wary. There were no darting shadows or ominous feelings, just the natural sounds of a peaceful forest.

"Fen just doesn't want to fly," Mati teased. "He's afraid of heights."

"I'm not scared," Fen retorted. "It's quicker and more efficient to have them beam us."

Mati laughed. "You're still scared."

Fen huffed at her and promptly changed the subject. "I'm glad to see you both. You caused quite the scene when you disappeared. I was afraid that Gruthlan and Clíodha weren't going to join us, after that."

"Well, it wasn't exactly how we planned to go," Asterion said. "We hear you've handled yourselves very well since then, mind you. Alik was very pleased."

Mati smiled shyly. "I haven't done much. Fen is the real hero."

"Not true," Fen huffed. "Mati's helped as much as I have. She's got a good touch for cooling down a situation. That's far more helpful when you're dealing with a bunch of hotheaded leaders. All I'm good at is swinging that damn sword around, and almost getting myself killed."

Mati's cheeks reddened and Asterion turned to her. "You make a good team. We knew you would pull through."

# Chapter 25

After reuniting with Trantu at the edge of the Terron, the stars beamed them all to the rebellion camp, a location that lay a safe distance between Duinan and the Meten Gate in a vast open plain mottled with sand and grass.

Mati was surprised that she only heaved up the contents of her stomach once before her body settled. Fen, on the other hand, still hadn't quite gotten used to traveling by starlight and was still doubled over with nausea. Mati laid her hand on his back and offered him the water skin, which he took gratefully.

She felt the sorriest for Trantu, who had thrown up several times and was currently laid out on the grass at their feet.

Fen wiped his lips and spit one more time before taking a swish of water to rinse his mouth. "Thank you," he said, handing the waterskin back to Mati.

"We really must be going," Dursten said. "We'll return as swiftly as our errand allows." And with those parting words, the stars burst into light and were gone once more.

After Trantu had composed himself, Trantu, Mati, and Fen started for the camp that lay a short walk away.

There were tents scattered all across the landscape, each one's origin obvious thanks to the different styles of the kingdoms that had erected them. The group headed for an enormous gray tent standing in the center of all the others. A flag or banner from each of the corresponding armies represented there had been erected by the door.

Alik came out of the tent as they approached. "You're back early! We weren't expecting you until late tonight or tomorrow morning."

"We ran into Asterion and Dursten," Mati explained.

"I thought I saw a bright light. Come in. We've got a lot to discuss."

Alik ushered them inside the tent where they were immediately greeted by Vrutuuk's imposing presence. They convened at a large wooden table like those in Duinan's eating hall, and when the others in the tent saw they were back, the table filled quickly. Clíodha was there, already flanked by Luciel and another banshee Mati didn't know. Vrutuuk sat down and was soon joined by Trantu, who still looked a little queasy.

"Good to see you again," Helian said to them as he and two other madrigal took spots at the table.

Faelinth, situated between a faun and an elf, also joined them at the table. He dipped his head to them. "It's an honor to be in your company again."

Fen and Mati nodded their heads in thanks as they too made spots for themselves at the table. Mati looked around with awe. She'd seen most of these people assembled before, at the Magnus Concilium, but this was different. At the Magnus, none had worn royal raiment or crowns, or any other indication of their status. They had met as equals. Here, though, they were representing the strength of their peoples. All now wore armor, crowns, and mantles that befitted their statuses as leaders, and all carried weapons at their sides, as if ready to go to battle at a moment's notice.

She sat awkwardly, the sword she wore banging off the seat and table as she lowered herself into the chair. In direct contrast, Fen sat gracefully, grasping his sword and moving it away as if it were an extension of his own body.

"You'll all be wondering about our visit to Hruguth," Fen started. "And you'll be pleased to hear that Gruthlan has promised his support."

"When will his forces be here?" Vrutuuk asked anxiously.

"Two days' time," Mati answered, determined to not be a hindrance in this meeting. "He's leaving immediately with the lycan army stationed in Hruguth, and has sent his general to gather the rest of the able-bodied. He promised eight hundred to the battle."

"We may not have that kind of time," Helian said. "Our scouts say that Syradax has been on the move with the dralin army. And only they know how many nuwu Ciksura is able to conjure."

"Well," Fen answered matter-of-factly, "we don't have much of a choice. They don't have a faster way to travel. Gruthlan made it clear that they would move as quickly as possible to uphold his oath to us."

"He'll likely turn back," Vrutuuk huffed. "Did you actually see his army leaving?"

"No," Mati retorted. "But we don't have any reason to doubt him. He was quite adamant that he would honor his commitment."

Vrutuuk hissed. "I mean no disrespect to your judgment, but the lycan are notorious for being very deceptive and selfish creatures."

Fen cut in, rejecting Vrutuuk's insinuation. "Maybe they have been in the past, but I will personally vouch for Gruthlan's sincerity. He and his army will be here. And we'll have to hope that Guyt holds off 'til they arrive."

"A few hundred more won't make a difference," Clíodha interrupted. "Guyt's armies are too vast. We don't stand a chance."

Fen leaped to his feet and smashed his fists against the table. The dignitaries' eyes went wide in offense. "Why are any of you here, then? Don't you have any trust in each other or in this rebellion?"

Mati could feel how upset he had become, but this time she didn't stop him from being a bit reckless. Hopefully a bit of his reckless nature was going to be what they needed to get their act together.

The leaders looked around at each other, bewildered and shocked, before Helian answered. "Fen, the two of you and the swords you carry are our only hope. Becca and I have faith in you."

Mati and Fen froze in unison. They traded looks and knew then what they needed to do. Mati rose to her feet beside Fen, no longer feeling like a hindrance.

"You're not here because of us," she began. "You're all here because you care enough about each other to stand up against Guyt, to reclaim your homes. We just showed you that."

"We have to work together," Fen added. "If not, then Guyt has already won, and you might as well all go home and wait for the inevitable. We need all of you to come together, to work together, or not even these swords will be of any use."

"You must have faith in each other." Mati said. "You can't go into a battle if you don't trust your allies any more than you trust your enemies. So please, can we stop bashing each other and work together to come up with a strategy?"

The room fell uncomfortably silent as Mati and Fen sat back down. The shock of being scolded was written on all their faces.

"I apologize," Vrutuuk said after taking a moment to compose himself. "They're right. We should be working together."

The room collectively nodded in agreement and Fen stood again, but before he could utter another word, a panting sykosee warrior burst into the room.

"Guyt's armies are moving down the Clerin," the warrior puffed. "At least seven ships that we saw."

"Shit," Vrutuuk cursed. "He's trying to encircle us."

"So, we don't let him," Becca replied forcefully. "Can we spare any soldiers to be stationed at the Clerin? We can face them head-on before they have a chance to come inland."

"I can send a portion of my forces," Vrutuuk offered. "We'll take our best archers and set their ships ablaze. That should at least keep them from coming ashore."

"That's the plan for now, then," Fen said. "I apologize for my ignorance, but do we have anything else that could sink the ships outright?"

Faelinth sat up straighter in his seat. "We brought six ballistae with us. We could use those to fire flaming, oil-dipped arrows at the ships. That will keep them too busy putting out the fires to launch an offensive."

"Perfect," Fen exclaimed. "How soon can you have them moving?"

Trantu and the elf beside Faelinth immediately raced out of the tent.

"My soldiers can be ready to fly in fifteen minutes," Vrutuuk replied.

"And I can have the ballista and a few soldiers ready in the same amount of time. It'll take the ballista longer to get there, however. You'll have to have your soldiers hold off the ships on their own for a while."

"They'll hold," Vrutuuk said.

Fen turned to Alik, who was standing off to the side by the tent flap. "Would you take control of the battle strategy from here? I'm afraid I'm not as skilled at battle plans as you."

Alik stepped forward out of the shadow he had been immersed in and bowed his head. "I'd be honored."

"Thank you." Fen scooted closer to Mati to make room for Alik to join them.

Alik moved over to the table to stand next to Fen and Mati. "Can I get a rough soldier count from all of you as soon as possible?" The table of leaders indicated they would. "Clíodha, I'd like your banshees on the front lines. Their powers will be more effective there." He turned to Faelinth next. "I want all your soldiers to head to the Clerin with the ballistae."

Faelinth nodded. "I'll have them ready and waiting for orders tomorrow morning."

"Good," Alik went on. "Vrutuuk, I want any soldiers you have left to be behind the front line. I'll need them armed with javelins and heavy belly armor; I want them flying overhead."

Vrutuuk gave a quick nod.

Alik turned now to his right. "Helian, I want your archers behind a line of javelins. Let's get Guyt pinned without anywhere to go."

"Consider it done," Helian replied.

"Be ready tomorrow morning. I want everyone up and fed before dawn every morning, ready to go. Weak and hungry soldiers won't do us any good. We need a watch on duty at all times; decide amongst yourselves to establish how to establish and rotate that. I won't have Guyt surprising us." He paused to take a deep breath. "And it is my honor to serve Vertrose—and all of you—once again."

Once the meeting was over, the leaders all stood, and those who didn't leave the tent immediately to attend to Alik's requests stayed only to discuss the watch schedule.

"Alik," Fen asked. "Can you give me and Mati a tour of the camp? I'd like to know all we have going on here."

"Not me," Mati cut in quietly. "I'm just here for moral support."

"Okay, fine," Fen said. "Just me, then."

"Of course," Alik answered with a dip of his head. "That's a good idea."

The others stood respectfully as the two left the tent. Fen felt anxiety creep through his bones. What would he have done without Alik? He owed a lot to him. "Thank you," Fen almost whispered.

"You're welcome," Alik replied, with a slight curl to his lip. "You're a very wise young man. Tanophis would be proud to know you're leading us."

That was a name Fen hadn't heard or thought about in a long time. "Tanophis?"

Alik turned them down a row of tents that looked suspiciously like the madrigals' pastons. "Yes. He and I were very close. And I think he'd like knowing that you and I are here now, trying to save Vertrose."

Fen sighed. "You really can't tell me what happened to them? Him and Paxis, I mean."

"We don't know what life, if any, they led after being cursed. But I do think they'd be pleased with how things are turning out. You remind me a lot of him." Alik clapped Fen on the shoulder.

A light sparked in Fen's head at that, sending his mind scattering in a flurry of thought. "Is that why Mati and I were chosen? Because we're Tanophis and Paxis reincarnated, or something?"

Alik stopped dead in his tracks and just stared at Fen, like he was waiting for something.

"Are you okay?" Fen finally asked. "Is that the curse?"

The surprise faded out in Alik's eyes, and it was like Fen was seeing the man's hopes dashed to pieces right in front of him. "No. I thought maybe you were on to something, but I guess I was wrong. Come; we have a lot of ground to cover."

Fen kept thinking about it, though, as he followed Alik. Whatever he had said, had left Alik reeling. He made a mental note to ask Mati about it later.

Alik walked Fen through the entire camp, visiting all the different encampments. The camp was far larger than Fen had anticipated, but Alik made sure he saw everything. They had no major artillery besides the six ballistae Faelinth had brought, but their arsenal included the javelins and swords of the sykosee, the bows and staves of the madrigal—who would double as armed cavalry—and the various melee weapons of Faelinth's soldiers.

"Alik," Fen asked as respectfully as he could, "what exactly can the banshee do? Do they have weapons, or magical powers?"

"The banshee are the harbingers of death," Alik explained in hushed tones. "They can make you see your death in your head before it happens, which can drive the fiercest of warriors mad. And if that doesn't do it, then their wailing cries are a constant reminder in your head of the doom that awaits you."

Fen shivered. "Put them down for mental warfare."

"They're not ones to anger." Alik turned the corner of a tent and they saw Faelinth and his soldiers preparing the ballistae.

The pair strode over to them, joining the group. Faelinth clapped Fen on the shoulder when he came close. "You've grown quite a bit since our last meeting."

"Did I have a choice?" Fen countered. "Thank you, though. I'm glad I'm not a complete disappointment."

"Far from it," Faelinth replied, smiling before striding off again to help move a ballista into position.

That night, after Mati and Fen had eaten dinner with all the leaders in the mess tent, Rena led them to the tent that would be theirs, just across the path.

"Here you are," Rena said, folding back the tent flap. "The sleeping quarters are through there." She pointed through to the room to another set of flaps.

"Thank you, Rena," Mati said, giving Rena a warm embrace. "For everything. I could use some of your tea, if you have any."

Rena beamed. "You're more than welcome. I'll go brew some right now and have it sent over to you."

Rena left them alone, letting the flap drop closed.

Fen and Mati exchanged relieved looks at being left alone. The antechamber was softly lit by a single hanging brass lantern, and the smaller room beyond the thick curtains was piled with blankets and pillows.

Fen's eyes were drawn to two sets of armor that had been set up against the wall. He walked over and looked at them in awe, watching the flames from the light above bounce off of the metal.

"I guess these are for us." His voice almost cracked as he reached out to run his fingers along the tooled leather and gold gilding. He'd obviously never worn armor before, but the gleaming metal and leather in front of him felt oddly familiar—like greeting an old friend after a long time apart. "It's all so real now."

"I know," Mati said quietly, taking in the sight. "I spent the day with Rena walking around the camp and I never had time to really think, until now. I'm scared, Fen."

"Me too," Fen admitted, fiddling idly with the leather straps on the breastplate. "It just hit me that I have no idea what I'm doing. I've never been in a battle."

Mati laid one hand on the bracers of her armor and the other on Fen's arm. "You'll do fine. You're a natural at this. Even Alik says so."

"Oh," Fen exclaimed, suddenly remembering what he'd meant to tell her. "I need to tell you something. I had a weird conversation with Alik earlier today."

"How so?" Mati asked, as she walked toward the adjacent room.

Fen followed Mati into the smaller bedchamber. "I asked Alik if we were Tanophis and Paxis reincarnated, and he got the strangest look on his face."

"What do you mean?"

Fen undressed and laid his clothes on a small wooden bench next to their plush pallet as he recounted the scene and Alik's behavior.

Mati undressed as well, climbing under the blankets. "That's odd. That can't be the thing that breaks the curse, though, because nothing happened when you said it. Right?"

"It was the way he looked at me," Fen mused climbing under the blanket next to her. "It just felt strange. Like he was expecting something to happen."

"Maybe you got close to what the curse is." Mati burrowed down under the covers and sidled up next to Fen. "Seems strange that he would act like that over nothing."

Fen wrapped his arm around Mati's shoulders and tucked her in as close as he could, kissing the top of her head. "It's going to bug me until I figure it out. I thought about asking him, but he was so startled that it caught me off guard."

Mati placed her open palm on Fen's chest. "Well, let's think about that, then. What do we know so far about them, or the curse?"

Fen sighed, placing his hand over Mati's. "We know that no one knows what happened to them after Guyt cursed them."

"Because they disappeared," Mati finished his sentence.

"What if Guyt has them locked up somewhere?" Fen theorized out loud.

Mati scrunched her nose up. "Maybe. That would explain why no one's seen them since. As far as we know, Guyt is the only one who knows what actually happened."

"Fuck," Fen cursed. "Why is this so stupid?"

"I think that was kinda the point."

Fen let go of Mati's hand to run his fingers through his hair. "I just want this to be over."

Mati leaned in and kissed his chest lovingly. "It'll all work out."

"I just don't get why Alik and the stars were so obsessed about us working together. They made it seem like a big deal—like if we didn't hate each other, the curse would be lifted. I really thought that would fix all this."

"I hate seeing you like this. We'll figure it out. Maybe not tonight or tomorrow, but one day. I think you need to focus on this battle instead. Is there anything I can do to help?"

Fen closed his eyes and breathed deeply. When he opened them, his focus landed on Mati's face, her bright, troubled eyes pleading with him. "You don't need to do anything. You're doing everything you can to help already."

"I don't do shit," she grumbled. "All I do is sit around and get in the way. I can't fight. I can't lead the way you do. I can't do anything useful."

"Self-deprecation isn't a good look on you," Fen frowned. "You're more useful than you know."

"Tell me one way I'm not a total sack of stones."

"You know how to calm a situation before it gets out of hand. And you give me confidence in myself. And you care so deeply for everyone, which rubs off on others. You keep me focused and on point—"

"Okay, okay," Mati cut him off. "But none of that is useful in the way *you're* useful."

Fen let out a barking laugh. "That's a good thing. If you haven't noticed, I haven't been getting into so many scrapes since you started looking after me. So, you've quite literally kept me alive. I think that's pretty useful."

Mati lightly punched his shoulder. "You know what I mean."

Fen squeezed her tight. "Mati, we're opposites for a reason. You're my other half. I may have you beat in the physicality department, but you are far superior when it comes to reading a room and dealing with people. I'm terrible at that. Stop comparing yourself to me."

Mati rolled her eyes. "I still wish I was more physically helpful."

A grin spread wide across Fen's face. "Trust me, you're very helpful physically. To me, at least." He nodded downward and Mati's gaze followed.

Fen had hardened while they lay pressed against one another, and the evidence could be clearly seen saluting Mati from under the blanket.

Mati burst out laughing. "Looks like making that happen is my one and only talent. I suppose I'll have to settle for that." She leaned over and planted a kiss on his chest, then another on his lips.

Fen rolled to his side and pulled her with him. "Still can't resist me…"

Mati rolled her eyes and smiled softly. "So cocky."

Fen looked down again and wiggled himself against Mati. "Yes. Yes, I am."

Mati burst out laughing again. "You need help."

Fen squeezed her tightly and sent a flurry of quick kisses down on her cheek. Mati laughed and returned his embrace. He loved the sound of her laugh. He gave her one more big squeeze and kiss on her forehead. "We'd better get some sleep."

"No extracurricular activity?"

Fen considered it, then sigh. "No. I think I'm going to be the bigger man and pass tonight. I'm actually exhausted."

"Me too," Mati agreed. She yawned and nestled in close to Fen's chest, closing her eyes. Having her there felt like a missing puzzle piece had been set back into its place to complete his life.

# Chapter 26

Fen and Mati woke before dawn the next morning, roused by the sounds of the camp coming alive for a new day. They heard the bustle of people scurrying from one place to another through dewy grass, and the clang of armor and weapons being polished and sharpened.

Fen reached over and pulled Mati close.

"This all seems like a dream," Mati said.

"I know," he answered. "I still can't believe we're here." He tucked her to his chest and buried his face in her neck. She scooted back, settling her butt against him. "That's just mean," he said.

Mati chuckled. "You started it," she teased.

Fen moaned and pressed himself closer to her, nuzzling further into her neck when a voice from outside the tent startled them both.

"My lord and lady," the voice called. "Your presence is requested."

Fen let out an irritated groan. "Thank you. We'll be there in a moment."

"Very good, my lord."

"No rest for the wicked," Mati said, and started to pull herself out of bed.

"Not yet," Fen protested, pulling her back against him.

"We have to go. We're needed, and I assume it's important."

"It can't possibly be more important than this." Fen kissed her neck and snaked his arms around her, like a snake constricting its prey.

Mati laughed, attempting in vain to wiggle free. "Come on. Get up."

Fen groaned again in protest, this time longer and far whinier. "Fine, but remember where we left off."

"Deal," Mati said, finally fighting herself free and sliding out from under the blanket.

A male faun outfitted in full armor waited for them in the antechamber of their tent. Fen was still yawning as he led them across the grass to the mess tent where all the leaders were already assembled and waiting.

"I'm sorry," Mati apologized as she sat down. "We didn't know we were meeting this morning."

Fen sat in the same spot next to Mati that he'd claimed yesterday. "Yes, we would've been up and ready if we'd known. Where's Faelinth?"

Alik stood as Fen sat. "This is an impromptu meeting. Faelinth is preparing to leave with his soldiers and the six ballista's, but what we have to discuss is too important to wait." He gave his attention to the rest of the group. "Our scouts returned this morning with reports that Guyt's armies are moving away from the Meten Gate. It seems they're keenly aware of where we are, and are coming out to meet us."

"It was only a matter of time," Clíodha said. "We weren't going to stay hidden for long."

"No," Alik continued. "But it does mean that we have to be extra careful. If history is any indication, then we know he favors the element of surprise. So, keep your watches on guard and I want numbers doubled."

"Gruthlan should be here today, assuming they didn't meet with any setbacks," Fen added. "Hopefully Guyt doesn't attack until we have the lycan army with us."

"True," Vrutuuk said, "Hope is all we have, it seems."

"None of that, Vrutuuk," Mati chided gently. "We need positivity and your expertise. Your warriors are the only ones here with recent experience fighting Syradax and the dralin. Alik and Fen will need your help to bring the others up to speed."

"Apologies, my lady," the great winged lizard said, bowing his head. "But as you said, my people have been the only ones fighting Guyt recently. I can't help but feel a little sting at that."

Mati reached over and placed a hand on his shoulder. "I understand that, and I can assure you that your people's sacrifices won't be in vain."

Vrutuuk nodded and let Alik continue his briefing. "She's right, Vrutuuk. I'll need to ask you for all you know about Syradax's fighting style. It'll help me anticipate his moves."

"I'd be honored," Vrutuuk answered.

Clíodha rose to her feet, gown and hair swishing about. "I must go. My banshees and I are holding a ritual this morning. I trust Alik will inform us of any major changes to the plans."

"I will," Alik replied. "I think that's all I had this morning, anyway. I'll call you all back if I have any other news."

The meeting adjourned as the leaders all dispersed, and Mati made a bee-line for Rena. After the strange interaction Fen had with Alik yesterday, Rena might be the only person able to shed some light on it.

"Rena," she called out, and Rena stopped to wait for her.

Mati dashed over, her sword clunking awkwardly on the belt. "I have to ask—or tell you, rather—about something that happened yesterday between Alik and Fen."

Rena's eyebrows raised. "I think I know what you're going to say."

They walked together out of the tent. "Alik told you, then?"

They crossed the camp toward Rena's tent, just out of earshot of anyone around. "Yes. You have questions, I presume?"

"Yes," Mati answered, hoping that Rena would be honest with her. "Why was Alik acting so strangely?"

"I think this conversation calls for tea. I already put some water on."

Mati was silent as they walked over.

"Sit," Rena motioned to a seat in her tent, and they settled in with their cups. "Now, what is it that you want to know?"

"I want to know why Alik acted like that, after Fen suggested we had been reincarnated."

"Ah," Rena breathed out, then as she took another sip of tea. "The nature of Guyt's curse isn't exactly clear to us, as you know. We aren't sure what the key will be to unlock it. So Alik thought maybe that—the two of you coming to that conclusion—could be the key."

Mati almost spilled her tea with surprise and quickly set the cup on the low table before she dropped it. "So, Fen was right?"

"Not exactly."

Mati was getting confused and irritated by Rena's brief answers. "If Fen wasn't even right, why did Alik react all weirdly?"

"Love, I wish I had all the answers, but I don't. The curse will break when it breaks. We told you to stop fretting about it, and this is why." She took another sip of tea.

Mati grunted. "But Fen and I can't move on until this fucking thing is broken and over."

The only indication that Rena had been caught off-guard by Mati's outburst was a slight widening of her eyes. "My dear, do you love Fen?"

It was Mati's turn to be surprised at such a blatant question. Every atom in her body wanted to throw up a defensive wall against this perceived attack. She wanted nothing more than to flee from Rena's question. She sat back, feigning calm. "No. Of course not. We're just... we're just... well, I don't know what we are. But in *love* is not it, I assure you."

Rena seemed visibly anxious as she pushed the issue. "But you are together?"

"Yes," Mati answered calmly. "I suppose so. We share a tent now, so I certainly hope that means we're together."

Rena set her tea down, looking flabbergasted. "But..."

Mati cocked one eyebrow. "Now *you're* acting like a nutcase."

"I'm not sure what a *nutcase* is, love, but if it means stunned, then yes."

"I don't understand," Mati said, now very confused by the whole scenario. "There's no way you didn't know. You practically sanctioned it that day you told me about your lost lover."

Rena picked her tea back up and sipped it, staring off into space. "Do you love him, Mati?" Rena asked eventually, this time with a stern bite to her words.

Mati was taken aback. "I... uh... I don't know. We haven't had any time to just be with one another. I think it might just be a mutual togetherness from being in each other's company so much."

Rena looked deep into Mati's face, her eyes narrowing as she searched for something. "You don't believe that, do you?"

"I don't see why it matters," Mati huffed. "This is exactly why I wanted to keep it a secret. I didn't want to answer silly questions, or have people stare. I just wanted to focus on breaking the curse. I don't know if I love Fen. I like him, sure. He's attractive and nice and funny. But... I don't want to talk about this. I just wanted everything to be calm and understated so we didn't cause a spectacle during a time when we, and everyone else, should be focusing on a battle."

Rena laid a hand on Mati's arm. "I'm sorry. Truly, I am. I didn't mean to pry. I know how much you value order, and I will respect that."

Mati took a deep, calming breath and took a gulp of tea, forgetting how hot it was. She swallowed hard just to get the burning to stop, and ended up with a sore throat.

Rena sat back in her chair, giving Mati space. "Calm down, love. I truly didn't mean anything by it. I was surprised, is all. We've suspected something was going on for a while, but we didn't want to pry. I won't bring it up again."

"Thank you," Mati said genuinely, setting the teacup on the table and rising to her feet. "I need to go. Thank you for the tea."

She felt very vulnerable after the talk and she hurried to leave, but Rena caught her arm. "Mati, love, please stop focusing on the curse. It will work itself out. I'm sure of it now."


Mati spent the remainder of the morning with Alik and Fen, patrolling the camp and making sure everything was in order.

"I want to see the battlefield," Fen said to Alik.

"Ah, yes," Alik replied. "I was going to show you that after lunch, but we can do it now."

They walked out into a field just over a hillock from camp. It was strange to Mati that Alik was so calm and nonchalant about war. She knew he was the god of war, but it still felt eerie and unsettling to her that someone could feel so much ease with that kind of mayhem.

Alik pointed to a spot on the horizon. "I'm hoping they'll come from that way."

Fen stroked his chin in thought. "Why don't we go for them while they're closer to the sea? Then we could cut them off and prevent them from sneaking down the coast."

Alik shook his head. "I would rather keep us out of range of the ships."

"But we have that taken care of," Fen protested. "I don't think we should leave ourselves so open. They could go right down the coast without us seeing anything, ambush us from behind, and go for Faelinth's ballistae."

Alik grumbled loudly. "I think this is my expertise, boy. I've been doing this a lot longer than you could imagine."

"Ha," Fen burst out. "But I think, technically, I outrank you."

Mati smiled at the nostalgic banter. The two men hadn't had a good argument in a while, and it was nice to hear their vexed conversation like she had so many times before when they were traveling.

Alik's face fractured in irritation. "Need I remind you that *you* appointed me in charge of this battle—"

"Well, what else was I supposed to do? You looked like a lost dog skulking in the corner during that meeting."

Alik threw his head back with a hearty laugh. "I can't believe you're trying to act like you don't need me."

Fen threw up his hands into the air. "Well, of course I need you, you horse-brained ogre. I couldn't do this without you."

"I knew it!" Alik pointed an accusatory finger at Fen's chest. "So, we'll be staying away from the sea."

Fen made a strange noise of disgust and seemed about to keep arguing, so Mati stepped in before he could say whatever it was that he had brewing on his lips. "Why don't you two ninnies compromise?" They looked at her with indignation when she started speaking, almost as if they'd forgotten she was even there.

Fen scrunched his brows together and turned back to Alik. "Fine. We move the battle slightly to the east, closer to the shore, and station a guard unit to patrol the coast."

"*That* is a plan I can agree to. I'll have Trantu place two of his soldiers there to do regular patrols."

And with that declaration, the argument was over and the three walked back to camp as if nothing had happened. Once they arrived, however, they saw several lycan collapsed on the ground as though they'd just run a marathon.

"Looks like Gruthlan's arrived," Fen noted.

"So it appears," Mati replied, pointing towards the mess tent where a lycan banner now hung outside alongside the rest.

The three headed into the tent to see Gruthlan himself being greeted by Helian.

Fen strode over to them and stretched out his arm to Gruthlan, who took it and linked their forearms. "Good to see you again," Fen greeted him.

"It's an honor to be here," Gruthlan replied. "We made good time. Rugrul will be arriving tomorrow with at least another hundred soldiers."

"Good to hear," Alik said. "We'll have to have a quick briefing."

Mati tapped Fen on the shoulder. "I'm going to head out. I think we both know how much I love war talk."

Fen smiled and leaned in to peck her cheek. "Okay, I'll see you later."


After leaving the meeting, Mati wandered the camp looking for something to do. Preparation for the battle was in full swing, but she had never felt more useless than she did while looking at all the weaponry and armor surrounding her. The harsh *tink* of metal and the *swish* of arrows could be heard everywhere in the camp as the soldiers of all the folk trained together. She wondered if she would even be any help when the time came to fight. She knew she couldn't and wouldn't stay behind, but she didn't want to be a hindrance, either.

From far off, she spotted a familiar face approaching between the rows of tents. Jaylin was walking toward her with a wide, friendly smile. "Mati," she called, "it's so good to see you again."

Mati returned her smile. "Are you here for the battle?"

"I am." Jaylin stopped next to her. "I thought I could at least help with the wounded. I'm looking for Rena. I assume she's here."

"Yes, she is. Follow me." Mati turned and led Jaylin through the camp, back the way she'd come. "So, I found out you're a god."

"Yes, goddess of nature and healing."

"Maybe I can help you during the battle," Mati said. "I'm not that great with a sword, anyway."

"Only because you don't yet know your full worth. You'd be more than welcome to assist me." Jaylin smiled at Mati. "But I'm sure you'll be wanted on the battlefield."

"I'll just be in the way."

"Maybe, but maybe not. You might surprise yourself."

Mati huffed. "I doubt it. I'm a hazard with that sword. I'd probably do more damage than help."

"There are more weapons on the battlefield than swords. Your mind can be your most useful tool."

Mati didn't answer Jaylin, deciding that she wanted to stew in her own irritation alone. They walked until they came to Rena's tent and Mati announced them.

"Rena," she called.

"I'm here," Rena answered from inside. "Come on in, love."

Mati pulled back the tent flap and Rena squealed when she saw Jaylin. She raced past Mati out of the tent, nearly tackling Jaylin. "All together again," she said happily.

The three sat down at Rena's tea table while she gathered cups and poured them each a cup.

Jaylin picked up her cup and held it close to her nose, breathing in deeply. "I've missed your tea." She looked up from the steam. "And you, my friends."

Mati sat in awkward silence as Rena and Jaylin caught up. They did try to include her in their chat, but it fell flat since Mati had no reference for most of the people in their stories.

Rena took a sip of tea and smiled. "Mati, you wouldn't believe the trouble Tanophis and Alik used to get into."

Jaylin set her cup down on the table, giggling preemptively. "The time they had a brawl, and both rolled into that mudhole. They smelled horrendous for a solid week afterward."

Rena cackled. "And we made them sit in another room entirely for all meals. They were furious with us."

Rena and Jaylin cackled like schoolgirls, tears rolling down their faces from laughing at the memories, and Mati found herself smiling as well. She couldn't imagine stuffy Alik brawling like a teenager.

Rena took a deep breath and picked her tea up again. "I miss those days."

Jaylin and Rena both fell into a quiet melancholy after that story. Mati tried to think of anything that could bring back the easy conversation. "What were your lives like before all of this? Did you all get along?"

Rena huffed a laugh. "No, not at all. We are all sets of opposites, and we fought constantly. But we also loved one another... until Guyt."

"I'm sorry," Mati said. "I didn't mean to bring that up."

Jaylin laid a hand on Mati's arm. "You're curious, and that's okay. It's just sad for us to remember the way things used to be."

Mati nodded. "How long was Guyt living here before he started taking over?"

"A hundred years, at least," Jaylin answered.

"A *hundred years?*"

Rena smiled. "You forget that we're gods. We live forever."

"So, how old are you all?"

The laugh Jaylin let out was light and airy. "Very, very old."

Mati mulled over the information when her own fate crossed her mind. "What happens to me and Fen when all of this is over?"

Rena sighed, fingering the rim of her cup. "Hopefully, everything will return to normal."

Mati looked down at the floor. "And Paxis and Tanophis will return?"

"Yes," Jaylin answered softly. "We hope. But enough of these sad topics. Let's talk about happier things."

"Yes," Rena agreed with a cheeky grin. "Pretend we're old friends, and tell us about yourself and Fen. Neither of us know exactly how it came to be."

Mati's face flushed. "What do you want to know?"

"Everything," Jaylin teased her giddily.

Mati beamed and agreed, and they fell into an easy conversation as she recounted how she and Fen had come to be in the relationship in which they now found themselves.

# Chapter 27

Fen steeled himself as he walked into the mess tent beside Mati. They had spent the previous twenty-four hours making all the last-minute preparations and plans for the coming battle, and that morning he and Mati had been woken up by an emissary with news of Guyt's movements. They dragged themselves sleepily out of their blankets and tossed on their clothes.

The others were all waiting in the dim morning light for them to arrive, sitting around the table in their usual spots. Mati took the seat next to Fen and stifled a yawn.

"What's the news?" Fen asked eagerly, looking around to anyone that would speak.

Clíodha straightened in her chair, drawing Fen's attention. "My scouts have reported that Guyt's army has made camp just over the hill. They moved in last night."

Fen was instantly on alert, leaning in to give her his full attention. "I want to know everything."

"The scouts stayed until it was almost too dangerous to leave. I could send them to the Hell Realm myself for being so reckless. But they did return with valuable information." The whole table was now all paying attention to what Clíodha was saying. "Guyt has brought with him thousands of gigantic carts full of dirt—"

Helian leaned over the table and interrupted her. "For Ciksura's nuwu, no doubt."

"And that is all they brought." Clíodha continued. "There are about a thousand other soldiers."

"Well," Gruthlan said, "at least we know where they are, and their current numbers."

"Is there any way to watch them?" Mati asked. "I imagine Ciksura won't create nuwu to just leave them sitting around for days. She'll create them right before Guyt plans on striking, right?"

"True," Vrutuuk agreed. "My scouts won't be useful. He'll see us approach, and surely has scouts of his own."

"My women are capable of the task," Clíodha said proudly.

"Good," Alik said. "We'll hold you to that. We'll need a constant watch placed on his camp and regular reports of anything that happens."

Clíodha nodded. "Consider it done."

⤜⤚ ⤙⤛

The next day was another inactive one, and left Fen and Mati going stir-crazy. Fen spent most of his day with Alik, leaving Mati to help Jaylin and Rena set up the medical tents. The air around camp was static-charged, making Mati's hair stand on end.

That night at dinner with all the leaders, Alik announced that he wanted everyone to be battle-ready at dawn, and to stay that way.

Gruthlan turned to Clíodha. "Did you receive word of Guyt assembling his army?"

"No," Alik interrupted. "But Guyt is a slimy bastard, and I don't trust him. He knows we're watching him. I don't want any surprises, so have your troops battle-ready at all times. I want them sleeping in their armor, if that's what it takes."

"That's absurd," Vrutuuk objected. "They'll get no sleep that way."

Alik's face hardened and he glared at Vrutuuk. "Then they had better learn to run on no sleep. Guyt isn't going to show us his whole hand. He knows he has the advantage, but he still won't be eager to pretend that we're not a threat."

Helian stood to address the group. "Alik wouldn't ask anything of us if he thought it wasn't necessary."

Mati looked at the group surrounding her and took a robotic bite of her food while she thought. Then the light bulb turned on. "What if Guyt has another army?"

"What do you mean?" Alik asked.

"I mean, how likely is it that Guyt wouldn't have other troops? Where's Syradax?"

Gruthlan huffed. "He must be on the ships, of course."

Mati laid her fork down and sat forward. "How do you know that? Have you seen them?"

"No," answered Vrutuuk. "We just assumed that that was who was on the ships, since they weren't in the camp. Where else would they be?"

"That's my point," Mati said coolly. "You don't know."

"She's right," Alik said. "We don't know that for sure. For all we know, Guyt has a third force on those ships, one that we haven't seen yet, and Syradax is skulking elsewhere."

"Fuck," Fen swore, running his fingers through his hair. "Which means we need another scouting party. Any volunteers?"

"I'll send two of my fastest runners," Gruthlan offered.

"Done," Alik said, then whipped out a map, shoving empty dishes out of the way to lay it on the table between them. "Send them around this way, and make sure he hasn't got any troops flanking us to the west."


That night, Fen put on his armor and sword together for the first time. It fit perfectly around every contour of his body. He stretched experimentally, and swung the sword to see how it all felt. Not too bulky, and it moved easily along with every movement he made. It was strange, he considered, that they'd had armor just laying around that fit him so perfectly. He turned to Mati and posed for her, comically statuesque. "How's it look?"

Mati stared at him in awe. "You look like a king."

"It fits me perfectly."

She stared at him in wonder, taking in all the details. "Yes, it does."

Fen grinned. "You're thinking dirty thoughts."

Mati snapped her eyes up to his with an incredulous look. "I—"

"Don't lie to me," Fen stalked closer to her, with a sinful smirk.

Mati pushed herself further into the pile of pillows under her.

Fen stood over her, that wicked smile still on his lips, and slowly knelt down to her level. "Tell me what you're thinking." he demanded, his voice caressing her.

Mati leaned up on her elbows, continuing to eye Fen. "I'm thinking of all the ways I'd happily let you destroy me while wearing that."

Fen let out a feral rumble and prowled closer to her, like a hunter toward his prey, his sights set firmly on the woman currently meeting his stare. His own eyes narrowed on his prize as she spread her legs apart, inviting him in to devour her.

Fen dropped onto all fours. He saw the way Mati's heart thudded in her chest, the flush that crept across her cheeks, and the way her breathing turned ragged.

He reached out his hand and slowly moved her tunic out of his way. Another low rumble of satisfaction rolled out of him when he saw how ready she already was. He flashed her a wicked grin before crawling up her body to touch noses.

Mati curled up one side of her lip as Fen took her chin gently with his whole hand. That sinful look sent a thrill through him. He kissed her then, so fast and hard it caught her by surprise and made them both fall back into the pillows.

"Fuck me," she whispered in his ear.

Fen hitched up her leg and smoothly ran his hand up her thigh. He pulled back for a moment to shimmy his pants down around his knees. He didn't have the patience to bother removing them, nor the greaves buckled around his shins. His singular focus was giving her exactly what she needed.

He lunged at Mati urgently, biting the side of her neck as he found a good handhold in the pile of pillows and blankets. She pulled him toward her, matching his need.

Fen obliged happily and thrust himself inside of her. They both let out a groan of fulfillment as he moved desperately inside her.

Mati reached down, stroking the nerves. Fen gave one more deep thrust that sent her over the edge with a loud cry. One so loud that he was sure the rest of the camp had heard her. In any other situation he might've tried to muffle her, but as it was, Fen only needed to feel Mati pulse beneath him. He thrust a few more times before he too let out a deep, satiated cry. He collapsed beside her, both of them breathless.

"So, you like the armor..." Fen grinned.

Mati laughed lazily. "Yes."

His body was exhausted, but his soul was happier than he'd ever been.

The next morning started with clamor, when Fen and Mati were awakened by Alik bursting into their tent. Mati sat bolt upright.

"Wake up," he demanded, urgency lacing his words. "Gruthlan's scouts have returned. Syradax is coming from the west... behind us."

"Shit," Fen burst out from under the blanket, fully clothed and in armor, as Alik had instructed. "How long do we have?"

"They should arrive within the hour. I've sent word to have two companies sent out to face them head on, before they can circle around and flank us."

Fen grabbed his spirit sword, which he'd set next to his side of the blankets the night before, and slid it into the sheath. Mati grabbed hers as well, a bit more clumsily, as they raced out of the tent into the very early dawn.

The camp had come alive like an anthill. Folks of all kinds were grabbing weapons, hustling from place to place with supplies, some stuffing the last remnants of breakfast into their mouths.

Fen held Mati's hand tight as he tugged her through the crowd. "Stay close to me," Fen warned her. She could hear the fear in his voice but didn't see it on his face. "Promise me."

"I can't," she answered. "I'm going to help Jaylin with the injured."

He stopped and turned to face her. "Then go, but *do not* come out to the battle." His eyes were almost black as he stared intently into hers.

She let a smile tug at one side of her mouth. "I'd be more offended if you didn't look so serious."

He didn't return her smile. "I *am* serious, Mati."

All sense of humor drained from her. "Okay, I promise."

Fen pulled her into a tight embrace and kissed the top of her head. "Go."

"Fen," Alik called from ahead.

Fen turned and started to walk away, and Mati felt a string tug at her gut. "Fen," she called out.

He turned back, but as Mati stared at him, the words she wanted to say refused to come out. "Be careful," she said instead, as tears welled up in her eyes.

Fen flashed her a familiar grin and turned away again, racing after Alik through the gathering soldiers. Mati watched him, and it seemed to her that time slowed somehow, a sense of foreboding settling over her as he turned and darted off into the chaos.

⤜⤜ ⤛⤛

Fen followed Alik through the rows of tents and out onto the edge of the field for which, only a few days ago, they had made their battle plans. Alik directed the battalions, and ranks formed up at his command. Four battalions would face Guyt's forces head-on and two companies were sent to head off Syradax and his forces. Clíodha and Rugrul led the two companies of banshee and lycan to the west, leaving Gruthlan, Vrutuuk, and Helian leading the four battalions.

"Alik," Fen called out, "We need a line further east, to make sure they don't skirt down the coast toward Faelinth."

"Fuck," Alik cursed, striding off and directing a line of soldiers to move further east.

Fen stood amidst the forming ranks and broke out in a cold sweat. He grabbed the hilt of the sword at his side and squeezed. He could see Guyt's army forming their own ranks on the opposite side of the field.

The morning mist lay low and still between them. Fen saw companies of nuwu rising together, led by Ciksura, with ranks of mingled folk standing before them. He took a deep breath to steel himself, and turned away to focus on Alik.

"We're as ready as we're ever going to be," Alik said, stopping next to Fen. "Follow my lead."

Fen nodded. "How long will this battle last?"

Alik shrugged. "I'm not sure. Hopefully longer than I think it will."

***

Faelinth and his soldiers waited on the banks of the Clerin, where they had been stationed for several days. Guyt's ships had been anchored off the coast since the previous night, making no attempts to land any troops, or to attack. He hoped that meant their plan had worked, but his gut hitched, telling him it was only the beginning.

There had been no movement on board for the whole morning, aside from a few deckhands, and Faelinth didn't feel right attacking a seemingly unarmed ship. He mulled the idea over in his mind before finally giving the order to fire one ballista as a warning.

The bolt whistled through the air and landed with a dull thud in the side of the lead ship. Faelinth waited for any reaction or sign that would clue them to what was going on aboard the vessel.

After a long moment, an elf beside Faelinth spoke. "My lord, they don't seem to have realized we struck them."

Faelinth pondered a few ideas through his mind. "Or they're ignoring it. But a merchant's ship would have skinned us alive for shooting at them, and a ship of soldiers would have fired back." He stood in silence for another moment the realization sent him reeling. How could he have been so witless? Guyt had tricked them.

"My lord?" the elf asked, awaiting further orders.

"Shit! Have the men form up. We're leaving. Guyt sent us on a fool's errand. These ships are empty. He meant to spread us too thin, and we fell right into his trap."

The elf scurried to obey Faelinth's order, and soon the company was marching at full tilt to rejoin the others back on the battlefield.

⋙ ⋘

Fen felt his stomach open a trap door and fall right down to his feet. Several thoughts ran through his mind as he stood next to Alik, looking out at the mist-covered field. He wondered how he'd ended up here, and considered just how quickly his life had changed. Only a few months ago he had been mucking out a farm, with no future, and now he was standing next to a god, holding a magic sword, on a battlefield in the early sunlight. He hadn't even realized the changes as they happened. They'd happened so fast, and at first he'd wanted them all. This was who he was now, on a battlefield in custom-made armor, standing next to Alik and Rena as their equal.

A low, rolling drumbeat sounded, pulling Fen from his daze. He shook it off and looked toward Guyt's army. Guyt's living forces erupted in a frenzy of activity as the drumbeat rolled on and on. They gestured and whooped, looking like agitated hornets as they beat their swords against their shields.

The army surrounding Fen erupted equally as powerfully, with howls, beating shields, and voices ringing with power that coursed through the crisp morning air. The sound was compelling and, unconsciously, Fen's voice joined with the others. He ripped his sword from its sheath and held it high, screaming like a demon unleashed. Guyt's challenge was officially accepted.

Guyt's army raced toward them across the field.

Alik stood next to Fen, eyes focused tightly on every slight movement in front of them. "Hold," he called to the madrigal archers, their bows drawn and ready. The opposing army drew nearer and nearer, until finally they crossed the midpoint of the field. "Fire!" Alik ordered, swinging his sword forward to signal the archers to unleash fury.

Arrows whizzed high above Fen's head, most of them meeting their targets. As the enemy fell, they disappeared beneath the light mist that swirled around their feet. His eyes narrowed, his stomach in knots, and he brought his sword to the ready. He pushed forward through the ranks of sykosee and lycan, some with their javelins braced in the ground like pikes and some with the weapons poised to hurl through the air. The lycan howled with victory as Guyt's mingled forces fell.

"How do you kill a nuwu?" Fen asked the female lycan standing next to him. The absurdity that he hadn't thought to ask before they had entered battle would've embarrassed him at any other time.

"Cut off their heads," the lycan answered as she held her javelin fast against an elf who had been so unfortunate as to run into their front line. She howled with triumph as the elf struggled to free itself, ramming the point further into its gut with a howling victory cry. She yanked the javelin out with brutal ferocity and stabbed the elf once more through the heart as it fell.

More and more of their enemies reached the javelin line, their personal fights ending on top of a growing pile of their own comrades. The few individuals who managed to escape the arrows and the javelins met an untimely end by sword point.

The mingled forces fell in piles, making it nearly impossible for their comrades to reach the front line. Fen heard, more than saw, the newest arrivals to the battlefield.

Ciksura thundered forward, followed by hundreds of nuwu. The unleashed terrors tore across the field in a frenzy, bearing down on Alik's front line and leaving Ciksura in their wake. The javelins were all dropped and the lycan and sykosee that made up the front line drew their swords instead. Guyt's mingled forces had been annihilated, and triumphant howls and whoops went up again as the front line prepared to face the nuwu.

"Cover," Alik called over the noise and confusion.

Fen and the others on the front line obeyed without hesitation. They fell to one knee as the madrigal easily leapt over them all and charged the approaching nuwu. They galloped through the ranks, expertly chopping off heads. The nuwu's bodies crumpled to dust once their heads were severed, creating a dust cloud that drifted through the mayhem.

The lycan rose on their hind legs and howled, immediately taking off onto the field behind the madrigals.

Fen stood beside Rena, whooping and cheering, their swords held overhead. Then they vaulted over the dead and mangled bodies of the enemy. Fen broke the line and raced after the lycan. He swung his sword with a battle cry and a nuwu head went flying, covering him in a fine gray dust that stuck to his sweat and to the splatters of blood.

The battle raged on for what felt to Fen like hours. For every nuwu they slew, two more took its place. Fen felt the inevitable fatigue set in, along with the deep hopelessness of a battle that they couldn't win, against a never-ending force.

"Fall back," Alik called out over the clatter and cries. "Fall back!"

Fen turned and fought his way towards Alik's voice. Their ranks had broken from the sheer force of nuwu crashing into them like the storm surge of a hurricane. He fumbled, trying to find his footing over the dead and dying, trying desperately to get to the safety that Alik's voice promised. He strained to look away from the faces of the motionless and pleading injured as he ran.

The nuwu fell back as well, and reformed a line much closer than when they had started out that morning.

"Why're the nuwu falling back?" Fen asked Alik breathlessly.

Alik stared at the reformed line and at Ciksura beside them. "I don't know what they have in store."

Alik's obvious unease set Fen's nerves on edge. They watched silently for a moment. No victorious howls or calls or shield-pounding came from either army. The only eerie sounds heard across the field were the subtle whimpers and cries of the injured and dying.

Then a horn blew loud and low across the hill and, in answer, the nuwu parted. Over the rise, through the fading wisps of mist, came the figure of a man. His broad shoulders shone in his golden armor and he wore a thick red cape that whipped heavily behind him in the wind.

Alik's face contorted in rage. He looked more like a lycan than a huma in the moment. "Guyt." And he surged forward to meet the catalyst of all the chaos in which they were embroiled.

Fen ran at Alik's side until he pulled ahead, now leading the charge.

The horns continued to blow unceasingly, accompanied by the low rolls of drums. Guyt was followed by Lavinia and Ciksura one to his left and one to the right, forming a triangle. Guyt saw Fen and a subtle smirk crossed his lip as he approached. Fen kept his face hard in answer.

Guyt stopped and kicked a dead lycan aside to create a small, unobstructed area of grass for himself to stand on. Growls could be heard behind them as the other lycan protested the disgusting move.

"Alik," Guyt started. "It's so nice to see you again."

"Shut the fuck up," Alik shot back.

"So abrasive." Guyt clicked his tongue before turning his attention to Fen. "It's nice to see you two together again. I nearly lost hope."

"What do you want, worm?" Fen spat. He had no real reason to hate this man, other than the stories that his friends had told him, but his mere presence made Fen's skin crawl, and feel like he'd been dipped in oil.

Guyt sneered. "I want you."

Alik stepped forward, blocking Fen.

"Alik, I really came out here to help you," Guyt continued. Fen and Alik made no move to speak, so Guyt continued. "You've lost so many already. We could end this here, you and me. I'll take Fen with me, and you can continue living whatever pathetic existence you've carved out for yourself in Lyserria, pretending that you're hiding from me."

Alik gave him a sneer that turned into a smirk. "You can certainly try to take Fen. But I think you'll be in for a fight."

Fen's eyes widened and he whipped his head around to stare in shock at Alik. "I'd rather die."

"Perfect," Guyt growled, a menacing grin on his face. He grabbed Fen's arm, latching on with so much speed that Fen barely saw him move.

Fen reacted instantly, twisting out of Guyt's grip. He slashed at Guyt, who bent easily out of the sword's path.

"Feistier than I remember," Guyt said.

Fen was caught off guard by that statement. He'd never met Guyt. What did that mean? He stood in thought, nearly stunned.

Alik shoved Fen back away from Guyt and took up his place in the void between them.

"Where's your little wifey?" Guyt taunted. Fen felt the air leave his body in an enraged huff. "Once this is all over, I'll make sure you get to watch—"

Guyt didn't get to finish his sentence before a fist flew. Fen leaped over Alik and grabbed a fistful of Guyt's robe. Alik dropped out of the way and Fen pulled Guyt to him, head-butting him so hard that Fen felt blood rise to his nose and stars dance behind his eyelids.

Guyt made a guttural sound of anger and whipped out a dagger that he had hidden beneath his robe. He slashed through the air. Fen leapt back and attempted to block Guyt's dagger, but it grazed his cheek. Fen was acutely aware of the pain of the cut as warm blood trickled down his face.

"Lavinia!"

They paused at the cry, turning as Faelinth made his way through the army toward them. "Lavinia," he called again.

Lavinia's face went blank and hollow as Faelinth came to a halt.

"How sweet," Guyt sneered. "A jilted lover, come to reclaim his prize."

Faelinth ignored Guyt's words. He only had eyes for his wife. His tortured face pleaded silently with her to answer him. "Please, Lavinia, you've let him poison your heart long enough. Come back to me."

"Yes, Lavinia—" Guyt said, mockingly.

"Shut up," Faelinth spat. "I'm talking to my *wife*." He held out one pleading hand to her. "Because that is still what I consider you... my wife."

Guyt scoffed at Faelinth. "You want to claim her, while I want to free her."

"How is she free now? You keep her tethered to you with your lies. She hasn't been free since you took her from me."

"I remember that day well, Faelinth, god of all things good, and I wasn't in the room when she left you. She made that decision on her own."

"It was your manipulation that made her feel unworthy," Faelinth snapped.

Lavinia stood in silence, listening to Faelinth.

Faelinth's face softened. "He made you feel unworthy, Lavinia. He preyed on you and turned you against me. And if I ever did anything that made you feel unworthy, then let me fix that mistake."

He stared at her pleadingly until she finally spoke, her voice low.

"You never made me feel unworthy," she said.

"Then please, wife, come back to me. Please."

Lavinia turned her face from Faelinth and squeezed her eyes shut. "I can't."

Guyt laughed in the silence that followed. "She made a blood oath to serve and obey me."

Faelinth uttered a primal scream and drew his sword to strike Guyt, but his swing was interrupted in midair. He looked up and saw Lavinia's outstretched arm, her sword blocking Faelinth's from reaching its target.

"Are you truly gone?" he muttered in quiet devastation, tears welling in his eyes. Their swords clashed again, sending a metallic trill through the crowd. They pulled apart, preparing to slash at one another one more time.

Guyt drew his sword, taking advantage of the confusion. He slashed at Alik's arm, leaving a long cut. Alik cried out, his hand convulsing and dropping his sword, bringing Fen's attention back to Guyt.

Ciksura disappeared into the company of nuwu that had now started moving forward again, while the sounds of Lavinia and Faelinth's swords still rang out.

Fen's eyes fell on the sword that Alik had dropped, and he grabbed it. The air felt like it left the battlefield. Fen's mind cleared as he prepared to do whatever necessary to end this, here and now. He raised both swords in front of him, ready to fight.

Guyt's eyes met his, and then his sword did the same.

# Chapter 28

Mati watched Fen race off into the dim morning light. She attempted to steel herself against that pressure building in her core, trying to release an emotion she wasn't fully prepared to show. Mati turned and hurried off to where Jaylin waited in the medical tents. A few others were already there, mostly older folks who scurried around making beds, starting fires, and making sure enough cloth was laid out for bandaging. The tent had a slight medicinal smell to it that clung in Mati's nose.

"Good," Jaylin greeted her, barely pausing as she set out her many salves and powders on the table. "I was hoping you'd get here soon."

"What do you need me to do?" Mati asked, forcing her mind to focus on tasks instead of the tears that strained to burst out of her.

"Nothing, currently. We'll have our hands full once they start fighting. This is the calm before the storm for us."

Mati wrung her hands and looked about at all the other volunteers being useful. "I need something to do."

Jaylin met her eyes and gave her a sad smile. "Alik will protect him."

"I know, but I still need to not think about it. And I need to not feel useless."

"Okay," Jaylin answered, and handed her a pot. "Then go fetch some water and get it boiling. We're going to need plenty of it."

Mati walked to the small creek that ran along the outskirts of the camp and filled the pot. The camp had gone silent now, but in the distance she heard the battle cries of both armies. The sounds sent a chill through her that almost made her drop the pot. She'd never heard anything so primal before.

"My lady," a voice startled her.

She turned, hand on her heart, to find a young female faun approaching from behind her, also carrying a pot. "Are you all right, my lady?"

"Yes," Mati answered. "I've never heard anything so terrifying."

The faun bowed her head. "I remember the great fall, even though I was young." Memory and fear and sadness showed on her face. "The sounds were terrifying. My matim—mother, as you would call her—she made me hide in the little shed outside our house. I remember the screams, and the sounds of the soldiers ravaging our house and my mother. My father had gone away to help fight. We had no one to help us." A few tears began to slide down her cheeks. "She survived physically, but she was never the same. I still think about that day."

She fell silent and Mati laid a hand on her shoulder. "I'm sorry you both had to go through that. We will beat Guyt this time. I promise."

The young faun looked up to Mati, wiping away the unfallen tears. "I hope so, my lady. I really hope so."

Mati linked arms with her and they started back. "I feel very dumb. You obviously know me, but I don't know you."

The faun smiled at Mati, her long-buried memories now put away behind the doors that kept them contained. "I'm Cleta, my lady."

"Well, Cleta, you can call me Mati." They exchanged another wide smile and Cleta nodded.

By the time they got back to the camp, the sounds from the battlefield had died down, and only the occasional loud cry or clang could be heard. As Mati entered the medical tents, wounded soldiers had already started arriving. Jaylin was rushing from one cot to the next, assessing injuries and giving orders.

Mati rushed to the side of another arriving wounded. The glazed eyes of a lycan met her gaze. The soldier had received a long fleshy wound that laid his thigh open to the bone. She stared at the injury in awe for a moment before taking a closer look. The wound was matted with fur and blue blood, and deep in the center she could see black bone.

"Put him here," Mati said, directing the elves who carried him to an open area next to Jaylin.

Jaylin turned her head while she stitched up another gaping wound. Sweat had started to bead on her forehead, and she shrugged it off onto her bicep. "Clean out that cut with water. I'll tell you what to do from there."

Mati rushed to grab a pot of steaming hot water and some clean cloths. The wound had mostly stopped bleeding, but the matted fur made it hard to see anything. She wet the cloth and gently wiped the hairs back out of the way. The lycan winced and took a sharp breath. "I'm sorry," she whispered, gritting her teeth.

"Good," Jaylin said. "Now I want you to go do that with everyone. If they need to be stitched up, put them over here with me. And if you can just use bandages, then bandage them up. I only want the worst of the injuries."

Mati nodded and took off toward the door to direct the traffic. She assessed all the injured as they entered, and promptly directed them to various tents. She saw soldiers with deep gashes, missing limbs, and cracked bones now coming in at an alarming rate.

After an hour or so of triage—she couldn't tell—she was covered in various colors of blood and bodily fluids. The tent had begun to reek of musty earth, piss, and the sweet metallic bite of blood. It would've made Mati heave if she'd had any time to stop and think about it, but, as it was, she wiped sweat from her brow with her sleeve, used an apron Cleta had given her to wipe off most of the blood from her hands, and kept directing the cots of wounded.

During a brief lull, Mati stepped out of the tent and filled her lungs with fresh, warm air. The sun had come up some time ago and started to warm the grass. The silence outside the tent disturbed her. All morning she had been surrounded by screams, whimper, and the murmurs of voices consoling the injured.

Another cot came around the corner laden with a sykosee warrior, his tail and wings dragging along the ground. Mati held out a hand to the lycan who carried the back of the cot. His fur was heavily matted in spots and smelled terribly of wet dog. "How... I mean... what's happening?" she stumbled over her words.

The lycan halted for a moment and looked straight at Mati—but also right through her. "Guyt has come out onto the field. All battle is paused while he talks to Alik and Fen."

"What?" Mati exclaimed and immediately turned and raced back into the tent. "Jaylin, Guyt is on the battlefield. I have to go to Fen."

Before Jaylin had a chance to protest, Mati fled the tent and sprinted toward the battlefield. Her sword bounced rhythmically against her leg as she sped past more injured soldiers on their way to the medical tent.

The world blurred as she ran as fast as her legs would carry her. The feeling in her gut pulled her desperately onward.

Faster.

Faster.

She must get to Fen.

⟫ ⟪

Once Mati reached the battlefield, her view was blocked by lines of soldiers. She shoved unceremoniously past them all, reaching the front line in time to see Alik fall to his knees, clasping his bloody arm. Fen had grabbed Alik's sword as well as his own and was now poised in front of a tall, broad man wearing a red cape.

She didn't scream like instinct told her to do. Instead, she clamped her mouth shut and shoved her way through the remaining crowd. Fear and rage fueled her. As the lycan and madrigal parted for her, they offered her an unobstructed view of Fen and Guyt. Fen charged forward, swords in both hands, but Guyt blocked his blows with a solid clang that vibrated under her feet. The two battled expertly, moving around and over the dead soldiers that lay on the battlefield. Mati's breath caught at the power the two men exerted during that dangerous dance.

Fen's eyes flashed toward Mati and, in that split second of distraction, Guyt kicked Fen's foot out from under him, knocking him off balance. Mati wasn't sure if the bloodcurdling scream she heard had come from her, or from the collective shock around her.

She was frozen, helpless, as Guyt's dagger slashed across Fen's throat.

Blood sprayed upwards, splattering across Guyt's armor. And as Fen fell, Guyt took his sword and thrust it into Fen's side, between the armored plates.

Guyt's expression was one of manic glee as he ripped and twisted the sword from Fen's gut. He staggered back, wiping the blood from his sword and armor with his cape.

Mati dashed toward Fen, falling to her knees and scooping him up against her chest. She cradled him to herself, rocking back and forth and crying out in despair.

Battle erupted around them once more and still Mati held Fen close, stuck in a bubble that was all their own.

⁓⟫⟫ ⟪⟪⁓

Fen felt the sharp pain in his gut and throbbing pain at his neck. His breathing came in fast and short spurts, each breath accompanied by a different shooting pain. He saw Mati above him, tears in her eyes, and more still pouring down her cheeks. He tried to speak, but all that came out was a cough of blood and searing pain in his throat. He had so much to tell her still. He didn't want the last thing he saw in this life to be her tears.

More than pain or panic, he felt anger. Anger that he wouldn't get the time with Mati that he wanted. Anger that she had to see him die like this. And burning anger that Guyt had bested him.

⁓⟫⟫ ⟪⟪⁓

"I'm sorry," was all Mati managed to repeat over and over as Fen's lips twitched and he tried to move. Blood gurgled from his mouth as she held him. She smoothed and stroked the hair away from his face compulsively. "You can't die... you can't! I won't let you."

He stared up at her, the realization that death was quickly approaching etched into his eyes. It frightened Mati to meet his gaze now.

Mati's tears fell onto Fen's face, creating tiny, clean rivers that dripped away into the grass.

"You can't die. Do you know why?" Mati paused, even knowing that Fen couldn't answer. His body had begun to get heavier and his eyes were glazing over with a faraway stare, seeing nothing. "Because I love you, Fen. I love you, and you can't die."

A bright light engulfed them, terrifying Mati. "No!" she bellowed. "You can't have him!" She refused to lose him like this.

The light barricaded them from the rest of the battle, the brightness around them like being inside of a star. Mati tried to see more, clutching Fen closer until the light began to pour from inside both of them as well. All around her, Mati saw vignettes, memories from hers and Fen's journey, mixed with scenes from a life she didn't remember.

Younger Rena and Alik laughing together, on a star-speckled evening high above a city.

Ciksura and Jaylin dancing across a marble hall.

Lavinia and Faelinth hugging beneath a red arch.

Their whole family sitting at a long table filled with food, and seeing Tanophis at the other end looking at her with overwhelming love.

Watching these moments flash by released a flood of further memories. Their friends, their people, their life. They all rushed through her mind, bringing her clarity, mixing with her memories of her new, second life.

Then a memory that had been locked away broke free of its chains and pushed to the forefront of her thoughts.

The day Ciksura had led them through the streets of Meten. Led them to Guyt. The day she had lost everything that truly mattered to her. The day that Guyt had broken her family, cursed her and Tanophis to mortal bodies, and stolen their memories.

Anger boiled up inside her, but then she looked down. Tanophis lay in her lap. He was still coated in blood, but his wounds had healed.

The light still surrounded them as Tanophis sat up on the grass in front of her. Her beloved other half. He looked at her with a love and longing that melted Paxis' heart, and the tears that streamed down her face now were happy ones.

Paxis laughed through her tears and stroked his cheek. "I thought I'd lost you."

Tanophis returned her smile. "You'll never lose me. I'm too stubborn to die."

Paxis' laugh burst the sphere of light encircling them into a million pieces, and suddenly they were back on the battlefield, surrounded by death.

⫸⫷

When the light burst, both armies stood frozen in awe and fear.

"You're back," Rena announced joyously, tears streaming down her face.

Guyt's eyes narrowed in anger as he looked at them, the realization of what had just happened etching deep, angry lines into his face. He raised his sword over his head in a flash, and he brought it down over their heads. Tanophis held up an arm, and Guyt's sword ricocheted away.

Guyt let out a guttural scream and took another swing. Paxis blocked the sword this time, and she and Tanophis rose to their feet.

"It's over, Guyt," Paxis said.

Guyt stepped back and swept his hair from his face. "This is far from over."

The armies resumed fighting as the shock wore off and tensions rose once more. Paxis shot a glance at Tanophis and, in a sweeping movement, unsheathed her green sword and attempted to hand it to him. As Tanophis reached out his hand to grasp the hilt, Guyt lunged forward and grabbed the sword instead.

Paxis halted, eyes wide. "Fuck!"

"I've never seen a sword like this." Guyt said, reading the scrolling runes that trailed along the blade before recognition spread across his face. "Where did you get this?"

"Funny story, actually," Tanophis quipped. "I'd love to sit and tell you about it sometime over tea." He lunged for his own sword that lay in the grass, just out of reach.

Ciksura and Lavinia stepped in front of Guyt, protecting him, as Tanophis reclaimed his spirit sword. Guyt held Paxis' sword in front of him, but closed his eyes and began to chant. Ciksura held a spiked metal scourge in each hand and Lavinia raised her sword as a barrier.

Faelinth joined Tanophis, standing at his side. "We have unfinished business, *wife*." He twirled his sword once before attacking. Lavinia reacted, taking her attention off Guyt as she parried Faelinth's blade.

Alik and Rena joined the fight as Ciksura began spinning their scourges, a wicked smile on their face. They lunged at Ciksura, who blocked both swords expertly.

Guyt still stood, chanting, with eyes closed. But the second Ciksura stepped away, he opened them with a flash. Tanophis and Paxis watched, waiting to see what he would do. Guyt's eyes had turned a pale white and, as he opened his mouth, they heard an ear-shattering roar.

From behind Guyt, a nuwu rose from the ground in the shape of a great dragon. Its wings spread and flapped as it lifted into the air above them, giving another thunderous roar. As it reached the apex of its flight in the clouds, it looked to the southern sky and gave an angry bellow. Guyt's eyes had returned to normal, but as he lifted his head to the sky, he cursed.

Tanophis and Paxis turned to see another dragon, this one flesh and blood, bearing down on them. Its scales glinted golden brown in the sunlight. "Morimas," Tanophis said, bursting with hope.

Morimas flew straight for the nuwu. Their fiery breaths, meeting in midair, exploded in a rain of sparks that descended onto the battlefield. Paxis had to shield her eyes.

Tanophis tried to use the momentary distraction to rush Guyt, but his blade missed its mark as Guyt countered wand parried his attack.

Tanophis and Guyt fought, trading blow for blow across the field, through the burning embers of the dragon fire. Each of their steps sent up little sparks and trails of smoke.

Paxis knelt, took the sword of a dead soldier, and raced after them. Guyt rolled away from them both and picked up a second sword as he came back up onto his feet. With unflagging ferocity the trio fought through the blood-stained grass.

In the sky above the battle, Morimas lunged at the nuwu with predatory accuracy. She sank her teeth deep into the mud-dragon's neck and ripped a chunk of its fleshy dirt from the nuwu. It let out a dreadful, angry screech as Morimas sank her teeth in once more, severing its head. The nuwu dragon burst with a dull thud, dust drifting down to cover the battlefield below.

Morimas twisted her body and head to look down, gliding toward the remaining dirt and clay in Guyt's camp, and crop-dusted it with blue dragon fire. The dirt and clay melted into a heap of slag. Then the great dragon swooped low, dragging enemy soldiers up into the air and dropping them from a terrible height, or ripping into them with her teeth.

⟫⟫⟫ ⟪⟪⟪

"Ciksura," Rena called out, through the metallic clashes of blade and scourge, "you don't need to do this. Stop fighting and we can work all this out."

Ciksura chuckled darkly. "You can't sway me with your sweet speech."

Rena twirled out of the path of a scourge's spikes. "Not even for friendship?"

"Is that what you call it?" Ciksura cried out, dodging Alik's blade. "I begged you *all* for help, and you *all* refused."

"What price did he make you pay?" Alik asked, thrusting with his sword at an opening.

Ciksura flipped backward through the air, evading Alik's blow. "A price I was willing to pay."

"What was it?" Rena pressed. "Lifelong servitude? Your soul? What was it, Ciksura?"

Ciksura's face twisted as they flung the scourge at Rena's face with more bite than before, then let out an angry wail. "My soul…"

"Did it at least bring you the peace you desired?"

"Why do you care?"

Rena and Alik both attempted to make stabbing blows at their friend. Alik manifested a ball of light in his hand, a clear sign his godly powers had been restored. He sent the ball of light toward Ciksura's chest.

"Because we love you, Ciksura," Rena said. "He manipulated you. Can't you see that?"

Ciksura avoided the light and recovered, drawing themselves upright again. "I see more than you know!"

Alik took another shot, sending light streaking toward them. This time the ball hit them squarely in the chest. Ciksura halted, the wind knocked out of them, and fell to their knees.

Tears welled up in Rena's eyes as she dropped to her knees before Ciksura. "I am so sorry, my dear friend, that we failed you."

Ciksura huddled on the ground, gasping for air, fighting for their words through choppy breaths. "You… made me feel… like I…was a monster."

Rena embraced Ciksura. "You are not a monster. I see now that we were too hard on you. How can we ever make it right?"

The light that had stunned Ciksura still glowed across their chest, holding them immobile. "You can't."

"Please forgive us," Rena pleaded. "We truly failed you. I wish now that we'd listened better. We didn't see you as a monster, but now I understand that's how you see yourself, and we contributed to that. We created this person in front of us now."

Ciksura closed their eyes and refused to speak any further.

⟫⟫ ⟪⟪

"What blood oath did Guyt make you swear?" Faelinth asked Lavinia between blocked blows.

Lavinia's eyes glazed over. "I swore to protect and obey him." She pushed him back with a loud clang of their swords and Faelinth spun away.

"You offered too much of yourself to him."

"Faelinth," Lavinia huffed. "I am a monster."

"I still love you, Lavinia. And I know our friends do, too. You could stop this madness. Look at Tanophis and Paxis... they are fated to be together as well, yet they have found true and undying love. The same love I have for you. I don't care that we are fated to be two halves of a whole. I will always choose you."

"I'm bound to him by a blood oath, Faelinth. Even you can't undo that." She chased him, leaping over several dead soldiers.

Faelinth caught her arm as their blades collided once more. "What if I told you we could?"

"Ha!" Lavinia scoffed. "How do you plan to do that? Guyt can't be killed."

"Maybe... or maybe not."

Lavinia's eyes flashed open. "How?"

Faelinth gave her a teasing smile. "Agree to come back to me and I'll *think* about telling you."

Lavinia returned Faelinth's smile, breaking free from his hold. She stood on guard, sword up, waiting for Faelinth's next move. "Only if you agree to let me kill any who cross us."

"Wife," Faelinth said, slashing at her, "you know I believe all people have some good in them. It's against my nature to kill."

"Well, it's my belief that sometimes that good is buried too deep." They exchanged several more blows, their deadly dance leading them across the field. "Let me punish those who can't be redeemed. And I'll *think* about coming back to you." She shot him a wink that curled half her lip into a smirk.

Faelinth grinned. "It pains me to say it... but alright. I'll agree to let you search souls and kill only those with black hearts, if that will make you happy."

Lavinia laughed lightly as she and her husband continued their fight. "I've never known you to be so eager to end our negotiations."

"You've been away for a long time, my love. I miss our late-night tête-à-têtes." He caught her by the waist and spun her around, pulling her back against his chest and folding her arms around herself, pinning them and the sword in place. "Come back to me," he whispered in her ear.

# Chapter 29

Clíodha and Rugrul led their companies into battle, surprising Syradax into a conflict he hadn't intended. Rugrul withdrew from the main group and led a howling group of lycan straight at the center of the dralin line. The dralin fumbled to get their weapons readied as the lycan barreled into them headfirst, ripping into their callused skin with no hint of mercy.

Rugrul hurtled through the air into Syradax, knocking him off balance. The lycan's claws extended, dug into the neck of his opponent, and separated muscle from bone. Syradax let out a low growl, fumbling around Rugrul's mass of fur to reach his sword. Rugrul fell back and pulled out his own sword, baring his teeth to Syradax in a snarl. They lunged at each other, metal crashing into metal with a *clang*.

Clíodha and the banshees stopped in front of the dralin. With a blood-curdling wail, the banshees dropped their cloaks and veils behind them, revealing their terrible, pure-white forms. The dralin squinted at the light and let out terrified screams, as the equally demonic and angelic figures glided toward them, wailing.

The banshees sliced their claws through the skins of their petrified enemies. The dralin were now realizing their deepest fears, locked in their own minds, while their guts hung out of their bellies onto the ground.

Clíodha stopped her attack on the dralin when she noticed a fog rolling in around her robes. It was terribly thick and jelly-like and it trailed and snaked through the fight, wrapping around the dralin's legs and pulling them down into its clutches. She could hear the muffled screams of the dralin beneath the supernatural fog as it choked them to death.

Syradax and his remaining army tried to escape the fog's wispy fingers, but it crept swiftly up their legs, wrapped around their arms, and yanked them down. Rugrul stood still as a statue, marveling at the horror—and the luck—of their strange new ally.

With the fog alongside them, Clíodha and Rugrul led their army back to the heart of the battleground.

⟫ ⟪

Sweat flew off Tanophis's forehead as he spun away out of Guyt's reach. He had been engaged in this fight for much too long.

Guyt still held the other green sword, and slashed with it at Paxis' unarmored back. She tried to turn away, but cried out as Guyt's blow carved a long gash down her spine. Tanophis saw Guyt's eyes sparkle as a knowing smile spread across his face. Terror struck Tanophis as he realized Guyt had figured out what the sword he held could do to immortals.

Paxis fell to the ground in front of Tanophis with an agonizing scream. His face twisted in anger, slashing harder and faster, but Guyt had doubled his efforts as well, now that he understood the power he held in his hand.

The two dueled with renewed fervor around and through the carnage. For each attack, the other had a counter. Their blades sparked with every clash.

Tanophis stole a quick glance at his wife's blood-slicked back. Grimacing, her jaw tight, she gathered all her strength and rose to her feet with a warrior's cry. She staggered behind Guyt, met Tanophis's eyes, and he understood her plan. Tanophis drew Guyt's attention with several more wicked attacks, luring him forward.

Paxis hit Guyt in the back with her borrowed sword.

The steel bounced off of Guyt's skin and he spun his head to look at his attacker. In the split second that Guyt's attention was diverted, Tanophis thrust his sword through Guyt.

Surprise and malice were etched onto Guyt's face as his gaze whipped back to Tanophis.

Guyt's eyes glazed over, and he gave a single, choked cough. Blood trickled from his mouth. He reached his hand up to touch it, pulling his hand away in shock. As Guyt looked at the blood staining his fingers, Tanophis twisted the sword and pulled it out of Guyt's torso with a grunt of victory. He stepped back.

Guyt dropped to his knees with a dull thud, then fell forward in horrified surprise.

Tanophis took a long, deep breath and made his way over to Paxis, who had dropped, panting, to her knees.

The enemy forces seemed to become more frenzied than ever with the loss of Guyt, so much so that Tanophis was forced to take up his sword once more. He continued to beat back the nuwu surrounding them. He was starting to worry that they could never thin out the enemy ranks enough, when a thick low fog started rolling in under their feet.

The fog trickled around the feet of the soldiers, some powerful force pulling down Guyt's army one by one. It seemed to be searching for something.

Tanophis spotted a chilling sight, a woman clad in a liquid black dress and hood. Her face was painted with symbols, surrounding her stunning white eyes. The mist seemed to roll out of her mouth as she glided toward them.

All eyes fell on her with wonder and terror. Her fog curled around nuwu throats, compressing and strangling, until their heads rolled away and their bodies turned to dust. The choking sounds of Guyt's dying army were now the only sounds to be heard on the battlefield.

She stopped in front of Paxis and Tanophis, who looked at her with curiosity. "I see my contribution did not go to waste."

"Gaia?" Paxis said, furrowing her brow as she struggled to stand.

"With my brother dead," Gaia said, her voice low and resolute, "I have fulfilled my oath to him. I could no longer wait idly by in my forest. I have kept silent for far too long."

The trio was now being slowly surrounded by all the great leaders who had followed them into battle. They were all covered with wounds, in blood, and gray ash. And all of them stared at Gaia.

"Thank you, Mother," Clíodha said, bowing her head low with reverence.

Gaia nodded, accepting her thanks, the deadly fog retracing its path back into her pores. "I hope, now, that my brother's madness will be unmade." And once the fog had retreated completely, Gaia herself vanished into a wisp of mist.

Tanophis helped Paxis up with a steady hand, only now noticing the blood trailing down her legs. "Get Jaylin," he pleaded, more than ordered, with anyone who was within earshot.

Rena sprinted away to the camp and returned within a few minutes, Jaylin in tow.

"Set her down here," Jaylin said to Tanophis. "I've never treated a magical wound of this nature, so I'll do what I can."

As Jaylin poked and prodded the wound, Paxis took several sharp breaths. Jaylin's hands started to glow and she closed her eyes, chanting quietly. Paxis sat as still as she could while Jaylin ran her hands up and down the gash. After making several passes, she opened her eyes and drew in a deep breath. "I've done what I can here. Take her back to my tent. I'll need to stitch it up, but this is a magical wound, and healing will take time. Just as much time as a mortal's wound, I'm afraid."

Jaylin stood with visible effort, as Tanophis and Rena eased Paxis to her feet and helped her start the walk to the medical tent. That was when Jaylin noticed Ciksura, still bound by Alik's light around their chest. Jaylin locked eyes with her sibling and slowly walked over to their side.

"I would have helped you, had it been within my power," she said quietly, cupping their cheek with one hand.

# Chapter 30

That night, the funeral pyres of the dead illuminated the low-hanging clouds, as well as the long process of burying Guyt's army. Celebrations of victory and order restored began two days later, once the somber task was completed.

The mess tent filled with the smell of alcohol and cooked meats as the armies cheered their success and toasted the victorious dead. Their own losses crept to the back of their minds, just for that night.

Tanophis entered the uproarious tent in a daze. Paxis was still in the medical tent, healing, but he couldn't spend one more moment there. The stench of healing wounds and medicine had started to drive him slightly crazy. He needed a night with alcohol to drown out the last few days—and last few years.

He spied Asterion and Dursten sitting at a table with Alik and he crossed the tent, weaving through the crowd. "Asterion, Dursten," he began with a wide smile. "I didn't know you'd returned."

Asterion set down his mug of whiskey. "Only this morning. We had to settle our disagreements with the Illustrus for helping you all."

"Thank you," Tanophis bowed his head reverently. "None of this would have been possible without your help."

The stars nodded and Dursten patted the seat next to him. "Sit, my old friend. I'm glad you're back."

Tanophis smiled, and grabbed a mug of whiskey for himself off a passing tray. "Didn't like me as Fen?"

Alik grunted into his mug. "It's not that we didn't like you. It's just that we didn't like you. I almost knocked your head off more than a few times."

They all laughed and Tanophis took a gulp from his mug. "I have definitely learned deference in my long years."

"And how to use your damn head, thank the Cosmos," Alik grumbled, but he smiled as he took another chug from his mug.

"Brother!" Rena appeared from within the crowd, carrying two exceptionally large mugs sloshing over with beer.

Alik peered over the rim of his mug at her and rolled his eyes. She didn't care that he didn't answer and plopped down on the bench next to him, nearly sliding off the edge. She chuckled loudly, slamming the beer down onto the table as she almost fell.

"Is there nowhere else for your drunken self to go?" he said flatly.

She slapped Alik on the back and leaned into his shoulder, laughing. "There's nowhere I'd rather be than here with you, brother. I've missed out on years of—"

Alik shrugged her off and gave her an annoyed sidelong glance. "Being a pain in my ass? A plague to my sanity?"

"I love you too, brother." Rena took a swig of beer, then looked up and spotted Faelinth and Lavinia entering the tent. "Come, friends! Come join us."

Faelinth grasped Lavinia's hand and gave her a reassuring squeeze before leading her over to the table.

"Grab a beer, La-La," Rena said almost slurring her words.

Lavinia winced at the nickname, but graciously snagged a mug of whiskey from another passing tray. She chugged the contents with ease then quietly traded her empty mug for another full one as another server passed. She locked eyes with Alik. The tension built between the two for a long moment, before Alik tipped his head respectfully to her and continued his conversation with the stars.

Faelinth laid his hand lovingly on her arm and leaned in close to her ear. "The worst is over, love."

Tanophis couldn't help but smile at the entire exchange. He was glad to have them all back.

Paxis wriggled deeper under the blankets of her cot. The light was low in the tent, and she could hear the noise of merrymaking wafting from the main tent. Her back had started the itchy healing stage and she was sick of laying on her chest. She had sent Tanophis away to get some much-needed fresh air, but right now she was feeling sorry for herself.

"What do you need?" she heard Jaylin ask from her other side.

"It's starting to itch. And I'm bored. Can't we go get just one drink?"

Jaylin frowned. "I'd prefer it if you didn't, but I know you're not going to listen to me."

"Please," Paxis begged. "I promise I'll be good. I'm healing really well, and I'll go slow."

Jaylin sighed and smiled. "Alright, then. Come on." She helped Paxis up onto her feet.

"You're going to go with me?"

"If I don't, then I'll be left alone here to brood about Ciksura's fate."

Paxis slid her arm under Jaylin's and linked their arms. She smiled softly. "Everything will work out, my friend."

The two walked slowly arm in arm to the main tent, where they were greeted by a cacophony of noise. Paxis scanned the tent for Tanophis and finally saw him sitting with the others.

Tanophis caught her eye and jumped to his feet as they approached, giving her his arm to lean on as well. "You shouldn't be out here."

Paxis smiled and sat gingerly on the end of a bench. "My adventure is Jaylin-approved."

"Paxis!" Rena announced, vastly inebriated, and holding up two mugs of foamy beer. "I love you!"

Paxis laughed. "Who's in charge of monitoring Rena's alcohol intake?"

Tanophis grabbed a fresh mug of ale and placed it in front of Paxis. "We nominated Alik—"

"I never accepted that position," Alik grumbled. "And you can see how well it'll go if someone tries."

Jaylin sat glumly next to Paxis and tried to smile at the others' shenanigans. It broke Paxis's heart to see her friend this way; their family was still missing one member.

"Go," Paxis said to her, leaning in to be heard over the noise. "No one is keeping them from you. Go talk to them."

⤜⟫⟫ ⟪⟪⤛

The tent Jaylin stopped in front of was wholly dark, and an ice-cold breeze swept out of it.

"Are you going to just lurk out there, sister, or are you going to come in?"

Jaylin pushed back the tent flap and entered. The air inside was so cold that it took her breath away. Ciksura knelt, praying in hushed tones, in front of a small pile of bones and ash laid in the center of a rug.

"You didn't change yourself?" Jaylin exclaimed quietly.

"Yes, I am still 'they.'"

"Why did you lead us to believe that Guyt had changed you?"

"No one ever asked," they stated flatly.

Jaylin knelt beside them and prayed. Their combined prayers lowered the temperature in the tent so much that ice began to form on all the objects around them, and their puffs of breath now appeared as little wisps of clouds.

Once their prayers were complete, the two stood and the air immediately warmed. Jaylin looked long and hard at her sibling. "Why?"

Ciksura brushed the ice crystals from their long cloak and met their sister's tormented eyes. "I needed to forge my own path. True, I followed Guyt for the power to change myself..." their voice trailed away as they brought a chair out for Jaylin, and the two of them sat. "But he never could change me. It was all lies. But by the time I discovered that, I was so hurt and angry that I couldn't leave. I couldn't let him know that he'd destroyed me. I searched all the tomes I could find, but nothing had the answer that I sought. It seemed I was destined to be stuck forever as I am, and that realization tore my soul to shreds.

"Guyt laughed at me when he found out what I was searching for. Laughed, and told me that there was no magic that could *fix* me. But he'd manipulated me into a blood oath by then, and I realized I was stuck. My world crashed around me. And that's when I realized it."

"Realized what?" Jaylin asked.

"I realized that I was normal. That there wasn't anything broken or missing. That I could just be me, and that was normal."

Jaylin sat quietly, her head hanging, as Ciksura fell silent. "Are you truly happy as you are now?"

"Yes," Ciksura answered softly, with a whisper of a smile.

"Then your journey was worth it. Will you join us in Meten?"

Ciksura looked away. "They don't want me there."

Jaylin reached out a hand and placed it on their arm. "They still love you. I still love you. I always have." She stood and started for the exit, then turned. "We'll all be here when you're ready."

⟫⟫ ⟪⟪

The sunlight outside the tent the next morning nearly blinded Tanophis. They had kept drinking into the wee hours of the night, and he was regretting every second of that decision. The armies were packing to return to their homes and the camp was filled with too many loud clatters and bangs.

"Good morning," Alik's voice boomed purposefully as he clapped Tanophis on the shoulder.

Tanophis winced and shot a disdainful look Alik's way. "Hushed tones, please."

Alik laughed heartily. "Still can't handle a hangover?"

"It's been a while since I've been able to drink properly. And I can handle a hangover just fine." Tanophis smoothed his rumpled pants and stood a bit straighter. "It's the light and noise I can't handle," he added quietly, squinting his eyes against the sun.

"Are you taking those swords back today?" Alik asked as they started walking.

"Yes," Tanophis answered. "I'll grab some breakfast and then I'll be off."

The tent was already pretty cleared out when they entered, the tables bare. They piled some of whatever had been left out from breakfast on their plates, and started to make their way over to an empty table. A familiar face strode through the tent toward them. Trantu had also come in for a late breakfast, and was now scanning the tables for a place to sit. Tanophis tossed up a hand and called to him.

Trantu sat down next to him with a smile. "It's an honor to be seated with you, my lord."

"Nonsense," Tanophis said waving his hand. "I'm glad to see you, friend. We owe you a lot. It's my honor completely."

Trantu nodded and took a large bite from the pile of various meats on his plate. "Trantu," Tanophis asked, "would you honor Meten by joining us there, and being an official guard of the gods?"

Trantu nearly dropped his utensil. "It would be the greatest honor to serve you, my lord."

Tanophis smiled. "Good. I hate to steal you from Vrutuuk... well, not really."

Trantu beamed and sat up a little taller. "You honor Vrutuuk by choosing one of his own."

"First order of business, can you fly me out to Naina? I have business with Morana and Osirim."

"Of course, my lord."

"Perfect. We'll leave after I make Vrutuuk a formal offer for your services."

"Very good, my lord."

"Second order... stop calling me *lord*. Tanophis will be fine." He smiled and took a bite of a mystery food.

Trantu returned his smile. "Of course." Tanophis was sure he heard an almost inaudible 'my lord' that Trantu muttered.

Tanophis took a deep breath of the cold, snowy air and closed his eyes as he exhaled. With the twin blades strapped to his side, he started up the mountain. The snow crunched under his feet and his mind started to stray as he climbed.

Memories and feelings of the last few months wafted dreamily through his head. He drew closer and closer to the ledge and magic portal until he stood before it, still lost in thought. This trip up Naina had been significantly different than the previous two. His immortal body stayed warm and untired, but the efforts of being mortal would have a lasting impact on him. He could serve his people better now, understanding their daily struggles.

The two spirits said nothing as Tanophis crossed the magical room and laid the swords silently on the ground at their feet. "Returned, as promised."

Osirim stood, picked up a sword in each hand, and the weapons disappeared. "We are glad to see you returned to us, King of the Gods."

"We couldn't have done it without your help. So many have contributed to our victory."

Osirim nodded in acknowledgment and acceptance. "Your blood oath is fulfilled."

Tanophis turned to leave, but was stopped by Morana's voice. "Beware, Tanophis, King of the Gods."

He spun on his heel. "Beware of what?"

"The universe requires balance... always."

Tanophis narrowed his eyes at her, then meaning struck him like a bolt of lightning. "Guyt isn't dead."

"Guyt—as you knew him—Is dead. But there will be another to take his place. There must always be balance. As long as a Gaia exists, there must be a Guyt."

# Chapter 31

Tanophis joined Paxis in their tent upon his return. He stopped at the entrance to their bed chamber, leaning against the post. Paxis hadn't noticed him come in and was sitting on their pile of blankets, brushing out her long brown hair. "You look gorgeous."

She turned and smiled at him. "Thank you, love. The swords are returned?"

Tanophis nodded. "And I've got more news."

Paxis frowned at him and stopped brushing. "What news?"

He crossed the floor and sat next to her, running his fingers through his hair. "I should've expected it, honestly."

"What has your mind in knots, love?"

"Guyt will return as a new god."

Paxis thought about that for a long minute. "But how?"

"The universe always demands balance. I feel pretty stupid for not thinking of it before."

Paxis leaned onto his shoulder and laid a calming hand on his arm. "We'll worry about that when—or if—it ever becomes an issue. Right now, let's go home."

Tanophis leaned into her touch. "Meten? Or do you still have plans to return to Earth?"

Paxis smiled at him. "No. I can't go back to Earth. Showing up on their doorstep unannounced a second time would be too much, I think.

I wouldn't even know how to explain to them what happened, or who I am. It would upset them too much. I already upended their world once. No need to do it again."

Tanophis reached for her hand and squeezed it.

"I am glad of one thing," she said.

"What's that?"

Her eyes filled with love as they stared deep into his. "I'm glad that we were able to experience life as mortals would. I believe we're better for it."

"I had the same thoughts on Naina. Although, I'm not so sure I enjoyed being so naïve."

Paxis let out a laugh that made the room sparkle. "I can agree with you. Although, I'm glad that we got to experience our love grow naturally again. Not many can boast that."

Tanophis barked a laugh. "I thought you hated me!"

"You are my opposite. Young and impetuous Fen was quite a handful."

"Young and stuck-up Mati was very boring at times."

Paxis scoffed. "You nearly got yourself killed several times. It's no wonder that the stars were worried about us in the Crescent Wood. We could easily have been a feast for those beasts."

"Nah," Tanophis waved her off. "I had everything under control."

"Ha!" Paxis let out a laugh. "If it hadn't been for me, you would have been killed by that nenad. I shudder to think what would've happened if a god had been killed. The chaos it would bring!"

Tanophis smiled boldly at his wife. His love. "And that is why we make a good team."

Paxis smiled lovingly at him. "I suppose it is."

Meten looked the same as before, but it felt different. The towers and streets had been shoddily rebuilt by Guyt. Their once-vibrant and nearly perfectly curated city would recover in time, as they all would, but they would all be tainted by the nightmarish experiences that Guyt had put them through.

The gods had all followed Paxis and Tanophis back to their old home, even Ciksura. It had taken a fair amount of convincing and apologizing on everyone's part to get them to agree, but they ultimately decided to travel with the others. For their sister's sake.

"It reeks of that bastard," Alik grumbled loudly, wrinkling his nose. "He better not have messed with my armory."

"It still feels good to be home," Rena said, looking around herself fondly, almost hugging the massive columns with her thoughts.

Faelinth led Lavinia to the wide staircase and started to climb. "Come, wife," Faelinth said to her lovingly, "We have a lot of missed time to make up for."

Alik pointed at them accusingly. "You two had better not keep me awake all night. I had enough of the sounds of your lovemaking back at that camp to last me four immortal lifetimes."

Faelinth flashed him a wicked grin and a wink. "Don't be jealous, Alik."

Alik's face turned bright red. "*Jealous?*"

"Alik," Lavinia added teasingly, "Faelinth didn't tell me you two had become so attached in my absence. I don't mind sharing."

Alik's whole body seemed to puff up in surprise and anger as he stomped up the steps after them. "I mean it! I'm not walking through the halls with my eyes covered for a millennium."

Their voices trailed away as they disappeared up the steps and down the hall, still mercilessly teasing Alik.

Jaylin turned to Ciksura, clasped their hand, and they too disappeared down a long hallway, leaving Paxis and Tanophis alone in the vast, echoing atrium.

"Well," Tanophis said, sliding his hand into hers. "Our family is all back together."

Alik's booming voice sounded in the distance.

"For better or for worse," Paxis laughed.

The fire in their old room had already been lit, and even though the room looked the same as when they'd left, like the rest of their palace, it had changed—in feeling, in meaning, and in smell.

"We need to have Jaylin cleanse this whole place tomorrow," Paxis said, wrinkling her nose.

Tanophis sidled up behind her, being careful not to press against her back. "In the meantime, I know something we could do to make it feel a lot more like home in here." And Paxis returned his wicked smile.

Dear reader,

Thank you for joining Fen and Mati on this journey. This is the finality of two years of work for me. Love, pain, and, at times, frustration were all poured into this story. This was my debut novel and I hope one day to have another novel to put out into the world for you. I have an idea but no final plans if I'll be writing another full novel again.

As a hobby writer, this was me being stubborn and proving to myself that I could do it. And I did! Thank you so much for giving a no name author from the Midwest a chance to take you on this journey. It means the world to me.

If you want to keep up with my life as a normie and be the first to know when/if I decide to write another novel, you can follow my account on Instagram @cosplayandtea.

Nicole